5

m

DEATH IN A DRY SEASON

JOHN WELLS

DEATH IN A
DRY SEASON

ST. MARTIN'S PRESS
NEW YORK

A THOMAS DUNNE BOOK.
An imprint of St. Martin's Press

Design by Ellen R. Sasahara

Library of Congress Cataloging-in-Publication Data

Wells, John.
Death in a dry season / John Wells.—1st ed.
p.   cm.
"A Thomas Dunne book."
ISBN 0-312-15509-3
I. Title.
PS3573.E4916D4   1997
813'.54—dc21   97-1184
                                          CIP

First Edition: July 1997

10 9 8 7 6 5 4 3 2 1

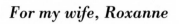

For my wife, Roxanne

ACKNOWLEDGMENTS

I wish to thank the people in Atlantic City and the Pine Barrens who generously shared their time and expertise with me. (Although none of these individuals has been depicted in the book, in one or two instances an actual person's title or job function has been attributed to a fictional character.)

Barry K. Durman, president of the Atlantic City Rescue Mission, and Jackie Nederberger, his administrative assistant, explained the challenges a mission faces in contending with the impact of so many slot machines and blackjack tables and kindly introduced me to a few of the people for whom they provide a safe haven.

Those who I met in the casino business were enormously helpful as well. In particular, Bob Sertell, assistant director of the Casino Career Institute at Atlantic Community College, and Joe DeRosa, casino shift manager at Trump Castle and assistant director of gaming at the Casino Career Institute, patiently answered my questions about day-to-day operations and gave me a layman's introduction to casino computer systems. Joe Gaimo, vice president and casino manager at the Showboat, explained, among other things, just who's watching who (and how) out on the casino floor. John Connors, vice president at Caesars, offered a behind-the-scenes look at one casino's security system. And Dick Ross, of Ross Security Consultants, arranged a lunch and an introduction, and provided some priceless Atlantic City anecdotes.

In law enforcement, Capt. James Barber of the Atlantic County Major Crimes Squad, and Jake Glassey, Atlantic City arson investigator, were invaluable regarding the ins and outs of an arson-homicide investigation. Dr. Lyla E. Perez, Atlantic County Medical Examiner, and Joe Dintino, Principal Forensic Scientist, New Jersey State Police, provided answers to my forensic and scene-of-the-crime questions. Thanks also to FBI Agent James Darcy and Robert Preston of Forrest Associates.

I am especially grateful to James Gowdy, assistant division forest fire warden, and Horace Somes, section forest fire warden, both of the New Jersey Forest Fire Service, who explained the behavior of fires in the Pines and helped find a way for Frank Sweeney to escape one. Also thanks to: Elaine and Roy Everett of the Pinelands Cultural Society; Mary Joan Wyatt, tax assessor, Town of Hammonton; and Pamela Wilson, secretary, Bankruptcy Judges Division, Administrative Office of the United States Courts.

A number of books were indispensable. In particular, *Pinelands Folklife*, edited by Rita Zorn Moonsammy, David Steven Cohen, and Lorraine E. Williams, and *One Space, Many Places*, by Mary Hufford. But it was John McPhee's *The Pine Barrens*, still the best book on that remarkably enticing place, which years ago got me thinking about writing a novel set in the Jersey Pines.

Finally, a special note of appreciation to Arnold Goodman, agent par excellence, who persisted, and to Robert Youdelman, attorney and mentor, who offered advice, encouragement, and friendship.

And what the dead had no speech for, when living,
They can tell you, being dead: the communication
Of the dead is tongued with fire beyond the language of the living.

—T.S. Eliot, "Little Gidding"

CONTENTS

PROLOGUE
JULY 1977

AFTER PUTTING THE last length of pitch pine in place, the old man circled the charcoal pit, checking the placement of each piece of wood one last time. Here and there he adjusted a log that seemed to be misaligned. When he was satisfied, he walked over to a small plywood lean-to where a decrepit mongrel dog lay waiting for him. Groaning slightly, he lowered himself into an old aluminum lawn chair, then reached down and pulled a pint bottle of whiskey out of a waterproof sack containing the day's food.

This would be his last day. He'd decided that months ago. It had been a hard decision. He'd been burning charcoal since he was a boy. But there was no profit in it anymore, none to speak of anyway. Occasionally he sold to a local artist or to some roofers who used it to heat their tar pots. But that was all. Still, coaling was what he did best, and building a charcoal pit gave him more satisfaction than anything he'd ever done working the seasonal cycle.

The pit—a kiln, really—looked like a tepee. It was conical in shape but rounded at the top. Although he'd never actually measured it, he knew it was about ten feet high and twenty-five feet in diameter at the bottom. It was constructed of three tiers of pine cordwood stacked vertically in an upside-down V-formation around a thick oak guide pole. At ground level there was an arched opening just big enough for a man to crawl through. It led to the center where the kindling was placed. Most of the other Pineys, the few who still worked as part-time colliers, liked to fire their kilns through a chimney in the middle, putting the kindling in from the top. He preferred a special kind

3

of arch pit that allowed him to crawl inside on the sandy floor, smelling the resin in the neatly stacked pine as he laid out each piece of kindling. He'd always liked things different. It was in his nature.

Over the years more serious eccentricities had cost him friends, even family. Which was why he lived alone now. People figured he wanted it that way. Except, that is, for the young girl across the road. She came over every now and then to help watch the burning. Still, she was the only one. That was fine with him.

After a measured sip of whiskey, he sat back and gazed around the clearing. It was a cul-de-sac about fifty yards in diameter, surrounded by thick woods of pine and oak to the north and east, and a cedar swamp to the southwest. A narrow sand road through the woods provided the only access. Unless you knew the Pines, that is. Him, he could reach the clearing from any direction, through the swamp if need be.

After two more sips of whiskey he took a sandwich out of the sack, ripped off a piece, and gave it to the dog. She reached for it, then dropped to the ground, clutching the morsel in her mouth. He ate what was left, chewing methodically, his eyes fixed on the pine structure in the middle of the clearing. When he finished the sandwich, he wiped his hands on his bib overalls, stuffed the paper wrappings inside the sack along with the whiskey bottle, and returned to the center of the clearing.

He circled the pit one more time. Then he walked over to a large pile of turf—a sandy mixture of sheep laurel, black huckleberry, and teaberry—and picked up a wide pitchfork about the size of a standard garden rake. Spearing a clump of turf with the fork, he carried it over to the kiln and spread it over an area on the bottom tier, patting it down with the back of a spade. Once the turfing was completed he would begin blacking the kiln, adding a layer of sand about four or five inches thick. After he had poked flue holes in the side, it would be time to lay the kindling and fire it up. In a week or two, when the burning was complete and the pit had settled, he would close the flue holes and turn the turfs over, letting the sand settle down in, cooling the pit. Then he would rake off the turf and sand and begin to bag the charcoal.

The panel truck had entered the clearing and come to a stop before he noticed it. There were two men in the cab. The one in the passenger seat had his head back, eyes closed. There was printing of some sort on the side of the van, but he couldn't make it out from where he was standing.

The man on the driver's side opened the door and stepped out. He was scrawny, average in height, and young. Very young. Couldn't have been much over twenty. He wore a rumpled felt hat with the brim turned up on each side. His tight blue jeans were tucked into black western boots decorated with elaborate white stitching. His spindly arms protruded from under a red flannel shirt and ratty down vest. In his right hand he gripped a shotgun just below the slide handle, resting the butt on his hip, the barrel pointed upward at an angle.

The collier stopped and stared. The man with the gun came toward him. He had a limp.

"Didn't know there was any Pineys left still did any coaling," said the young man.

"There's a few."

The young man didn't speak for several seconds, then pointed to his hat. "You can call me 'Cowboy.' " He reached inside his vest for a small flask and took a long drink from it.

"Wrong time a year to be doing any lawful huntin', ain't it?"

There was no response.

" 'Course," said the collier, "never heard of a Piney who didn't use the law a little now and then." He looked the other man up and down for a long time.

Cowboy kicked at some leaves and pine needles near his feet, then looked up at the tops of the trees. "Awful dry right now. Bit windy, too."

"Ain't never started no forest fire yet. 'Sides, I'll be here mosta the time watchin' it."

His right leg dragging behind him, Cowboy walked over to where the collier was packing turf onto the pine understructure. He bent down and looked through the arched opening.

"Like this better'n a chimney pit?"

"Suits me," said the collier.

5

"Yeah, me too." Cowboy grinned.

He had the face of a child, thought the collier, but there was something wild about him, like an untamed animal. When he smiled he looked away from you, all the while baring his teeth like some damned hyena on the prowl. The rest of the time he acted smart, like he knew something you didn't.

"Who's your friend?" the collier asked.

"Ain't none of your business," Cowboy barked. Then, changing his tone, he said, "Just a friend." He moved away from the kiln, lowering his shotgun a little. "What's your name?"

"What's it to you?"

"You're real friendly, ain't you."

"Ain't got no need to be. I don't bother nobody and they don't bother me."

"Live alone, do ya?"

"Like it that way."

Cowboy took another swig from his flask. "Got a man wants to see inside your kiln."

"What?"

"Man in the truck back there, he wants to see inside." Cowboy pointed his gun at the opening.

"Ain't much to see. 'Sides, I ain't finished yet."

"I'll be the judge of that."

"Look, mister, I ain't gonna—"

Cowboy had aimed his gun at the collier's chest.

"What the hell? I don't know who you are but—"

The blast reverberated across the clearing, slicing off the top branches of some cedar trees about thirty yards behind them. Cowboy had fired about a foot above the collier's right shoulder. The old man looked dumbstruck. Cowboy picked up the spent casing, then pressed the barrel of the gun into the collier's groin.

"What in God's name do you want?" His voice was shaking now.

"Dammit, now you've gone and got me mad," said Cowboy. "Get inside." He pointed at the kiln.

"What?"

6

"You're going to show my friend. Maybe he can learn how to build one of his own."

"There's barely room for one in there."

"Plenty of room." He pressed the barrel of the gun hard against the collier's testicles. "Better do what I say."

Still shaking, the collier got down on his hands and knees in front of the opening and turned around to back into the kiln.

"Head first," said Cowboy.

"Can't see your friend if I do that. No way to turn around in there."

"Get inside, old man."

"Why? Why're you doing this?"

Cowboy drove the butt of the gun into the collier's right side, just below his ribs, knocking the wind out of him. He fell forward into the sand, stunned but still conscious.

"Didn't hurt ya," said Cowboy. "Now move it."

Moaning, the collier managed to get up on his hands and knees and make his way into the narrow passageway.

"All the way," said Cowboy. He crouched down and watched the collier inch his way toward the center of the kiln. "Now don't ya move."

Cowboy stood up and drank some more from his flask. Then he walked back toward the van, looking over his shoulder every now and then at the entrance to the charcoal pit. At the van he opened the door on the passenger side and began pulling and tugging at the white-haired man sitting there. The man was about seventy years old, dressed in an expensive three-piece suit. His eyes were half-closed. He wasn't able to walk on his own so Cowboy draped the man's arm around his shoulder and dragged him to the kiln. He dropped the limp body in front of the opening to the kiln, where the sound of the collier's moaning had grown louder. Cowboy sat the man up, his back to the opening, and pushed him backward so that his torso fell into the kiln. Then he picked up the man's feet, bent his legs at the knees, and shoved the bottom half of his body through the opening as well. Finally, he sat down in front of the kiln and kicked with both feet, cramming the man all the way in.

"I can't move," the collier screamed, his voice muffled by the other's body. "How'm I supposed to get out! Jesus God, what are you doing to me? Oh, sweet Jesus."

"Too bad you had to be here," Cowboy said. "Didn't expect to find nobody way out here, for chrissakes. Too bad."

Cowboy looked around. Noticing a pile of leftover pitch pine, he picked out six pieces, each about four feet long. After laying the wood down in front of the opening to the kiln, he walked back to the van and returned with an ax and a long-handled sledgehammer.

"Name's not really Cowboy," he said, speaking into the kiln. "Want ya to know that. Don't like telling no lies."

He began hacking away at the pitch pine with the ax, shaping a rough point on one end of each piece. When he was finished he picked up one of the stakes and shoved the pointed end into the sandy soil directly in front of the opening. Once the stake was standing on its own, he drove it into the ground with the sledgehammer. When it was in far enough to satisfy him, he stopped and did the same with another stake. He did this two more times until he had blocked off the opening to the kiln. The body of the man on the other side was barely visible though the cracks.

Cowboy stopped to catch his breath and listen. All he could hear now was a faint whimpering noise. It sounded like a child who'd lost his mommy, that's all.

"Like I said, too bad you was here. Didn't have to be this way."

Putting the unused stakes aside, he picked up his shotgun and eyed the old dog, who was sniffing around the base of the kiln. The dog saw him and whined. When Cowboy moved in her direction, she stopped and fell to the ground, bearing her aged teeth in a pathetic snarl.

"Nice doggy, nice doggy."

He raised the shotgun. Sensing what was coming, the dog turned tail and headed for the woods, whimpering pathetically. She was no match for Cowboy's speed and steady aim. The buckshot blew her hind legs off, and she collapsed in a heap on the grassy edge of the clearing, bloody and immobilized. She made one feeble attempt to crawl forward, then stopped breathing. After first picking up the shell casing, Cowboy walked over to the dog and poked at its head with the barrel of the gun. Satisfied, he grabbed the carcass by the neck, dragged it back to the charcoal pit, and tossed it on top of the pine logs. He noticed the moaning and crying again. He'd been right. It sounded like some little kid who'd lost his mommy.

Back at the van he placed the shotgun on the seat, went around to the back, opened the rear doors, and dragged out two five-gallon cans of gasoline. He carried each can to the kiln, then stood back a moment, studying the structure and listening intently. The sounds coming from inside had stopped. He took the top off the spout of the first container and dragged the can around the pit, pouring the liquid onto the dry turf that covered the lower tier, stopping several times to bend over and let the acrid vapor fill his nostrils. When he'd emptied half the container, he picked it up by the bottom with both hands and sprayed the gasoline back and forth over the top half of the kiln, making sure to get some on the dog. He did the same with the second can, dowsing the lower half of the kiln until the can was light enough to lift over his shoulders.

When he was finished he thought he heard a new sound. It was a rhythmic monotone this time. It didn't sound like the collier. But it couldn't be the businessman either. Not with all that horse in him.

He backed away from the charcoal pit, making sure to keep the wind, which was coming from the direction of the van, behind him. When he was about thirty feet away, he stopped and again reached inside his down vest for the flask. He could still hear the sound. A chill went through him. The old man was praying, praying out loud. He hated it when people did that. Prayer was a private thing. You were supposed to keep it to yourself. He emptied the flask and put it back inside his vest.

From his other vest pocket he took out a book of matches and a small spool of solder. He ripped off one of the matches, held it between his front teeth, and folded back the cover of the matchbook, tucking it behind the rest of the matches. Then he unwound an eight-inch length of solder and bent it back and forth at the joint until it broke off. Holding one end of the solder against the back of the matchbook, he wound the thin string of malleable lead around the middle, tucking in the last loose end, making sure to leave the abrasive scoring pad uncovered. When he was finished he held the matchbook in his right hand and tossed it lightly into the air to check its weight and stability. It was just right.

By now a familiar ringing filled his ears. It ought to have felt uncomfortable, even painful. But he rejoiced in it. His release was near.

He took the match from between his teeth, struck it, then touched the flame to the rest of the matches. After a few seconds he tossed the makeshift torch in a low arc toward the kiln. It landed precisely where he'd intended, midway up the side, just above the lower tier of turfing. A ripple of flame ran laterally around the conical structure, setting the exposed pitch pine ablaze and quickly engulfing the body of the dead dog. In several seconds the edges of the dry turf caught as well. Within half a minute the entire kiln was crackling and blazing.

He no longer heard the screams coming from inside the kiln. He had surrendered to the rapture.

The flames leapt into the air, sparks and embers flying out in every direction. Most dropped short of the undergrowth of ferns and huckleberry bushes that preceded the tree line. But every now and then the wind caught an ember and carried it up over the collier's watch cabin and into the cedar swamp where it dropped with a hiss into the gray-red water or landed on the damp sphagnum surface of the bog's edge and died out. Still the kiln roared and crackled, the fire gathering strength as it reached each new layer of pitch pine. Eventually a spark landed atop one of the pond pines at the edge of the clearing in the transitional area between the swamp and the thick woods adjoining it. The crown of the tree went up as if it too had been dowsed in gasoline. The fire spread quickly to two neighboring cedars, then to several shorter white pines below. Sparks began dropping onto the underbrush that surrounded the clearing. Soon a semicircle of flames worked its way along the ground to the collier's small lean-to, which burst into flames and was consumed in less than a minute.

Cowboy stood and watched until he couldn't stand the heat any longer. When he finally turned and headed for the truck, a damp stain covered the front of his jeans.

With one hand pressed against his crotch, he drove the van down

10

the narrow sand road, staring straight ahead. After about fifty yards, he stopped and turned around in his seat. The flames had spread beyond the far side of the clearing. He picked up a small camera on the seat next to him and got out. From the road he took three photographs of the fire.

"Be okay," he said out loud. "Long as the wind don't change, it'll be okay."

THE CITY
BOOK ONE

1

Lucy the Elephant watches disdainfully out of the corner of her eye as if I'm just another gawking day-tripper down from Philly. Probably wondering what I'm doing here in the off-season. The fact is, I'm waiting to meet a stranger, a man who calls himself "Cappy." Said he'd be here at five. It's nearly six, and so far I've seen two kids on bikes and a white-haired matron in a Cadillac who pulled over on Atlantic Avenue to give me the once-over. And twice some scraggly vagrant in a raincoat and red Phillies cap has walked by, pausing each time to glance my way. Sizing up a mark, no doubt—though the neighborhood's hardly good pickings for panhandlers. This part of Margate's strictly upscale and residential. No stores or shops and, except for one enormous man-made elephant, nothing to attract tourists. Most outsiders simply drive on by. A few slow down to stare at Lucy or ogle the moneyed Georgian homes along the beach. It's well patrolled by the Margate City police, too. Margate residents don't take kindly to having to contend with the spillover from Atlantic City's homeless.

From the end of the cul-de-sac where I'm waiting, the ninety-ton Lucy looks like an outsized Disney cartoon creature, her gaudy expansiveness an affront to the ordered dullness of the neighborhood. She's six stories high and almost as long from trunk to tail. Her old howdah, an airy two-story canopied basket, looks like an oversized Hindu hot-dog stand. It's fixed on her back atop an ornate blanket of salmon-colored paint that reaches down thirty feet on each side. One can "tour" Lucy, examining exhibits from her past, peering out to sea through the dark, circular windows that are her eyes, ending by taking in the panorama of bay and ocean from her howdah. You enter through a door in one of her bulbous rear legs. Open weekends, 10 A.M.–4:30 P.M., so the sign says.

15

I check my watch again. It's well past six. The day's cooling down, the thermometer having reached eighty earlier. It's been tantalizingly warm for mid-April. Unseasonably dry, too. A light breeze drifts in off the ocean, bringing with it a pungency, like dead fish.

I'm going to give it another ten minutes, then get some dinner. The guy's probably a crackpot anyway. On the phone he sounded drunk. Wouldn't tell me anything. Only that he was "Cappy, a friend of Nick's." And that odd statement at the end: "I told Nick too much."

So I wait. It's one of the things I do best.

I like to think I possess a historian's cast of mind, which is not a bad thing for a private investigator to have. If you're curious about the way events unfold, you're more likely to get it right for the client than one of those New Age techno-dicks who uses nothing but the latest audio telescope and miniaturized video camera to do the job. Spying and eavesdropping are necessary evils in this business, but they merely capture people at a certain point in time. *Why* people do what they do is what interests me. Schlegel said the historian is a prophet in reverse. The same's true of a good investigator.

All of which is why I pride myself on my memory. I've always had an unusually retentive one. In college after the first week of General Chemistry, I could recall the entire periodic table, and by my sophomore year recite verbatim most of T. S. Eliot's poetry. (Eliot's my personal choice for Poet of Memory.) I can also tell you what Richie Ashburn hit in each year of his career with the Phillies, as well as his last with the '62 Mets (it was a superb .306, but for the Mets it was an *annus horribilis,* the first of many). I also remember the price of every antique I've ever bought or sold. But enough. It sounds as if I'm boasting. Besides, as someone once said, memory's a crazy woman who hoards colored rags and throws away food.

Mixed in among the rags I've collected over the years are details of Lucy's past. I've been coming to the Jersey shore for forty-six years and know her history as well as I know that of my native Philadelphia. At least I thought I did until this morning. I've always believed this location to be the site where Lucy was erected 113 years ago. But the fact is—you could look it up, as Casey Stengel said, and I have:

16

twenty-six years ago Lucy was placed on wheels and moved here from a spot two blocks away to undergo extensive rehabilitation. What can I say? Maybe in recent years my mind's been too focused on Lucy's future, on what's to become of her now that Mammon's been enthroned in Atlantic City. As the Queen said to Alice, "It's a poor sort of memory that only works backwards."

The old man in the Phillies cap has returned. He's a block away on Atlantic Avenue, eyeing me from underneath his angled brow like a hungry vulture appraising fresh roadkill.

Did I forget Lucy had been moved, or have I simply been misinformed all this time? Most people wouldn't care. They don't take Margate's notorious elephant seriously, not anymore at least. But for me she's a cultural icon, always has been. Gazing out to sea with those playful disk-shaped eyes of hers, this amiable giant is pure camp, wonderfully excessive in the innocently boastful way that characterized so much of Atlantic City in its heyday, when Steel Pier had diving horses and the Boardwalk advertised freak shows featuring premature babies and two-headed women. Back then Lucy was one of the reasons people came to the Jersey shore.

But things have changed. Consider Meryl Sarbanes.

Meryl's a quadriplegic who, until last month, earned a substantial income on the Boardwalk playing the electric keyboard with her tongue. At the instigation of several casinos, the city fathers recently banished her. Meryl, who has two children, a fact of some consequence as far as I'm concerned, has since disappeared into whatever void it is that swallows up Atlantic City's outcasts. What no one seems to understand is that this has always been a town of freaks. And even among freaks, distinctions must be made. Some, like Lucy and Meryl Sarbanes, can be liberating, even life-giving. Others, like those encaged in the Boardwalk's glittery debtors' prisons called casinos, are society's hollow men, capable of throwing away personal fortunes on a roll of the dice, convinced all the while that the rest of the world envies them. They're the truly deformed.

The vagrant is across the street now, shuffling slowly back and forth, tracing and retracing the same route in front of Lucy. He begins to back away, as if to take in the long view. When he reaches the curb,

17

he steps down and continues edging away from the elephant, his back to me all the while. In the middle of the street he's no more than fifty feet away from me and my car. After a final gaze at Lucy, he turns and looks directly at me.

"You Mr. Sweeney?" he shouts, as if I were deaf. Coming still closer, he says, "You a cop? Heard you were a cop."

Besides the baseball cap, he's wearing raggedy Converse high-tops, a pair of stained and torn brown corduroy pants, and a crisp, new tan raincoat, buttoned up to the neck. London Fog, by the look of it.

"Used to be. Who're you?"

"Cappy. Didn't you figure that out?"

"How'd you know I used to be a cop?"

"Nick told me. Didn't figure that out either, huh? You're a little slow, Mr. Sweeney. Maybe that's why you're no longer a cop, huh?"

"Look—"

"How about buying a man a drink, Mr. Sweeney? Then we can talk."

"Talk about what?"

Now it's his turn to stare at me. "You'll see. This yours?"

He moves in close to my car, a white Range Rover, and begins to examine it, his hands trembling slightly as he runs them along the surface of the hood.

"Yeah." I watch him closely. "Okay, look, I can give you a few minutes."

He turns abruptly toward me, hands shoved deep in the pockets of his raincoat.

"A few minutes? I assume you didn't come down from Philly just for the air. Bear with me, Mr. Sweeney. I may be an old man down on his luck, but I'm not cracked. At least not yet."

"Tell you what, I'll buy you a meal. If I like what you have to say, I'll throw in a drink."

He thinks about it a moment. "Okay, but make it some place decent. Mission food isn't exactly Bookbinder's, you know."

I glance down at his pants and sneakers. "No, I guess not."

He smiles, revealing a mouth full of remarkably fine teeth. "Don't worry. We'll find a place without a dress code."

"Yeah, sure. Come on."

Inside the car he looks the interior over carefully. "Nice. Used to have one of these myself. Except mine was green. Hunter green. You like yours?"

I start to say something but end up laughing. "Yeah, Cappy, I like it."

"So you're really not a cop?" asks Cappy.

"Not since last year. I own an antiques shop in Philly. As a sideline I do a little PI work."

I find things for people. Sometimes I find *people*. Here and there a Hepplewhite chair or a Chippendale desk. Once in a while a father who's overdue on child support. This week it's a missing brother, Nick D'Angelo. Lately, however, it's as if something's been trying to find me.

Cappy pushes aside a plate that held enough fettuccine to feed me for a week. I'm still working on a Caesar salad and coffee. We're in Atlantic City at Franco's, a no-nonsense working man's eatery off Pacific Avenue. Cappy recommends it "most highly."

Watching him eat gets me thinking about Lester, a homeless man in north Philly, and was one of my best informants back when I was a homicide detective. I would meet Lester once a month and take him to a diner for some decent food. He always began by asking the waitress for a mug of hot water. Then he would proceed to shake the contents of a ketchup bottle into it, stir everything around, and drink the whole mess as if it were soup, slurping loudly all the while. Even though I was paying, he'd never order soup from the menu. Cappy hasn't developed such street behavior. At least not yet.

He studies me intently.

"Do you believe in our country's tax laws, Mr. Sweeney?"

If this is some psychotic's idea of a character test, he's going to be disappointed. I've never had any patience for playing games with pathological types.

"Do I have a choice?"

"We all have choices, Mr. Sweeney. A policeman, of all people, should know that the tax laws are immoral. Especially the one that established the invidious withholding tax."

He lowers his voice, looking over his shoulder, and it occurs to me that until now I've never met a vagrant capable of using the word *invidious* in a sentence.

"You may not believe this," he whispers, "but I haven't paid any taxes since 1980."

His smile is faintly ironic, his mannerisms formal, almost ceremonious. Despite the stubby growth of beard and the unkempt hair, he has the look of a washed-up Shakespearean actor, a member of the Old Vic who's a touch too much of the sauce taken.

"Really? You're right, I don't believe it."

"Please don't mock me, Mr. Sweeney. It's uncalled for."

Apologizing, I ask him to continue but make no attempt to conceal how impatient I'm becoming.

"Are you a baseball fan, Mr. Sweeney?"

"Ever since I first set foot inside Shibe Park. I was eight years old at the time."

He looks taken aback for an instant. "Really? Nick dislikes the game. But I insisted he go with me. He needs to get away more often."

"Don't you want to take that off?"

He still has the raincoat on, buttoned up to the neck.

"Too risky," he says, patting his chest. "All my valuable papers are here." Again he lowers his voice. "IRS would have a field day if they could get their hands on what's in this coat."

"I see. Okay then, when was this ball game you and Nick went to?"

"Opening day at the Vet."

"You're both reduced to living in a rescue mission and yet you found the means to get all the way to Philly for a ball game?"

In the car, Cappy, who wouldn't tell me his full name, explained that he and Nick met at the Lighthouse Mission, in Atlantic City's Inlet area. The mission's a refuge for the homeless, the unemployed, and, in Nick's case, anyone who's spent too much time at the blackjack tables. According to Cappy, Nick moved there three weeks ago, right after losing his job as a security guard at the Poseidon. In this town if you work at a casino you don't gamble there. Nick never did respond well to rules and regulations.

"Nick was busted, flat broke. It was on me. Do you have a problem with that?"

"How'd you get there?"

He gives me that enigmatic smile again.

"I have my ways. Something happened after the game, something important. Do you want to hear about it or not?"

"Shoot."

"An apt choice of words, Mr. Sweeney. As we came out of the stadium there was a drug deal of some sort taking place in the parking lot. I don't know how Nick spotted it but he did. I guess you cops have your ways. Anyway, he saw these crackheads, or whatever they were, off behind some cars. They saw him looking their way and someone pulled a gun. He got me down just as shots were fired. Then he pushed me under a car and took off after them."

"Did he nail them?"

He shakes his head. "They got away. Besides, he didn't have his gun. Pawned it weeks ago."

This takes me more by surprise than the news that Nick's living in a shelter. Even after he left the Camden PD, Nick would sooner have walked naked down Broadway than go anywhere without a piece.

"It did buy him a two-day run at the tables," says Cappy, reading the expression on my face.

Two days. And after that, what? Pawn your clothing?

Cappy looks jittery. "Could I have that drink now?"

I motion to the waitress, who's been watching us closely, afraid we're going to make a run for it. She comes over to the table and Cappy orders a double Absolut on the rocks. Mission life hasn't kept him from developing a taste for the good life. I order a draft and hand the waitress a twenty, which she walks off clutching like an insurance policy.

When the drinks arrive Cappy takes a large swallow of vodka and sits back, scratching his beard contentedly. I'd guess he's sixty-five or seventy, although behind all that facial hair he could be eighty. As the alcohol enters his system, his eyes brighten, making him suddenly younger.

"To return to my little tale. As I said, Nick couldn't catch the perps—isn't that what you call them?—but when he returned and helped drag me out from under the car, I realized he'd saved my life."

He pauses, savoring more of the silvery elixir.

"I owe Nick a large debt of gratitude. That's why I got in touch with you, Mr. Sweeney."

"How'd you find me?"

"I learned you were at Nick's old rooming house inquiring about him. You left your Beach Haven phone number with the manager there. He's an old friend. So I called you. I want you to help Nick. That *is* why you're down here, isn't it? To help Nick?"

"His brother Bernie's my best friend. I'm trying to put the two back in touch with each other."

Bernie hasn't seen or heard from his brother in six months, not since Nick ran off and left his wife and kids back in Camden for the glory of a gambler's life. Bernie's worried. But the truth is he's also feeling guilty at having turned down Nick's last request for cash. Bernie's like that. He'll say no and then hate himself afterward. What he doesn't seem to understand is that he would have hated himself even more if he'd said yes.

"Then, as far as I'm concerned, you're trying to help."

Something in his tone has changed. He looks tense again.

"Is Nick in some kind of trouble?"

Cappy finishes his drink and I motion to the waitress for another. My beer is still untouched.

"I tried to help him in my own way, to repay him. I told him certain things. That was a mistake. Now you've got to get him out of here."

"Why?"

"Why ask? You came here to take him back, didn't you? So take him back."

"Tell me what happened."

The waitress arrives with the second vodka. He lifts the glass in a quick salute and swallows.

"I made a big mistake, Mr. Sweeney." He pauses to look down at his glass. "You see, sometimes when I drink I say things. Things I shouldn't." Suddenly he leans across the table toward me. "I never asked. Are you married, Mr. Sweeney?"

"No."

He studies me a moment and then goes on.

"Trust. That's what it's all about. Nick trusts me. Oh, he trusts others at the mission, too. Lady René. Sister Felice. Especially Sister Felice. But he and I are close. That's why he's asked me to hold certain papers for him." He lowers his voice to a whisper. "I think he's becoming paranoid. But with good reason." He pats his raincoat. "His papers are safe with me."

"What is it you said to Nick?"

He doesn't hear me.

"What sort of cop were you? Vice, drugs, what?"

"Homicide. Look, are you listening to me? What was it you told Nick?"

"Nick? He only wants his old job back. That's all. He means no harm. He's no high roller, you know."

"Is that what you talked to him about, how to get his old job back?"

"In a manner of speaking."

He holds his empty glass up in the waitress's direction. Before I can wave her off, she's at the table with another.

"Last one," I say to her, as she walks away.

He shakes his head. "On second thought, you can't help Nick."

"Why's that?"

"He doesn't want it. He's sick. You can't help a man like that, not unless *he* wants it. He tried GA but stopped going to meetings weeks ago. Still . . . like they say, it only takes one win to make you well." Then he's off on a new tack. "Nick's not much of a player. He needs an edge."

"What do you mean?"

"You gamble?"

"I've played blackjack a few times, yeah."

"Then you know the game. You know there's a basic strategy. And you know there's a way to manage your money. When you're losing you don't double or triple your bets, trying to recoup your losses. Well, Nick, he doesn't know that."

"He's a steamer."

"Exactly. That's why he needs an edge. All he wants is to get his old job back. He was at the Poseidon a few days ago trying to convince them. Who knows, maybe it'll work."

"And you gave him the edge he needed with the Poseidon? Is that what this is all about?"

An impish gleam fills his eye. Then he shakes his head. "Nick'll tell you everything when you see him."

I'm stymied. "Cappy, look—"

"Did I mention that Nick got a phone call this morning?"

"A phone call? At the mission?"

"That's right. I think it has him worried."

"Why?"

"What time is it?"

I look at my watch and tell him it's seven-thirty.

"He's meeting someone right now. At the lighthouse. He doesn't know who it is. I almost followed him but then I thought, no, this Mr. Sweeney, he's the man for that." He throws his hands in the air in a gesture of frustration. "It's all my fault. Sometimes I say things I shouldn't."

2

ABSECON LIGHTHOUSE in the Inlet area is one of the few landmarks from Atlantic City's glory days still standing. The neighborhood's mostly rundown apartment buildings and rubble-strewn lots now, although here and there you see a new high-rise going up. The red-and-white beacon itself has been treated for years like a condemned building, the romantic appeal that once made it the most visited lighthouse in the country overshadowed now by the glitzy allure of blackjack, craps, and slots. Closed to the public (it attracts only vandals these days), it nevertheless stands as a lofty tribute to the town that gave us the Ferris wheel, the picture postcard, and saltwater taffy. I understand there's a plan afoot to restore the structure and open it to visitors again. Maybe someone finally realized there's not much to do here anymore, other than watch your money disappear. Still, the old Atlantic City is gone forever, and that's everyone's loss. Truth is, some things really *aren't* as good as they used to be.

Looking down Pacific Avenue past the Showboat, I can make out the flashing lights from a police barrier looming in the early darkness. At Rhode Island Avenue I'm waved over by a uniformed officer with a luminescent baton.

I pull over abruptly and get out. I'm wearing chinos, hiking boots, and a light windbreaker, so this calls for a little chutzpah.

"Lt. Frank Sweeney, Sergeant. Philadelphia PD."

I hold my old ID wallet, half-opened, in my hand. He never even looks at it. Cops seem to recognize other cops, even ex-cops. It has something to do with the stride, the tone of voice, the mannerisms. Some say it's the swagger and the arrogance. My guess is we're talking about the same things.

"You here to see Captain Talley?"

I nod. He's young so I push my luck.

"Who got the call?"

"Fire department, sir. Half hour ago. The arson boys are in there now. Northfield's here, too."

"Northfield?" A mistake. Too late to correct myself.

"Major Crimes Squad." He's studying me now.

I go on as if nothing's happened.

"Where's the captain?"

"Over there," he says, pointing.

Three men appear to be talking to two kids by the curb at Rhode Island Avenue. Behind them, emergency flashers intermingle with the spotlights trained on the lighthouse. It looks like a night launch at Cape Canaveral. Everyone's wondering if the old beacon's going to make it off its rickety launching pad.

Ducking under the web of yellow police tape, I get a dirty look or two, but nobody tries to stop me. Which is just as well because my mind is elsewhere. I've had my share of dealings with the Atlantic County Major Crimes Squad. There's a paved, high-speed crime corridor just sixty miles long between A.C. and Philly, and it's been heavily traveled since the casinos opened. I know what's going on here. These guys from Northfield didn't show up merely to assist in an arson investigation. If they're on the scene it means there's a body.

I make my way through a maze of hoses and fire paraphernalia spread out on the street. At the curb near one of the fire trucks the three men are talking to the two kids straddling their bicycles.

"No, no. *I* saw it first, mister."

The boy's speaking to a man wearing a fire helmet and turnout coat. An arson investigator.

"Maybe he did, maybe he didn't," says the other kid. "Don't matter. It's the dude in the Mercedes called it in."

"What's your name, kid?"

"Sir Charles."

"Yeah, dat's his name." The second boy looks at the first. "Mine's Nails."

"Sir Charles and Nails. Right."

"Know what I'm talking 'bout for sure. Saw him stop the car right in front of dat lighthouse and stare out the window like he jest seen Elvis or somethin'."

"So what'd he look like, Nails?"

The investigator winks at the other two men. One's in a chief's uniform. The other, Talley, wears a rumpled blue suit, white shirt, and no tie. He's fifty-nine. Looks forty, with a tight gut and the wrinkle-free face of a man who knows how to take care of himself. Some say he takes *very* good care of himself, doesn't pull his own weight. Talley calls it "delegation of responsibility." Whatever it is, Jake Talley's a good cop.

"Some old guy. Funny sort of lopsided hair and a slimy little cigar.

Called somebody on his phone. Must've been 911. That's what it was, 911, like on TV. Why else'd a rich white dude pull over and stop in this neighborhood?"

"Sure weren't looking for no girls," says Sir Charles, "not here."

"No pussy round here," says Nails, looking at the other.

"Jesus, you two talk like you personally took a census of all the Inlet snatch."

Talley moves closer. "So where'd you see the Merce?"

Nails points to the curb. "Right here."

"He pulled over and stopped? Didn't just cruise by?"

"Stopped."

"Color was it?" asks the arson investigator.

"White," says Nails, "all shiny, like new."

"And then you saw him talking on his car phone," says the chief.

Sir Charles, still straddling his bicycle, moves in close, edging Nails aside. "That's what he said, Mr. Fireman. But I saw the fire, saw it first. Saw it all red like. Like a glow, you know? And the smoke was black, I think."

"Gimme your names." The investigator reaches inside his pocket for paper and pen.

"Just did."

"Your real names. None of this bullshit play-acting."

"You sure none of you kids made the call?" the chief asks.

Sir Charles and Nails shake their heads in unison.

A fireman comes out of the lighthouse, yells in this direction.

"Captain Martindale, they're ready for you."

Martindale, the investigator, looks at the chief.

"Get their names, willya Tony?"

Turning, he and Talley walk back toward the lighthouse. I keep behind them, waiting to be noticed. We reach a small fenced-in area that surrounds what was once the lighthouse visitor's center.

Martindale is seething. "What a fucking day. First I hear I'm getting audited. Then a fire in a fucking lighthouse. Jeees-us, a lighthouse! And a little acne-faced white kid thinks he's Charles fucking Barkley, for chrissakes. What's the world coming to?"

"They're just kids, Ray," says Talley.

"And the black kid, *he* thinks he's Lenny Dykstra. They got it all bass-ackward, Jake."

"They may be able to tell us something."

"Shit, in my neighborhood we'd never let no pimply-faced cracker pretend he was Wilt the Stilt. What's the world coming to? Don't let the little cons go nowhere. I'll talk to them later."

He disappears through the front door of the old visitor's center.

"Captain?"

Talley looks at me, uncomprehending for a moment. Steel gray eyes beneath a wide, sloping forehead.

"Frank Sweeney, is that you? Jesus, how the hell are you? What're you doing here?"

"A long story, Captain. Guess Bernie never told you. I left the department just before Christmas."

"What?"

"Yeah, I'm working solo now. Run an antiques shop on Walnut Street. Do a little PI work when it comes along."

"I'll be damned. I never thought I'd see the day."

"You hear about Bernie? He just had bypass surgery."

"Oh, no. Christ, nobody told me."

"He's trying to keep it quiet. Thinks he's going to go back to work in a few days and nobody'll be the wiser."

"Sounds like Bernie. He's okay, though?"

"They say he's going to be fine. He's going to have to make a few changes in the ol' lifestyle though."

"So what the hell are you doing here?"

"I'm trying to find Bernie's brother."

"What? Nick's missing?"

"You've got a body inside, am I right?"

"Yeah, looks like we have a homicide on our hands."

"Any ID yet?"

"Not yet. When Martindale's finished in there we'll know."

I reach inside my shirt pocket and take out a photograph.

"Bernie gave me this. You may want to check it against your victim."

28

"What the? . . . What makes you think it's Nick D'Angelo in there?"

He looks down at Nick five years ago, holding his seven-year-old. The slick black hair, nearly all gone now, was just beginning to thin out then.

"I just talked to a friend of his. Says Nick was supposed to meet someone here this evening."

"Yeah, but . . . oh, shit." He looks up at the lighthouse.

A station wagon driven by the Atlantic County medical examiner begins inching across the grass toward us.

"I UNDERSTAND THERE'S a body. Is that right?"

A tall, thirtyish woman in blazer and slacks has materialized next to me. Both hands clutch the straps of a brown leather rucksack slung over her shoulder.

"I haven't been inside."

"You a cop?"

"You a reporter?"

"Yeah, actually. *Atlantic City Star.* Your turn." She moves closer.

In the residual light, I can make out penetrating brown eyes and long champagne-colored hair gathered up in the back. She has the self-assured brashness of the young feminist warrior. It's in her body language, the way she presumes.

"I'm an interested party, that's all."

"Interested in what?"

I turn around. Martindale's cause-and-origin men have come down, carrying plastic evidence bags. The body appears next, under a sheet on one of the ME's gurney's. When I turn back the reporter's gone.

TALLEY, MARTINDALE, AND the ME stand in the doorway behind the body. The captain looks in my direction once, then turns away. Whatever's under that sheet is cruelly misshapen, as if it's been rolled up and tied in a knot.

At the ME's station wagon I take a look before the two assistants can lift the gurney in.

Fire can do grotesque things to people. Most victims are found in what's called the pugilistic attitude, a defensive boxing pose that looks something like the fetal position. It's caused by the stronger muscles being exposed to intense heat, making them contract drastically, pulling the limbs in toward the body. The hands are cupped like claws, the fingers drawn in toward the palms. If a badly burned body is not in this position, either it was caught in a flash fire or rigor mortis set in beforehand. In the latter case, you can be sure burning wasn't the cause of death.

"Those are flame burns. I'd guess he died from smoke inhalation."

I turn to find the medical examiner standing next to me. She's a portly, middle-aged woman, her hair prematurely white, exuding a motherliness that's reassuring under the circumstances.

"Is that supposed to be good?" I say, fending off anger with sarcasm.

Nick's body isn't completely charred. Which isn't saying much. His hair, what there was of it, is gone, his facial features partially hidden under raised and blackened skin. Some of his clothing has been consumed, but you can still read the label on the undershirt he was wearing. The pugilistic attitude is only partially developed. His fingers are open slightly and extended, as if he were reaching for something when he died.

"Dead is dead." She holds Nick's wallet and the photograph I gave Talley. "I understand you knew him."

"Not well. He was by best friend's brother."

"I'm sorry. Wallet ID's him as Nicholas P. D'Angelo. Is that right?"

It's him, all right. Nick had one front tooth capped in gold. The victim's lips are pulled back over the gums in a rictus of intense terror. There's no mistaking the yellow metal revealed by the corpse's death grin.

"That's right, it's Nick."

Satisfied, she glances at the photograph one more time, then returns it to me.

"I'll do what I can. Have some results as soon as possible."

Talley and Martindale wait for me in front of the visitor's center.

"Frank Sweeney, this is Capt. Ray Martindale. He's our chief arson investigator."

Talley looks like he wishes he'd been out of town for this one.

Martindale and I shake hands. He's a burly black man who gives the impression of contending with a restless energy he can't quite control. He's tall, too. At eye level I find myself staring at the collar of his turnout coat.

"Sorry, Sweeney," he says, more angry than sad, which pleases me.

"Yeah, me too," says Talley. "This is going to be tough on Bernie."

There's an awkward silence, which Talley finally breaks.

"What was his brother doing down here, anyway?"

"Nick had a gambling problem. Lost his job with Camden PD. Left his wife and kids months ago, too. Apparently he's been living at the Lighthouse Mission for several weeks."

Martindale looks at me. "Jesus, I thought the name sounded familiar. I think I met him once at a GA meeting."

There's another awkward silence.

"So, Sweeney," says Talley, "want to tell us what you know?"

There's a window of opportunity here and I take it.

"I'd like to see inside first."

To me it's a simple matter of professional courtesy but Talley balks.

"Jesus, Sweeney, it's not like Philly down here. The DA could have my badge for letting a PI in on an official investigation."

"All I'm asking for is a little chaperoned visit. For Bernie's sake?"

Talley owes Bernie big time. I've got him over a barrel and he knows it.

"Give him the nickel tour, Ray. Then we'll talk."

"Let's go," says Martindale, "shouldn't take long." He looks at me. "Hope you're not afraid of heights."

He bends down, picks up two battery-powered spotlights, and hands me one, aiming his at the door.

"We start here."

The rusty door to the visitor's center has been swung back. There's a portable exhaust fan in the doorway, blowing straight at us. He turns it off and closes the door, showing me what's left of the two shackles.

31

"When we arrived this was locked up tight as a drum. Had to smash the padlocks off to get in. *Two* padlocks, I might add."

He swings the door back open and walks through, the top of his head brushing the transom. I follow him and the first thing I notice is the smell. Martindale, as if on cue, explains.

"Gasoline, turpentine, and oil-base paint are what you smell. Gasoline was the primary accelerant. Arsonist brought that with him. We found the can inside. The turpentine and paint were already on the premises. They were fixing up the old place."

The onetime visitor's center is nothing more than a small utility building connected to the base of the lighthouse. I scan the walls with my spotlight looking for a light switch. All I can find are open receptacle boxes with the wires tied off. Inside the door, immediately to the right, is a small room that once served as a gift shop, back when the city fathers still cared about attracting tourists, not just high rollers. I can make out a damaged display counter and behind it, against the back wall, some empty shelves. Shattered glass from the display case lies on the floor. Some chipped red bricks have been stacked in a corner. To my left is a small storage room. It's filled with cans of paint and turpentine, most still unopened, as well as a cardboard box containing brushes, scrapers, and other tools. Litter and plaster debris are scattered about on the concrete floor.

I follow Martindale down a narrow arched hallway about twenty feet long. Red bricks show through the white paint on the walls, indicating we're now in the original lighthouse structure. There's no sign of the fire having reached this area. At the end of the hallway I can see why. There's an arched doorway like a hatchway on a ship, only this one is full-size and reaches to the floor. Martindale runs his light around the arch for my benefit, and I test the door. The doorjamb and the door itself are made of solid iron.

"I presume this was closed?"

He nods.

We walk through, closing the door behind us. Now we're in a small alcove about ten feet from the foot of the spiral staircase going to the top of the lighthouse. The fire has blackened the brick walls enclosing the alcove and stairs, and there's water everywhere from the interior having been hosed down. The smell of gasoline mixed with turpentine and paint is nearly overpowering.

Martindale points to the other side of the arched door. Its gray paint is gone, covered now with a layer of black carbon. He kicks at several charred lumps of metal at the foot of the stairs.

"Cans of paint and turpentine, all melted from the heat," he says, his voice bouncing off the walls. "There was one other can that held the gasoline. It had a few drops left in it. We may be able to do something with that. I'll have the lab at Hammonton take a look at it."

He points to the one window on this level. It's been broken. Pieces of glass are scattered about on the floor.

"We found it like that. Killer must have broken it from inside beforehand. He broke a window at the top near the lens room, too. Later, after your buddy had climbed the stairs, the killer spread the gasoline around, went outside, closed all the doors behind him, and walked around to this window. Then he tossed in his lighted torch. With all the accelerant splashed around in here and all the paint and turpentine stored upstairs on the landings, there would've been an incredible flash, then an instantaneous venting straight up to the lens chamber. It's called the chimney effect. Heated gases always rise, but in a building like this it would happen so fast you probably couldn't move more than a few feet before it got to you. The open staircase sucked the flames straight up, and the broken windows guaranteed him a draft. This son of a bitch knew what he was doing."

He walks over to the base of the wall, a few feet from the first metal step on the spiral staircase.

"Here's our point of origin. This is where the torch landed. See the V pattern, how it starts down here near the floor and spreads upward, branching out as it goes? Here on the concrete floor, this is called spalling. It's pitted from the heat drawing the moisture out of the concrete."

My spotlight finds a white area on the opposite wall that the fire seems to have missed. It's in the vicinity of the iron door. Right in front of it is a wooden stepladder that has been thoroughly blistered.

"What happened there?"

"That's not unusual in a flash fire like this. The heat was so intense the soot couldn't adhere to the wall. But look what it did to the wooden ladder. See the alligatoring, those large rolling blisters? More effects of the intense heat."

"What's this 'torch' you keep referring to?"

"Show you when we get back outside. Come on, I'll take you upstairs."

I put my head next to the thick newel post and look straight up, sighting along the vertical support of the staircase. The iron stairs and landings, although they've been designed with triangular holes to lessen the weight, completely fill the core of the lighthouse, obscuring any light source that might be above.

"How could Nick have seen anything? Did he have a flashlight on him when you found him?"

"There was one next to the body."

"And other than that there was no light source in here?"

"There was one other. It's probably what drew him up there in the first place. Come on, I'll show you."

Carefully, I begin to follow him up the stairs.

"The entire structure's 171 feet above grade," he says. "There are 228 steps to the base of the light fixture and another twelve to the light room itself. I know, I counted. And six landings, with a window on each one."

By the time we reach the second landing, I can feel the walls closing in on me. The open staircase doesn't help any. It makes me feel as if I'm hanging in midair. Add in the two beams of light bouncing about, along with the caustic smell of gas and turps permeating my nostrils, and I'm beginning to wish I'd stayed below.

"One more landing to go," he says.

When we get there I have to sit down, take a few deep breaths, and put my head between my knees. I can feel Martindale grinning behind me.

"This is where we found him."

He aims his light at a small wooden bench below a recessed window with a metal grill over it. The bench is black with soot and charred paint, except for a gray spot where the body was.

"Found him with his fingers gripping that grillwork on the window."

"Like he was trying to pull it out?"

"Exactly."

He aims his light down at the landing.

"And this is where we found what lured him up here. A Coleman lantern with twin fluorescent tubes. It gives off 360 degrees of illumination. Down on the ground you can see it several blocks away. I went down and checked. Lights up this window pretty good."

"How do you know the Coleman wasn't Nick's?"

"Not likely he'd bring something that expensive along. Besides, we found the flashlight next to the body, like it'd fallen out of his hand."

"So what are you saying?"

"Talley says you told him D'Angelo came here to meet someone. Well, it was a trap. Our arsonist put the lantern up here to make it look to D'Angelo like someone was waiting for him. I figure it this way. Once D'Angelo gets all the way up here, the killer, who's been hiding out somewhere in the bushes down below, sneaks in and splashes some accelerant around, locks everything up, and goes back outside to light the fire through the window. It wouldn't take more than a minute or so to do all that. Remember, earlier he'd broken the windows up top and down below. D'Angelo wouldn't have paid any attention to that, not the way the rest of the place already looks. Anyway, so D'Angelo probably hears something downstairs. Maybe he heads back down, thinking it's Mr. X arriving for the meeting. Then he smells something new. It's not paint and turpentine. It's gasoline. Now he's worried, and he doesn't have very long to take evasive measures. Then he hears something new, an explosion—a popping noise, followed by a whooshing sound. Next he feels a gust of searing hot air, then the smoke and flames. He probably panics and starts back up the stairs. He's disoriented now, gagging and hyperventilating. It feels like his lungs are on fire, like there's something burning inside his chest. He makes it back to this landing where he grabs the window grill and tries to pull it out in order to break the glass. But it's too late. And there's nowhere else to go. Even if he makes it all the

35

way to the lens room at the top, it won't do him any good. There's no way out."

It's good to hear this. It gives me something to focus on. Gives me a reason for being here, the first good reason I've had in months for doing my job. Suddenly, whatever's been pursuing me for the past year has backed off a little. It's nice to be on the offensive for a change.

"How long you figure it took?"

"ME figures the smoke got him within a minute or so. Since the structure's mostly metal and brick, the fire itself didn't last very long. But it was long enough for the whole structure to be inundated with smoke."

Martindale begins to make his way back down the stairs. I take one last look around with my light. One of the open electrical boxes on the wall above the window bench catches my eye. The wiring is exposed, as if the repairmen never got around to covering it up. Hanging over the bottom edge of the box by a fraction of an inch is something so brightly colored it stands out in the flickering shadows. I take a handkerchief out of my back pocket, stand up on the bench, and take it down. It's an orange casino chip—a wheel chip, to be precise—with a raised image of some kind on it. Under the light I can make out the familiar figure of a mythical Greek god.

DOWNSTAIRS, THERE'S a new arrival.

"This is Detective Petrillo," says Talley, looking uneasy. "He'll be the case detective on this one."

I shake hands, trying not to stare. Petrillo's a baby. I put his age at twenty-five, maybe less. He's dressed in baggy khakis, a blue denim shirt, and an obnoxious necktie made to look like a fish. He doesn't look old enough to vote, let alone conduct a murder investigation. Is it embarrassment I detect in Talley's face? I certainly hope so.

I hand Martindale the handkerchief with the casino chip and explain where I found it.

"It's a wheel chip," I tell him.

"Shit, I know what it is," he says. "I bought my share of them over the years, for Christ's sake. The question is what the fuck was it doing up there?"

36

"I'm not sure. Could have been left there by Nick."

"A dying man's message," says Detective Petrillo.

"Shit," Martindale says again, frowning at him.

"Where's it from?" asks Talley.

"Well, the image *is* the Greek god Poseidon," I say.

"Then it must be from the Poseidon Casino," says Petrillo.

Another deduction like that and he'll make sergeant in no time.

"Did D'Angelo gamble there?" Talley asks, eyes averted.

I nod. "He had a job there. As a security guard. But it's odd. Nick didn't play roulette. His game was blackjack."

"We'll dust it for prints," says Petrillo, plucking the handkerchief out of Martindale's hands.

I look at Martindale. "Can I ask what this torch is you've been referring to?"

He walks over to his car and comes back with a plastic evidence bag. Inside is what looks like a ball of fused metal.

"Found it on the floor near the point of origin. I'm sure it's the ignition device. It's some kind of metal wrapped around a matchbook to give it weight. He could light the matches and then toss the whole thing in through the broken window."

But Talley's patience has worn thin.

"Okay, Sweeney, now let's hear what you have to tell us."

3

IT'S AFTER 10 P.M. when I finally arrive on the floor of the cardiac recovery unit at Philadelphia Memorial. I have to keep telling myself it's okay to be here. After all, Bernie's been out of intensive care for two days, having progressed to taking several strolls a day up and down the hallway. And he did claim on the phone yesterday that he felt fine. But then that's what he said the day before his doctor found 90 percent blockage in three arteries, too.

In his room the light's on over the bed. He's on the phone, talking in hushed tones, looking grim-faced. There's a copy of *Dr. Dean Ornish's Program for Reversing Heart Disease* on the table by his bed.

"That was Michelle," he says, hanging up. "I wanted to be the one to tell her. She's taking it badly."

"How'd you find out?"

"Talley called me."

"I'm sorry, Bernie. I wanted to tell you in person."

He stares out the window at the night lights on the west Philadelphia skyline. When he looks back at me there are tears in his eyes.

"Bernie, it's not your fault. You couldn't have saved him."

"What're you saying? Trying to save my own brother was a mistake?"

Trying to *save* anybody is the mistake, but he doesn't need to hear that right now.

He slumps back against the pillows. In the other bed his roommate kicks at the sheets and continues snoring.

"Are you up to a little stroll?" I ask.

He gets up slowly and puts on slippers and a wine-colored bathrobe.

"There's a little lounge area down the hall," he says, gamely. "They've got a coffee machine there. You can put it on my tab. Me, I'm not allowed. No more caffeine, no more pizza, no more beer. My life's over, Frank."

On his feet he looks worse than he did in bed, more unstable, less sure of himself. I imagine the foot-long scar running down the middle of his chest.

With him clutching my arm, we make our way out into the hall, past the glaring nurse at the desk, and down the middle of a dark corridor toward the hum of a distant coffee machine. The doors to most of the rooms are closed, but every now and then I can see a patient sitting up in bed, staring blankly at the lonely glow of a television set.

"Nick just wanted to be a player, Frank, a winner. That's all he ever really wanted out of life. It's pathetic but true."

I agree, on both counts. As a gambler Nick had the same shortcomings he had as a cop. He was lazy and impatient. He wanted the quick fix, the short cut to success. Maybe that's what got him killed. That and his bad luck.

"He was a good man, Frank. A good father and a good brother. He loved Michelle and the kids. He would've sooner cut out his own heart than leave them with this . . . this memory."

Now he's reconstructing the past, something I know a lot about. It's a common tendency among the grieving. The Nick D'Angelo that Bernie is remembering is the same man who three years ago cashed in his wife's insurance policy and "borrowed" his son's first communion money so he could drive to Atlantic City and blow it all on two hours of blackjack. He's the same man who two years later lost his job as a vice cop because he stole cash out of his buddies' lockers. The same man who walked out on his wife and kids eight months ago to be closer to the action in Atlantic City. True, he hated himself for what he did. In the end I think he just hated himself period.

At the end of the corridor Bernie sits down on a small couch next to the coffee machine while I fish around in my pocket for some coins. It takes several tries for the machine to work. When I finally get my coffee it arrives in a little paper cup with playing cards on it. Aces and tens. A full house. Nick would have been pleased.

"Look, Bernie, about the arrangements, you're in no shape—"

"Michelle says she'll do it. She insists. It's part of her 'penance,' she says. The question is, what's mine? What do I do to atone for this, Frank?"

Nothing's changed.

I met Bernie on a Lenten retreat the year I graduated from Villanova. That was thirty years ago. He was in his second year at St. Charles Borromeo Seminary and had been asked to run a Saturday-night session on "Faith and Sexuality." In those days for a young seminarian to be given an assignment like that meant someone in the diocese had plans for him. What Bernie didn't realize was, it was also a test. And he failed. He was having grave doubts about becoming a priest. We talked about it until three in the morning. Afterward, I knew he'd never be ordained. Five months later, after I'd gone off to grad school to study art history, he entered the police academy, getting a three-year head start on me as a cop. Bernie had a jump on me in the guilt department, too. He never thought of himself as *worthy,* worthy to be a priest, a brother, or even a friend. You name it and Bernie has agonized over it at one time or another. With one exception. I never saw Bernie D'Angelo reveal the faintest glimmer of self-doubt about being a cop. I guess even the conscience-stricken sometimes find a refuge from their anguish. But it's rarely the Church that provides it.

"Dammit, you can't keep punishing yourself for someone else's—"

"Someone else's what, Frank? Michelle and I *are* the ones who wouldn't help him out. His own wife and brother, for God's sake! All he wanted was a few hundred. A man died, Frank, because we wouldn't give him a lousy three hundred dollars."

Now I'm angry.

"You don't know that. We don't have any idea why he died. Besides, how many other times did you give him money? Did it ever help? Did it ever do him any good? Did he ever change?"

I lose him for a few moments as he stares down the dark hallway. This time when he returns from visiting his private demons, there aren't any tears in his eyes.

"I want you to do me a favor, Frank."

"Anything, Bernie. You know that."

"Don't say that until you know what I'm going to ask."

But it's true. I'd walk backward into Hell for the man. Besides, I already know what he's going to ask.

"What is it you want me to do, Bernie?"

"I want you to find out why he was in that lighthouse . . . why he died."

What he really wants is for me to play priest, to absolve him, if not of guilt, at least of the temporal responsibility for his brother's actions. That's a heavy burden to lay on a man who wants nothing more to do with priests or the Church.

"Nick was a decent man, Frank. A bad gambler but a good man. He didn't deserve to die. Not like that. Not trapped like a helpless animal."

40

"No, Bernie, he didn't."

The truth is, at fifty-one I've reached a point in my life when I don't believe *anybody* deserves to die, although it would be unfair to foist my midlife angst onto someone recovering from bypass surgery and now the loss of a brother. Nevertheless, I don't share Bernie's lofty opinion of his brother's character. Somebody wanted Nick dead, and I doubt it was because Nick was about to be named South Jersey Citizen of the Year. But Bernie's a big boy and ought to be able to handle the truth. Besides, there's more on my mind than protecting him from his brother's past. By the time I walked out of that lighthouse a faint but discernible electric charge had begun running through my system. For the first time since Catherine's death I'm able to look beyond the next twenty-four hours and not feel an attack of the black dog coming on. It's a hell of a thing to have to say, but Nick's murder has jolted me back into the land of the living.

So I let Bernie in on my meeting with Cappy, recounting the bizarre conversation over dinner at Franco's. I describe my tour of the lighthouse. And I tell him about the wheel chip.

"What's a wheel chip?"

"They're used in roulette. They have no particular monetary value like other chips. That's why there's nothing on them but the casino's emblem or logo."

"I don't get it."

"In roulette each player's assigned a different color chip to bet with. You choose the value of your particular color before you begin to play. Then you buy into the game for however many of those chips you want."

"I still don't get it. Nick didn't play roulette. He thought it was a sucker's game, no control over it. That's why he played blackjack. He always said *he* was in control with blackjack."

"I know. Cappy said the same thing."

"Then what's the point? And how do you know this chip was left there by Nick in the first place?"

"I don't. But the prints should answer that question. My guess is it was his insurance."

41

Bernie looks mystified.

"In blackjack they have a bet called 'insurance.' When you think the dealer may have a natural, which is an ace and a face card or ten, you can place what's called an insurance bet. You're betting that he actually has blackjack, or twenty-one. If it turns out he does, you still win something with your insurance bet. The appeal of it for the casinos is that the player thinks he can't lose."

"So you're saying Nick was trying to hedge his bets?"

"Think about it. You're meeting someone, probably a stranger, up in a lighthouse. You used to be a cop. You know all about setups and ambushes. But you're thinking one of two things. Either you're thinking you've got the upper hand or what you stand to gain is so big it's worth the risk. Maybe you figure it's both. Then, probably at the last minute, you decide it would be smart to cover yourself somehow. So you leave a wheel chip at the scene. Just in case. It's the best you can come up with on the spur of the moment. If you'd taken the time to think about it, maybe you would have done something more obvious, less chancy. Maybe you wouldn't have gone up into the lighthouse at all."

"Nick loved taking chances. Besides, he wasn't capable of thinking ahead."

"Maybe, but he had to have put that chip there before he realized he was going to die. From what the arson investigator says, he wouldn't have had time to do it once the fire started."

"So what's it mean?"

He stands up and we start the slow walk back to his room.

"I'm not sure yet. My guess is it's some kind of plea for help. But all we know for sure is that it's a roulette chip from the Poseidon Casino, and roulette wasn't Nick's game."

Bernie stares at the floor a while, then says, "Find out what happened, Frank."

I nod, trying to look reassuring. Bernie looks up. Something else is on his mind.

"I expect to pay you for this, Frank."

"Just concentrate on getting better, Bernie."

"I'm serious, Frank. Consider this a business arrangement between friends. Besides, I know you can use the money."

He's right about that. Just about everything that belongs to me I inherited from Catherine, and none of it came unencumbered. The antiques shop is mortgaged to the hilt. I'd have sold it off right away if it weren't for the fact that I like the kind of people you meet in the business. They're interesting people. People with a sense of history. People with money. The Range Rover's not paid for either— twenty more payments to go. I ought to trade it in for something I can afford, like a used bicycle, but I've decided I look good in it. Toss in the fact that my daughter starts medical school in the fall and you'll have a sense of my once and future indebtedness. I've considered getting back into teaching, but I left the classroom in the first place because it didn't suit me. In short, financially speaking, it's decision time—either downsize or find some new markets. Which brings me back to Nick D'Angelo.

"We'll talk about it later," I say.

"Nothing to talk about. I'm paying you for services rendered. I'll call Talley in the morning and see if I can't get him to cut you a little slack down there."

"I don't think there's much slack to cut. It's too risky for him to feed information to a PI. Think about it. Would you do it?"

"He owes me, Frank. I don't usually call in my chits, but this time I'm making an exception."

There's a long silence as we approach his room. I can tell his thoughts have moved into new territory.

"It's two years next week, isn't it, Frank?"

"How'd you remember that?"

"Mother of God, Frank, I was there. I held you up at the graveside when you nearly collapsed. Or have you forgotten?"

As we reach the door to his room, I stop and let him go in alone.

"Get some rest, Bernie. I'll be in touch."

4

I₁ was 2 a.m. by the time I made it back to Beach Haven and into bed. Five hours later the clock radio clicks on with the seven o'clock weather forecast. Mostly sunny, high in the seventies, chance of rain near zero.

After a quick shave and shower, and a pot of strong coffee, I'm ready to attempt the drive back to Atlantic City. Outside, the air feels tepid and motionless. The tide is low; I inhale the boggy bouquet of Barnegat Bay's salt marshes as I leave the island. On the mainland it looks more like late fall than early spring. The grass along the Garden State Parkway, usually a rich parrot green this time of year, has the appearance of dry straw. It's the middle of the cruelest month and we've not had a drop of rain since early March.

On the bright side, I remind myself that the parkway isn't the Schuylkill Expressway, at least not yet, not even at eight a.m. on a Friday morning. Down here the stiffest competition a commuter faces comes from the processions of glitzy limos and chartered buses rolling relentlessly toward the casinos like floats in an endless high-roller's parade.

I make it to A.C. around nine, after the swing shift has headed home and well before the hordes of eager bus people have begun to pull into the casino parking garages. On Pacific Avenue the lighthouse has been cordoned off with police tape, the door to the visitor's center sealed with a chain and padlock, scant challenge for any enterprising locals.

The mission, several blocks from the lighthouse, is oblivious to any redevelopment being undertaken elsewhere. Here abandoned buildings bleed loose bricks and shards of broken windowpanes. Vacant lots are clotted with gravel and chunks of dry concrete. It's greed's own wasteland, T. S. Eliot country. *Winds in dry grass. Rats' feet over broken glass.* In the distance, across a barren landscape to the south, the first of eleven oceanfront casinos glitters enticingly, as faraway and out of reach as the green light seen from Gatsby's dock.

The mission itself is a flat, rectangular, one-story building that years ago used to be a thriving neighborhood supermarket. Angelo Valenti, the building's original tenant, went out of business soon after the first casino opened in the spring of '78. What's left of the store's sign— ANGELO'S MARKET, it reads—hangs precariously over the sidewalk like an untended grave marker. Rocks, bottles, and an occasional .22 bullet have destroyed much of its red-and-white plastic facing. As if deferring to Angelo's memory, the new occupants, rather than replace the old sign, have chosen a hand-lettered cardboard one, taping it to the inside of the storefront's large plate-glass window. It's yellow now from exposure to the sun and salt air.

Inside, a dozen people sit or lie about on the tile floor of the lobby. In front of them a young man with a beard stands with a clipboard, checking off names. He's wearing a black T-shirt bearing the image of a lighthouse that radiates four white beams. Above the light it says, LIGHTHOUSE MISSION and below it, HE SAID 'I AM THE LIGHT OF THE WORLD.'

Behind the bearded man there's a glassed-in reception area where a staff member is speaking to two men through a sliding window. Hand-lettered signs have been taped to the glass proclaiming various mission services and events. FREE HIV TESTING—CONTACT TED IN ROOM 11 ON TUESDAY MORNINGS. AA MEETING, THURSDAY AFTER LUNCH, IN THE CHAPEL. GA MEETINGS EVERY TUESDAY AND SATURDAY, 8 P.M., IN THE CHAPEL.

Something touches my right boot. Someone in tattered Nikes has placed a foot next to one of my new Timberlands.

"Good morning," says a white-haired man.

I put his age at seventy. He's small and wiry, about my height, dressed in soiled tan slacks and a rumpled white dress shirt. He smells of mildew.

"Good morning to you, too."

"We're about the same size, don't you think?"

"So we are."

"What's your name?"

45

"Frank Sweeney. What's yours?"

"Tommy. They call me Tommy the Toe." He extends his hand, looking down at my shoes again. "Sure would like to have them boots."

"They're all I've got."

"No problem. Get you another pair out back where they keep the donated stuff."

I try a different approach. "How long have you been in the mission, Tommy?"

"Too long."

"Did you know Nick D'Angelo?"

He nods. "Yeah. I knew Nick. It's a shame what happened. He was a nice man."

"Tell you what. You answer a few questions for me about Nick and I'll get you a new pair of Nikes."

He shakes his head. "I like yours better. I collect things, see. You know, things other people give me. It's good luck. See these?" He points to his pants. "Mrs. Babson, one of the trustees, gave me these. Used to be her son's. And this?"

He pulls his shirt sleeve back, revealing a plain Timex wristwatch.

"Mr. Abelson, the banker, gave me this."

Suddenly he seems to lose interest.

"Know why they call me Tommy the Toe?"

I shake my head.

"Show you."

He finds an open area on the floor and lines his feet up, one behind the other, on the linoleum tiles.

"Watch."

He begins to walk along a line where the tiles meet, his arms extended out from his sides for balance. After going the length of the lobby, he pivots on his toes, still on the line, and returns along the same path. When he reaches the spot where I'm standing, he smiles, claps his hands, and bows. No one else, I notice, seems to be paying any attention to this.

"I can do acrobatics, too. Used to have a high-wire act on the beach. Back in the fifties. Near Steel Pier? You remember it?"

"Don't think I ever caught it."

" 'Baby Titus, Child of the High Wire.' That was my billing. Actually, I wasn't a baby. I started on the wire at ten. 'Tommy the Toe' came later. You remember the Mechanical Man?"

I smile. "Yeah, I do."

"He and I was pals. Used to drink together." He anticipates my next question. "I'm sixty-nine."

"Well, you sure don't look it, Tommy."

"You're probably wondering what I'm doing here, huh? Slots. That's what did it. I don't work much no more. Brother Stephen, he sets me up with an odd job every now and then. But whenever I get any money it goes right into the slots. It's better if I don't work. You hungry?"

"I could use a cup of coffee."

He smiles as if I've just offered him *two* pairs of Timberlands. A connection has been made.

"Follow me."

He takes me across the lobby toward a hallway leading to the back of the building. We pass several small offices and meeting rooms as well as a lounge, where I can hear the muffled sounds of a television. At the end of the hall we can go right or left. He takes me right.

"Those are the dormitories down there," he says, pointing the other way. "Cafeteria's this way. Breakfast's over, but they let us have coffee and doughnuts during the morning. Until it's time for chapel, that is. Then they put the food away till lunch. There's coffee in the lounge, too—but it's more private back here. You ever been in a mission, Frank?"

I shake my head. "This is my first time."

"It's not so bad. They'll take care of you long as you want. Gotta do some scut work though. Ain't much around that's free no more."

He whispers to me. "It's not so bad," he says, averting his eyes, "once you get over the humiliation." Then he's back to his normal voice. "You a gambler, Frank? Lots of gamblers here. Been a real boom in mission work since the casinos come to town. I used to work at a casino. Got fired though."

We turn through a side door and we're in the kitchen. An obese black man, his forearms encased in yellow rubber gloves that reach to his elbows, stands at the sink scraping plates.

"Julius, this is Frank. He's my guest. He'd like a cup of your best."

"Frank, you say? Like in Ol' Blue Eyes?"

I deny any relationship to that other Frank, but Julius isn't interested.

"Heard him once. Live. I was a cook at the Sands. Good job. Lost it. Too much of this." He motions with his hand, downing an imaginary glass of something. "That Frank, he likes to put down a few, too. Don't see him doing no dishes in no mission kitchen. No sir, he's got it knocked."

Tommy hands me a Styrofoam cup filled from a Mr. Coffee machine in the corner. We walk through another doorway and take a seat in the empty cafeteria.

"This Brother Stephen you mentioned, who's he?" I sip some of the bitterest coffee I've ever tasted, trying not to cringe.

"You never heard of him? He runs the place. A good man. He'll help you through anything. Long as he thinks you're trying to help yourself. Hates gambling, though. With a passion. Don't get him started on that. It makes him weird."

"Did he know Nick?"

He thinks a moment. "Well, I'm sure he must have. He makes a point of getting to know everybody who's here for more than a night or two. And Nick, he was here a good while before . . . before what happened."

"You know Cappy, too?"

"Cappy? Sure. Everybody knows Cappy."

"Is he here? I'd like to talk to him."

"The cops were asking about him last night, too. Haven't seen him since late yesterday, though. You a cop?"

"A friend of Nick's."

He digests that.

"Ah, I see. Well, Cappy, he sometimes goes away for days." He lowers his voice again. "He's got a little problem with the bottle, too, you know. Like Julius. He and Julius go out and tie one on pretty regular. Brother Stephen, he doesn't like that either. But as long as you get to AA afterward, he's okay with it. Then he lets you stay."

Sounds a lot like the church I left behind. Sin one day, confess and rejoin the fold the next.

"Any idea where I might find Cappy?"

"He drinks just about anywhere. But he'll probably end up at the Hotel Underwood."

"The Hotel Underwood?"

Someone else has come into the cafeteria. He's standing near the door, watching us.

"Sol, come over here and meet Frank."

Sol takes short, quick, little steps in our direction, as if he has something urgent to report but is afraid we'll hurt him.

"Frank, this is Sol."

He stops about six feet away and just stands there. I nod at him. "Nice to meet you, Sol."

"You tell him about me?" he asks Tommy.

"Sol used to be a card counter," Tommy says, winking unabashedly. "He's been blacklisted by the best casinos."

Sol smiles and nods in agreement. "It's been six years since they first spotted me. Haven't lost my touch, though. Want to see?"

I shake my head. "Thanks anyway. Did you know Nick D'Angelo, Sol?"

"Nick? Sure. Awful blackjack player. Couldn't manage his money."

"Did either of you talk to him yesterday, before he left here?"

They both shake their heads.

"Didn't see much of him at all this past week or two," says Sol. "He was out running around, everywhere but here, it seemed."

"Doing what?"

"Said he was on to something. That's all he told me. Man never could gamble. Hope he wasn't trying to work out a new system. Won't work. Only counting works."

Tommy glares at him. "Sure as hell don't matter now."

"Who were his friends?"

"Not us, that's for sure," says Sol.

"Besides Cappy and Sister Felice, I'd say Lady René," says Tommy. "He wouldn't have much to do with the rest of us."

49

"Sister Felice is with the mission?"

"She's the chaplain," says Tommy.

"And Lady René?"

"Come on, I'll introduce you," says Sol, turning and shuffling toward the door.

"You want to talk again some time," says Tommy, "you know where to find me."

"Thanks, Tommy, I'll remember that. By the way, you ever been up in the lighthouse?"

"Not lately."

"Not last night?"

"Hell, no. What're you getting at?"

"Guess *you're* not afraid of heights, are you Tommy?"

THE LOUNGE, like the rest of the mission, is little more than old supermarket floor space partitioned off with two-by-fours and wallboard. You can see the markings on the tile floor where grocery shelves and freezers once stood. A few rooms have old-fashioned paneled doors transplanted from abandoned buildings; the lounge has nothing but an opening for an entrance.

About forty people—men, women, and children—have filled the large but sparsely furnished room. Nearly everyone's drinking coffee or juice out of Styrofoam cups and munching doughnuts from a plate on a table in the corner of the room. A few have grabbed one of the folding chairs or tattered recliners. The rest are standing or sitting cross-legged on the floor. There's not a lot of talk. Nearly everyone's watching some new morning talk show on a television bolted to the wall. Below the TV set is a hand-lettered sign that says, THIS TV DONATED BY O'HARA MOTORS.

Sol introduces me to Lady René, then goes and stands in the doorway. She's sitting in a corner, her bulk overflowing one of the room's two upholstered chairs. She's an obese woman of indeterminate age dressed in an enormous gray sweat suit with a bright yellow kerchief around her neck. I crouch down on the floor next to her.

"Man's a nuisance," Lady René says, glaring at him. "I suppose he told you he used to be a card counter?"

I smile and nod.

"That's bullshit. Don't you believe it. Man's a born loser. Couldn't count past ten if his life depended on it." She looks around the room. "Everybody's got his own story, I guess, but when you get right down to it, we're *all* losers here. Since the casinos arrived, half the outcasts and rejects of Atlantic City have come through the doors of this place. You gamble, Frank?"

"Once in a while. I like to watch the people more than anything else."

Catherine was the one I enjoyed watching the most. She said she loved the tingling feeling in her stomach as the ball rolled around the roulette wheel just before it dropped. It made her giddy, transformed her into a child. It's an image of her I've come to cherish.

"Don't understand what everybody sees in it. Why not just flush your money down the crapper?"

"Less fun, I guess."

"I suppose. Me, my weakness is Gallo Hearty Burgundy. Tried AA, but it doesn't work, not for me. Know why?" She turns her head a little so she can look me in the eye. "They expect you to stop drinking."

Her laughter bounces off the walls, enlarging the room. She reminds me of a chubby nun I had in the fifth grade, Sister Mary Aloysius, the only sister I ever remember wanting to please. She would tell us funny stories about the priests and hand out candy when the Mother Superior wasn't looking.

After a moment Lady René is serious again.

"I hate the casinos. They ran me out of business. Pushed me right off the Boardwalk. Last place I had was this pathetic little closet off on a side street. No one could ever find it. In the old days I'd do eight, maybe ten readings a day. The last year I worked I was lucky if I did one or two a week. Now every two-bit amateur who comes into this city's got his own system. So here I am, can't feed myself or pay the rent. What's a gal to do? Life's a bitch."

I tell her I agree, life's a bitch.

"I'm not the only one who hates the casinos," she goes on. "There's a bunch of us from the old days. People like Harry LaRue, the magician, and Busty Barkley, the fan dancer. And Tommy the Toe, too. We've got ourselves a self-help group going. Call it the Boardwalk Irregulars. All you got to do to belong is you got to have worked the Boards at one time or another. Brother Stephen lets us have the chapel once a week for our meetings."

I interrupt to ask her about Nick.

"You a friend of his?" she asks.

"I knew him, but not well. His brother's a good friend."

"You're doing somebody a favor." She states it as fact, not conjecture. "Okay then. Nick would come to me for a reading when he was about to hit the tables. Last week he consulted me three times. But it was different. It wasn't about cards or money. There was something on his mind. He was excited but, you know, afraid at the same time?"

"What was he afraid of?"

She thinks a moment. "I gave him his last reading the day before he died. But the man wouldn't listen."

"Why not?"

"He didn't like what the cards had to say. That often happens. But the cards can't lie."

"What did they say?"

"The card that came up for him was the Knight of Wands. Do you know what that means, Frank? The Knight is Lord of the Flame and Lightning, King of the Spirits of Fire. He represents activity, generosity, impetuosity, pride, and impulsiveness. Unpredictability, too. That was Nick to a tee. He'd been transformed by something. I don't know what it was, but if the Knight's your significator, it means you can turn bad. Especially if you're doing something that energizes you in an evil way. That's what happened to Nick. I didn't need no cards to tell me that." She stops and takes a breath, her chest heaving with emotion. "And he died by fire, too, didn't he. What's that tell you?"

"What do you think it was that changed Nick?"

"He was up to something is all I know. You could see it in his walk. And that cocky little grin he had. Before that he'd been down so low he walked around like he was ready to give it all up. He was getting up the courage to do something. Wouldn't say what. And he wanted

52

the cards to tell him it was okay. He asked if I thought he was in danger. I told him he didn't need a Tarot deck to know enough to stay away from the casinos."

"What'd he say to that?"

"He said it wasn't like that. It wasn't about going back to the tables."

"Did he say what it *was* about?"

"All I know is, he said his luck had changed and he wouldn't need me no more. Except we'd still be friends, of course. He just wanted his reading, his final send-off. That's when the Knight of Wands turned up, all engulfed in flames. He didn't so much as blink. Just asked me if I could tell whether he'd get his old job back. Didn't even care about the Knight."

"Tell me, besides Cappy, did Nick have any other friends?"

"Why don't you try Monica? Maybe she can help."

"Who's Monica?"

"Don't know her last name. Works with some escort service. He took her with him to the casinos. There's no one else I can think of." Then she stops and raises a finger. "Wait, there is one other person you might talk to."

"Who's that?"

"Harriet."

"Who's Harriet?"

"Can't miss her. She's always out front by the telephone. Never leaves her spot, except when her check comes in. Then she's off to the slots."

I stand up and stretch my legs.

"Would you like a reading before you go? No charge. I like your face." She reaches down for a plastic shopping bag on the floor by her side and pulls out a deck of Tarot cards.

"How about a rain check?"

"You're not a believer?"

"I don't have time. Besides, you might tell me something I don't want to know."

She smiles. "That's right. I just might."

———

53

HARRIET IS OUT in the lobby by the pay phone. She's the grand-motherly type, white-haired and solicitous, and she's in a wheelchair. On the floor next to her are two department-store shopping bags containing everything she owns.

"It's truly a shame about Nick," she says after I introduce myself. "I just can't believe it. He was such a nice man. Do you know what he did for me once? He came and got me at the Taj. Sometimes I play the slots so long I forget what time it is. Then I just pass out. Usually the guards take me off to the infirmary and call the police. The police always bring me back here. They're very nice. Well, a week ago, this guard, he just called the mission right off. And Nick came and got me. Wasn't that nice?"

As she talks she clutches a large, wide-mouthed plastic cup bearing the Taj Mahal's insignia. She keeps it at the ready, as if expecting a jackpot of quarters any moment.

"Did you know Nick well?"

"He would stop and talk with me once in a while. That's more than some around here do." She looks around the lobby as if to determine if anything might have changed in that regard. "Of course, I never go in the lounge where everyone else hangs around. So it's hard for them to be with me. Never leave my spot right here, except to eat, sleep, and go to the toilet. And chapel. I never miss chapel."

"Why is it you never leave here?"

"Don't want to miss my phone call. It's my son, Albert. He'll be calling soon. To take me home."

This stops me short. "I see. Tell me, did you talk to Nick yesterday?"

"Well, sort of."

"I don't understand."

"I was right here all morning waiting for Albert to call. But I guess it was one of his busy days. He's a stockbroker, you know, and they're real busy. Well, anyway, the phone did ring. But it was for Nick. So I sent someone to fetch him while I held the phone."

"Who was it?"

She shakes her head. "Don't know, but it was a man's voice."

"Young or old?"

"Middle, I'd say. Not young, not old."

"Did he have an accent or sound like anyone you know?"

"No one I know. No accent. Sounded white to me. Of course, all he said was, 'Is Mr. D'Angelo there?' "

"And what happened when Nick took the call?"

"He didn't know who it was either. I could tell that."

"He acted surprised?"

"Not so much that. More like he'd never heard of the man before."

"Then what?"

"Nick didn't say much. He mostly listened."

"Like he was being told to do something?"

She ponders this. "Yeah, like that."

"And what was it he was being told, could you tell?"

She shakes her head.

"Did Nick say anything else you can remember?"

She fiddles around with her coin cup and then looks up quickly. "There was one thing. A name. Nick said a name to the man."

"A name? What was it?"

"Jonah."

"Jonah who?"

"No idea. Don't know any Jonah myself. Never heard Nick mention one either."

"And you can't recall what Nick said about this Jonah person?"

"Nope. I couldn't hear every word anyway. Nick was turned away from me some of the time. I never moved though. Don't care whether or not it bothers people I'm here. Don't want to lose my spot. Got to be here when Albert calls."

"But you do go to the casinos, don't you? What do you do about the phone then?"

"Oh, that's only once a month. On check day. I get $436 a month from the government, you see. When that comes I pick a casino and leave the name where I'm gonna be with one of the girls here. They'll get word to me when Albert calls. Anyway, I'm usually back the next day."

"I guess it doesn't take long to lose $436."

"Not usually. Once, though, I had a big winning streak. At Bally's. Got comped and everything. Got to eat in their best restaurant and stay in a room all my own. Lost everything the next day. I hate gambling."

"Why do you do it then?"

"Makes me forget everything." She pauses and looks away. "Even my own son."

She's near tears.

"Have you tried Gamblers Anonymous?"

Her mood turns black. "GA's not for people like me. It's full of a bunch of sharpies and hoodlums."

I nod sympathetically. "Harriet, did you tell the police what you told me about Nick's phone call?"

She shakes her head. "They never asked. Hardly spoke to any of *us*. Only seemed interested in the staff."

5

THE MISSION'S OFFICES, four small rooms down a short hallway, are in the back of the building, around the corner from the chapel. Hand-lettered paper signs have been taped to the wall next to each door. BUSINESS MANAGER, ADMINISTRATIVE ASSISTANT, DIRECTOR, and CHAPLAIN, in that order.

I stop at an open door. STEPHEN LEEDS, DIRECTOR. Inside, an elderly woman—Mrs. Wellstone, according to her nameplate—sits at a desk outside the closed door to an inner office. She's working at a Macintosh computer.

"Do you know how to work one of these?"

She moves the mouse about cautiously on its little gray Apple pad, glowering at the screen.

"Sorry, I never touch the things."

"We just got it. It's not like my old IBM at all."

A framed print of DaVinci's *The Last Supper,* the first religious icon of any kind that I've noticed here, hangs behind her on the wall. A length of narrow linen fabric, like an altar cloth, has been draped over it. Some nondescript electric-acoustic harp music burbles out of a tape player in the corner of the room. Somebody appears to have invested a little time and money in the decor. The walls and doors are painted a pleasant light blue. There's even carpeting, also blue, several shades darker than the walls. A small couch and two upholstered chairs line the wall across from the desk. Some magazines and books have been set out on a coffee table. Over the couch a poster filled with clouds and sunbeams proclaims to all, EXPECT A MIRACLE.

"Would it be possible to speak with the director?"

"Brother Stephen's with someone right now, I'm afraid. And at ten-thirty he has chapel. Could you come back?"

I give her my name and decide to wander around for a while.

Down the hall, there's no one in the chapel yet. It's a plain, windowless room, much larger than the lounge, with off-white walls and the same worn tile floor. A hundred or so folding chairs have been arranged in parallel rows in front of an old mahogany pulpit. Most of the wall behind the pulpit is covered with a kitschy mural that stands out like a drunk at a garden party. More or less in the style of Norman Rockwell, it's not a picture that counts on subtlety to make its point. A haggard and exhausted man sits slumped over a blackjack table, head propped up with one hand, eyes fixed on the dealer's cards in the foreground. Physically wasted, the bleary-eyed wretch has the expression of someone who's just been given twenty-four hours to live. His hair is mussed up; his white dress shirt, with tie askew, is stained and open at the collar; and his complexion is red and blotchy. On the table to his right is an empty cocktail glass and an ashtray full of cigarette butts; next to them is the single chip that remains for his final wager. Lest some dullard miss the point, painted in bright red capital letters at the bottom is THE LOSER. On an adjoining wall I envision a complementary painting called THE WINNER by, say, Mark Twain. It would show a Christian holding four aces.

A little before ten-thirty, I move to the back by the door and watch people begin to straggle in. Though not especially talkative, they're an uneasy and restless bunch as they cram together on the gray metal chairs, jostling each other for space, swearing and cursing whenever something or someone irritates them. A young Hispanic in a T-shirt and dirty jeans shoves aside an old wino and proceeds to pace up and down the middle aisle, shouting every now and then at the person nearest to him. Nobody pays any attention except two little boys who leave their mother's side to stand in the aisle and stare. Up front two middle-aged women, one white, one black, argue over a sweatshirt being pulled back and forth between them. A male staff member intervenes, separates them, and walks off with the shirt. At this, Lady René, who is spread out across two chairs in the front row, laughs raucously and applauds.

Harriet enters the room, her wheelchair pushed by Tommy the Toe. He steers her down the middle aisle and parks the chair at the end of the front row.

Then another wheelchair enters the room, this one under its own power. It takes a second before I realize it's Meryl Sarbanes. She's able to control the electrically powered chair with her fingers and steer it over to the left side of the chapel where someone has set up her electronic keyboard. It would appear Lady René has another candidate for membership in the Boardwalk Irregulars.

A fortyish woman in a red denim shirt, jeans, and tennis shoes walks up the middle aisle carrying a Bible. The commotion subsides. Heads turn. Smiles and affectionate greetings all around.

"Hi, Sister!"

"How's it going, Sister?"

Sister stops to greet people, patting some on the back, squeezing the hands of others, occasionally bending down to give a hug. She makes a point of speaking to several of the children before going to the front of the room where she places the Bible behind the pulpit.

An old man in the back row yells out, "You preachin' today, Sister?"

Sister stands back and shakes her head, a contrite smile on her face. The group lets out a collective moan that she stifles with a stern glance. When she's gone the room becomes expectantly quiet.

In another minute a man appears at the pulpit: Brother Stephen, presumably. About forty, in jeans and a white cotton oxford, at first he looks too much like the other men in the room to be mistaken for a person of authority. But when he glances up I notice the feverish, darting Elmer Gantry eyes. He stands quietly for a moment, motions for everyone to stand, then turns to his right and nods.

I begin edging toward the door, then stop.

Meryl Sarbanes, leaning toward her keyboard, tongue fully extended, has begun to play something. I think it's "Amazing Grace" but can't be sure. Whatever it is, it's only the melody, a series of single tones, blank and emotionless except for Meryl's furious energy. Everyone else in the room seems to recognize it. As Meryl's head jumps up and down, spearing notes with her tongue, people begin to sing along, not an easy thing to do given the unpredictable pauses between notes. Then, as everyone reaches the middle of a line, Meryl loses her place.

. . . that saved a wretch like—

The song's staccato progression is broken. All singing stops. At first it appears the assembly, too, has lost its place, but glancing around I realize it's an act of charitable solidarity. Everybody's waiting patiently for Meryl to find the right note. When she finally does, the singing resumes.

When the song's concluded, Brother Stephen takes a deep breath and looks out over his congregation. There's a moment of uneasy silence before he reaches behind the pulpit and retrieves the Bible.

"My fellow players, lay down your cards and your dice and listen to the Book of Job: 'Naked came I out of my mother's womb, And naked shall I return thither; The Lord gave, and the Lord hath taken away; Blessed be the name of the Lord.' "

He marks his place, then looks up.

"This is a difficult time. As you know, we lost one of our own last night. Nick D'Angelo was not with us a long time, but this morning I'd like to dedicate my remarks to his memory. 'The Lord gave, and the Lord hath taken away.'

"How many know the story of Job? Well, let me tell it to you this morning. 'There was a man in the Land of Uz, whose name was Job; and that man was blameless and upright, one who feared God, and turned away from evil—' "

Something tugs at my elbow. I turn to find last night's reporter from the *Atlantic City Star* standing behind me in the doorway.

"Getting a little religion, are we?" she whispers in my ear.

"I like a good sermon. It's a lost art."

"So's witch-dunking."

"You disapprove?"

"I've heard it all before. He does this weird thing with the Book of Job. Twists it all around. The whole Bible's just some kind of goofy allegory about gambling to him."

I turn back to Brother Stephen. He's describing Job as a high roller who's run out his luck.

"My friends and fellow players, in the Book of Job God has made a wager with Satan. God, it appears, is a betting man."

"I thought God didn't gamble," the woman behind me whispers, "isn't that what Einstein said?"

"Einstein said he could never believe God plays dice."

She looks at me. "I was right about you."

She's near enough for me to pick up her scent. It's not perfume but something natural. She's wearing an ankle-length skirt, a long tunic sweater, and a hat of crocheted straw. Catherine never wore perfume either.

"Satan challenges God, taunting him, telling him that if he will inflict physical suffering on his servant Job then Job'll 'curse thee to thy face.' The Lord goes along with the test, putting Job in Satan's power. So Satan sees to it that Job loses everything, his oxen, his sheep, his belongings, even his own children. And he's afflicted 'with loathsome sores from the sole of his foot to the crown of his head.' Job's wife, wanting an end to the suffering, suggests to her husband that he get out now, cut his losses. 'Curse God, and die.' "

Brother Stephen pauses to stare down at the faces in the front row.

"How many of you ever got out? Is there anybody here who ever broke even and *walked away* from the tables or the slots? Anybody here who ever cursed the casinos and lived with the consequences? Are there any *free* men or women here?"

Heads begin to nod in agreement. A few "amen's" begin to be heard. The group is primed.

"Job's three friends show up, and Job curses the day he was born: 'Let the day perish wherein I was born.' Who here, after a big loss, has not felt the same way? 'I am not at ease,' said Job, 'nor am I quiet; I have no rest; but trouble comes.' Was ever a better description written of the disease of gambling, of the curse of addiction? And what *comfort* do our friends offer? Can they be of any help? Beware, my fellow players, of the false comfort of Job's 'friends'! They are like every casino host, every pit boss and floorman, every casino manager you ever knew."

Behind me there's a derisive snort. When I turn to look, she has her hands in the air and is shrugging dismissively. She heads for the hallway, motioning for me to follow.

"Trust me, you're not missing anything," she says, coming toward me out in the hall.

"He always like that?"

"You should hear what he does to the Sermon on the Mount." She smiles at me. "You're the Range Rover parked out front, right?"

She looks me over unashamedly. It's not an unpleasant feeling, being checked out like this, but my cop brain can't help recalling that the last time a woman looked at me this way she had to be wrestled to the street after producing a .45 automatic from her purse.

"That's me. And you, you're with the *Star*."

"You *do* remember. At first I wasn't sure you would. You never answered my question last night, you know."

"What question was that?"

"At the lighthouse you said you were an 'interested party.' Interested in what?"

"I'm helping a friend. His brother was the one murdered last night."

"Really?" She reaches into the rucksack for her notebook. "Brother of the victim? Nicholas D'Angelo, right? What can you tell me about him?"

"What can *you* tell me about this place?"

"Lots. Want to trade?"

"Maybe."

"Sounds exciting."

Her smile is mischievousness, and she has a presumptuousness about her, a way of moving in close. It feels like a test, as if she's trying to determine if I'm worth her time.

"You do know Brother Stephen, don't you?" I said.

We begin walking in the direction of the offices.

"I met him once. He bored me."

"He's supposed to meet me after he finishes chapel."

"Fine, we can compare notes after that. How about lunch?"

6

GAUNT AND EARNEST, Brother Stephen looks like someone who's just returned from forty days in the wilderness. He has a fifties-style crew cut and the physique of a marathon runner, with lean, muscular arms and a stomach as flat as a well-planed board. His deeply recessed blue eyes flicker intensely—bright candles at the end of two long tunnels.

"Mr. Sweeney? You wanted to talk to me?"

"I'd like to ask you a few questions about Nick D'Angelo."

"I already spoke to the police—"

"I'm a friend of the family's." I follow him into his office, then show him my ID. "Nick's brother is a close friend. He's asked me to look into what happened."

His face darkens. "I had hopes for Nick. Obviously I wasn't quick enough. Have a seat."

I take the chair next to his desk. "What do you mean?"

"The best thing any compulsive gambler here can do for himself is to get away. You can go to all the GA meetings in the world, but as long as you're still in this town the casinos will draw you back."

"You're suggesting his death had something to do with his gambling?"

"It wouldn't surprise me if it did. But I only meant that if we'd gotten him back with his family he might be alive today."

"He came here after losing his job at the Poseidon, is that right?"

"One of the few good things that casino's ever done was fire Nick."

"I gather he was pretty far gone."

"He'd hit bottom. Lost his family, his job. . . ." His gaze wanders, then seems to focus on some Abstract Truth in the ether about us.

"There's something else?"

His attention returns.

"I don't think he ever realized how far gone he really was. He couldn't let go. He was always chasing the big win."

"That sounds like Nick."

"Maybe you've heard the joke about the compulsive gambler who said he had five hundred dollars and was going to lose it if it took all night? Well, that was Nick. Gambling's a sickness, Mr. Sweeney, just like alcoholism and drug addiction. Believe me, I know."

I nod. "Saw the mural in the chapel. Heard some of your sermon, too."

He looks at me earnestly, those distant candles flaring up.

"Then you understand. St. Augustine said the devil invented gambling. Well, I believe that. I also believe the better the gambler the worse the man. Everything we're trying to do here—all the efforts to save bodies *and* souls—it's all for nothing if you're in the grip of an addiction like gambling. Nothing's possible until that hurdle's overcome." Then he leans forward and says something odd. "Personally, Mr. Sweeney, if I ever had to choose between the devil and gambling, I hope I'd have the good sense to choose the devil."

" 'Curse God, and die'?"

"Precisely."

No doubt Brother Stephen really believes what he says. Some people live by hyperbole. It reminds me of a snobbish art-history professor I had in grad school. He despised imitations and boasted he'd rather own a piece of cheap dime-store schlock than possess a near-perfect copy done in the style of a master. Fatuous thinking can keep you from finding your way in life.

"Tell me, do you have any idea what Nick might have been doing in the lighthouse?"

"Not a clue. It makes no sense."

"Did he say or do anything in the days before his death that might explain his behavior?"

He shakes his head. "As I told the police, I don't see the residents as often as I'd like. Lately, I've been out a lot, giving talks, trying to raise money. I don't remember seeing Nick this past week at all, in fact. You may want to talk to our other staff members. They—"

The door to the adjoining office opens.

"Steve, are we still going—Oh, I'm sorry. I thought you were alone."

It's the woman in the red denim shirt from the chapel. She's clearly embarrassed. More so than necessary, it seems to me. There's an awkward silence before Brother Stephen speaks.

"This is Mr. Sweeney. He's here about Nick D'Angelo. He's a friend of the family's."

"Oh, I see. I'm Sister Felice, the mission chaplain. We're all truly saddened by what happened."

I get the impression she means it. She's a plain woman with graying hair and tiny age lines around the mouth. Obviously older than "Steve," she nevertheless gives the impression of having enough energy for two.

"Did you know him well?"

She looks surprised by the question. "I know every client who's here for more than a few days. It's my job."

"Then perhaps you can help. Did he say anything to you during the last week he was here? I mean, was anything bothering him?"

She takes a long time before responding.

"My role here is much like a priest's or a counselor's, Mr. Sweeney. I'm not in a position to talk about what our clients confide to me in private."

"The man's dead, Sister."

"Even if I revealed something about a deceased person, no matter how trivial it might be, I'd risk losing the confidence of our other clients."

She may or may not have a point. But the fact is, confidentiality is always a convenient defense for those unwilling to cooperate.

"What about his activities? Do you have any idea what he did with himself these past few weeks?"

Brother Stephen intervenes. "Obviously we can't account for anyone's time when they're not here."

"Was he out looking for work? Was he gambling?"

"He did mention he hoped to get his old job back," says Sister Felice. "I guess I can say that much."

"Why would he have thought he was getting his job back?" I ask.

"I've no idea," she says.

"Did he ever mention someone named Jonah?"

She shakes her head. "I'm sorry."

"He never mentioned any Jonah to me," says Brother Stephen.

Sister Felice looks at him. "Sorry to have interrupted. You and I can talk later."

And with that she's gone. For a moment, Brother Stephen looks both relieved and disappointed.

"Okay, thanks for your time, Brother Stephen."

Getting up to leave, I notice some framed black-and-white photographs on the wall at the end of his office. He follows my eyes and points to one in particular.

"That's the old Chalfonte-Haddon Hall," he says. "It became Resorts International back in 1977, the end of an era."

I glance at the other pictures: old aerial shots of the Boardwalk and the crowded summer beach, Steel Pier in the fifties, Miss America contestants in old-fashioned bathing suits posing by the water's edge, quaint Boardwalk storefronts, and the eccentric human comedy that has always walked the Boards in the summer. There are a few recognizable faces: south Jersey celebrities and old vaudevillians who once appeared regularly before summer audiences. One faded 8 × 10 glossy shows a teenager from the 1940s. He's in tights on a high wire, and the picture's been signed, "To Brother Stephen, with much gratitude—Baby Titus, Child of the High Wire (alias Tommy the Toe)."

"You look a little young to have been around when these were taken."

He smiles self-consciously.

"I love the old days. I'm very fond of this town. Or, I should say, the way this town *used* to be."

"You've been here all your life?"

"I was born not too far away, near Nesco. When I was a little boy, my father would bring me here to see the Boardwalk. But when I reached thirteen, my mother and I moved to Africa to work for the missions. That's how I got started in this work."

"I see."

"Nothing lasts," he says, looking at his photographs. "It's like Sodom and Gomorrah here now. It cries out for a cleansing, Mr. Sweeney. This town is ripe for conflagration. It's coming. Mark my words, it's coming."

"*What's* coming?"

Are we talking about *real* conflagration here? The kind that raged through Absecon Lighthouse last night?

"I don't know what it'll be like, but we'll all know it when it's here."

I never know how to respond to apocalyptic types. You'd think it'd be enough for them that no one's ever gotten it right predicting The End.

On the way out he points to some more photos on the wall behind the door. One shows him posing with a group of hunters in front of a small lodge. There's a sign on an overhang above the men that's been cut off by the camera. Another picture shows Brother Stephen in full camouflage attire, kneeling behind a five-point buck. There's a shotgun resting in the crook of his arm.

"Do you hunt?" he asks me.

I get the feeling he's looking for company, or at least a convert.

"Only people."

He stares at me. Finally I smile.

"It was a joke," I say.

"Oh."

"There's one other thing. Can you tell me where to find Cappy? Tommy said he might be at the Hotel Underwood."

"I wouldn't go there, if I were you."

"Why not?"

"Only homeless people live there. And they don't like outsiders."

"Where is it?"

"Under the Boardwalk. That's how it got its name. Anyway, he's probably moved on by now. Come back later in the day. By then his hangover will have worn off and he'll be hungry. He always returns then."

Outside in the hall there's a line of people waiting to see Sister Felice. I walk by and find that the door to her office is closed.

7

THE REPORTER'S NAME is Gwen Olin. Coming out of the mission, I find her sitting on the curb in front of my car looking over her notes. She's in "a water mood," she says, so I follow her rusty green Toyota down Pacific Avenue to a parking lot on South Carolina.

"You like chili dogs?" she asks, once we've parked.

"Love them."

"Place down from Resorts has the best on the East Coast."

Five minutes later we're on the Boardwalk placing an order at the window of Lou's Dogs and Suds. We take our chili dogs and root beers and sit on a bench at the edge of the Boardwalk, facing the water.

It's a brilliant day, the air light and translucent, the temperature already over seventy. People are everywhere, even out on the beach. I can see the tops of waves breaking in the distance. Overhead, hungry gulls scream raucously. Down the Boardwalk someone with a trumpet is playing "Bye, Bye, Blackbird."

It was on a Friday afternoon like this that Catherine and I arrived in Cape May for our honeymoon. We'd gotten married on the spur of the moment and had only the weekend before I was due back at work. We walked the beach, ate lobster and lemon meringue pie for dinner, and made love until 3 A.M. By the next morning the barometer was dropping, the skies darkening. But we set out anyway in my '59 Chevy to explore the Pine Barrens. It was to be an adventure. To ignorant outsiders the Pine Barrens have always been terra incognito, home to the Jersey Devil and an indolent, slow-witted race of people who marry their cousins and prey on unfortunate city people whose cars break down on the way to the shore. We were going to prove everybody wrong about the Pineys, but Catherine insisted we drive the whole trip with the doors locked, "just in case." I kidded her, loving every minute of it. The storm hit in the middle of the afternoon, and we nearly lost our way in a downpour somewhere near Chatsworth. By the time we made it back to the inn at Cape May we were all over each other. To this day, stormy weather still makes me think of sex.

"Hoagies here are good, too," says Gwen Olin, managing to speak with a mouthful of chili dog.

"Do you live around here?"

It seems like a logical point at which to begin.

"Atlantic City? Hell, no. I have a small place on the Mullica River."

"You mean in the Pines?"

"Anything the matter with that?"

"This is weird."

"Why?"

"No reason."

"Tell me."

"It's nothing. Are you a genuine Piney?"

"I'd like to think so, but the truth is I'm really a newcomer. I'm a north Jersey girl. I've only lived here for four years. My ex-husband's the native. The house is his gift."

"Gift?"

"More like payback, I guess, for the three shitty years he put me through. What about you, you from around here?"

"No, Philadelphia."

"You married? Divorced?"

I shake my head. "My wife died two years ago."

I expect the usual clichés, perhaps an "Oh, I'm sorry." Instead, she looks at me for a moment, then asks, "Do you miss her?"

"We were married twenty-one years," is all I can think to say. And then, à la Lady René, "Sometimes life's a bitch."

"I know, and then you die. My father always says that."

Suddenly I feel ancient. Mercifully, she changes the subject, putting her soda down on the bench first.

"I know it's none of my business, but were you close to this D'Angelo?"

In the sun she looks older than she did in the shadowy mission hallway, but the deep brown eyes stand out more in the light, underlining her youthful intensity. She has a long, thin nose and wide, full lips, which she bites nervously when she's about to ask a question.

"Like I said, I'm a friend of his brother's, that's all."

"Isn't that enough?"

"Enough for what?"

"Enough to feel involved."

"I'm not involved. I'm here on business."

She studies me a moment. "Are you a private investigator? Of course you are. I should have known. You have the look."

"What look is that?"

"Inquisitive."

"I'd have said that applies more to you than me."

She gives me another searching examination, as if considering just how far to take this, whatever "this" is.

"I *did* zero in on you last night, didn't I? Thought maybe you were somebody who could give me a slant on the story. You know, 'Long Lost Relative at the Scene of Lighthouse Murder.' Something like that."

Her expression says something else now. Suddenly, it's more relaxed, less taunting, as if she's decided I'm okay. Or harmless. Not that she isn't still fishing for something.

"And you, what are you?"

"Assistant editor."

"An editor, really?"

"It's a misleading title. I'm *very* junior, really. The *Atlantic City Star* is not *The New York Times*."

"What do you write about, besides lighthouse murders?"

"Actually, crime's not my usual beat. I was sent over there last night because I happened to be in the neighborhood. Normally, I get assigned to do warm, fuzzy feature stories."

"Like what?"

"Oh, once I interviewed some candidates for the Miss New Jersey contest. My editor didn't appreciate my slant on it, though. I got one of the girls to admit she'd once cheated on a test in high school. After that I was assigned to do baby parades and garden parties for a while. My real interest right now is the mission."

"In what way?"

"Well, ever since the casinos opened, the *Star*'s been doing articles about the impact of gambling on the city, but the stories always seem to have an economic slant. I figure people matter more than the economy or the tax base. So I suggested to my boss that we finally take a look at the mission. That's why I was there last night. I had an interview with Sister Felice."

"Really? What can you tell me about her?"

"Oh, no. Now it's your turn. What'd you learn from Brother Stephen?" She rummages around in her rucksack for a notebook and pen. "He have any idea who might have killed your friend's brother?"

"No."

"Really?"

"You sound surprised."

"Well, there *are* some strange people staying at that place. Surely he must have something to say about one or two of them."

"Nothing he was willing to tell me. All I know for sure is the man hates gambling. Says he might have been able to help Nick if there'd been more time."

"What'd you think of him? Personally, I mean."

"He's intense. Single-minded. Charismatic. Has an apocalyptic outlook. And no sense of humor. Seems angry."

"Yeah, he has a temper. I saw him blow up at one of his own residents once. It was some fat woman, used to be a fortune-teller or something."

"Lady René?"

"Yeah, that's the one."

"What was it about?"

"As far as I could tell, nothing. Brother Steve just has a short fuse, is all. They say that's why he left Africa and came back to the States. Everybody there was tired of his shitty attitude. So did you talk to any others?"

"Sister Felice walked in on us while we were talking."

"What'd she say?"

She chews on her lower lip, eyes wandering over her notebook.

"She claimed confidentiality."

"She's pulled that with me a few times. What'd you think of her?"

"We didn't talk long. I can only give you my gut response."

"That's the best kind."

"She's your basic compassionate type. The kind who'd do anything for you, as long as you appreciate her in return. And, I think she and Brother Stephen have got something going."

She looks at me. "What? No, wait. My God, you could be right."

"You didn't know about it?"

She shakes her head. "No, but now that you've said it, it makes sense. She's one of those nuns who never got over the sixties. Left the convent but couldn't quite bring herself to leave the Church. She's trapped in a middle-aged body, needing a man, still hoping the Church will ordain women someday."

"She needs a reality check."

"Yeah, somehow she's managed to avoid the real world, even outside the convent. I mean it's not like the woman hasn't had the opportunity. Before the mission she was with Covenant House in New York."

"Storing away all that repressed sexuality."

She grins at me. "You know about that sort of stuff, do you?"

"I'm not as old as I look. Besides, I learned it from nuns like her."

"Ah, you too. Well, I scrapped that view of the world years ago."

"You're studying to be a free spirit?"

"Something like that."

I can't quite figure out the look she's giving me. It's a cross between filial admiration and journalistic curiosity. I don't much like either one.

"Tell me," I ask, "do you know any of the residents at the mission?"

"I've interviewed a few so far. They're a sad lot. And weird too, at least a lot of them seem so to me. But not murderers, at least so far as I can tell."

"Who've you talked to?"

"Well, there's Harriet, the slot addict in the wheelchair."

"Right, the one who's waiting for her son to come get her."

"She's got a long wait. He died a teenager, thirty years ago, according to Brother Stephen."

"You're kidding."

"Died in a drug raid in Newark. Harriet was off somewhere gambling at the time. Now she can't remember anything about it. Nice, huh?"

"Any others?"

"I interviewed Meryl Sarbanes. Now there's a profile in courage. I'd like to do an entire piece on that lady."

"What about Tommy the Toe? You meet him yet?"

"The old guy, used to do a high-wire act? Yeah, I talked to him. Shows you what the casinos can do to people's lives."

"In what way?"

"He had an act at the Poseidon back in the eighties. Too old-fashioned, I guess. No topless bimbos. He never found work again."

"Do you think there might be any connection between the mission and the Poseidon Casino?"

"A connection? What do you mean?"

She looks at me, suddenly curious.

"Just wondering. I know most of the charities in the city look to the casinos for help."

"That's true. And, God knows, the mission needs money. But then so does the Poseidon. They've been in Chapter Eleven for over a year."

"I know."

The Philadelphia papers have been running stories on it for the last two years. It makes for good reading, that is if your taste runs to theater of the absurd. The casino and hotel were on the verge of closing down a year and a half ago, but Tony Dante, the Poseidon's president and head of its parent body, the Angelina Corporation, was able to "restructure," which for Dante apparently means "screw the creditors." Since then he has been less than diplomatic in his dealings with his suppliers, the unions, and the Casino Control Commission, just a few of the groups that can, if they choose to do so, help push him under. But this is a man who, in his own words, "could give a fuck" about his public image. You might think this an unusual attitude for someone in the casino business, an enterprise that these days thinks of itself as only slightly less public-service-oriented than the Red Cross. But Tony Dante is not your average casino executive. He didn't work his way up from dealer, and he didn't get an MBA from the Wharton School. In fact, he never finished high school. Tony got his education in the streets, whacking heads. Getting in people's faces is all he knows.

Gwen finishes her chili dog and picks up her pen and notebook again. "Okay, your turn again. Tell me about the scene of the crime last night. What'd they find?"

"Didn't they tell you?"

"The Major Crimes Squad isn't into *sharing* with the media. Most they'll let on is, there was a fire and a man died in it."

"I'm as much in the dark as you are."

"What about the arson investigators? They have anything to say?"

"They're sending samples to the lab in Hammonton, that sort of thing."

"No leads of any kind?"

"Two kids saw the fire and ID'd the guy who called it in from his car."

"They already told me that. No theories?"

"Not a one. I'm on my way to Northfield after this. Maybe something'll turn up there."

"Okay, I give up." She puts her pen down and studies me a moment. "You going to be around for a while, Sweeney?"

"For as long as it takes."

"Where you staying?"

"Long Beach Island. My wife's parents have a house in Beach Haven. They're letting me use it for a while."

"Maybe I'll look you up."

8

THE OFFICES OF THE Major Crimes Squad are in Northfield, on the mainland or, as Atlantic City residents say, offshore. They're part of what's called the Atlantic County Facilities at Northfield, a sprawling complex of nondescript three-story brick buildings that look as if they once comprised the campus of a mental institution or an antiseptic state college. Talley and his people are in the rear of this government village, on the first floor of one of the older-looking structures. If floor assignment is any indication of official importance, Talley and his men had better watch their backs. Closing in on them from the second floor is the Mosquito Control Unit, which every year exterminates far more evildoers in Atlantic County than Major Crimes could eliminate in a lifetime. In south Jersey it pays to keep your priorities straight.

Talley greets me with a forced smile. Some of the vibrancy has gone out of his well-tanned face. He ushers me down a dimly lighted hall, past half-a-dozen small rooms that look as if they were last painted sometime during World War II. His own office, reflecting no sign of his rank, is as dark, dingy, and cramped as all the others.

"Captain D'Angelo called this morning," he says, tilting back in his chair.

So today it's "Captain" D'Angelo. What happened to "Bernie," the man Talley has known since their days as rookie cops in Philly, the man who helped him fish his teenage daughter's life out of the toilet before the judicial system could flush it into oblivion? Taking the only other chair in the room, one wedged between the desk and door, I look him in the eye, searching for an explanation. He turns away.

"He told me he'd call you," I say. "I saw him last night in the hospital. He looks terrible, by the way."

"Yeah, he sounded kind of tired last night when I phoned him."

"Triple bypass surgery'll do that to you."

"Look, Sweeney, I know what the man's been through. I got a brother-in-law traveled down that same road. Now let's cut the chitchat."

"I do something to piss you off, Captain? I figured the least you could do—"

"The least I could do is what I'm doing. I owe Bernie a favor. Otherwise you wouldn't even be in this building right now."

A *favor*? Is that what he calls it? Bernie and I managed to keep Talley's daughter from facing charges after a drug sweep in west Philadelphia three years ago. From some reports the kid was just an innocent bystander, but that doesn't diminish the magnitude of what we managed to do for her, or for her father. She could be doing serious time right now. The way I look at it, Jake Talley owes Bernie and me an all-expenses-paid trip around the world. And that's just for starters.

"What's the problem?"

"Frank, you know how it is. My hands are tied. Shit, we had a state trooper down here lose his job last year because he talked to a PI about an investigation. Believe me, the DA watches us real close."

"I believe you. So, what're you saying, that you've got a nasty murder on your hands and I'm taking up your time?"

"Yeah, *officially* that's what I'm saying. *Officially.*"

The meaning of the pained expression on his face finally sinks in. This isn't just a cover-your-ass situation for Talley. He *does* want to help. But what he really wants, and won't get, is for someone, anyone, to walk into his office with proof that Nick D'Angelo died a hero, maybe trying to pull a helpless child from the fire, something like that. Anything but what he suspects to be the truth, which is that Nick was into something dirty and got wasted because of it. For that reason, he'd probably rather have *me* investigate the case than his own men. It might avoid a lot of pain between him and Bernie in the end.

"Captain, you should understand something. Bernie's not asking you to solve his personal problems for him. He only wants to find out what his brother was doing in that lighthouse. The way I see it, that's my job. Yours, as I view it, is to find the son of a bitch who did it and arrest him. I'll do my damnedest to stay out of your way.

Meanwhile, if there's anything you can do for me, *unofficially,* I'd appreciate it. I *know* Bernie would appreciate it."

He stands up, his face contorted with anxiety.

"Look, why don't you go down the hall to our conference room, have yourself a cup of coffee, read some of our brochures, shit like that. Who knows, maybe somebody'll drop in to see you. You know, give you a little briefing on how we handle law enforcement here in Atlantic County. That *is* why you came to see me, isn't it? To learn about our law-enforcement techniques for your PI operation?"

I nod my understanding. "It certainly is, Captain. And I appreciate you taking the time to let me in on how you do things down here."

"By the way," he says, "you're not carrying, are you?"

I open my windbreaker for him to see.

"I know your gun laws down here, Captain."

In the state of Pennsylvania a private citizen can get a permit to carry a gun for one dollar. In New Jersey you have to apply to a prosecutor's office, take a psychological exam, pass a firearms test, post bond, and then get approval from a superior court judge. Those are some serious hurdles, even for an ex-cop. Given the short notice of this case, I had no choice but to come unarmed. And Bernie wouldn't appreciate it if I got arrested for illegal possession of a firearm while in his employ. He's particular about such niceties. So am I, for that matter.

Out in the hall I bump into young Petrillo, Boy Detective, and his fish tie. At least he's changed shirts. His hair is closely cropped and parted down the middle. And he's wearing what, back in the sixties, people used to call granny glasses, with round metal frames. Maybe fashion trends have come full circle, but there's still a generation gap here. Actually, it's more like a gulf.

"Lieutenant?" he says, stopping me. "You don't mind if I call you Lieutenant, do you? Captain Talley told me all about you. He says you were one of the best."

Were one of the best?

"Call me whatever you like, Detective. How's the case going so far?"

"Looks like plain old, down-and-dirty detective work from here on."

I decide to let that one pass. My guess is the kid doesn't have a clue what to do next. As I try to move by him, he puts his hand out to stop me.

"Look, Lieutenant Sweeney, I know this must be hard for you."

"What do you mean?"

"You know, being on the outside and all."

"I'll manage."

"I'd help you if I could. I want you to understand that. But you know the rules."

"I know the rules."

"And if there's anything you can tell *us,* I'd like to hear from you. I mean, you know, if you have any leads of your own you want to share, I'm here for you."

I'm right. He doesn't have a clue.

THE CONFERENCE ROOM down the hall is empty. I pour myself some murky coffee and take a seat at a battered walnut library table. After a few minutes Ray Martindale walks in.

"Hear they're giving you the red-carpet treatment," he says, closing the door behind him. He's holding a manila folder in his right hand.

"Nothing but the best."

Martindale's eyes flit about the room as if he were a caged animal. He reminds me of Jethro Jackson, a varsity tackle at Penn State when Bernie was there. Jethro was a giant of a man who made up for his lack of speed with the best peripheral vision I've ever seen in an athlete. Martindale's big and slow-moving, too, but when he's talking I get the impression that, like Jethro Jackson, he knows exactly what's going on behind him.

He looks at his watch. "There's a full briefing in here at two. That's why I'm over here. Thought maybe I'd drop in on you and shoot the bull. Captain tells me you're interested in learning how we do things around here."

I smile at him. "Yeah, it's never too late to learn new techniques."

"Damn straight."

He puts the file folder on the table in front of him and takes a seat.

"Jake's asked me to help you. *Unofficially.* As far as anyone's concerned, this meeting never happened."

"Understood."

"I guess he figures since I'm in A.C. arson I'm one office removed from everybody here in Northfield. So I'm your 'unofficial liaison' or some such shit like that. If that's good enough for you, I'll do what I can. Not that you have a hell of a lot of choice. Nobody's making any other offers."

I smile at him. "I couldn't ask for anything more."

"You got that right. You gotta understand something. Jake, he's not the enemy. Me neither. I'll help you all I can, long as it doesn't fuck me with Jake. I've got to work with the guy after you're long gone."

He pauses to study the back of his hands.

I look at him. "Is there something else going on here?"

"I remembered some more about Nick D'Angelo last night after I got home. Met him at a GA meeting a few months back. He was an okay guy. He wasn't gonna make it, I could tell that, but he *was* a fellow addict. And you came down here to help the dumb bastard out. That counts for something with me. You know how much sympathy gambling addicts get? Zilch. It ain't fair." He pauses a moment. "Besides, I think Jake's on the spot with this case."

"What do you mean?"

"Petrillo. The way he got assigned to the squad. It's all political. The kid's father is some hotshot lawyer in A.C. He works for the mayor. Jake didn't have any choice. That say enough for you?"

"Says it all."

"With Petrillo on the case, the way I look at it, we can use all the help we can get. Even if you ain't a cop no more. You get my slant."

"Yeah, I do. And thanks. Nick's brother, Bernie, thanks you too."

"I'm here to serve." He gives me a toothy grin and picks up a sheet of paper from the file folder. "Here's what we got so far. ME says smoke inhalation was the cause of death. No surprise there. We knew that last night. Soot was in his mouth, nose, the upper respiratory airways, the works. No blows to the head or body, no wounds, nothing like that. Smoke killed him sure as shit. For whatever it's worth, your buddy was dead before the flames got to him. The charring the ME found on the body was post mortem, all flame burns."

"I suppose it's better than burning to death."

"Never having had the pleasure, I can't say."

"What about prints?"

"There were hundreds everywhere. Petrillo seemed surprised by that. I mean, shit, it *was* a fucking lighthouse for God's sake. Thousands of tourists been through that place over the years. Our people focused on the doors and windows, stuff like that. We're using the FBI to run checks. Nothing yet."

"What about the Coleman lantern?"

"Wiped clean. We've got someone checking with local stores that sell the things. No luck so far."

"And the gas can?"

"The same. Wiped clean."

"And what about the flashlight next to Nick's body, and the wheel chip?"

He gives me his best smile. "Those particular items had only the victim's prints on them."

"You were right then, about the flashlight being Nick's, but not the lantern."

"Never doubted it."

"And the wheel chip was Nick's insurance bet."

"Question is, what's it mean?"

"What else do you have? Anything from the lab in Hammonton on that torch or the gas can?"

"Nothing yet."

"What about canvassing the neighborhood? The mission? Nick's last place of employment?"

He shakes his head. "Nothing there either. We've talked with the neighbors living near the lighthouse. There are men at the Poseidon right now taking statements about Nick. And Petrillo himself has been to the mission."

"Bully for him. What about the guy who called in the fire?"

"Traced him through 911. Some tourist checking out the sights."

"And what about jitney drivers?"

"What about them?"

"One of them might have picked up the killer. Did anyone check it out?"

Obviously not, from the expression on his face.

"I'll mention it to Petrillo."

He makes a notation in the file.

"Never hurts to check. So, tell me, Ray, what's your personal take on the case?"

He looks at his watch. "Another few minutes and people are gonna start walking in here. Okay, my take on it is this: your killer's a pro, a hit man."

"How do you figure?"

"The guy knows fire, knows how it works, and how to use it. The accelerant, the broken window, the locked door, the updraft, the lantern as a come-on. I mean, it wasn't the most sophisticated job I've ever seen, but then you don't need a thousand dollars worth of high-tech shit to burn somebody alive. This guy knows his business. He's done this kinda shit before. He left no prints but he didn't waste time trying to cover up his work, either. He knew we'd figure it for arson so he didn't bother getting rid of the gas can. He was there to kill D'Angelo, pure and simple."

"Sounds reasonable."

"One other thing, Frank. Since you're gonna be involved, you oughta keep it in mind."

"What's that?"

"This guy gets his jollies torching people. I mean he *enjoys* it."

"How do you know that?"

"Think about it. There are a hundred ways to blow away an easy mark that are less chancy than trapping the poor bastard in a locked-up lighthouse. It's real iffy. Why go to all that trouble unless you get off on it?"

"What's your point?"

"My point is: watch your back. Don't piss this guy off. He likes to burn people alive."

9

Aᴏᴛᴇʀ I ᴄᴏᴀx ʜɪᴍ a little, Talley agrees to let me use the phone in his office while the briefing in the conference room takes place.

Leafing through the telephone book on his desk, I learn a few things. Like the fact that Atlantic City, once billed as the East Coast's most popular family resort, now lists twenty-one escort services in the Yellow Pages. Featured are names like "Absolutely Discreet," "Sparkles," "Desire," "Aphrodite," and "Adorable Doll." The ads promise "youth," "beauty," and "discretion," and guarantee prompt twenty-four-hour service seven days a week. Well, everyone said the casinos would be good for business.

There's nothing to do but settle back and start dialing. My story goes something like this. I'm a private investigator working for the family attorney of Nicholas D'Angelo. Nick, God rest his soul, recently passed on, leaving behind a sum of money for a certain "Monica," an escort girl who touched the heart of the dearly departed during his last days. Nick never was very good with names. He mentioned "Monica" in his will but neglected to give her last name or the name of her employer. Could your service be of any help? Is there anyone named Monica working there? If so, did a Nick D'Angelo ever hire her?

Some of this is a bit implausible, but I keep in mind the intended audience. I'm not likely to encounter any Bryn Mawr graduates on the phone. Besides, over the years I've learned the power of certain words. If I throw in some legal terms like "probate" and "intestate" and mention an imaginary law firm like Crabtree, Burnitz, and Burnitz, things ought to move right along. And move along they do. Right through nine different escort services. Only one person laughs at me. The rest either don't employ anyone named Monica, or if they do, they have no memory of any Nick D'Angelo having used their service.

With call number ten I come up a winner. At Classy Lady Escort Service, Monica Poole answers the phone. She's the owner. In a matter of minutes I'm out of the Major Crime Squad's building and headed back to A.C.

Classy Lady turns out to be one and the same as Monica's Hair Salon, a plain storefront on a side street off Bacharach Boulevard. Monica, bewigged and heavily made up, closer to forty than thirty, employs three younger hairdressers who double as escorts when duty calls.

Business must be good because in the back room the phone rings twice before I can begin my pitch. We're in a combination sitting and dressing area, furnished with two soiled upholstered chairs placed next to a Formica-topped coffee table. One wall has been given over to racks of exotic and fancy clothing—high- and low-cut dresses, pants outfits, designer jeans, and skimpy blouses. On a wall in the corner a hand-painted sign offers this therapeutic message: HAPPINESS IS A GOOD SCREW.

"I heard 'bout Nick," Monica says, offering me a glass of iced tea after getting off the phone. She's dressed in some kind of shocking-pink caftan with little Disney figures all over it. "It was in the paper. Awful, just awful. He was such a nice man."

"Did you know him well?"

"Do you mind if I smoke?" she asks, lighting up. "Yeah, I knew him real well. We spent lots of time together. He took me to shows and everything."

Not likely. Nick hated floor shows. As far as he was concerned, you only went to a casino for one thing.

"Could you give me your full name? The attorneys will need it for probate." I take out a notebook, intending to give her her money's worth.

"Monica Frances Poole. That's Poole with an 'e.' Most people don't spell it right."

I scribble her name on my pad. "Now, Monica, when did you first meet Nick?"

She thinks a moment. "Couple of months ago, I think. He called me up. Said he got the name out of the phone book. Wanted an escort for the night. He was going to go play blackjack, he said. Well, our other girls was all busy so I went along myself. I'm semiretired, you know. Don't usually go out myself anymore."

"And Nick took you along to watch him gamble?"

"You know Nick, he thought he was a real high roller. Always had to have a pretty girl on his arm at the tables. Said I made him lucky. We were kind of a couple, you know? 'Bout once a week or more he'd call me up and I'd go along and watch him play."

"That's all?"

"Course that's all, whaddya think? Nick was a gentleman."

I nod understandingly. Actually, I believe her. From what Bernie told me, gambling was about the only passion Nick could muster toward the end.

"And when did you last see him?"

"How much money am I going to get?"

"I'm sorry, didn't I explain? I'm just the investigator. My report goes back to the law firm. They'll be in touch."

"I see."

"So when did you last see him?"

She thinks a moment. "I'd say it was a week and a half ago. The ninth. Tuesday, I think. Yeah, Tuesday, the ninth."

I jot down the date. "And he played blackjack as usual?"

She shakes her head. "No, not that time. He didn't want to."

"But he took you to a casino?"

"Oh, yeah. We went to the Poseidon. First time. He never took me there before."

"Then what did he do?"

"Played roulette."

"Roulette? I didn't know Nick played roulette."

"He didn't. He hated it. Said it was stupid. Only for losers."

"Then why?"

"Don't know. Look, what's all this got to do with Nick's will?"

I make a big thing out of putting my notebook aside and looking directly at her. "May I ask you something before we proceed? It doesn't have anything to do with the will or the money."

She looks confused. "Sure, I guess."

"Nick's family is devastated. I'm sure they'd ask you this if they were here. What was he like that last night? I know they'd like to have a memory to cherish."

"What was he 'like?' "

"You know, how'd he behave? What'd he do? Did he win, lose, or what? Did he talk to anyone special? It would be consoling to the family to know how he spent that last night with you."

"To be honest, he wasn't much fun. But you don't have to tell them that."

"Why wasn't he much fun?"

"It was the damnedest thing." She leans forward as she speaks. "It's like he wasn't interested in gambling at all. He bought this little pile of chips and then he just tried to hold onto them."

"You mean he only bet the minimum?"

"Yeah, that's it. He just bet the minimum. I could tell he really wasn't interested."

"Why was he there then?"

She lowers her voice. "He was watching somebody."

"Really? Who was it, do you know?"

"Some old guy on the other side of the table."

"Do you know his name?"

"Nick never said. And I'd never seen him before."

"Did Nick ever say anything about someone called Jonah?"

She shakes her head. "No."

"Okay, so you're at the roulette table and Nick is watching some guy. Then what happened?"

"Nick watched for a while and we left. That's all. He dropped me off early."

"What'd this man look like?"

"Like I said, old. Sixties, maybe seventies. I remember him because he was dressed real good. You know, suit and tie. He had all his hair, too. No hairpiece. I can tell those things."

I stand up to leave. "Look, Monica, it's very important to the family to verify Nick's activities on that last night you spent with him. Are you sure it was Tuesday, the ninth? Because I can check. All I have to do is have the casino pull its videotapes of that roulette table for the night of April nine."

She looks at me. "Am I in trouble or something?"

"No, you're not in any trouble. You've been extremely helpful."

"This isn't about Nick's will at all, is it?"

"It's about catching whoever killed him."

She thinks that over a moment, then walks over to a small chest of drawers. With her back to me she takes something out of a drawer and studies it. I can hear pages turning. She replaces the book and turns back to face me.

"Like I said, the last night I saw Nick was Tuesday, the ninth, at the Poseidon Casino. I'm sure of it. Does that help?"

"That helps a lot, Monica."

"I could of used the money, ya know," she says, as I'm going out the door.

I REACH PETRILLO from the cellular phone in my car.

"Lieutenant Sweeney, what can I do for you?"

"You said you wanted a lead."

"Yeah, you got something?"

I can hear his voice change, like a kid whose father has just told him he has a surprise waiting for him in the garage.

"Yeah, I got something. Write this down. Tuesday night, April nine. Roulette. The Poseidon Casino."

I wait while he lays down the phone and fumbles for pen and paper. When he picks up again I repeat the information.

"Okay, Mr. Sweeney, now what?"

"Now what? What the hell do you think? Get a warrant. For the surveillance tapes for all the roulette tables at the Poseidon for that night. Nick D'Angelo will be on one of those tapes."

"How do you know that?"

Like I said, he's clueless.

"Look, I'm going to give you my Beach Haven phone number. I'd appreciate a call after you get hold of the tapes. Trust me, Detective, this is the lead you've been waiting for. Better get moving."

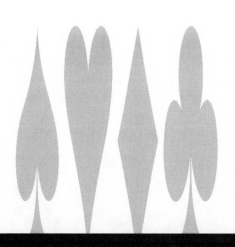

THE CITY
BOOK TWO

1

B<small>ACK IN</small> B<small>EACH</small> H<small>AVEN</small>, I can feel a sense of normalcy return. There are no boardwalks on Long Beach Island, no escort services or high-rises. The only gambling is Saturday-night bingo at the Catholic church. There's a small amusement park catering to kids under twelve and a would-be mall of sorts that will never be a serious alternative to the beach except in foul weather. Anyone favoring an active vacation itinerary with options such as golf and trendy all-night entertainment will be disappointed. Which is why so many people like me love the place. The only drawback is that in the summertime too many people love it. But these days, I guess, overcrowding is the price you pay for getting away from it all.

Catherine's parents' house is a Victorian three-story affair (not counting an airless and gloomy unfinished attic and a dungeon of a cellar), complete with an old-fashioned porch that wraps around two sides and looks out over the dunes, lots of gingerbread trim, half-a-dozen ornate dormer windows, and two Romanesque corner turrets facing the ocean. When last I counted, it had fifteen rooms, most of which are closed off. The Cordells have received dozens of offers from people who'd like to convert it into a bed-and-breakfast, but so far they've chosen to keep the house in the family. To them I'm still part of the family, which means I get free run of the place whenever it's vacant. It's an arrangement that meets certain emergent needs of mine. One of the side effects of marrying into Catherine's family was that it raised the level of my theretofore middle-class aspirations. I can't go back now to staying in one of the Jersey shore's ubiquitous look-alike duplexes. And I could never afford a place like this on my own.

Two things about the house particularly appeal to me. One is the furnishings. Locksley Hall with Chippendale, I call it. These are not your run-of-the-mill antiques. No reproductions for the Cordells. I'm especially fond of the Queen Anne dressing table, circa 1770, in the master bedroom on the second floor. It's museum quality, and I was the one who located it for them. Since acquiring it, they've had to put the house under the year-round protection of a local home-security company.

The other attraction that draws me here is the well-equipped kitchen. I'm learning to cook, in my middle years. A few months after Catherine died I signed up for a night course, "Zen and the Art of Cooking," at a local community college. I thought it might keep me from sitting at home and brooding, maybe pull me out of the slough of despond I'd fallen into. It hasn't quite done that, but the course has taken some unexpected turns. Rami, my teacher, claims cooking induces a state of mindfulness. He says if I work at it I should be able to do my best thinking when I'm making a soufflé or chopping vegetables. The kind of thinking he has in mind isn't like your typical self-conscious ratiocination. What takes place when you cook, Rami says, is less controlled and more spontaneous than that. It's a kind of unpremeditated meditation. If you try to force it, to *make* it happen, you invariably get flat, uninspired, linear intellectualization of the worst sort. "When you look for it, you can't find it." Or so Rami says. Maybe that's what Yogi Berra meant when he said you can't think and hit at the same time. Well, I'm not there yet but I'm working on it.

For now my attention is on *l'omelette roulée*. Reflections on arson and murder will emerge when the conditions are right. The beginning's extremely important. According to Rami, all genuine cooking involves a Zen-like element of ceremony, a process that appears to be mindful in the way that, for example, a Japanese tea ritual is. If everything isn't just so at the outset, if the preparations are sloppy or incomplete, then what follows will be equally imperfect. The process can't be forced. Something will happen, or it will not happen, according to some unnameable inner power. The trick is to remove as many obstacles as possible and let things transpire as they will. To cook is to be.

I take the omelette pan, already carefully scrubbed, scoured, and rubbed with cooking oil, from its shelf underneath the island in the middle of the kitchen and sprinkle some salt in it. Then I heat it slightly and rub the salt around with a paper towel. Setting it aside for the moment, I begin opening drawers and cabinets, laying out the necessary cooking implements. This takes some time because not only is there a specific place for each item on the countertop, there's a sequence in which you're supposed to retrieve each one. The final preparatory step is to take a dinner plate out of the cabinet and put it in the oven to warm.

With these preliminaries completed, I can turn to cutting up some *fines herbes,* a mixture of parsley, tarragon, chives, and chervil. I chop the chives and the chervil separately with a large chef's knife. For the parsley I use a two-bladed rocker. Then I scoop about a teaspoon of each herb into my hand and drop it all into a small stainless-steel bowl. I take three large eggs from the refrigerator, but manage to drop two on the floor. After cleaning up the mess and retrieving two more, I break them all into a glass mixing bowl, adding salt and pepper. Blending the yolks and whites lightly with a fork, I toss in the mixture of herbs and beat everything together, trying to count precisely thirty-five strokes. I often have trouble with this part. I find it difficult to focus on counting and still have my mind remain blank so as to be receptive to the universal oversoul.

Putting the bowl aside and turning up the gas burner under the frying pan, I hear a noise outside.

There are two places on the front porch with loose floorboards. Each gives out a distinctive creaking sound that can be heard from nearly anywhere in the house. What I just heard came from the beach side, where the loose board is near the swing. Putting everything down, I turn off the gas burner and toss aside my cook's apron.

One side of the living room faces the ocean. It's possible to stand next to a window there and look out without being seen, taking in most of the porch and adjoining dunes. It's still twilight, so visibility is no problem, but I don't see anything, even though I have the distinct sensation of movement outside. I move into the light of the window to get a better view. At the same moment the phantom of the porch materializes on the opposite side of the window, peering in eagerly with unabashed childlike curiosity.

"Jesus, Sweeney," Gwen shouts through the closed window, "you hearing-impaired or what? I've been pounding on your front door for the last five minutes. Can I come in?" She holds up a bottle of wine as an inducement.

Once inside, she stalks the living room like a critic from *Architectural Digest,* examining each piece of furniture up close, standing back to study the paintings and prints on the wall, all the while clutching the bottle of wine to her chest. When she's finished, she walks over to a wing chair and flops down. She's wearing powder-blue jeans and an oversized, lightweight burgundy sweater, which isn't so big that I don't notice the firm outline of her breasts.

"This is bloody unbelievable. I never knew people lived like this down here. I mean this *is* the shore, for chrissakes. Can you imagine anyone running around in here with sandy feet and wet bathing suits?"

"I like it."

"I bet you do," she says, setting the bottle on the floor and pushing up the sleeves of her sweater.

"Sorry I didn't hear the door. I was in the kitchen cooking dinner."

"You cook? My God. I suppose next you'll be telling me you support the Equal Rights Amendment."

I shake my head. "A foolish idea. Give women any more rights and pretty soon they'll want the good jobs, too. Like newspaper editor."

She winces. "Yeah, the glass ceiling's really low where I work."

"How'd you find me?"

"Beach Haven police. I stopped by, showed them my press credentials. Said I was here to interview you for a story. Didn't even have to show them a little skin or anything."

"So is it true?"

"Is what true?"

"That you're here to interview me?"

"I went over my notes from this afternoon, Sweeney. I got zilch from you, fella. And after I poured my heart out to you." She gives me a coy, little-girl smile.

"You always bring wine to an interview?"

A frown appears. "Truce, okay? This *is* really just a social visit. Seriously. Look, no notebook or anything."

She holds up empty hands and then opens her rucksack so I can look inside. Ever the gentleman, I refuse the offer.

"You hungry? I was making an omelette. Easy enough to make it for two."

"Thought you'd never ask. Here." She gets up and hands me the bottle of wine. "I must be a mind reader. It's Chablis. Just right for omelettes."

"I'll stick it in the freezer for a quick chill."

"You have a little-girl's room?"

I direct her around the corner from the dining room and down the hall. Once the door to the bathroom closes I go over and open her rucksack. The tape recorder is on the bottom, underneath a change purse, a large clump of tissues, and a small plastic Tampax container. I turn it off, flip open the lid, and pop out the tape cassette. Then I close the lid and reposition the recorder at the bottom of the rucksack, putting the cassette in my pocket. It was easy to spot. The little silver button-microphone stands out once you notice all the rest of the fittings on the rucksack are burnished brass.

In the kitchen I put the wine away to chill, stick a second plate in the oven to warm, and return to the living room at the same time she does.

"Come on, you can help."

She follows me into the kitchen, putting the rucksack down on the floor next to the island. I add three more eggs to the glass mixing bowl, turn the gas burner back on, and drop a tablespoon of butter into the pan.

"What can I do?" she asks.

"What kind of bread do you like?"

"I don't know, what kind do you have?"

"There's some French there in the drawer. How about garlic bread?"

"I can handle that."

I hand her a bowl of butter with the garlic already mixed in. She begins slicing the long loaf into thick pieces.

"This isn't the least bit healthy, you know." She holds up a piece of bread spread generously with garlic butter.

"My philosophy on egg dishes is that when you're already con-

93

suming so much cholesterol you might as well go all the way."

"Makes sense to me."

When she's finished wrapping the bread in aluminum foil and has placed it in the oven, I resume with the omelette. Holding the buttered pan over the heat, I tilt it back and forth in a circular motion so that the sides are covered with a greasy film. Some of the butter drips from the pan into the flame and flares up, forcing me to drop the pan abruptly onto the burner. I stand back and wait. Once the butter is the right color, I pour in the mixture of eggs and herbs.

She stands next to me, watching every move.

"Tell me," she says, "how'd you come to be at the lighthouse last night at the very moment the police were there?"

"A friend of Nick's tipped me off."

"Who?"

"Someone he met at the mission."

"I don't suppose you'd be willing to give me a name?"

"Thought this was a social call."

"It is. But you owe me, remember?"

"Off the record?"

She thinks a moment and then nods.

"Say it," I insist.

"Okay, it's off the record."

"He's some old eccentric named Cappy. He looked me up. Wanted me to get Nick out of Atlantic City and back to Philly."

I hold the pan over the burner with both hands, pushing and pulling it back and forth at a slight angle, then around in a circle. The eggs begin to thicken and come loose from the pan. It doesn't look right yet so I increase the angle of the pan. As the omelette begins to roll over onto the far lip, some of it falls over the edge and into the burner. I change the angle quickly before I lose any more. Eventually, it begins to take on a rolled shape. When everything looks right I turn off the burner and put the pan aside.

"Nicely done, Sweeney."

"I need practice."

"Looks fine. So why'd this Cappy guy want D'Angelo out of town?"

94

"If I knew the answer to that one, I might know why Nick was killed."

"What does Cappy have to say, now that his buddy's dead?"

"Can't find him. I went back to the mission this afternoon, but he hasn't shown up yet. Apparently he goes on long binges and doesn't return for days."

"Brother Steve must see some potential in this guy. Usually, he kicks their butts out if they don't stay sober or go to AA." She stops for a moment, lost in thought. "And you don't have any idea why this Cappy wanted Nick out of town?"

Taking the bread and plates out of the oven, I point to a cabinet behind her.

"There are some wine glasses down there. Why don't you get two for us."

I begin dividing up the omelette. By the time she's found the glasses and put them on the oak trestle table, she's forgotten her question and moved on to another subject.

"So how'd your visit to Northfield go?" she asks, taking the wine out of the freezer and placing it on the table.

"The cops don't have diddly."

"They never do." She sits down at the table and takes the bread out of the aluminum foil.

"Careful," I say, inserting a corkscrew in the wine bottle, "I used to be one."

"You? A cop? You're a man of many surprises, Sweeney."

I smile and pour us each a glass of wine.

"I guess I should've known," she says.

"Known what?"

"That you were a cop once."

"How, from my flat feet?"

"No, you don't give much away."

I nod slightly and try to look secretive, which elicits a smile.

"Why'd you quit?"

That stops me for a moment.

"Hard to say. Everything was different after Catherine died. It seemed like the time to change some things."

95

We each take a long, slow sip of Chablis and let the silence build.

"Oh, this is fabulous," she says, after finishing a forkful of omelette.

Actually, the underside is burned. Gwen may be prepared to ignore it, but I doubt Rami would give me high marks for a crispy omelette. On the other hand, grades and Zen don't seem to go together. Isn't there something about the trip being more important than the destination?

"So what else is it you're keeping back about yourself, Sweeney."

"Jesus, you're pushy."

"You mean because I asked about your wife this afternoon?"

"That, for starters."

"Want to talk about it?"

"What, being a widower?"

"No, your wife."

"Not much to talk about. It's been two years. She was a wonderful woman. We had a good life together."

"How'd she die?"

I guess sooner or later someone had to ask. But that doesn't make it any easier.

"She killed herself."

The expression on her face is difficult to describe. It's not shock, although I sensed a hint of that the moment after I spoke. What I see now is more like sadness. For an instant she actually seems to be in pain. She doesn't say anything. She doesn't have to.

"She had breast cancer. It was terminal. They operated. It left her deformed. She hated that more than the dying. She didn't want me or our daughter Diane to see her like that. One afternoon a few days after the surgery she left the hospital on her own, against doctor's orders. I came home that night and found her in the garage, slumped over the steering wheel of her car, the motor still running."

"I'm so sorry, Sweeney." Then she surprises me again. "I hope you don't blame yourself."

"Why do you say that? How did you. . . ."

"It would take a saint not to."

Then the phone rings and another death intrudes.

2

Curled up on the damp sand next to a piling, Cappy's grotesque corpse looks like an enormous barbecued fetus that washed up with the tide. The body's in the full pugilistic position. Everything has been blistered by flames, his face, hands, clothing, even his Converse high-tops. The only thing not burned is his baseball cap, which lies next to him in a pool of seawater. The hat is why I'm pretty sure it's Cappy. Otherwise, this could easily be a four-thousand-year-old mummy without the wrappings.

Our killer—I'm assuming it's the same son of a bitch who took out Nick—likes accelerants. Next to the body he left an empty bottle of cheap 150-proof rum, the kind so many winos rely on for what little solace is available to them. In New York City, bored young sociopaths with nothing better to do sometimes use it to set a sleeping bum on fire in the subway, dousing the helpless drunk with his own booze, then tossing a lighted match before making a run for it. It's noteworthy that Cappy didn't favor cheap drink, at least not in my presence, but that doesn't necessarily mean anything. He could have been broke or could have gotten the rum from one of the others here at the Hotel Underwood. Or maybe the killer brought it along with him. No matter how you figure it, it's a wretched way to go.

"Last time I saw him he was drinking Absolut on the rocks," I say to Martindale, standing next to me.

"For his sake I hope he had plenty of *something* in him."

Martindale watches as the ME examines the body. After turning the corpse over, she gets up and walks over to us.

"Look familiar?" she says to Martindale, holding something in her gloved hand.

"Sure as hell does."

It's the same kind of "torch" Martindale showed me last night. This time the matchbook is distinguishable from the fused metal, the entire device having fallen away from the body once the fire got going.

Martindale goes with the ME to take a look at what's left of Cappy. I turn and walk over to Talley, who's being briefed by the case detective, Ted Cox, a wispy-haired, middle-aged man with a large paunch. Talley ignores me while Cox watches me out of the corner of his eye but keeps on talking. I'm only here because Martindale had the courtesy to call, although I *am* a witness of sorts in this case. How long I'll be allowed to stay around is an open question.

Around us police floodlights have created an eerie haze probing the misty night air under the Boardwalk. Here and there among the pilings, the paraphernalia of the homeless protrudes from the shadows: large cardboard lean-tos, clotheslines draped with blankets to form makeshift tents, old pieces of timber stacked for firewood, and plastic bags of cast-off food scavenged from Dumpsters.

"We've got no witnesses," Cox says.

Talley looks incredulous.

"Jesus, Sergeant, there are thirty, forty bums living down here. One of them musta seen something."

Cox shakes his head. "Someone probably did. Finding him is another matter."

"What?"

"Anyone who was awake would've taken off when he realized what was going down. The ones left behind were drunk to the world. They wouldn't have woke up if the whole fucking Boardwalk had been on fire."

"They've got to come back sometime, don't they?"

"What for?" I interject. "To pick up their mail?"

"These people aren't exactly permanent residents here, Captain," Cox says. "The population turns over every couple a days. My guess is if anybody saw something he's going to be scared shitless. He'll probably take up residence someplace else."

In the distance ten of the Hotel Underwood's residents, most of them drunk or semiconscious, have been grouped behind a police tape in the vicinity of a large floodlight. Two cops from Major Crimes are trying unsuccessfully to penetrate the alcoholic stupors with a few simple questions. Somewhere beyond them, held back by another police tape, is a group of onlookers that includes Gwen, who followed me here in her Toyota, ecstatic at the good fortune of being in on a breaking story. Her enthusiasm waned heading out the door when I handed her the unused tape cassette. No apologies, no explanations, only a terse "shit" escaped her lips, followed by a quick look in my direction.

Cox is saying something about trying to identify the body.

"If I'm right, his name was Cappy," I interject.

"Jesus, you mean you knew him?" says Talley.

"He's the one who contacted me about getting Nick out of town."

"What can you tell us about him?" Cox asks.

"Age about seventy, maybe older. It was hard to tell with the beard. Lived at the mission off and on. That's where he met Nick. He was eccentric, paranoid, but sharp and intelligent. He had a taste for good food and good vodka. And he liked baseball."

Cox, who can't decide whether or not to write all that down, asks for Cappy's full name.

"He wouldn't tell me. The man was a mystery. About the only thing I'd venture is he was no bum."

Cox and Talley turn away, consulting sotto voce, so I wander off and hang around on the perimeter until I can get Martindale alone.

"Has anybody got a plan of attack?" I ask.

"Talley's convinced someone here knows something. So he's got Cox questioning all of them again. They've sent a couple of men up to the Boardwalk to see if they can find any witnesses there."

"Have they thought to talk to anyone at the mission?"

"They'll get around to it eventually."

I look at my watch. It's after ten. "What are you doing now?"

"Well, they don't really need me here. What'd you have in mind?" asked Martindale.

"What do you say we pay a visit to Brother Stephen?"

WORD OF A DEATH at the Hotel Underwood has already reached the mission. Noisy groups have begun to congregate in the lobby. Several people stop us as we pass through, looking for some confirmation from the outside. When we make our way to the back of the building, Brother Stephen is standing in the hallway outside his office with Sister Felice and Tommy the Toe.

"Have you heard?" asks Tommy, looking at me. "Someone died under the Boardwalk tonight."

"I know. I was there."

"Who was it?" he asks.

Martindale intervenes. "Brother Stephen, can we see you in your office?"

"So who was it?" he asks, once we're seated around his desk.

"We think it was one of your residents, a man named Cappy," Martindale says.

"Cappy? Are you sure? But who . . . why?"

Martindale shakes his head. "We don't know yet."

"My God."

"What can you tell us about him?" I ask. "What was his full name?"

He drops his head a moment, then gets up and walks over to a file cabinet. He returns with a manila folder.

"I guess you need to know," he says, "otherwise how will his family. . . ."

He takes a document of some kind out of the folder.

"This is a terrible loss," he says, his attention riveted to the piece of paper, "just terrible."

Martindale looks at me. I reply with a shrug.

"Cappy was going to save this mission," says Brother Stephen. He still hasn't looked up from the document in his hand.

"Just who is it we're talking about here?" I ask.

Finally he looks up. "His full name was Theodore Capetanakis."

He waits for it to sink in.

"Jesus Christ," says Martindale.

My sentiments exactly.

In Philadelphia the name of Theodore Capetanakis is synonymous with two things: money and mystery. On the financial side of the equation, Capetanakis, born in Greece and raised in the City of Brotherly Love, is, or was, a wealthy trucking magnate. His largest company, Capetan Transport, provides trucks and other vehicles to construction outfits from Boston to Baltimore. In recent years he's gotten into the rental business too, giving U-Haul and Ryder a run for their money in the region. Since the casinos opened, a new subsidiary, Capetan Coaches, has emerged, buying up a number of bus companies and capturing the largest market share of the routes between Atlantic City, Philly, and New York. It'd be difficult to find a major transportation corridor in the Northeast that doesn't have a few dozen vehicles driving on it with a Capetan logo.

Then there's the mystery part. For years Capetanakis has been Philly's Howard Hughes. No one knows what he looks like. The last known photograph of the man, the one the newspapers always use, is from 1951. A bachelor, he's said to move about constantly, always incognito, rarely staying in one spot long enough for anyone to identify him. The word is that the old man has turned the day-to-day management of the business over to his brother just so he can stay on the move. He has a shadowy past, although, based upon the reports I saw when I was in the police department, he's never been tied to organized crime. The thinking is, the old man's so paranoid he'd never link up with any organization that could take control out of his hands. Recently there've been rumors that he's giving away money to offbeat charities, which, if the Cappy I knew really was Capetanakis, explains Brother Stephen's anxiety. One thing I recall leads me to think Stephen is telling the truth. It's from a talk I had some years back over a few beers with an FBI buddy. Capetanakis is reputed to despise the IRS so much that defying it has become an obsession with him. My agent friend told me—and here I recall Cappy's bravado at dinner—that Capetanakis hasn't paid any personal income taxes for the past fifteen years, and still the IRS is having trouble nailing him.

Brother Stephen pushes the document across the desk toward us, and I glance at it before handing it to Martindale. It appears to be a legal agreement of some sort.

"We just got this from his lawyers. Once our attorney looked it over we were going to have a private signing ceremony here in my office."

"Can you summarize it for us in layman's terms?" I ask.

"Cappy was to give us twenty-five thousand dollars for temporary repairs on this building. But the big thing was that he would include the mission in his will. It would have been enough for us to put up a brand-new building."

"So now you'll get nothing?"

If he notices a touch of sarcasm in my voice, he doesn't show it.

"Nothing's been signed. And he wasn't going to change the will until this agreement was worked out."

"Why'd there have to be anything in writing?" asks Martindale. "I mean why didn't the guy just *put* you in his will?"

"He had ideas, ideas about what the new building should look like. He didn't want to leave us the money unless we agreed in advance on how it would be used. His ideas were kind of weird, but we'd gotten him to tone most of them down. We were only days away from signing."

Martindale hands the document back. "Do you have any idea who might have wanted to kill him?"

Brother Stephen shakes his head. "Hardly anybody knew him. That was the way he wanted it. His only friend was Nick."

"What can you tell us about that relationship?" I ask.

He shakes his head. "They were friends, that's all I know. I think Nick did a favor for Cappy, or something like that."

"Saved his life, at least that's what Cappy said."

"Really? Well, it would be like Cappy to want to do something big for Nick after that."

"What might he have done? Given him money?"

"I doubt it. Cappy knew Nick had a gambling problem. He wouldn't have wanted to make matters worse. His own gambling was recreational, not compulsive. He did have a serious drinking problem though, which was why I was so worried about this agreement."

"I don't understand."

"When he was drinking Cappy often did things he didn't remember later."

"And you were afraid that he'd agreed to help the mission when he was under the influence."

He nods his head. "There was no way to be sure. You could never tell how much he'd had. He never seemed to show it."

I wonder now if Cappy ever remembered talking to me. But more than that, I wonder what it was he told Nick in that condition that resulted in Nick and him being incinerated.

"Did he have *any* enemies that you know of?"

"He was terrified of the IRS, the FBI, that sort of thing. But I never heard him even hint at having any personal enemies."

"Tell me, where were you earlier this evening?"

"I haven't left the building all day. Surely—"

Martindale jumps in. "It's just a routine question."

But I've saved the big one for last. "Besides you, who knew who Cappy was?"

He shakes his head again. "I've been very careful not to let it get out. I haven't even told the board of trustees yet."

"But who did know?"

"Well, our attorney, of course."

"Anyone else?"

"Just one other person. Sister Felice. Cappy told her himself."

On the way out, Martindale and I stop at Sister's office, but it's late and she's gone for the day. Coming down the hallway we bump into Tommy again.

"Frank, is it true? Was it Cappy who died?"

I nod at him. "It looks that way."

"How'd it happen? I mean, you know, *how'd* he die?"

I glance at Martindale, then back at Tommy. "It was a lot like the way Nick went, I'm afraid."

Tommy makes the sign of the cross. "Jesus, Mary, and Joseph, have mercy on us."

When we're outside, Martindale stops in front of his car and looks at me. "What do you make of that honky, *Brother* Stephen?"

"I think he's going to miss Cappy."

"You've got that right," says Martindale. "It's truly inspiring to be witness to such compassion among the missionary brethren."

"You notice what Tommy asked us?"

"Yeah, why?"

"Well, it's interesting. Remember how Tommy and Brother

Stephen and the sister were all talking things over when we arrived. That tells me that if Tommy didn't know how Cappy died, then Brother Stephen probably didn't know either."

"Yeah, so?"

"Well, Brother Stephen never even asked. Wouldn't you think he'd at least ask how his biggest donor had died?"

3

Early Saturday morning Petrillo lets me into the Major Crimes building. He has the look of a college freshman who's just pulled an all-nighter. A day's growth of beard is beginning to show, and his eyes are watery and bloodshot.

"Thanks for coming, Lieutenant. I know it's early."

"I'm an early riser. But you look like you could use some sleep."

He smiles weakly. I follow him down the hall to the conference room. At first it appears he's working solo. There's no one else in sight when he ushers me into the room, where a VCR and television monitor have been set up. But someone forgot to empty the ashtrays and clear away the Styrofoam coffee cups. From the looks of it, half-a-dozen people sat around this old walnut table during the wee hours.

He gets right down to business. "Let's try this one first," he says, appearing to pick a videotape at random from a cardboard box, then inserting it into the VCR. He looks too tired to play games so I'll give odds Nick makes an early appearance.

The tape opens with a title frame that reads DIVISION OF GAMING EN-FORCEMENT—POSEIDON CASINO. It gives the date, the time (in military style), the camera number (in this case it's 42), and the table number (11). The action begins at 19:00 hours, 7 P.M. Everything's in black and white.

"We have videos from three different cameras for this table, each from a unique angle," he says. "Okay, I'm going to move through this tape. I need your help confirming the ID. Tell me if you see D'Angelo."

From a quick scan of the gamblers, three of whom are women, it's clear Nick isn't playing. Petrillo fast-forwards the tape, and I watch as the minutes fly by. By the time the clock reaches 20:00 hours, three players have left the table and have been replaced by three others. Still no sign of Nick. At 20:39 one of the two dealers goes on a break and is relieved by a substitute. At 21:00 the other dealer goes on her break and is relieved by the dealer who left earlier. By now the players have settled in, with only two having left, to be replaced by two others. Table 11 is full, and a number of onlookers have pushed in close to watch the action, creating a substantial crowd.

At 21:33, or 9:33 P.M., Nick, his arm around Monica Poole's waist, appears on the screen. At 9:55 P.M. a place frees up at the table and Nick's ready to buy in. By the time he begins to play he appears to have forgotten about Monica, who's left standing behind him peering over his shoulder. His face is haggard and thin, and there are bags under his eyes. He looks seventy instead of fifty-six.

"That's him."

"That guy there?" He points to Nick on the screen.

"Yeah, that's him."

Petrillo takes a seat next to me, and we watch together for a few minutes. Finally, he can't stand it any longer. "What's he doing?"

"Playing roulette."

He glares at me. "You know what I mean. You notice anything unusual?"

I do. Monica was right. He's not interested in gambling. He has bought into the game with a hundred dollars and is playing it safe as can be, each time placing only the minimum bet, one ten-dollar chip, on either black or red. At that rate, theoretically at least, he could play a long while before losing it all. But it's not Nick's suddenly conservative betting habits that interest me. It's his eyes.

"Looks to me like he's getting a feel for the table," I say. "You know, playing it safe at first, waiting to see which way his luck's going."

Petrillo ponders this as I return to watching Nick's eyes. Directly across from him there are four other players, two men and two women, surrounded by half-a-dozen onlookers. Ignoring the two women, I concentrate on the men. But from this angle it's hard to see their faces in full. Both men are in their sixties and well dressed. One's so bald he has nothing left but a few thin strands along the side. The second man, in Monica's words, has "all his hair." He's the one who interests me.

Petrillo's interest has been piqued, too. He leans forward. "Who's the broad?"

"The broad?"

"The woman standing behind D'Angelo."

"Interesting," I respond.

"What?"

"I'm not sure. Can we play a tape from another angle? Maybe if I see her from the side it would help."

He takes another tape from the cardboard box, inserts it into the VCR, and fast-forwards it to 21:33 hours. Now I can see the full face of the man with all the hair. His eyes are deeply set, and his nose is long and thin with a keen edge to it, like a shark's dorsal fin. I'm no expert but the hair does look natural. The telling feature is that there's a slight receding of the hairline, something you'd expect to be concealed if he were wearing a hairpiece. It's been styled by a pro, all fluffed and teased to give it a wild, "natural" appearance, as if its owner has just come back from climbing Grand Teton and hasn't had time to use a comb. Everything about the man is hirsute. He has a pencil-thin mustache. And he possesses the largest pair of untamed eyebrows I've ever seen on a Homo sapien. Their dominant feature is an upward curve, extending half an inch or more up toward his forehead.

"So what do you think?" Petrillo asks, his eyes on Monica Poole.

"Monica. It must be Monica."

"The broad? Her name's Monica?"

"Nick used to mention her. I think she's with some escort service."

"What's her full name?"

"Nick never said."

Which of course is true.

At this point a new figure appears on the screen. He wears a gaming license on his lapel and holds a piece of paper that he hands to the hairy Mr. X. Mr. X writes something on the paper, returns it, and resumes play. Picking up a handful of chips, he places two at a time on a dozen different numbers. I've never understood the allure of roulette. There's absolutely no skill involved. It's a sucker's game, just behind Keno and the big six wheel in the extent to which the odds favor the house. You're even at a disadvantage simply betting black or red, odd or even, all of which pay even money, because the house wins if the ball lands on 0 or 00, giving you eighteen ways to win and twenty to lose. But Nick's Mr. X isn't interested in such relatively "safe" bets. Undaunted by the house advantage, he's picking individual numbers, placing bets that face 37 to 1 odds while paying 35 to 1.

"Did he say anything about her," Petrillo asks, "where she works, anything like that?"

"I don't believe so."

"No problem. We'll find her."

As Petrillo scribbles something in a notebook, Ray Martindale sticks his head into the room.

"Mind if I talk with Frank, Detective?"

Petrillo, his mind elsewhere, heads for the door.

"Just called your place," Martindale says, one gnarled black hand wrapped around a Dunkin' Donuts paper coffee cup. "No answer so I figured you might be here. Brought you some news from the lab. Unofficially, of course."

"Of course."

"It's the ignition device. I sent the one used on Cappy over to Hammonton last night. No surprise. It's identical to the one used on D'Angelo. Primitive but very effective."

"What is it?"

"Here, I'll show you."

He puts his coffee cup down on the conference table and reaches into his pants pocket, producing a book of matches and something in a cellophane package. Placing the matchbook on the table, he opens the package and takes out a spool of solder. He measures off a piece about a foot long, bends it back and forth until it breaks, and proceeds to wrap it around the matchbook.

"There, see? Makes a handy little torch. Costs a buck ninety-five. It's nothing more than ordinary 40/60 solder wound around a book of matches. All our friend has to do is light the matchbook and toss the sucker. The solder gives it weight. This way the bastard can spread a shit-load of accelerant around and keep his distance when he lights it."

"Fascinating, but what does it tell us?"

"Maybe nothing. Maybe a lot. I've seen these used in the Pines by arsonists. Sometimes it's electrical wire instead of solder. Works fine either way. Sicko wants to torch some woods, he can drive by and throw this from his pickup. Then he just keeps on truckin'."

"What're you saying, our hit man's a Piney?"

He considers that for a moment, taking a long drink of his coffee. "Not necessarily. But he might have started a few fires there. Fact is, this is the first time I've seen one a these things anywhere else."

"Well, it's something."

"Trust me, Frank. This is more than 'something.' This is *ev-ee-dense.*"

"What else do you have?"

"Only what we already knew. The lab confirmed that gasoline was the accelerant used in D'Angelo's death."

"What about the residue in the gas can left behind?"

"They're still working on that. But it won't do us much good unless we can track down the source."

"Why's that?"

"Well, if we can discover where this guy gets his gas, the lab can do a dye comparison and tell us if it's the same as the residue left behind in that can. The residue by itself gets us nowhere."

"What about Cappy? Any positive ID yet?"

"We're talking to the brother, trying to track down some dental records. The prosecutor's office is not happy, though. Isn't good for our image to have Theodore Capetanakis burned to death under the Boardwalk. They're all praying it's somebody else."

"Anything from the residents of Hotel Underwood?"

"Two old winos say they think they might've seen something moving in the distance near where Cappy was sleeping. But that's it. No descriptions, nothing. Everybody else has either skipped the neighborhood or was blotto at the time. Oh, and Cox is pissed. Talley's got him working with Petrillo—on the assumption that they're both looking for the same killer."

"Have you seen these videotapes?"

"No, and I'd rather not."

"Do you suppose you could watch just a few minutes of Nick at the roulette table? I need your help with this, Ray."

He sips some more coffee and thinks it over for a moment.

"What're you after?"

"Anything you can tell me."

He stands up, walks over to the coffeemaker in the corner of the room and refills his Dunkin' Donuts cup with something thick and muddy.

"Okay, but make it quick. It'd kill me to watch a bunch of assholes pissing their money away when I know I could do a much better job of it myself."

I rewind the tape and hit "play." Martindale watches the screen without saying anything, an expression of intense discomfort on his face.

"Doesn't look like your buddy was in the game that night."

"No," I say, "looks like he had other things on his mind."

"Who's the guy with all the hair?"

"I was hoping you'd tell me."

"D'Angelo's certainly interested. Never takes his eyes off the guy."

"You don't recognize him?"

"Never saw him before."

"Okay. I've got one more thing I'd like you to look at."

"Jesus, Sweeney, I'm a compulsive gambler, for chrissakes. I'm not even supposed to think about this shit."

"Won't take long. Trust me."

I fast-forward the tape to the spot where the casino employee appears.

"What's happening here?"

Martindale smiles. "That's Charlie Bishop. He's casino manager at the Poseidon. Haven't seen him for a while. Miss the slick bastard."

"What's the paper he's giving Mr. X to fill out?"

"Oh, that. It's probably just a CTR."

"What's that?"

"Stands for Currency Transaction Report. You have to fill one out whenever you're in a game for over ten thousand. IRS likes to know where all the cash is going."

"What's on one of these CTRs?"

"Name, rank, and serial number, that sort of thing."

"So we'd know who this guy was if we could see that CTR?"

"Yeah, assuming he told the truth about himself. But you can be sure Charlie Bishop ain't gonna tell you the dude's name. That's confidential information."

The tape continues to roll. Charlie Bishop stays to observe Mr. X bet. In turn, Nick watches Charlie Bishop. Bishop finally walks away. Then Nick prepares to leave the table as well. He says something to the dealer at the wheel, hands him a handful of chips, then leaves, with Monica close behind.

"Your friend was a big tipper," says Martindale.

"Liked to think he was a high roller."

"He's no whale."

"What's a whale?"

"A *serious* high roller, guy who's prepared to risk a million or so every time."

"You're right. Nick was no whale. He wasn't even a porpoise."

"Well, I'll tell you one thing, though, your Mr. X is in the big leagues."

"Because he has to fill out one of those CTRs? Exactly what I was thinking. Tell me, do you think the dealer'd know his name?"

"Shit, yeah. I know that dealer. Name's Billy Loo. He'd pay close attention to someone like Mr. X. Dealers score their biggest tokes off guys like that. They know *all* those high rollers by name. And one other thing."

"What's that?"

"Charlie Bishop's the head honcho on the floor. He doesn't waste his time going around asking players to fill out CTRs. That's the floor-person's or the pit boss's job."

"What're you saying?"

"I'm saying this hairy Mr. X must be one very special dude."

4

I WAIT OUTSIDE in the parking lot while Martindale gets Billy Loo's address for me. When he comes out I ask him what he knows about the Poseidon.

"Anarchy rules, from what I hear."

"How so?"

"Being near bankruptcy all this time has made people a bit testy. No one there believes the place's going to make it. I've heard all sorts of rumors."

"Like what?"

"Pilferage, rudeness to the guests, dealers defying pit bosses, that sort of thing. The casino's losing cash daily. Business in the hotel's way off, too."

"So you don't think it'll survive?"

"License's up for renewal. They've got to get that approved first."

The New Jersey Casino Control Commission, which decides such things, isn't exactly known for getting in the way of the casinos. I mention this to him.

"Yeah, that's true. But to keep your license you've got to be financially healthy. Even the CCC can't ignore a bankruptcy. According to the newspapers, they're waiting to see what the bankruptcy court will do. Word is, if Dante doesn't get some relief there, he's fucked."

"How the hell did he ever get in this fix? I mean how can a casino *lose* money?"

"Tony Dante's not exactly known for his business smarts."

"So I've heard. Have you ever met him? What's he like?"

Car keys in hand, he's standing next to a 1980 Buick pockmarked with rust and corrosion from the salt air. It takes him a while to decide whether or not to answer. When he finally does, he pockets the keys and leans back against the car door.

"Tell you a story. Dante gave a speech to the city employees last year. It was the mayor's idea, part of a series of monthly pep talks. Supposed to make us all feel grateful for having thankless jobs, some bullshit like that. Well, Dante, he was there representing the casinos. He was supposed to show his appreciation for all the hard work we'd done making the city run so fucking well, that sort of shit. So what does this asshole do? He tries warming us up with a Polish joke. A few retards down front where I'm sitting laugh a little and then there's silence. Dante thinks his timing must be off or something, so he tries a gay joke. A few titters. So he hits on Jews. Then Japanese. And Puerto Ricans. And finally women's libbers. By now *no one's* laughing. He hasn't tried any nigger material yet, but by this time I'm giving the bastard the evil eye. I've got myself zeroed in on him like a deer in my headlights. I mean, *man,* he's in my *crosshairs.* No way he can miss seeing me down front dissing him like I am. But just in case the dude ain't getting my message, I get up out of my seat, stand there, and stare right at the white motherfucker."

"What did he do?"

"Motherfucker froze. I stopped that white bastard in his tracks. From then on all he said was a bunch of bullshit platitudes. Told us how wonderful we were to be helping him do *his* job, shit like that. But no more fucking jokes. He cut that shit once he got an eyeful of me. That casino of his ever catches fire, I'm gonna see the trucks get lost on the way."

I used to know someone like Martindale. He was a talented assistant DA in Philly on the way up, and he wouldn't take crap from anybody. Eventually it backfired on him. Now he's in business for himself in a Podunk town in central Pennsylvania. Once every couple of years, if he's lucky, he gets a personal injury case. Otherwise, he drafts wills and fills in as public defender when business is really bad, which it is most of the time. It takes real chutzpah to face down powerful assholes, and a considerable amount of luck and skill to get away with it. Trouble is, guys like Martindale have a habit of drawing a line in the sand with every two-bit sleazebag who comes along. Not all assholes are equal. Which is to say, not all assholes are worth throwing your career away for.

As Martindale gets into his car, he turns to ask me a question.

"You think this D'Angelo got caught up in the Poseidon's bankruptcy problems somehow?"

"Seems unlikely. I mean he was only a security guard."

"And what about the guy on the videotape? Who do *you* figure he is?"

"Haven't a clue. But I know one thing."

"What's that?"

"Cappy was involved somehow."

He thinks this over, then says, "You think maybe he put D'Angelo onto this guy at the roulette table?"

"The thought has occurred to me."

BILLY LOO WORKS the swing shift and lives on the beach near the northern end of Ocean City's boardwalk. His apartment is above a place called Jeremy's, a combination restaurant and rental shop for bikes and beach equipment. The restaurant hasn't opened for the season yet, but there are a few adults with their children at the shop, checking out Jeremy's family-size three-wheelers.

I take the outside stairs to the second floor. A middle-aged man in red bikini briefs answers the door. He's a jowly Hispanic, a good ten or fifteen years older than the dealer I saw on the videotape. For some reason, he behaves as if I'm expected, motioning me inside.

I wait in a kitchenette area inside the door. It's a cramped apartment, with one bedroom, a bath, and a combination kitchen, living, and dining area. Places like this rent for a song during the off-season, but the price soars after Memorial Day when the summer crowd moves in. The average working stiff like Billy, unless he's making a hell of a lot more than the typical dealer, is forced to move out and find someplace else until Labor Day.

After a minute or two Billy appears, wearing a tattered black silk bathrobe.

"Already answer police questions," he says, defensively.

113

I underestimated Petrillo. He, or one of his men, has already been here, which means that he'd already studied those videotapes thoroughly before I was asked to look at them. It was the identity of "the broad" that he was after, not Nick D'Angelo.

"Sorry to wake you. My name's Frank Sweeney. I'm a private investigator. I just want to ask you a few questions about Nick D'Angelo."

I show him my ID.

"You PI?"

"That's right."

"Like in movie?"

Suddenly he's deferential. The man's been kissing up to too many high rollers.

I shake my head. "Sorry. No movie star. Just an investigator."

"You want tea?"

"I'd love some."

He goes over to a small sink, pours some water into a kettle, then places it on a burner. The skin under his neck is flabby. From this angle he looks older than in the videotape, closer in age to the man in the red briefs than I'd first thought. He's a little on the short side, about my height, five-eight, and has thin black hair with a small bald spot in the back like a tonsure. At least I still have most of my hair.

"What I do for you, Mr. PI?"

He takes a seat on a torn vinyl couch, letting the skimpy robe fall open around his bare legs.

"You remember Nick D'Angelo?" I ask.

He hesitates a moment. "Yeah, I remember Nick."

"What is it you remember about him?"

"He good guy. Bad player, nice man. Police already ask me questions 'bout him."

"I understand, but there are a few things *I'd* like to ask, too—if that's okay."

"Why I have to talk to you?"

"Look, you should understand something. Nick's brother is my best friend. I knew Nick from the time he was a rookie cop. I'm here as a *friend*."

He gives a little bow. "Okay, okay."

"Did you have any idea why Nick was murdered?"

"Like I tell police, Billy Loo just deal. I no mess with private lives." He shakes his head vigorously. "No way."

"You were a dealer for Nick, weren't you? Did you deal blackjack for him?"

"Right. Nick bad blackjack player, you know."

"Why was he playing roulette that Tuesday night, a week and a half ago?"

He shakes his head. "He do it one time, you know. But that only time I see."

"But do you know *why* he was there?"

"No."

"Did you notice anything unusual about him that night?"

He thinks a moment, then nods. "Now you say it, he bet funny. Like he don't care, you know."

"Anything else?"

He shakes his head.

"There was another man there that night. Across the table from him? Do you remember him? About sixty, sixty-five, with a moustache, real bushy eyebrows, and lots of gray hair."

Billy's expression changes.

"Don't want no trouble, no trouble."

He gets up and goes into the kitchen area where he buys some time getting the tea ready.

"Who is he?" I ask, when he returns with two cups of tea. "What's so special about this guy?"

Billy sips his tea and looks at the floor. "You know casinos, Mr. PI?"

"I've gambled a little."

"You know 'bout high rollers?"

"What about them?"

"Dealers can't go talkin' 'bout high rollers. Mr. D., he lose business real bad that way, you know."

"This is a murder case, Billy."

That doesn't work so I try another approach.

"If you don't cooperate, Billy, you could lose your license."

From the expression on his face, I'd say I hit a nerve. If he's like a lot of the foreign nationals in Atlantic City, he doesn't have a hell of a lot of other skills, and this is probably the only job that's ever paid him a decent wage. Lose the license and he might as well leave town, maybe the country.

"Don't know. That the truth."

"This guy doesn't have a name?" I say.

"Everybody call him Mr. Smith. Not his real name."

I move over to the couch where he's sitting.

"Okay, Billy, then tell me what you do know about Mr. Smith."

"Mr. Smith, big player. Usually come every Tuesday night. That's how come I see him so often, you know."

"Does he stay in the hotel?"

"No. No comps for Mr. Smith."

"He's a high roller and he doesn't get comped?"

"Bring him Cutty and water. That all."

"You always deal roulette on Tuesdays?"

"Mr. Bishop want me. Say I Mr. Smith's personal dealer." He smiles with pride at this.

"So you're assigned to be Smith's dealer? He doesn't play at anyone else's table?"

Billy smiles again and shakes his head. "Only my table."

"Why do you suppose that is, Billy?"

"Mr. Bishop like me, you know. Say I'm best dealer."

"How long have you been doing this for Mr. Bishop?"

He thinks a moment. " 'Bout three, four month."

"How long does Mr. Smith play when he's in town on Tuesdays?"

He frowns. "Very long time, very. All night."

"What else do you know about Mr. Smith?"

"He play like Nick."

"What do you mean?"

"He bad player."

"You mean he loses a lot?"

"All the time."

I move a little closer to him.

"What has Mr. Bishop told you about Mr. Smith?"

"Only tell me he take care of me."

"I'll bet he did. Billy, how long have you been in this country?"

"A while, you know."

"You got your green card?"

He looks offended. " 'Course I got green card. How else I work?"

"Okay, Billy, I'll be going. Thanks a lot for your help."

As I put the tea cup in the kitchen sink, another question occurs to me.

"Tell me, Billy, are you the personal dealer for any other players?"

"Deal twenty-one for Mr. Jones sometimes."

At first I take it as a joke, but then it hits me he's not kidding.

"What's this Mr. Jones look like?"

"Real old guy. Like a bum, you know?"

"He wear a raincoat and baseball cap?"

"Yeah, that's him."

"Any others?"

He shakes his head. "No, just two."

"I don't suppose Mr. Smith or Mr. Jones have first names, do they?"

He smiles. "Funny thing. Both names same."

"Oh?"

"Both name Jonah. Funny thing."

5

COMING UP FROM the parking garage, the Poseidon's elevator ascends to the beat of two conflicting messages, played alternately over a concealed ceiling speaker. In the first, the voice of a nameless, middle-aged man broadcasts a compulsory caveat heard in all the casinos. *Welcome to the Poseidon. Remember, if you sweat it, don't bet it. If you think you or someone you know has a gambling problem, call 1-800-GAMBLER.* Then, in counterpoint, a youthful Frank Sinatra beckons sensuously with "I've Got the World on a String." So who ya gonna believe, the killjoy with the toll-free phone number or Ol' Blue Eyes himself? Well, you came to play, didn't you? Like an old priest friend of mine used to say, you don't go to a whorehouse to listen to the piano player.

The Poseidon suffers from a number of design flaws best appreciated from the Boardwalk, so getting off the elevator I buck the foot traffic going to the casino and pass through the lobby and out into the open air. Here the Chairman of the Board greets me again, this time from speakers under the canopied entrance.

I want to see if anything's changed since I was last here. It hasn't.

One of the Poseidon's shortcomings is that it's situated on a relatively small parcel of land. So the casino's designers were forced to build upward, in three tiers, in order to create sufficient floor space for gambling. Then someone made a bad situation worse by constructing the casino façade, as well as that of the twenty-story hotel above it, with reflecting glass. As a result, restless players and those with second thoughts will find themselves distracted by the people out on the Boardwalk or by the glimmering blue-green Atlantic in the distance. No casino wants to give its gamblers an opportunity to do anything but lose their money. Yet that's just what the Poseidon has managed to accomplish.

Then there's Tony Dante's plastic god, Poseidon, the nonsectarian totem looming over the entrance. It rests on a fifteen-foot canopy extending out over ten opaque-glass doors. According to Dante's publicity brochure, it's more than twice as tall as the eighteen-foot-high Caesar Augustus that greets gamblers outside the entrance to Caesars several blocks down the Boardwalk. Clad in a Roman toga and bearing the Italian word FORTUNA in gold lettering across his chest, the bearded Greek god holds a trident in his right hand and an exposed pair of playing cards—an ace and king of spades—in the other. The trident, or so Tony D.'s brochure claims, is made of "real metal," and not the combination of fiberglass and plastic that makes up the face and body. He must be telling the truth because from where I'm standing I can see large patches of rust on the tines of the three-pronged spear. The exaggerated Italianate features of Poseidon's face are said to bear a striking resemblance to Dante himself, although Dante goes to great lengths in his publicity material to inform visitors that any resemblance between "the god out front" and its merely mortal owner inside is "entirely circumstantial." Tony D. writes his own material, too.

I've seen enough. It's time to find Charlie Bishop.

Inside, the bells and flashing lights, the frantic chug-chuggings of the coin-guzzling slot machines are almost enough to convince you of the Poseidon's claim that there's "a jackpot every forty-five seconds." ONE PULL CAN CHANGE YOUR LIFE, say the billboards along the Atlantic City Expressway. Believe that and you'll believe Tony Dante's ludicrous motto, too: "At the Poseidon you win even when you lose." There's another of Dante's mistakes. It's an ironclad principle in the casino business that you never mention the words *lose* or *loser*. But Tony D., like Francis Albert, prefers to do it his way, and proof of this—like Sinatra's music—is found everywhere in the Poseidon.

The first tier of the casino is all slots, and many are sitting idle. Not a good sign. I stroll along the elevated walkway that spans the length of the room, looking down each row of machines for someone above the rank of security officer or change person. Halfway past the sixth aisle I spot a young man in a dark blue suit wearing a casino badge on his lapel. He directs me to the Neptune Casino, level three, where there's a poker tournament going on.

The escalator in the middle of the casino takes me past the table games on the second floor to level three where a sign warns, POKER TOURNAMENT ONLY. I head in that direction, Sinatra's "April in Paris" in the air. Most of the tables are covered. But what the Neptune level lacks in gamblers, it makes up for in tropical fish. The room's three inside walls are lined with large glass tanks, each containing dozens of exotic species, all circling submerged replicas of Poseidon, plastic underwater traffic cops with upraised tridents in hand.

At the far end of the casino, people are seated around five poker tables. Three management types in suits stand off to one side talking, eyes fixed on the tables. If I hadn't known Charlie Bishop from the videotapes, I could have spotted him by the kiss-ass expression on the faces of the two underlings standing next to him.

"Mr. Bishop?"

"Yeah?"

He looks me over quickly, determining what, if any, level of attention I merit. The halfhearted smile tells me he's already written me off. Must be the chinos and no-name polo shirt.

"Name's Sweeney." I show him my ID. "I'm investigating Nick D'Angelo's murder. I'd like to ask you a few questions."

He hesitates, pretending not to understand.

"D'Angelo? Oh, the security cop. You want Jack Coyle. Jack's head of security. He was D'Angelo's boss."

"Coyle can wait. Right now I'd like to speak with you."

"Who are you?"

"Told you, I'm a private investigator."

He lets that register and decides it's not good enough.

"You still want Coyle."

I glance at the two men next to him, then give him a curt smile.

"Look, Bishop, I've seen the videotapes of Nick gambling here on Tuesday, the ninth. You remember, the night he played roulette instead of blackjack? You're the one in those tapes—not Coyle. That's why I want to talk to you, not him."

He says something under his breath, sending the two sycophants off to check out the poker tables.

"Follow me," he says.

I trail along, wending my way around vacant craps tables, staring at the back of his crisp blue Italian suit. When he reaches a door that says STAFF ONLY, he holds it open for me. I walk past him into a long, narrow corridor. He pulls the door shut, then walks by me and down the hall. I follow, still staring at his back. At the end of the corridor he turns left, leads me down a different hallway, and stops in front of a door that says PERSONNEL—INTERVIEWS. It's a small, nondescript room containing nothing more than two chairs and a small desk with a phone on it.

Bishop takes a seat behind the desk and motions me to the other chair in front. Now that he's alone he looks less sure of himself. He's heavyset, about forty, with dark, thinning hair and large blue-gray eyes. He could stand to lose at least twenty-five pounds. A formidable double chin protrudes above a shirt collar that's at least one size too small. He has the florid complexion of a man whose blood pressure ought to be checked, and soon. If I were his doctor I'd recommend a less stressful line of work.

"Now what's this about a videotape, Mr. Sweeney?" He runs his finger around the inside of his collar, releasing the pressure on a roll of pink flesh.

"The tape in question is for the night of April nine, Nick's last night here before he was killed. He was playing roulette. Which was quite unusual."

"I never knew the man, but I understand roulette wasn't his game."

"Do you know *why* he was playing it then?"

"Look, Mr. Sweeney, we've told all this to the police. D'Angelo lost some money here. Apparently he lost money everywhere he played. I gather the man had a problem. That wasn't our concern. After we let him go we had no reason to keep tabs on him. I've no idea why he was here that night."

"Had you ever seen him play roulette before?"

"Like I said, I didn't know the man."

"Why was he fired?"

"That's not my department. You want Jack Coyle."

"Tell me about Jonah."

The question catches him with his index finger between his collar and neck again. His hand hesitates and his expression changes slightly, but he makes a quick recovery, ending by looking only mildly curious.

"Jonah?"

"There's a man called Jonah on that tape. Who is he?"

"I don't know anyone by that name. But if I did and he was one of our regulars, I certainly wouldn't reveal it to you. That sort of information's confidential."

"This is a murder investigation."

He picks up the phone in front of him and calls someone.

"This is Mr. Bishop. Is Coyle there? . . . Then get him, I'll wait." He holds the receiver aside and says to me, "You're really talking to the wrong man, Mr. Sweeney. The man you want is—Jack? Charlie here. I'd like you to come up to personnel. I've got a private investigator here inquiring about Nick D'Angelo. I think you're the one to

121

speak with him. . . . Good. We're in interview room three-twelve."

He puts the phone down and heads for the door.

"I'm very busy, Mr. Sweeney. I'm sure Mr. Coyle will be able to answer all your questions."

He walks out, leaving the door open. About sixty seconds later someone new is standing in the doorway.

"Mr. Sweeney? Jack Coyle, head of security." We shake hands. He takes the seat behind the desk and lights up a cigarette. "What can I do for you?"

In his late fifties, he has the leathery complexion and raspy voice of a lifelong smoker. His face is rumpled sandpaper, his eyes black walnuts.

"What can you tell me about Nick D'Angelo?"

"You're a PI, right?"

"That's right."

"Our personnel files are confidential."

He looks uncomfortable in his oversized green suit and brown tie, as if he doesn't belong. Coyle's a transplanted working man, not supervisory material. He belongs down on the casino floor, quieting drunks, hustling hookers out the door.

"I presume you've shared that file with the police."

"You're not the police, are you?"

"Mr. Bishop led me to believe you'd be cooperative."

He leans back in his chair, blowing a ring of smoke over his head, peering at me from behind the dark slits that are his eyes.

"Did he now?"

"Why was Nick fired?"

"That's a matter of public record. He broke the rules. No gambling at the casino you work for, not in this state."

"Was that the only reason he was fired?"

"Isn't it enough?"

"Not for me."

"Maybe that's why I'm head of security and you're a PI, Mr. Sweeney." He jabs in my direction with his cigarette, dropping ashes on the desk top. The phone on the desk rings and he sits forward.

"Coyle here. . . . Yeah. . . . Right. . . . Okay. . . . Sure, whatever you say."

After he puts the phone down, he sits up in his chair, grinding the cigarette out in an ashtray.

"This is your lucky day, Mr. Sweeney."

"How's that?"

"Boss wants to see you."

"The boss?"

"Tony Dante. He wants to talk to you."

6

JACK COYLE'S A different man escorting me to his boss's office. One phone call has turned the head of the palace guard into an attentive host. Nor does he seem curious about the sudden change in my status. His not to reason why.

The elevator opens into a large reception area whose walls are covered in a rich maroon fabric. On the facing wall, foot-high brass letters proclaim,

THE ANGELINA CORPORATION'S
POSEIDON HOTEL AND CASINO

and underneath, in equally ostentatious lettering,

ANTHONY P. DANTE,
PRESIDENT AND CHIEF EXECUTIVE OFFICER

There are stacks of the Poseidon's much-traveled publicity brochure everywhere. Sinatra's voice continues to cloy the ether like cheap air freshener. Recessed into the walls are dozens of gilt-framed glossy photographs of Vegas and A.C. entertainers. I glance at a few up close.

All small-time opening acts, all autographed "To Tony D."

Coyle winks at a heavily mascaraed receptionist, who ignores him. He leads me past her, through double mahogany doors, down a long, carpeted hallway. The decor is brothel red outlined in imitation gold-leaf. Up and down the hall, every thirty feet or so, someone has placed gilded replicas of Louis XIV console tables complete with faux marble tops. Anachronisms abound. The console tables have imitation Tiffany lamps on them, while at the other end of the hall a Federal-style grandfather clock, of the kind to be found at your local Ethan Allen store, presides loftily over the entire ersatz mélange.

"Mr. D., he likes to collect stuff," says Coyle.

"Does he now?"

"Yeah, he's got this guy in Philly gets it for him wholesale."

"I'm not surprised."

In the middle of the hall Coyle pauses before some double walnut doors, imperceptibly catches his breath, then leads me through and into another reception area. A young woman—girl, really—of the MTV generation is seated like a hotel concierge at someone's idea of a gilded eighteenth-century side table. She doesn't seem to notice Coyle but greets me with a smile that, if I were twenty years younger, I'd consider wantonly inviting. She picks up the receiver of a simulated French antique telephone, dials a number, murmurs a word or two, then puts it back on the hook.

"He's on a call," she says, still eyeing me, "but says to go in."

Coyle leads the way down a small connecting hallway to the door of his boss's office. Dante's sitting at a walnut desk the size of a craps table, the phone to his ear. He waves at me to come in, directing me to a large conference table in the middle of the room. Coyle doesn't say anything but, as if by some signal, turns and disappears.

While I gaze around, Dante covers the mouthpiece of the phone and winks conspiratorially.

"Fuckin' suppliers," he says, "think they can fuckin' hold me up just cause some court said—"

He returns to the phone. Grin changing to frown. He's well tanned and has a high, broad forehead, wide shoulders, and suspicious eyes.

"Who the fuck says that? . . . I swear to God . . . you gotta be pullin'

124

my chain . . . Jesus, I'm like a fuckin' fool down here. . . ."

I walk past his desk over to the floor-to-ceiling glass wall that faces the ocean. It's a dizzying perspective, up and down the beach and out to sea, with nothing between me and the Boardwalk below but some tinted glass and the tips of Poseidon's rusty trident. I touch the glass to reassure myself, causing my stomach to do a little flip. For a moment I'm up in the lighthouse again, floating free of earthly tethers.

Dante keeps his eyes on me but goes on talking.

"Who? . . . Him? He's like a nothing, a fucking nothing. . . . Listen what I'm saying. . . . Did I ever lie to you? . . ."

Behind his desk there's a walnut credenza holding a computer monitor and keyboard. On the screen is the casino's full-color logo, a surprisingly accurate reproduction of the plastic god that I can see from the window facing out to sea below. The wall next to his desk contains an array of black-and-white television monitors. The screens in the top row reveal the cashier's cage and the count room from a number of different angles. One shows people at a large table with stacks of bills and coins in front of them. Dante sees what I'm looking at and grins, fingering imaginary money between his thumb and fingers.

"Tell me. I want to know who's saying this shit . . . tell me, for chrissakes. . . . Yeah? Yeah? No shit? . . . I'll break his fuckin' head . . . yeah, yours, too. . . ."

The office decor is as much a hodgepodge as the hallway outside. The walls are covered in dark walnut, the floor in a thick checkered carpeting of burgundy and green. A small sitting area features uncomfortable modernistic metal-frame chairs upholstered in black leather, situated around a glass coffee table. The conference table and chairs in the center of the room are simulated Regency, faux calamander veneer combined with imitation gilding. As awful as everything is, somebody went to a lot of expense to have it made. When it comes to taste, sometimes the bad costs just as much as the good.

"Whaddya saying? . . . You know me. I never hear nothing. It's forgotten. . . . I told you. It's forgotten."

A Chippendale-style combination desk and bookcase in the far corner of the room catches my eye. It's worth a closer look. The doors on the top are conspicuously open, revealing a few old volumes, which appear to be valuable. There are first editions of Machiavelli's *The Works,* Hemingway's *For Whom the Bell Tolls,* and Melville's *The Confidence-Man: His Masquerade.* Interspersed among them are a few copies of the Harvard Classics and several Reader's Digest Condensed Books. Our Tony's a man of eclectic tastes.

I stand back to examine the desk and bookcase. At first glance it appears to be the real thing, late eighteenth century. It's a three-part piece—the desk, bookcase, and a broken pediment—with a patterned mahogany veneer. Pulling the top drawer out, I check the width of the veneer. It's quite thin, machine-cut. The dovetail joints are machine-made, too. Drawer linings are oak, with the sides rounded at the top. And the brass drawer handles have the hardness and distinct coloring of a much later period. It's a fine piece of work but definitely made sometime within the last century.

"You want something done," Dante says, coming up behind me, "you gotta do it yourself, you know what I mean? Sorry about the interruption. So, you like my bookcase? Paid fifteen grand for that baby. It's genuine Chippendale or something. My man in Philly tells me it's dated like seventeen fucking eighty."

I shake my head. "Afraid not."

"What're you saying?"

"I'm saying this is nice work, but it was made long after 1780."

"How the hell you know that?"

"It's my business. Trust me, this isn't eighteenth century."

"You shitting me? You saying I been screwed?"

"Well, I wouldn't put it that way. It's a fine piece of work. It's not worth fifteen-thousand, though."

"Jesus Christ. I'll have that fucker's balls on a plate."

"Will Rogers once said he'd rather be the man who bought the Brooklyn Bridge than the man who sold it. Look at it that way."

"Fuck Will Rogers."

So much for the antiques lesson.

According to the newspapers, Dante is sixty-two. From a distance he could pass for forty. His face, though scarred and pitted, is largely wrinkle-free. And he has a full head of jet-black hair, combed straight back. But up close there are a couple of giveaways. Such as the distinctive spacing between clumps of hair. It's not the worst implant job I've ever seen, but it does leave the front of his head looking like a carrot patch. The telltale creases in his neck are another tipoff. The man's a walking advertisement for the latest in cosmetic rejuvenation.

"Can't fuckin' trust nobody," he says, turning and walking over to the conference table. "You know how many fuckin' MBAs I got working here? Well, they ain't worth shit. Everybody tells me I gotta have 'em, but you can't fuckin' trust any a them. What do they know? You can't run a operation like mine with a bunch of Ivy League dickheads. You wanna know how you make it in this business?" He taps his chest. "It's all in here. You gotta go with your instincts."

"Then why keep all these people on?" I ask, standing across from him.

He ignores my question, his right hand fondling the Rolex on his left wrist.

"Know what else it takes? The personal touch. Me, I'm a people person."

"Which is why you're taking the time to talk to me, right?"

"Fuckin' right. We're a small company. Everyone out there wants to turn us into one a these big corporate conglomerations, you know what I mean?" He points in the direction of his Ivy League dickheads out in the hall. "I don't believe in that shit. Look what it's done to the other casinos."

"What *has* it done?"

He pauses, this time giving my question his full attention.

"Lookit the Golden Nugget," he says. "Steve Wynn, he sold out and went back to Vegas."

"He didn't exactly take a loss, if I remember correctly. And he *is* coming back to the city."

"Lookit Trump. Yeah, lookit The Donald. There, see. Am I right or am I wrong?"

I've got to admit it's hard to argue with that kind of reasoning.

"Mr. Dante, look—"

"Call me Tony, everybody does."

"Look, I don't want to waste any more of your time. Perhaps we could talk about Nick D'Angelo?"

"You want something?" He punches a button on a speaker phone on the table in front of him. "Beth, honey, be a doll and bring us some fruit."

"Just coffee for me. Black."

"Stuff'll kill ya. Me, I'm a veggie-tarian. Body's a temple, ya know." He punches a button on the speaker phone again. "One coffee, Beth. Put a little snort in that, too, babe. You look like you need it, Frank. It is 'Frank,' isn't it?"

"The name's Sweeney."

The buzzer on the phone goes off. He hits a different button and the voice of Charlie Bishop comes on."

"Tony? Charlie."

Dante glances at me and says, "We got us a Jap whale, Frank. He's out to break the house. Fucker can't wait for the courts to close us down, he's got to do it himself." To the phone he says, "Yeah, go ahead."

"I'm in the baccarat pit. He's up nine hundred now."

"Shit. He change his bets?"

"He never changes. Five thou each hand."

"You have Jack check him out?"

"He's been watching him all morning. Can't find a thing."

"Fucker's got to be cheating."

"Tony, look—"

"You try changing dealers?"

"We do that and he'll walk. We're down nearly a mil now."

Dante stares at the ceiling a moment and then smiles.

"Got an idea, Charlie."

Silence on the other end.

"Charlie, you there?"

"Yeah."

"He still drinking orange juice?"

"Yeah."

"Change waitresses. Send in one with big boobs. Try that Rhonda. She's got tits out to here. Tell her to stick 'em right in the little Jap's face. That doesn't work, have her drop her panties."

"Tony—"

"Let me know how it works."

He turns off the speaker and taps himself on the chest again.

"Like I said, Frank, it's all here. Instincts."

Beth, eyes riveted on her boss now, enters the room with a large tray of fresh fruit, several bottles of Evian water, and my coffee. Dante gives her a slap on the behind as she leaves, then grins at me like a kid who just got a peek down his sister's blouse. I take a small sip of the whiskey-laced coffee to be polite, then set the cup aside.

"Look, about Nick D'Angelo, did you ever—"

"Know what people call me, Frank?"

He picks up a silver paring knife from the tray and cuts into a mango.

"What?"

"The Book. Tony the Book. Know why?"

"Because you read Machiavelli and Melville?"

"Because of what I've got up here." This time he taps his head. "I got this encyclopedia for a brain. It's like a book. I know all sorts a shit. And I never forget. I never forget, Frank."

"What sort of things don't you ever forget?"

"I'll tell you a story. When my father, God rest his soul, opened this casino, he didn't know dick about the business. Shit, he sold cosmetics all his life. Admitted it himself. 'Perfume ain't craps,' he used to say. I swear to God. But he learned. He learned by watching and listening. And he never forgot a thing. You do him a favor, he remembered. You fuck with him, he remembered that, too. Only way to do business. Am I right or wrong? One day that first year we had a dealer who was swinging. The guy was copping chips from us, the bastard. My father, he took care of the prick. Fucker never worked in this town again. My father, he saw to it I learned from that. I swear to God. It's a fucking art doing business like that. You got to be respected. You got to remember everything. Me, I'm like that. Treat me fair, I'm your friend. Fuck with me, I'm your worst nightmare."

"So what are you saying? Nick D'Angelo fucked with you?"

"Nick D'Angelo? Who said anything about Nick D'Angelo? But

since you mention it. This Nick D'Angelo, he was a flea, a desperado, a *nothing*. Man didn't belong here. Some people, they don't belong in the casinos, it's outa their league, know what I mean? Man oughta have stayed a vice cop. Am I right or wrong?"

On that one point at least, he and I are in agreement. Nick did *not* belong here. He *was* small-time, a flea. But he was important enough for Dante to do a little checking around, enough to find out at least that Nick used to be a vice cop. So why would a self-styled casino luminary like Anthony P. Dante waste his time on a petty, out-of-control compulsive gambler like Nick D'Angelo?

"So what did D'Angelo do, Tony?"

His face is blank, a lunar landscape of pockmarked indifference.

"I don't waste my time. He worked for Jack Coyle. Talk to him."

"I already have."

"Good." He stands up. "You know why I'm a success, Frank? Some guys, they're always sticking their tongues up their ass. They never make a beef. They never have a little sit-down when there's a misunderstanding. Me, I speak my mind. That's why I asked you up here today. What can I say, I'm a good talker. It's my, how do you say, my 'fortay.' Am I right or wrong?"

Who am I to contradict Tony the Book? Still, I decide to lob one last grenade.

"You know a high roller named Jonah, Tony?"

"Never heard of him. So Jack, he show you the Eye?"

"No—"

"Shit, you gotta see the Eye."

7

COYLE'S ON HIS third cigarette since picking me up at Dante's office. Something's on his mind. He wants to talk. And he isn't the type to blow his nose without instructions from Tony Dante.

"You know D'Angelo had a gambling problem?" he says, leading me down an unfinished hallway that runs under the ground floor of the casino. We're in a basement of some kind, surrounded by concrete walls, ventilation ducts, electrical cable, and a ceiling of flickering fluorescent lights. The surreal lighting has turned Coyle's florid complexion pale and opaque.

"Yeah, I know."

For some reason this seems to surprise him, so he tries another tack.

"You know he was a lousy fucking thief, too?"

"What did he steal, your good name?"

"Tried to take a tray of chips from us. Worth maybe twenty thou. Jesus, and him a security guard! Man was a fucking loser."

I can see Nick looking for an angle, maybe an edge with one of the dealers. But he wasn't stupid enough to rob a casino. He wanted to hit it big but not by stealing. Besides, Nick didn't really care about money. What he cared about was winning. A lot of gamblers are like that. And Nick was like a lot of gamblers.

"That what you told the cops?"

"Had to," Coyle says, suddenly somber. "Can't lie to the cops. I ought to know. I used to be one."

"Really? Tell me something. When'd you last see Nick?"

"Hardly ever spoke to the guy. He was just a security guard."

"He did work for you, didn't he?"

"Yeah, he worked for me, when he managed to show up. Guess he had other priorities, if you know what I mean. That's another reason we let him go."

"The way I heard it, he came here a few days ago trying to get his old job back. You must've seen him then."

"Actually, yeah, I remember now. He did show up at my office door one day. He was desperate. Said he'd do anything, clean toilets if that's all we had."

"What'd you tell him?"

"Told him he had his three strikes. Wasn't no way we were going to take another risk with that guy."

"And that's all he said, that he wanted his old job back?"

"That's all he said."

At the end of the concrete corridor we turn right and go up a short flight of stairs to a green metal door bearing a sign that says AUTHO-RIZED PERSONNEL ONLY. Coyle raps twice on the door, then once more, and a security guard lets us in.

Inside the Eye in the Sky there are TV monitors and VCRs every-where, hanging from the walls, laid out on long tables. Security staff sit watching, occasionally fiddling with the controls. Coyle, lighting up another cigarette, gives me the tour, occasionally looking over someone's shoulder to point something out.

"We got five, maybe six, cameras on every game. We can get all kinds of angles. See, watch this."

He reaches down past a woman who's sitting at one of the moni-tors and turns a dial. The camera angle changes. He turns another knob, and the camera closes in on the hands of a man at one of the craps tables. I can make out the initials on his signet ring.

"Very impressive."

"We can read the serial numbers on a hundred-dollar bill."

"Is there always someone watching each table?"

He laughs. "Look around. It look like we got that many people here? No, we watch real close when we think something's going down. Otherwise, we jump around, try to check every table on a regular basis."

"You remember the night of April nine? Was anybody watching table eleven that night?"

"I gave all that to the police."

"Any reason why you can't give it to me, too?"

"It was a slow night. We didn't have many staff on."

"From the tapes I saw, it didn't look all that slow at table eleven."

"Look, Sweeney—"

"Who's Jonah?"

"What?"

"I said who's Jonah?"

"I don't know any Jonah."

"Know anybody named Cappy?"

"No."

"So tell me, who else gets to sit down here and observe the activi-ties at the tables? Does Dante ever come down here to watch?"

132

"Mr. D.? Why would he want to waste his time down here?"

"Don't know. What about Charlie Bishop? He ever come down here?"

"Once in a while, why?"

Something on one of the monitors catches my attention.

"You keep cameras on the slot machines, too?"

"Hell, yes. Just as many cheaters there as anywhere else on the floor. Maybe more."

"How the hell do you cheat at slots?"

It's a stupid question, but it keeps Coyle busy while I study the screen in front of me. At first I didn't recognize him because he's wearing a raincoat, but he's short and has a distinctive way of walking. I remember Tommy the Toe's little prancing steps. He stands out, pacing up and down the row of half-occupied machines. Then I recognize another figure, this one in a wheelchair. It's Harriet, pulling the handle of one of the quarter machines, blissfully lost to the world of faithless sons and cruel misfortune. Tommy stops his pacing long enough to stand behind her chair for a moment, but she doesn't seem to know he's there. He leaves and moves to the intersection of two aisles. A man is standing there. Tommy stops a few steps away from him, arms folded, half-facing the man's back. Nothing happens, and then it hits me that the two are talking. After a while, the man in the aisle turns to face Tommy. It's Charlie Bishop. He glances over Tommy's shoulder, then walks off in the other direction.

All this while Jack Coyle has been explaining to me about spooning, stringing, handle slamming, and rhythm play. The man's been to slot mechanic's school, and I've given him a chance to show off a little.

"So tell me, Jack, where's the best place to eat around here?" I say, cutting him off in midlecture.

BYPASSING THE elevator, I take the stairs two at a time to the first floor where I walk the length of the casino, looking down every row of slots. No wheelchair in sight. Nor anybody in a raincoat. They must have come on foot, so I go out onto the Boardwalk. There I can make them out in the distance, heading in the direction of the mission,

Tommy in his raincoat pushing white-haired Harriet.

Back inside I look for Charlie Bishop, but no one, not even the floorpersons, seems to know where he is. I decide to take Coyle's advice and try the Reuben sandwich at the Seahorse Deli.

8

I T'S NEARLY SIX when I get back to Beach Haven. There's a note taped to the front door.

> Stopped by to see if you wanted to 'do' lunch. Back
> around 7 to take you to the Homestead. Hope you like
> real country music. All is forgiven.
> Gwen.

The lady has a sense of humor, I'll grant her that.

Later, when we're on our way off the island in her Toyota, she asks, "So who was that watching us from across the street?"

"Just a nosey neighbor. Name's Gordon. He checks out all the babes who come to see me." She glances over at me but I go on. "So what's this 'Homestead' place all about?"

"Piney music, that's what it's about. Good for what ails ya. A little country, a little bluegrass, and some old-time gospel sprinkled in for good measure. All acoustic. None of that phony electronic stuff. Real music played by real people."

"Well, I'm certainly glad it's genuine."

She shoots a look at me again.

"You'd better like it. I don't do this for everybody."

"I'm flattered. You performing?"

"Me? Nah. But I put your name in for a solo on the wooden spoons."

"I never perform with cookware. Shows a lack of respect for the tools."

134

So far we're doing a pretty good job of avoiding the events of last night, which is okay with me. I'm patient. She can apologize when she's ready.

"So what'd you do today?" she asks.

"Met Tony Dante."

That gets her attention.

"Jesus, how'd you pull that off? Took me two years to get an interview with that prick."

"I asked his underlings a few questions about Nick and word got back. Doesn't take long at a place like that."

"What'd you think of him?"

"He lived up to his advance billing."

I tell her Martindale's story about Dante's speech to the city employees.

"That's our Tony all right."

"You ever hear of the CEO of a corporation being on the phone with his suppliers?"

"That what he was doing?"

I nod. She thinks about it a moment.

"Means things must be pretty bad. On the other hand, that's Dante's style. He thinks he can do everybody's job better than they can."

"What about an ex-cop, name of Jack Coyle, you ever hear of him?"

"Red-faced Irishman with a raspy smoker's voice? He's the head of security, isn't he?"

"That's the one."

"He was in and out of Dante's office the day I had my interview. Does whatever Dante tells him, far as I can tell."

"Where's he from, you know?"

"No, but I could find out."

I let the offer pass. It's fine with me if she wants to get back in my good graces, but I'd prefer it wait until I really need her help.

"What about a guy named Charlie Bishop?"

This time there's an imperceptible freezing of the eyes before she responds.

135

"What about him?"

"You heard of him?"

"Yeah, he's the casino manager. He's okay."

"What's that mean?"

"I heard he's okay, that's all. By the way, I got a big story coming out."

"About the murder?"

She frowns.

"There're other things going on down here besides *your* murder case, you know."

"Okay, so what is it?"

"Read the *Star* tomorrow. You'll see."

She turns thoughtful. By the time we're off the island and onto Route 9, the silence has become a presence in the car.

"So, you gonna tell me what happened last night," she finally asks. "Who was it got fried to a crisp under the Boardwalk? Your cop friends aren't talking. We had to run a story this morning without the victim's name."

"Cops don't know who it is. Not for sure."

She looks over at me quickly.

"What about you, do you know?"

"I might."

"Shit, I knew it."

After another extended period of silence, she tries again.

"Look, I know you don't exactly trust me after last night but—"

"No, I *don't exactly.*"

"Well, check my bag then, dammit. It's in the backseat. No tape recorder. You want to frisk me, check me for a wire? Here, I'll stop and you can search me right now."

She pulls the car onto the gravel shoulder just past a Dairy Queen, and begins to open her door.

"Get back on the road. If I ever decide to tell you anything off the record again, *then* I'll frisk you. For now let's just enjoy the evening. That *is* what you invited me along for, isn't it?"

"Of course it is."

But it isn't, and she is *not* happy. We head south down Route 9 to-

136

ward Barnegat. It's another half mile before she speaks again.

"So tell me more about your wife."

It sounds like she's inquiring about what I had for lunch, not about the woman I lived with for twenty-one years.

"Just what is it you want to know?"

"Breast cancer runs in my family," she says in a whisper, answering a different question.

"I see."

"Believe it or not I admire what your wife did. I've always told myself if it happened to me, I'd kill myself, too, before—"

"You don't know what you're saying."

"What do you mean?"

"Suicide never solves anything. It just. . . ."

Suddenly it feels as if I'm falling. As my body stiffens, my mind grasps at images. Eliot again. *The memory throws up high and dry a crowd of twisted things.*

"It just what?"

"It robbed me of all the good memories."

"You're angry with her. That's natural."

"How could I be angry with someone who suffered so much?"

"Trust me, you can. How'd you two meet?"

So I tell her.

We met at a charity fund-raiser for inner-city kids. I'd been chosen, along with a few other cops, to show the departmental flag on behalf of improved community relations. She was there out of some civic obligation felt by Philadelphians of a certain social standing and, I later learned, because she loved children. "Do you come to these things often?" I asked, clutching at clichés in the buffet line. She wore a simple tweed skirt and a silk blouse that looked as if it would cost a month's pay. Velvety yellow-brown hair reached nearly to her shoulders. Her smile calmed me. I had no idea who she was.

"If it's for a good cause," she said, filling her plate, oblivious to the fashionable anorexia of the other women in line. "And you?" She stopped to look at me, waiting for an answer.

"It's my first time," I said, self-conscious in my dress uniform.

She seemed surprised. "Really? You look so . . . so in charge."

We found a table to ourselves and talked right through the speeches and awards. She'd gone to Bryn Mawr and was just back from a year in France. I had worked my way through Villanova and grad school at Penn, then spent two years teaching art history at Temple before joining the Philly PD. Her father was an investment banker, mine a furniture maker. She lived with her parents on a "small estate" in Haverford. I rented an efficiency apartment above a liquor store in West Philadelphia. She'd been raised on Bach and the ballet; I'd grown up with Elvis and "The Ed Sullivan Show." But we both loved antiques, the Jersey shore, jazz, and trashy thrillers. We were made for each other, we decided. After a four-week courtship, we exchanged vows before an old priest friend of mine and slipped off to Cape May for the honeymoon. Only Bernie knew where we'd gone.

"After she died, our parish priest wouldn't bury her," I tell Gwen. "The same man who confirmed her as a young girl wouldn't put her to rest in consecrated ground."

"God, that's awful."

"I had to call in an old debt with a priest in the city. He held a service for her, and she was buried in Germantown. Father Bogan—the bastard—wouldn't even attend the service. I haven't set foot inside a church since."

"I can imagine how you feel, Sweeney, but you can't blame God for all the assholes in the world."

"I don't blame God. Just the Church. That's where assholes go to be sanctified."

Gwen slows down at a faded wooden sign. It says THE HOMESTEAD and has a hand-painted arrow pointing toward a narrow hardtop road leading into the woods. She makes the turn, and in a quarter of a mile we come to a gravel road on the right. A hundred feet back is The Homestead. It's nothing more than a plain, one-story stucco building with a low sloping roof. Everything's been painted dark blue— walls, windowsills, and doors. There are no decorative highlights, not even a little trim around the casement windows. Only a large plastic sign over the door distinguishes it from a thousand other nondescript buildings scattered across south Jersey.

"Used to be a hunting club," says Gwen. "There're hundreds of the damn things in the Pines. Ought to know. My ex belonged to one. He'd disappear every deer season and wouldn't return for a month."

"Thought deer season only lasted a week or so."

"Serious male bonding requires time, so I'm told. God knows, it requires a lot of drinking and hunting. And gambling, too. That was his specialty."

Dozens of vehicles are parked in the sandy lot along the side of the building. She drives around to the back and parks next to a Ford pickup with a bumper sticker that says STOP CRIME—BUY A GUN.

Inside the door two teenage girls sit giggling behind a small table, waiting to collect the admission fee of $2.50 per person. A hand-lettered sign on the wall behind them directs musicians to make their presence known in the office if they want to be given a place on the evening's schedule.

"It's on me," says Gwen, giving one of the kids a five.

The Homestead's decor is genuine World War II. Hanging near the ceiling is a large wooden propeller and under it, mounted on plain plywood plaques, are three altimeters. At eye level there's a framed front page from the *Times* for December 8, 1941, along with something called "A Pilot's Creed." Off in the corner is a poster of more recent vintage, POW*MIA—YOU ARE NOT FORGOTTEN.

"Old Bill Dennis—the guy who started this place—was a fighter pilot in the second world war," explains Gwen. "He flew P-47s, I think. He's something of a hero around here. Died a few years ago. This was his deer club."

It's a single rectangular room furnished with an upright piano and several hundred folding chairs facing an elevated platform at the far end. The stage is a simulated Pine Barrens lodge constructed of log walls. The backdrop features a large painting of the salt marshes of Barnegat Bay, framed to look like a picture window. On the wall next to it hangs an American flag.

A young man in blue jeans, white shirt, and black Stetson kneels in front of a row of microphones testing the sound system. A few in the audience stand around chatting, but most of the seats are already filled with people.

Gwen leads me to a table where coffee and cookies have been laid out. She's wearing faded jeans and a burnt orange V-necked tunic sweater that highlights her brown eyes and champagne-colored hair. While she's pouring each of us coffee, the first group is introduced on stage—two middle-aged men on guitar, a younger one on the bass. The two older ones are wearing funky western hats with feathers projecting jauntily from leather hatbands. The younger one's in a faded cap with a small American flag on the front. They begin with something called "Ocean County Breakdown."

Gwen nods and smiles at a few people in the audience, then waves to a man in a black leather cap who acknowledges her before turning back toward the stage.

"That man who waved? That was Virgil, Virgil Applegate. A real old-timer. You'd like him. He can tell you all you'll ever need to know about the Jersey Pines."

Clutching our coffees and some chocolate chip cookies, we find seats in the back row. Two women are up next, one with a guitar, the other a banjo. They begin with something called "A Piney's Lament," about the sorry effect of progress on the Pines, then move on to "A Home in the Pines," a paean to the hardships and rewards of life in the south Jersey pinewoods. After two more songs they finish, promising to be back at the end of the evening. Someone named Father Will follows and launches into several brisk bluegrass tunes, employing a mandolin and a harmonica that's attached to a metal brace hanging from his neck. After that it's a five-piece band called the Lonesome Pineys playing "Nellie Bly," followed by "Jersey Moon" and "Beautiful Barnegat Bay." When intermission comes, it's none too soon.

"Come on," Gwen says, "let's go outside and get some air."

I grab another cup of coffee and follow her outside. Somewhere in the distance someone's practicing on a banjo. Gwen finds Virgil Applegate off by himself, standing next to a rusty pickup truck. He's drinking something out of a green plastic cup.

"Virgil, how're you?"

"That you, Miss Olin? I saw you back in there. You lookin' good, you lookin' good."

Virgil is somewhere between sixty-five and seventy. He's tall and angular, with a full head of grizzled black hair. His face is walnut-brown and deeply furrowed. Bulging cheekbones protrude over a sunken jawline that draws in sharply to a pursed mouth, making it look as if he's been sucking on a lemon.

"Virgil, this is Frank Sweeney."

"Glad to meet you." I offer my hand. His is half again as big as mine and feels like shoe leather.

Nodding noncommittally, he eyes my Timberlands, chinos, and windbreaker as if I've crashed the party in a tux. Along with his black leather cap, he's wearing stained black work pants, a faded red flannel shirt, and a pair of L. L. Bean gum shoes.

"You ain't from 'round here."

"You can tell, can you?"

"I kin tell. But that's all right. Miss Olin here, she ain't done so well with men from this part of the woods so—"

"Frank's a professional acquaintance, Virgil. He's a private investigator down from Philadelphia."

"Private investigator? You mean like that Travis McGee or that Lew Archer fella?"

"Something like that, only what I do isn't quite as exciting."

"Really? Well, that's too bad. Man's work should always be something worth getting up for in the morning. My father, he was a bayman. He always said if a man can't get no satisfaction clamming or corking boats or carving decoys then he must be sick in the head. Me I still work the cycle mostly."

"The cycle?"

"He means the seasonal cycle," says Gwen, as Virgil looks on, amused by my ignorance. "What's that old saying, Virgil?"

"You can always make a buck in the woods and a dollar in the bay," Virgil replies, nodding and reaching into his truck for an old brown bottle. "This here's a little applejack from down the road. Like to try it? Make you happy as a clam at high tide."

Gwen and I decline. Virgil takes another sip from his green mug and resumes talking.

"Yeah, I been working the pinewoods mosta my life. As the seasons gone by I done different things. Done everything mostly. Like the cranberry season, that's only two months at most. And then in the winter I might cut wood. And I done trapping. Done some pineballing, too. Come deer season I guide a few hunters. In the spring now, I knock huckleberries and then I go to pulling moss. When things get bad you can go work for one a the growers. Or the state highway sciencing a road. But my father, he was a bayman. Done that all his life. Mostly clamming. Now that's an art in itself, clamming."

"Where do you live?" I ask, beginning to fall under Virgil's spell.

"Place called Fox Chase Ridge. You know it?"

"You'll never find it on any map," Gwen says to me. "People here have a way of picking their own place names."

"Going north, it's just past Hog Wallow."

I stare blankly at him.

"It's near Jenkins," says Virgil. "You heard of that?"

"No, but tell me anyway."

"Well, off the county road about a mile there's this fingerboard and about another half mile there's this ridge."

"Fingerboard?"

"You know, it's like a point."

"Where several roads come together," Gwen explains.

"Anyway, used to be we'd have a fox chase 'round there every year. Everybody'd meet at the fingerboard. Them hounds'd take off and have a grand old time. More than once they'd run the fox right up the ridge. So that's how it got its name. Fox huntin' ain't for me though. I can't rightly see it. Don't care what they say 'bout fox huntin' being sport and all. Can't do it. But I like to watch. I live up the road from there. It's called Fox Chase Ridge."

People are heading inside. The three of us stroll back together.

"So what you think of our little place in the country here, Mr. Sweeney? You like the music?"

"Yes, I'm enjoying it."

"You sure you're not one of them college types, here to study us Pineys? Write us up in some book? We get a lot of those 'round here."

"No, my college days are over."

"Never too late to learn, though, is it?"

He winks at me, as if there's more to his comment than I'm able to grasp.

"No, Virgil, it's never too late for that."

9

Sunday morning I make a point of picking up a copy of the *Atlantic City Star*. Gwen and I are going antiquing in Cape May later, and I'd like to know what the woman's been up to before we see each other again. It doesn't take long to find out.

It's at the bottom of the front page and features a byline. The headline reads

UNDERAGE AND ADDICTED:
LOCAL GIRL A COMPULSIVE
GAMBLER AT FOURTEEN

The local girl is Sandra Greenberg, daughter of a prominent attorney in Linwood, one of the mainland's more upscale communities. Sandra, it seems, has run away from home. After finding her at the Poseidon Casino for the fifth time in a year, her father had returned Sandra kicking and screaming to his $700,000 English Tudor home, only to have her slip out during the night. "She's had a gambling problem for two years," the father is quoted as telling reporter Olin. "The people at the Poseidon know that. I told them. How can they let her keep coming back? I just don't understand what this world's coming to." Gwen's bombshell is an interview with the missing girl, whom she managed to track down somehow. "I hate my life and I hate my father," the addicted teenager says. "I just want to get back to the tables. It's the only place I'm happy." Sandra says she has tried Gamblers Anonymous, "but it's just a bunch of miserable old men." Gwen goes on to quote an expert in the field of compulsive gambling who says, "this disease can affect anyone at any age." Then she launches into a full court press against the Poseidon and Tony Dante, concluding with the statement that the incident is "something the Casino Control Commission can be expected to look at closely in the next few days as it decides whether or not to renew Mr. Dante's casino license." Wishful thinking on her part, I'm afraid.

Another story on the front page suggests that Sandra Greenberg is the least of Tony Dante's problems. It seems Dante has withheld a scheduled pay raise from his union employees for the second time in two years. The writer of the story, George Germaine, confirms that the Poseidon has a debt payment totaling $2.8 million due next month, with only enough cash on hand to pay half. In fact, Germaine claims, the Poseidon is suffering a net cash *outflow* of nearly $24,000 a day. The casino's financial vice president refused comment, and Dante himself could not be reached. The head of the local union, which represents most of the Poseidon's hotel, restaurant, and bar employees, is "outraged," and quoted as saying, "Dante got away with this a year ago, but it won't work again."

All in all, yesterday wasn't a good day for Tony the Book.

There's also a brief follow-up piece on Cappy's murder. A spokeswoman for the Major Crimes Squad says the body hasn't been identified yet. Nor has it been determined whether there's any connection to the recent murder in Absecon Lighthouse. The investigation is ongoing, etcetera, etcetera.

Before heading off to pick up Gwen I decide to call Bernie and tell him about Cappy's murder.

"It looks like a hit," I say, "probably the same guy who did Nick."

"Jesus, a hit? Why?"

"I'm not sure." Pausing to take a deep breath. "I have to tell you, Bernie, it looks like both Nick and Cappy pissed somebody off big time. Something was going down, and your brother was involved."

Silence on the line.

"Bernie? You there?"

"Yeah. So what do you figure it was, Frank?"

I tell him about the two Jonahs.

"You saying Nick caught this one 'Jonah' character in a scam of some sort? What about this Cappy? You saying he was called Jonah, too? I don't get it. Besides, Nick wouldn't—"

"There's more."

"What?"

"Cappy's real name was Theodore Capetanakis."

"*The* Theodore Capetanakis?"

"The same. Listen, Bernie, are you up to doing a little discreet calling around for me?"

"You want me to see what I can find out about Capetanakis?"

"See if you can find out what the guy was up to before he died."

"I'll make some calls. It shouldn't be too taxing. I'm going out of my mind with boredom anyway. I'd walk out of here this minute and catch a bus to the shore if you asked me."

"When do you go home?"

"Another day or so. It's a little scary, returning to the outside world."

"Just be sure to do what the doctors tell you, okay?"

"Oh, sure. You know what my doc said? He said I could resume normal sexual relations whenever I wanted. He must know something I don't."

Bernie, who's never been married, claims not to have had a serious sexual relationship in his entire life. The last time he and I talked about it he said he suspected he was gay but that, being a devout Catholic, it'd be best if he continued to live in ignorance about the whole matter.

"Maybe you should follow the doc's advice."

"What's that supposed to mean?"

"It means find somebody, for God's sake. Find a man or find a woman. It doesn't matter which. And stop worrying about what the Pope's going to think. You're too old to live the rest of your life alone."

"*Thanks,* Frank. Just what I needed to hear. And what about you?"

"What *about* me?"

"You know what I'm talking about. Forgive me for saying this, Frank, but you can't let anyone new into your bed until you get Catherine out of it."

"It's only been two years, Bernie."

"That's time enough. Letting go, Frank, life's all about letting go. I'm just learning that. Think about it."

"I *have* been thinking about it . . . for several days now."

"Oh?"

"Take care, Bernie. And call me when you get something on Capetanakis."

"Will do. And you watch your back. I figured to be your employer in this case, but I didn't take out any fire insurance."

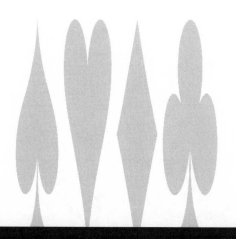

THE CITY

BOOK THREE

1

WHY DIDN'T YOU tell me you'd already talked to this Monica Poole?"

It's early Monday morning, and Petrillo is scurrying about among the file cabinets and office machines like a spider after a fugitive fly, pausing long enough to harangue me and take a gulp from a plastic Dunkin' Donuts coffee mug. His other hand grips a thick sheaf of computer printouts.

"There wasn't any need for you to talk to her. She'd already given me the date when Nick was last at the Poseidon. I passed it on to you."

"*I'll* be the one to decide who I need to talk to and who I don't."

He looks a bit embarrassed at this outburst of assertiveness. I notice he's switched from the fish tie to a standard paisley. He wears it with a microchecked button-down shirt and baggy chinos. It's the J. Crew look. I can visualize him during off-hours in one of those trendy band-collar shirts and a pair of stonewashed jeans with frayed edges and slashes at the knees.

"Look, I gave you what mattered. Don't forget, I *was* the one who pointed you toward those videotapes."

While he ponders that, I go down the hall to the conference room where Martindale's pacing back and forth. The room is shrouded in a haze of morning light from a single dirty window. A Manila folder lies on the table.

"Thanks for doing this, Ray. I know it's early."

"Actually, it's better for me this way. I have to be at a meeting in Linwood at nine."

"You and Talley still okay with this?"

"What, filling you in on our latest crime-fighting techniques? Sure. But I think we'd better limit it to a few discreet phone calls from now on. You've been seen here a lot."

"Right. But—"

"I know, the photos. Want some background first?"

"Fire away."

"For starters we have a positive ID. It was Capetanakis, all right. His brother faxed the dental records down here last night. It all checked out." He opens the folder on the table. "Here," he says, handing me a three-page document stapled together. "It's the ME's report. Read it for yourself."

I scan the pages quickly. Cappy died from second- and third-degree flesh burns that reached his upper respiratory region. The face, hands, and most of the torso were totally burned, while the legs as well as the back of the body, which was resting on the sand, were relatively untouched. No carbon monoxide was found in the blood, meaning he died from the heat of the flames, not the smoke. The blood alcohol level was a staggering .30. Thank God for that. The ME had to remove the jaw in order to x-ray it for comparison with available dental records. I'd rather not have known that. Everything fits so far. But I'm looking for something else. What interests me is the level of cutaneous burning of the torso. It's quite deep, given the fact that Cappy was fully clothed. I flip to the end of the report, looking for an inventory of clothing and possessions. Nothing.

"If you're wondering about the empty rum bottle found next to the body," Martindale says, "it was wiped clean."

I wasn't, but that's good to know.

"What about the photos?"

He reaches into the folder and comes up with half-a-dozen black-and-white glossies. The first one shows Cappy faceup, the way I saw him when I arrived at the Hotel Underwood. What I never got to see was the body after it had been turned over. The photos from that angle tell me what I need to know. I can make out Cappy's corduroy pants and a plaid shirt. But no other clothing. The raincoat is nowhere to be seen.

TOMMY ISN'T AT the mission, so I try the Hotel Underwood. It's nearly ten by the time I park and walk the three blocks to the beach. The tide is up, and the residents of the Boardwalk's least-expensive guest house have pulled up stakes and stashed their makeshift tents and cardboard boxes back in the dark forest of pilings. The area's deserted except for an old man filling a shopping cart with clothing and plastic bottles. For the price of breakfast he tells me Tommy just left. I should be able to catch him heading down Pacific Avenue.

Back in the car, I spot him five blocks away, standing in front of a bar. He's talking to two hookers who look as if they've had a long night. Tommy's wearing the same outfit he had on Friday, dirty tan pants and a wrinkled white dress shirt.

As I pull over, the two women descend upon the car. One of them paws at the window, while the other gets up close to the glass and begins whirling her tongue around like a lariat.

"Sorry, ladies," I say, rolling the window down, "it's him I want."

"Mr. Sweeney, that you?"

Tommy spots me and edges the women aside.

"Get in Tommy, I'll buy you a cup of coffee."

"Hey, what 'bout us?" The hooker with the contortionist's tongue gives off a loud nasal whine.

"Whatsamatter, mister, you only like old men?" the second one says, with an exaggerated wink. "Hey, how 'bout *all* a us? We could all do ya."

"Sorry, maybe next time. Right now I can only afford Tommy."

"So how ya doing, Mr. Sweeney?" Tommy says, after we're back in traffic. "Say, ain't it terrible about Cappy?"

"Where's the raincoat, Tommy?"

"What?"

"Cappy's raincoat. I know you have it. I saw you wearing it at the Poseidon on Saturday."

"You saw me there?"

"On the security cameras. So how you'd get it, Tommy? You steal it? Steal it off a helpless drunk?"

He stares at his feet.

"I . . . I didn't mean nothing bad. He was just lying there. Dead to the world. I mean drunk, you know, not really dead. We were under the Boards. And it was cold at night. And I always wanted a coat like that. I never had one. I—"

"Tell me where it is, Tommy, and maybe I can keep your ass out of jail."

"It's back at the mission. They give us a place to keep stuff. I'll show you. I didn't mean nothing by it, honest."

AT THE MISSION everyone's at morning chapel. Tommy leads the way past the lounge to a small unlocked storage room in the back.

"I didn't mean nothing by it, really I didn't," he says, pushing aside dozens of moldy-smelling coats and jackets hanging on a long rack. Cappy's raincoat is hidden in the rear, behind an old navy pea coat. He takes it off its hanger and hands it to me as if it were contaminated, standing back quickly.

I take it out into the lighted hallway and lay it on the floor. There's nothing in the front pockets, but then I didn't expect to find anything there. Cappy must have had some alterations done on the inside. Two zippered pockets have been added, one on each side of the coat. They're sturdy, durable, and well concealed. They're also empty.

"Where are the papers that were here, Tommy?"

He moves away from me, shaking his head, rocking back and forth as if he's slipped into some kind of catatonic state.

"Tommy! Snap out of it!"

I clap my hands. He stops and looks at me.

"I didn't mean for him to die, Mr. Sweeney. It wasn't my fault. All I did was borrow his coat. I didn't mean for nothing to happen to him."

"Nobody said you did. Now where are the papers?"

"I'll get them."

This time he returns from the back of the closet with a dilapidated briefcase. It's so old and shabby it's held together with a piece of twine. He puts it on the floor and unties the string. The briefcase is Tommy's scrapbook. It's filled with memorabilia from the forties and fifties, photographs and souvenirs from his days as "Baby Titus, Child of the High Wire." There's also an expired passport, dozens of old driver's licenses, and a pack of letters held together with a rubber band. Off to the side are three Kraft business envelopes. Tommy takes them out and hands them to me.

"Is this everything?" I ask.

"Just those three. I didn't look inside them, I swear. I collect things, that's all. They came with the coat so I just kept them. I didn't mean no harm."

The envelopes are still sealed. Only one has anything written on the outside. It says "N. D." in large bold print. I shove all three inside my windbreaker and roll up the raincoat.

"So tell me, Tommy, what were you doing at the Poseidon on Saturday?"

"Nothing much. It was check day for Harriet, so I took her down to the casinos. I needed the exercise. Saw that she got back, too."

"Don't con me, Tommy. Since when were checks given out on a Saturday? Offices are closed on weekends."

"I ain't bullshitting you, Mr. Sweeney."

"I watched you on TV, Tommy. You spoke with someone near the slot machines. Looked like a meeting to me. Is that why you were there?"

"It wasn't what you think, I swear."

"What *do* I think, Tommy?"

For a moment he doesn't say anything. Then he makes a decision. "I can't talk no more. I'm sorry."

With that he turns and heads for the chapel.

2

IT TURNS OUT THAT the same man who drank Absolut vodka at my expense could have hired a fleet of chauffeur-driven limos to take me and the entire Lighthouse Mission to Bec Fin's for dinner. What's more, he could have paid for everything in cash. What motivates a wealthy man to pose as a homeless vagrant while carrying $10,000 around inside a raincoat? That's the amount in hundred dollar bills that I found in one of the envelopes. An elderly Irish uncle of mine used to say, "Enjoy your money while you have it, my boy, because shrouds don't have pockets." Well, Cappy's certainly did.

Another envelope is crammed full of personal papers. There's a two-year-old will, which doesn't mention the mission but does include a number of charities and nonprofit organizations like Citizens Against Taxes and People for a Free Country; an up-to-date passport stamped within the past year in London, Amsterdam, and Zurich; several lists of names and phone numbers printed out meticulously in a minuscule hand; and half-a-dozen newspaper clippings featuring reports of alleged abuses by the IRS.

The third envelope, the one containing the papers Cappy was holding for Nick, is the one that gets my undivided attention. It's stuffed with photocopies of newspaper articles, most from the *Atlantic City Star*. There's also a one-page computer printout. It's dated April 11, two days after Nick played roulette at the Poseidon and a week before he was murdered.

POSEIDON CASINO   4/11/96

MODE: PLAYER MARKETING INFORMATION   19:09:33

──────────────────────── NAME: SMITH, JONAH ────────────────────────

CUSTOMER ACCOUNT NO.: 10350A   CUSTOMER SOC. SEC NO: 078-00-1120
BUSINESS ADDRESS CITY: 00000   ST: 00000   ZIP: 00000
FAVORITE BEVERAGE: CUTTY/WATER   FAVORITE CIGARETTE: NONE
JACKET SIZE: IGNORE   SHIRT SIZE: IGNORE

──────────────────────── COMPANION INFORMATION ────────────────────────

COMPANION LAST NAME: IGNORE   FIRST:
FAV BEV: CIG   FLOWER: ANNIV DATE: YRS MARRIED:
BIRTH DATE:

──────────────────────── SPECIAL INTERESTS ────────────────────────

FAVORITE GAMES: ROULETTE, BLACKJACK
FAVORITE MUSIC: IGNORE
FAVORITE ENTERTAINMENT: IGNORE

──────────────────────── COMMENTS ────────────────────────

NOTIFY MR. BISHOP IMMEDIATELY WHEN GUEST ARRIVES.

Casinos routinely collect this kind of information on their important players, who have big egos and expect to be catered to. But "Jonah Smith," or Mr. X, has given the Poseidon precious little to work with. He likes roulette, blackjack, and Cutty Sark, and apparently gambles alone. No personal interests, no companions. This printout wouldn't have told Nick anything useful. Except for one thing. The social security number's a phony. There's never been a "00" group number issued, something Nick would certainly have known. It's an old "pocketbook" number, originating from the sample social security cards that used to be inserted in wallets and pocketbooks sold back in the thirties. Since then thousands of fraudulent cards have used this or a similar number. So, Mr. X has given the Poseidon a phony name, a fraudulent social security number, no address, and revealed very little else about his interests. Yet he's important enough that whenever he's on the floor of the casino he demands the immediate attention of the casino manager, Charlie Bishop. If Nick suspected the Poseidon had some sort of arrangement with "Jonah Smith," this printout would have confirmed it.

As for the newspaper articles, the earliest one is dated June 9, 1975.

ATLANTIC CITY BUSINESSMAN
ATTACKS ANTICASINO GROUP

Harry Morrow, local restaurateur and investor, said yesterday in a speech to the Kiwanis Club, that "those who oppose casinos in this town are living in the dark ages." Speaking about the defeat of the November 1974 statewide gambling referendum, Mr. Morrow lashed out at "religious and other self-proclaimed morality groups" who, he said, "misquote the Bible and talk about Jesus as if he didn't even know how to have fun."

Without mentioning it by name, Morrow apparently had in mind the organization, Christians Against Casinos (CAC), a local coalition of lay and religious leaders headed by Felice Singleton, which recently stepped up its opposition to any effort to have a second referendum placed on the November ballot next year.

"The voters have already spoken," Ms. Singleton said, in

a press release issued following Morrow's Kiwanis speech. "It would be a waste of the voters' time and money to try to put it on the ballot again."

A number of state and local leaders have been pushing for a second gambling referendum that they characterize as "Atlantic City only," in contrast to the statewide effort that was defeated in 1974.

"The first vote failed at the polls because we didn't focus on this community," Mr. Morrow said in his speech. "Next time we'll get it right."

A second article is dated June 10, 1978, soon after the opening of the first casino by Resorts International. It's a lengthy piece, focusing on the city's much-anticipated economic revival. Most of the story is devoted to discussion of the plans to convert the Howard Johnson's Regency Motor Hotel on the Boardwalk to Caesars Boardwalk Regency and to comments by Steve Wynn, then owner of the Golden Nugget in Vegas, about his possible interest in opening a casino on the Boardwalk. Someone has circled one paragraph near the end.

> Amidst all the talk in the business community about Caesars and the Golden Nugget, rumors have surfaced in the last few days of the pending sale of the Ocean View Motel on the Boardwalk to the Angelina Corporation. Joseph Dante, president and CEO of Angelina, a Miami-based cosmetics firm, is reported to be negotiating with Henry Bass, local attorney and owner of the Ocean View. Bass, who is said to be planning to leave the area to practice law in New York City, had no comment last week on the rumored sale. However, Dante's son, Anthony, who operates a local trucking company, was a little more forthcoming. "Whatever happens," he said, "I promise it'll be good for the city."

That name—Henry Bass—sounds vaguely familiar, but other than that, the news item rings no bells.

The other articles in the envelope trace the highlights of the Dante family's history in Atlantic City: the opening of the Poseidon Hotel and Casino in 1981; the death of the family patriarch, Joseph, in 1983; the immediate accession of the older son, Vincent, to head of the corporation; his conviction on charges of tax evasion in 1987, and, finally, the ascendancy of Tony the Book in 1988.

I'm impressed. Nick always hated detective work. When he needed a lead his usual inclination was to shove a pimp or a pusher up against a wall and beat it out of him. But the computer printout and the news clippings suggest Nick actually got his feet wet on this one. Still, to make any sense of it I need what I can't have, which is what Nick had, a straw in the wind from Cappy.

"Sweeney, that you? Where are you?" Gwen asked.

"In my car."

"I should have figured. What's up?"

"You remember how you offered to help me with a little research?"

"It's payback time, huh?"

"Something like that."

There's a long pause.

"What do you need?"

"For starters, have you ever heard of Harry Morrow? He's a local bigwig. Or at least he was in the seventies. Apparently he was in the restaurant business back then. I've come across a story from your paper that mentions him. It's from June 9, 1975. He may have been part of the campaign to get the casino gambling issue placed on the ballot in '76."

"That was before my time. But I can do some checking. What do you want to know about him?"

"Anything you can dig up. What he's up to now, for starters."

"Fair enough. I'll do what I can. Anything else?"

"How about Sister Felice at the mission? Do you know her last name?"

"Yeah, it's Singleton. She goes by Sister Felice Mary Agnes now."

"Do you know if she ever headed up an anticasino group called Christians Against Casinos?"

"Yeah, now that you mention it, I do recall her saying something about that. You want me to check that out, too?"

"I'd appreciate it."

"You better. Gonna be home tonight? I'll let you know what I find."

"Stop by. I'll cook you dinner."

"It's a deal."

"YOU'VE BEEN A busy man, Mr. Sweeney."

"I get around."

"Apparently. But why on earth would you be interested in something I did nearly twenty years ago?"

"The big question is, why was *Nick* interested in it? He's the one who had Cappy hold the clipping for him."

"I see your point," Sister Felice says, with perfect equanimity.

She's impassive, more amused than surprised at me being here. There's a peaceful repose to her demeanor. This one isn't at all like the sisters I grew up with. The nuns of my youth usually exhibited far more zeal than Zen.

"Then you won't mind telling me about Christians Against Casinos."

"No, I don't mind. There's very little to tell. I was young and thought I could save the world, or at least this wonderful old town. A good many people felt the same way. There were a number of groups like ours back then. We succeeded in '74. The voters supported us that time."

"You succeeded because you convinced people around the state that organized crime would take over if gambling came in. That argument didn't work in 1976? How come?"

"Because the second referendum applied only to Atlantic City. And a lot of money was spent by the procasino people the second time. Millions of dollars. Whereas our little group managed to scrape together an advertising budget of two-thousand or so. The result was, the voters around the state believed Atlantic City *wanted* gambling. People said, 'If they want it down there, let them have it. Better them than us.' So it passed."

158

"And what about this Harry Morrow? Was he part of the procasino campaign?"

"Harry? Yes, he campaigned for the referendum. But he wasn't all that active. He didn't have time. He had his own businesses to worry about."

"And you and he were enemies?"

"Enemies? That's not a word I'd use, Mr. Sweeney. I liked Harry. He was a nice man, for a capitalist."

"You said *was* a nice man."

"Harry died soon after the referendum passed."

"I see. And what happened to your group afterward?"

"Oh, we all went our separate ways. I left the area for a while. Then I came back a few years ago to work here." She pauses to direct a faint smile in my direction. "I discovered that mission work is my calling. I have a passion for it, you see."

Passion is not a word that readily comes to mind in the case of Sister Felice. Hands folded calmly in her lap, she's barely moved a muscle since we began talking. I try to imagine her with Brother Stephen. He's excitable, charged with barely restrained feelings. She seems beyond fervor, both the spiritual and the fleshly kind.

"So I understand. And you were close to Nick and Cappy, I believe?"

"They confided in me. I told you that."

"Did either one explain the significance of this newspaper clipping?"

"I don't recall it ever coming up."

"Would you tell me if it had?"

"Probably not."

"You do understand we're talking about two brutal murders, Sister?"

"I understand perfectly. But my attitude toward death and violence is quite different from other people's, Mr. Sweeney."

"In what way?"

"I believe there's great significance in the way each of us dies. It's all part of the greater meaning of our life. We live many, many lives, and each of us, if he hasn't already, will experience what Cappy and Nick experienced."

"And what about the person who *murdered* Nick and Cappy, Sister? What's in store for him?"

"Quite a bit, I'm afraid. His is a very troubled soul."

3

I T'S A LITTLE AFTER six when Gwen arrives. I'm still working on dinner.

"Something smells good," she says, handing me a bottle of chardonnay she's brought.

"It better. I've been working on it for an hour." I take the wine into the kitchen and put it in the fridge.

"I waved to Mr. Gordon on the way in. I think I scared him. He disappeared from his front window like he'd seen a ghost."

"He's not used to seeing pretty women around here. His place and this are the only ones occupied this time of year."

She's holding a legal-size Manila envelope, which she places on the kitchen table. I notice she doesn't have her rucksack with her. Her hair is different, too. It's down around her shoulders, held together in the back with a leather barrette. Its color in the indoor light is variably amber, then honey, depending on where she stands. She's wearing jeans and a white cotton sweater.

"That the results of your research?"

I resume making the salad, and she takes a seat at the table.

"That's it. Tell me something, what put you onto this anyway? Why the sudden interest in Harry Morrow and the Christians Against Casinos?"

"I told you, I came across a newspaper clipping."

"The 1975 story?"

"Right. Why?"

"Because two years after that story ran, Harry Morrow was murdered."

I guess Sister Felice was holding something back. Never trust a nun, I always say. But then maybe I didn't ask the right questions. I glance at Gwen. Her expression is slightly accusatory, as if it's my fault this guy got whacked.

"Tell me all about it."

"There were a number of references in our index. He was a community leader, active in the chamber of commerce, that sort of thing. He ran a popular restaurant out on the Black Horse Pike. A place called The Tudor House. It went out of business after he was killed. He wasn't a politician, but I guess he mattered to those who were. The local media liked to quote him because he always spoke his mind. Apparently he owned or was a partner in a bunch of other businesses in the area. I didn't have time to check all that out because I got sidetracked by his disappearance in 1977."

"What happened?"

"One day after a Rotary club luncheon he got in his car and drove off. He was never seen again, at least not alive. They found what was left of his body in the Pines near Hammonton a few days later."

"Wait, don't tell me. He was burned to death, right?"

Her jaw drops visibly.

"But how? . . . "

"Come on, Gwen. Remember Nick D'Angelo? Remember the murder under the Boardwalk? Things are starting to connect."

"But the Morrow murder was nearly twenty years ago."

I just look at her. "Tell me what the cops found."

"There was a forest fire. It wiped out a few hundred acres. When it was over they discovered the remains of two humans and a dog in the ashes of an old charcoal pit."

"*Two* humans?"

"Yeah, two."

"Who was the other one?"

She opens the Manila envelope and takes out several photocopies of newspaper articles.

"He was never identified. The body was completely burned."

"Didn't they use dental records?"

"I don't know. Wasn't anything in the articles about it."

"Sounds like somebody was in the wrong place at the wrong time."

"What do you mean?"

"I mean it sounds like somebody took Morrow into the Pines to murder him and this other poor bastard got in the way."

"It's possible, I suppose."

"How'd they determine it was murder?"

She picks up one of the photocopies and reads from it. "A spokesman for the New Jersey State Forest Fire Service said today that the Hammonton fire was of 'suspicious origin. We have evidence that last Tuesday's fire was started with gasoline,' said Sandy Maclean, section fire warden. 'This is clearly a case of arson.' "

"And they found traces of gasoline *in* the charcoal pit?"

"That's what it says."

"So how'd it turn out? Were any arrests made?"

"None. Morrow's murder was never solved."

Hammonton's just inside the western tip of Atlantic County, which means the Major Crimes Squad would have handled the case. I hope Talley's predecessors kept good records.

"What about Sister Felice and the Christians Against Casinos? You find out anything about them?"

Gwen has nothing new to tell me about Sister Felice. But it turns out the animosity between the CAC and Harry Morrow was more extensive than the good sister led me to believe. Nor did Sister say anything about the innuendoes the CAC had to endure after Morrow's murder.

"I guess there was a lot of bitterness between the religious organizations and the progambling groups back then," says Gwen. "One story even quoted an anonymous source, saying that the CAC had every reason to be pleased that Morrow was dead."

"Did anything come of the story?"

"How could it? It's too incredible to believe. Can you imagine Sister Felice killing somebody, or having them killed?"

"I can't even imagine her getting angry."

"So what's this all about?" Gwen asks.

"Bad people doing bad things to each other."

"Seriously, what's your theory? You do have one, don't you?"

"I need more information."

"Me too. I'm going to do a little more checking around about Harry Morrow. I gotta tell ya, Sweeney, this is *definitely* interesting. It beats doing stories on homeless families at the mission." She pauses to give me a coquettish smile. "So, what do I get for being such a good girl?"

I stop what I'm doing.

"How's chicken dijonnaise, wild rice, and spinach salad with basil dressing sound? I'll try not to burn the chicken."

4

THE NEXT MORNING at the mission, Sister Felice isn't in her office.

"She's at a meeting," says Brother Stephen, seeing me in the hallway. "She shouldn't be long. She's in the chapel with a group Tommy and Lady René have organized. It's quite interesting, actually."

"What about you, do you have a minute?"

"I suppose so. Come in."

From behind his desk, Brother Stephen says, "Felice tells me you were here questioning her yesterday."

"Yes, about the organization she ran back in the seventies."

"Christians Against Casinos?"

"That's the one."

"It was a noble cause, Mr. Sweeney."

"Were you part of it?"

"No."

"I figured you to have been involved in the antigambling campaign."

"I was still in Africa with the missions then. By the time I returned to the country the referendum had already passed. Believe me, I would have helped Felice if I'd been here."

"What can you tell me about Harry Morrow? Did you know him?"

He stops playing with a paperweight and looks up. His distant blue eyes have turned steel gray. The muscles around his jaw are clenched.

"I never met him. But I know what happened to him."

"He was burned to death," I say, "just like Nick and Cappy."

"Death and the dice level all distinctions."

More platitudes. He's about to say something else but stops himself.

"Some people tried to link Sister's anticasino group with the murder," I respond.

He smiles. "You've met Felice, what do *you* think? Does she strike you as a murderer? Besides, Morrow was one among many. When it comes to the justifiers of gambling, their name is legion."

"Did you ever talk with Nick D'Angelo about Morrow?"

"I never talked with Nick about anything but his gambling problem."

"What about Cappy? He ever bring up the subject of Harry Morrow?"

"Cappy? Why should he?"

"Then why do you think Nick would be interested in Morrow's death? Or in Sister's anticasino group?"

"What makes you think he *was* interested?"

"Tell me, did Cappy ever show you any of his personal papers?"

He leans across the desk, not bothering to hide his curiosity.

"What personal papers?"

"He carried them around with him."

"Where? In that raincoat of his?"

"Yes, in the raincoat."

"Then they must have gone up in flames with him."

"Then you *do* know how he died."

"Of course. The police told me."

"You didn't seem interested in that the night Captain Martindale and I were here."

"No, I'm afraid I was too shocked."

"Shocked by the loss of such a big donor?"

164

"To be honest, yes."

For some people honesty's a relative concept. Sometimes it makes for a useful diversion to be frank about some disagreeable truth, drawing attention away from something even more unpleasant.

"You didn't answer my earlier question. Did Cappy ever show you his papers, or tell you about them?"

"He told me once he was collecting material on the IRS. That's all I know."

"He never showed you his will?"

"His will? Good heavens, no. Are you saying he carried his will around with him?"

"I'm not saying anything. Tell me, did you know Tommy was at the Poseidon on Saturday?"

"I was the one who sent him there."

"You *sent* him there?"

"That's right. To find someone."

"And Harriet, did you send her along, too?"

"I didn't learn she'd gone along until later. As it turned out, the trip was unsuccessful. But it all worked out in the end. The person they went looking for ended up at the mission anyway. Something I could have predicted."

For some reason I flash on Gwen's front-page story in the Sunday *Star,* and it hits me what he's getting at.

"Sandra Greenberg, the teenager with the gambling problem? Is that who you're talking about?"

"Yes, she's here, and by her own choosing I might add. You might like to meet her. It would help you to understand what's happened to this town."

"Does her family know she's here?"

"She'll get in touch when she's ready. She has all the family she needs right here at the mission. The residents have taken her in as one of their own."

He gets out of his chair and walks around the side of his desk.

"Gambling has destroyed this girl's childhood. It's a true tragedy."

"Look, this really isn't—"

"Ah, here's Sister now."

I turn around. She's standing in the doorway to the office.

"Something's happened, Stephen. Sandra's gone."

WHILE BROTHER STEPHEN and Sister Felice discuss what to do about the missing Sandra Greenberg, I walk down the hall to the chapel. From the looks of it, the meeting of the Boardwalk Irregulars is breaking up. Most of the people are standing around, preparing to leave. Lady René, sitting astride two folding chairs, sees me in the doorway and motions for me to come in. Tommy, who's about to leave, glances away quickly, then walks by and out the door without saying anything. I take a seat in the back.

Besides Tommy and Lady René, the group includes about ten others, all well along in years. One elderly man is doing a card trick for an even older man who watches with the jaundiced eye of someone who's seen it all before. Lady René is talking to a tall blond-haired woman standing in front of her. The others are heading for the door.

When all but Lady René and the blond are gone, I get up and walk over.

"Hello, Frank," Lady René says. "I'd like you to meet Miss Barkley."

The blond turns toward me, extending her hand.

"Everybody calls me 'Busty.' "

Busty's in her seventies, still flaunting the expansive chest that gave her her stage name. She wears a loose-fitting yellow wig. Strands of gray-white hair have fallen out and are dangling down around her neck.

"Busty used to have an act on the Boardwalk."

"You heard of La Troc?" Busty asks. "That's where I appeared. 'Busty Barkley and Her Fantastic Fans.' There's a parking garage there now."

"I know the place. Sorry, but I never caught your act."

"You missed Harry LaRue," says Lady René. "I could have introduced you."

"The man doing the card tricks?"

"That's him. Too bad. So did you come back for a reading?" she asks.

"I came back for a few more answers."

Busty waves goodbye as I grab a chair and situate myself across from Lady René.

"Answers," she says, wheezing slightly, "everybody wants answers. But nobody has the right questions."

She's got a point there.

"So what *are* the right questions?"

She studies me a moment.

"In your case, I'd say the first question ought to be, 'Why's this bunch of old Boardwalk has-beens meeting here in the mission chapel?'"

"Okay, *why* then?"

"Because we're dead and don't know it, Frank. We died years ago, the day the first casino opened. Now we meet here each week to bitch and moan and gripe about stupid, asinine things. Things we can't do nothing about. This ain't no city to grow old in, I can tell you that. Ghosts, we're all a bunch of ghosts." Her huge torso heaves with the effort, and she throws her head back, sucking in mouthfuls of air.

"What did you 'ghosts' talk about today?"

"You wouldn't believe it."

"Try me."

"We talked about Ronald Harrison, the Indian who buried himself alive on Steel Pier. You ever heard of him?"

"Yeah. He was a Sioux, wasn't he? It was back in the fifties sometime—1952, I think. He buried himself in a concrete box. It had a glass top on it so people could look in on him. He was fed liquids through a tube."

"Sweet Jesus, Frank, you're amazing."

"I have a good memory. And just what was it about Harrison that you talked about?"

"How long he was in there. Nobody could agree. I say it was six weeks. Tommy says only four. Busty and Harry LaRue think it was two months."

"It was six weeks, as I recall. Somehow he survived."

She grins at me. "I knew I was right. Anyway, you see? What'd I tell you? We're all dead! A bunch of old farts lost in the past. Trying to dig up the memory of some crazy Sioux who buried himself in concrete, for God's sake!"

"Look at it this way. You're all exercising your memories, keeping them in shape. And you're preserving what's worth preserving to you."

She smiles and nods at me.

"You're okay, Frank. So what is it you're *really* here for? You didn't stop by to discuss ancient history with the older generation."

"Tell me about Tommy. Does he often do errands for Brother Stephen?"

"Oh, you're talking about Saturday. No, he doesn't often do that. Fact is, Tommy hates the Poseidon. Even if he had any money of his own, he'd never gamble there."

"Why's that?"

"He used to work there. Back in the eighties. He got fired."

"What kind of work? And why'd he get fired?"

"I don't know exactly. Tommy doesn't like to talk about it. But I think he did the same kind of thing your friend did."

"You mean Nick? Was Tommy a security guard?"

"Yeah, I think that's what it was. But he hated it. He wanted to get back into the business. You know, show business. But he was past that a long time ago. Tommy just can't accept it. Like I said, we're all dying. Some of us just don't know it."

"Did Tommy and Nick know each other well?"

"No, I don't think they knew each other at all. Nick wasn't the friendly type. He looked down on Tommy and the rest of us. He thought he didn't belong here. Shit, nobody *belongs* here. Another walking dead man, that Nick."

"Thanks. You've been helpful."

"Think nothing of it. Sure I can't read your fortune? On second thought, maybe *you* should read mine." Her laugh caroms around the chapel.

"Maybe another time. We can do *each other's* fortunes."

5

LADY RENÉ'S RIGHT. Nick was a 'walking dead man.' Bernie and Michelle and I, we all should have seen that. But Nick made it hard for people to figure him out. He took the offensive if you got too close. He kept you at arm's length by using you. It was in his nature. Still, it's the kind of character trait that makes my job easier. The way I figure it, Nick took advantage of Cappy. Once Nick knew Cappy felt obligated to him for having saved his life, he milked it for all it was worth. It would have been out of character for him not to. But this time he did the legwork. This time he didn't wait for someone else to hand him the entire package, wrapped up and tied with a bright red ribbon. And that leads me to the printout. To come up with that, Nick had to have connected with someone at the Poseidon who could get into the casino computer. It wouldn't have to be a senior executive, merely someone who knows how to log on to the system, someone willing to show Nick how to do it, or maybe do it for him.

Which brings me back to Billy Loo.

This time I find him awake. He answers the door barefoot, in black pants and a white T-shirt.

"Billy, remember me? Frank Sweeney?"

"I remember. You fuck me, Mr. PI. You fuck Billy real bad."

"What do you mean?"

"You talk 'bout me, right?"

"I didn't talk about you to anybody. What's the matter, are you in trouble?"

"Billy in big trouble. Billy out of job."

"What happened? They fire you?"

"That's right, Mr. PI."

"Billy, I swear I didn't talk to anyone."

"All I know is I outa work. Now what I gonna do?"

He turns and walks back into the apartment, leaving the front door open. I follow him into the kitchenette.

"Who fired you, Billy?"

"Mr. Bishop talk to me. But it was Mr. D. who fire me, I know that. Mr. Bishop, he not want to do it."

"Did they give you a reason?"

"Business bad. Not enough players. All bullshit. Was Mr. Bishop say I best dealer." Taking the whistling tea kettle off the burner, he nods in the direction of the bedroom. "He leave, too. Gotta have job, you wanna keep boyfriend. You want tea?"

We sit in the living room with our tea, Billy on the vinyl couch, me across from him on a frayed lounge chair.

"Billy, maybe I can help."

"How you can help? They say Poseidon gonna close down, you know. What you saying? Maybe I get job somewhere else?"

"Maybe. I know somebody. I can't make any promises, but I'll speak to this man for you."

He looks over at me, tears filling his eyes.

"I really 'preciate that."

"It's the least I can do for you, Billy." I take a long sip of tea. "Maybe I can also get you some satisfaction."

"What kind satisfaction? It pay big bucks?"

"No big bucks, Billy. Just plain old satisfaction. Like when the bad guys get it in the end."

"You mean like in movies?"

"Right, Billy. Like in the movies."

He thinks about that a moment or two.

"What you want me do?"

"Tell me about Nick D'Angelo. Did he ever come to you for help?"

"Once he ask for help. Only once."

"What'd he want you to do?"

"Information. He want information."

"Like the kind of information that comes from a computer?"

"Don't know nothing 'bout computers."

"But you know someone who does, don't you Billy?"

He nods his head.

"Who was it, Billy? I need to talk to him."

"How I know I can trust you? This dangerous shit, man."

"Look, Billy. I don't have to know any names. I don't even have to meet this guy. I just want him to get me some information, too—like he did for Nick."

"My friend afraid. He don't want to lose job, too."

"Would you at least call him for me? I'll tell you what to ask him. You don't have to tell me his name or anything."

"What you want to know?"

I try to explain it as best I can. Then I give Billy the account number from Jonah Smith's printout. He stands up and goes into the bedroom, closing the door behind him. Five minutes later he comes out.

"He want to talk to you."

"Thanks, Billy."

The phone sits on an old trunk next to the bed. It's the only piece of furniture in the room, other than the mattress on the floor. The room is cluttered with piles of clothing and cardboard boxes containing personal effects.

"Hello, this is Frank Sweeney . . . hello, anybody there?"

"Yeah, I'm here. What do you want?"

"I thought maybe you could provide me with some information."

"What made you think that? Do you know who I am?"

"No."

"Good. Let's keep it that way. You can call me . . . 'Joe.' It's not my real name."

"I understand."

"What do you want?"

"I thought since you helped Nick D'Angelo once, maybe you'd help me. I'm an old friend of Nick's brother. I'm trying to find Nick's killer."

"Nick was fucked up. I knew him in GA. He mighta made it if he'd stayed away from the damned tables."

"I know. Will you help?"

"What's the name of Nick's brother?"

"Bernard. Bernie."

"How'd you get that account number Billy gave me? From Nick's printout?"

"Yeah."

"You gonna help Billy?"

"I'm going to try. I know somebody. But I can't make any promises."

There's a long silence on the other end. I wait it out.

"You know how to use a computer?" he asks when he resumes.

"I know enough."

"I can give you the password, but you'll need an access code. You can't use mine. They'd know how you logged on."

"How do I get one?"

"It's the employee's casino license number. Five digits plus a letter. But it has to be someone who's approved to log on, like a floor person or a pit boss or something."

"Will the casino manager do?"

The phone goes silent again for a moment. Then I hear a faint laugh at the other end.

"Yeah, his'll do just fine."

"Consider it done. Now what?"

"I'll tell you where to meet me."

6

ON THE WAY BACK to Atlantic City, I stop at a diner in Somers Point and grab a cup of coffee and a sandwich to eat in the car. The coffee's cold and the sandwich is stale, but I didn't eat breakfast so I'm too hungry to care.

At the Poseidon I track Charlie Bishop down near the dollar slots. He's talking to one of the floor persons, looking just as harried as he did on Saturday.

"Mr. Bishop, you remember me?"

"Yeah. Sweeney, right?"

He signs a piece of paper and gives it to the floor person, who walks off.

"That's right."

"You here to see me? I'm busy as hell."

"You know Tommy the Toe, don't you? He used to have a high-wire act on Steel Pier back in the old days."

He studies me closely for a moment. I can tell he's going to try a bluff.

" 'Tommy the Toe'? This some kind of joke?"

"Funny name, huh? I thought maybe you might know him."

"Why would you think I'd know somebody named Tommy the Toe?"

"Because I saw him talking to you. Right here on Saturday. You know, after you and I talked? I got a tour of the Eye from Jack Coyle. That's how I saw you. On one of the TV screens down in the Eye."

"You're jerking my chain, right?"

"What about Sandra Greenberg, you know her?"

He studies me one more time, then decides to continue stonewalling. I half-admire him for it.

"I don't know what you're talking about, but if you think—"

I raise my hand. "It's okay. Look, here's my take on this. The way I figure it, you're trying to help this Greenberg kid out. I don't know if you got in touch with the mission or they came to you. It doesn't matter. Either way it makes you one of the good guys around here. I figure you may even be the one who talked to that reporter. What's her name? Olin? You know, the one who wrote the story on the kid for last Sunday's paper?"

"Jesus Christ, look—

I raise my hand again, this time taking a quick look at the license number on his plastic ID badge.

"Like I said, in my book this makes you one of the good guys. Don't sweat it. I'm not ratting on you. Besides, you've been more help than you can know."

I move away as if to leave, then come back to where he's standing.

"There's something you should know. She's gone. Sandra Greenberg skipped out on the mission folks. You may want to keep an eye out for her."

"Joe" is fortyish, balding, and has a bad case of the jitters. His real name, according to his ID badge, is Leonard Pitkin. For the sake of his nerves, I pretend to ignore the badge and resist the temptation to call him "Lenny." Since meeting me outside the Seahorse Deli, it's been nothing but nonstop nervous chatter. His talk is all of "bottom lines" and "spreadsheets" and "cash flow." He's probably an accountant or some other kind of number cruncher. Either that or he's a bookie.

"So you knew Nick through Gamblers Anonymous?"

"Yeah, you got a problem with that?"

"No problem. How well'd you know him?"

"Not well. He singled me out at a meeting one day after I caught a lot of flack from the group for still working in a casino. He came to my defense. It's not like I've got a choice, for Christ's sake. Not if I'm gonna pay back my debts. Man's gotta work."

Good ol' Nick, ever true to form. Even at a GA meeting he managed to find a way to use people.

"He ever talk to you about personal things? Things that were on his mind?"

"Nick? Nah. He'd tell you all the safe stuff. Like how he used to be a cop, things like that. And the name of his brother. He mentioned that once or twice. That's how I knew to ask you. It was sort of my safety check, you know? Like they do in the movies when the guy wants to see if the other guy's legit? But Nick, he never like really shared, you know what I mean?"

"Yeah, I know. So you don't have any idea why he wanted that computer data?"

"He never said. But shit, he got me curious, you know? So I did some checking of my own."

"What'd you find out?"

"Zilch. He was on some kinda wild fuckin' goose chase, far as I can see."

"Maybe so. So now what?"

"I'm gonna take you to a room. Hardly anyone uses it. It's got a few computer terminals and that's all. No printer or nothing. I can't chance that again. There are no cameras there either. Not in the room anyway. Out in the hallway, that's another question. There are gonna be cameras there and everywhere. Once we go back inside the casino, we're gonna be on TV the whole way. So you gotta stay behind me. Don't even look at me. Ya know, like we're not together?"

"What if I'm seen going into this room?"

"What can I tell ya? It's a risk. You're the one's gotta decide if it's worth it. They spot you, you got three minutes, five tops, to get outa the room. After that somebody's gonna come checking up on you, and you sure as fuck better not remember you ever saw me."

"Don't worry. So what's the password?"

"*Samson.*" He spells it out for me. "You enter it after the access code. You got a code?"

I tap the side of my head. "Right here."

He looks dubious. "You sure? Okay. Now listen, let me give you some advice. You wanna find out about a guy, right? One of the high rollers?"

"Right."

"Go straight for 'Player History.' It's got the most data on all the rated players. After you log on there'll be a list of things to choose from. Just hit the key number for 'Player History.' "

"Thanks. By the way, why are you doing this?"

"It's Billy," he says, averting his eyes.

"What do you mean?"

"They fucked him good. I'm gonna fuck them back. This is just the beginning."

"Just watch yourself."

"Shit, this place's already going down the tubes. We'll *all* be on the street eventually. I got a couple of job prospects. What about Billy, you think you can help him? He's counting on it."

"Like I said, I'll do what I can."

7

Keeping a safe distance ahead of me, Leonard Pitkin, aka Joe, leads me to the third floor. I follow him down the same hallway Charlie Bishop took me to on Saturday. He passes the personnel interview rooms, turns right down a long carpeted corridor, then right again into a narrow passageway with a bare tile floor. It appears to be a corridor of storage rooms. I can see the surveillance camera at the other end of the hallway.

The plan calls for Leonard to scratch the back of his neck as he passes the target room. He assures me the door will be unlocked. I'm holding a piece of paper, as if it contains directions someone's given me. I keep looking back and forth from it to the numbers on the doors along the hallway. Two-thirds of the way down the hall Leonard scratches. By the time I reach the spot, he has disappeared from sight. I go right in and close the door behind me.

It's a small windowless room, about a hundred square feet, almost entirely taken up with boxes of IBM computer equipment stacked on top of each other. A narrow table sits against one wall. It holds three computer monitors and keyboards, apparently for testing. They're connected by cables to special jacks in the wall. According to Lenny each of them has access to the players' files. He's seen to it that one is turned on. Right now the screen shows the Poseidon's logo.

I glance at my watch. It's 12:10 P.M. Pulling up a chair, I hit the return key on the keyboard. The logo disappears and a command appears on the screen.

ENTER ACCOUNT NAME:

I type in Charlie Bishop's name. The next command materializes.

ENTER ACCESS CODE:

I enter the five digits and single letter of Bishop's casino license, triggering yet another command.

ENTER PASSWORD:

After I type out SAMSON, a menu of ten different program options comes up. I choose PLAYER HISTORY, which brings up another screen offering four ways to start the search.

1 LAST NAME, FIRST
2 PLAYER SS#
3 PLAYER ACCT. NO.
4 LIST ALL

When I enter Jonah Smith's account number, his name appears at the top of the screen along with eight different options covering his history at the Poseidon.

1 TRIP HISTORY DISPLAY
2 PLAYER RATINGS
3 DETAIL RATINGS
4 COMPS DISPLAY
5 PLAYER MARKETING INFORMATION
6 GIFT LIST/COMMENTS
7 CASINO CALENDAR
8 CREDIT HISTORY

I already have Nick's printout of the Player Marketing Information, so I opt for Credit History. A screen comes up showing fields for home and business addresses, home and business telephone numbers, credit-card numbers, names of banks, and so on. But there's no data. The fields are empty. I go back to the previous menu and enter one for the Trip History Display. As soon as that screen comes up I can see that it would take me an hour to figure it out so I go back and call up the next one, Player Ratings. This one's a little more decipherable.

PLAYER RATING

ACCT: 10350A							CREDIT LMT: 0	
CITY/ST:							AVL. CREDIT: 0	
DOB:							DEPOSIT: 0	

DATE	TIME PLAY	AVG BET	CASH BUYIN	CREDIT BUYIN	W/L	THEO. LOSS	COMPS	GM/PIT TABLE
4/09/96	2:56	550	8440	0	5400-	2534	40	R0611
4/02/96	2:34	399	7345	0	567	1976	70	R0611
3/26/96	:52	500	5000	0	5000-	478	20	R0611
3/19/96	5:18	303	12500	0	12500-	5900	95	R0611
3/12/96	3:34	345	5950	0	235	5430	25	R0611
3/05/96	:59	950	2800	0	45	600	15	R0611
2/27/96	1:39	155	1500	0	455	90	20	R0611
2/20/96	:48	45	550	0	550-	35	35	R0611
2/13/96	4:43	678	17890	0	16995-	8295	95	R0611
2/06/96	2:41	780	23450	0	21340-	7595	105	R0611
1/30/96	3:67	895	28565	0	27460-	9832	105	R0611
1/23/96	1:57	445	7650	0	650	2578	20	R0611
1/16/96	:57	560	2500	0	18900	790	10	R0611
1/09/96	2:31	605	9050	0	175	3565	15	R0611

What strikes me first is that Mr. X, high roller that he is, has no line of credit. Gambling's entirely a cash enterprise with him, which is only logical if he intends to remain anonymous. Otherwise, he'd have to supply detailed information about his bank accounts, credit history, and, ultimately, his identity. A number of other details emerge. First of all, the last time Mr. X gambled at the Poseidon was April 9, the date we have him on videotape being watched by Nick. Tuesday's his regular night at the Poseidon, as the dates in the first column indicate. But he wasn't here last Tuesday, the sixteenth, suggesting he knew Nick was on to him. From the indicators in the last column, it's clear he only plays roulette and always at pit 6, table 11, Billy Loo's table. And Billy Loo was right. Mr. X costs the casino very little in the way of complimentaries. The paltry dollar amounts in the next-to-last column must be for Cutty and water, which he clearly drinks in larger quantities when he's losing.

Billy Loo's also right about another thing. Mr. X doesn't know when to quit. If you regularly spend three or four hours at the roulette table averaging $500 a bet, then you've got a problem. Either that or you've run out of rat holes to shove your money down. In Mr. X's case, I'd say he's got a *big* problem. It's all there in the W/L (won/lost) column. On four different occasions during the past three months he lost dollar amounts in the five figures. For all but one of those dates the time of play was over two-and-a-half hours. In two instances it took four or more hours. Mr. X just keeps on playing no matter how much he's losing. He's what's called a "soft player." He plays until the money runs out. And on several occasions it ran out big time. By my rough calculation, during this three-month period he lost nearly $90,000 to the Poseidon, winning back a little over $20,000. If Tony Dante's in the red, it's not because of assholes like this.

I check my watch. It's 12:16 P.M. I decide to push my luck. Exciting from the Jonah Smith file, I return to the PLAYER HISTORY menu and choose LIST ALL. This produces an alphabetically arranged list of all the Poseidon's rated players. There are hundreds of them. The screen shows last name first, social security number, and account number. I scroll down to the Jones's. There are dozens but only one Jonah. When the name appears, I type in the number next to the name and get the same menu as before.

    1   TRIP HISTORY DISPLAY
    2   PLAYER RATINGS
    3   DETAIL RATINGS
    4   COMPS DISPLAY
    5   PLAYER MARKETING INFORMATION
    6   GIFT LIST/COMMENTS
    7   CASINO CALENDAR
    8   CREDIT HISTORY

This time I choose Player Marketing Information, calling up for Jonah Jones the same screen that Nick had printed out for Jonah Smith. But there's no more here than there is on Jonah Smith. True,

Cappy, aka Jonah Jones, drinks Absolut instead of Cutty, and plays blackjack, not roulette. But that's the sum total of the personal information. Like Mr. Smith, Mr. Jones employs a phony social security number and commands the immediate attention of Charlie Bishop as soon as he arrives in the casino. I try the Player Ratings screen.

POSEIDON CASINO

PLAYER RATING

ACCT: 10350B   CREDIT LMT: OPEN
CITY/ST: AVL. CREDIT: OPEN
DOB: DEPOSIT: 800550

DATE	TIME PLAY	AVG BET	CASH BUYIN	CREDIT BUYIN	W/L	THEO. LOSS	COMPS	GM/PIT TABLE
4/02/96	:26	50	0	300	45-	50	20	B0515
3/17/96	:34	70	0	250	98	53	35	B0515
3/02/96	:42	95	0	200	148	60	60	B0515
2/23/96	:18	65	0	300	100-	35	25	B0515
2/03/96	:34	80	0	300	205-	52	35	B0515
1/21/96	:49	45	0	200	135	58	65	B0515
1/10/96	:20	35	0	200	200-	49	25	B0515
1/02/96	:38	50	0	250	250-	57	45	B0515

A few things stand out. First of all, Cappy had an "open" line of credit, something unheard of, as far as I know. And before his death he had more than $800,000 on deposit with the casino. Yet he spent little more than half an hour at the blackjack table during each session and never bought in for more than a few hundred. If it weren't for all that money on deposit, he wouldn't have been important enough for the casino to keep tabs on him. Nobody, but *nobody,* turns over that much money to a casino without putting it in play. That is, unless . . . unless he wants to use the casino as a bank.

It's 12:23 P.M., well past Leonard's recommended quitting time, and I still don't know much of anything about Mr. X. I need to get back to Jonah Smith. As I'm exiting from Cappy's file there's a noise outside the door. I quickly hit the log-off command.

The Poseidon logo appears on the screen at the moment the door to the room opens and the florid face of Jack Coyle fills the doorway.

"Sweeney, how nice of you to pay us a visit again."

Tony Dante stands in front of one of the security monitors by his desk, staring at a picture of the hallway Leonard Pitkin just led me down.

"Ain't all this high-tech shit something?" he says, waving Coyle out of the room. "And them fuckin' computers, too! Am I right or wrong?" He turns in the direction of the monitor on the credenza behind his desk. "Did you know, when one of my people logs on to these fuckin' things, I know it, too? So it was kinda odd when this screen here showed Charlie Bishop logged on and he was standing right here in the room talking to me. Can you believe it? They're watching us every second, Frank. I swear to God. It's all we can do to grab a little pussy in private and not get caught, ya know what I mean? Only the paranoid survive, am I right?"

"Look, Dante—

He raises a meaty hand to silence me. He's out of uniform today, dressed in beige slacks and a silk sport shirt, open wide at the neck to display an array of gold chains clinging to a well-tanned chest.

"Never apologize, Frankie, that's my motto. Just makes you look bad. I'll tell you a story. I once had a blackjack table was losing dough like you wouldn't believe. It was like there was a fuckin' hole in the drop box or something. I swear to God. I had our security people on top of that table twenty-four hours a day. Shit, we had the fuckin' dealers followed. Checked up on their wives, girlfriends, everything. Me, I personally don't go in for that kinda shit, but the security boys, they say it's necessary, you know what I mean? I'm sure you understand. Well, security had squat. Nada. So I figured it out. It had to be some other cocksucker in the pit crew. Probably there was a whole bunch of the scumbags in on it together. Maybe even the pit boss himself. So you know what I did? Know what I did? Take a guess. Go ahead, take a shot."

"You fired everybody."

He looks at me as if I've just guessed his age and weight.

"The fuck you know that? Who told you?"

"It's exactly the kind of half-assed move you'd pull."

"Yeah? Well, it worked, dickhead. Wasn't any fuckin' losses in that pit after the whole crew got canned. But that ain't my point."

"What's your point?"

"Point is half the cocksuckers in that pit crew came to me and apologized. Begged for their jobs back. Christ, they were confessing to shit I didn't even know about."

"I'm not here to apologize, Tony."

"Fuck you're not. You're ready to shit your pants right now."

"Do I look scared?"

"Tell you another story, Frankie boy. It's about an ex-cop who turns PI and shows up down here in A.C. trying to help a buddy. The dumb shit comes down here thinking he's still a cop. Thinking he can go anywhere he fuckin' wants. No search warrant, no invite, no nothin'. Guy just strolls into places uninvited and pokes his stubby Irish nose into business that ain't his. Can you believe it? And you know what else? He meets this young bitch reporter. Can you picture this? Him, an over-the-hill ex-cop running around with this young broad. Tits out to here. She'd give ya balls the size of cantaloupes. I swear to God. Was she a good lay, do you think? Man his age's gotta be real appreciative of young pussy like that, huh? But a man in his profession's also gotta be real careful hanging around with reporters. You never know when you might end up in the papers."

"Who's Jonah Smith, Tony? I know who Jonah Jones was. I met him, you know. Name was Theodore Capetanakis. Yeah, that's right, I know all about him. I know they were both murdered by the same killer, too. Even this dumb Irish PI figured that much out. So just tell me who Jonah Smith is and how to find him, and I'll go quietly. Or maybe you'd like to call the cops and press charges against me for breaking into your computer system?"

It's not in character for a man like Tony D. to go speechless all of a sudden, but that's what's happened. We appear to have reached an impasse. At the door I turn around.

"One last thing, Dante. You have anybody else follow me or Gwen Olin and you can kiss that casino license of yours goodbye."

What can I say, he pissed me off. Just hope I didn't hurt his feelings.

8

I KEEP AN EYE OUT all the way to the parking garage. When I get to D Level it seems darker than before. As a precaution I circle around and come at the car from the opposite direction. Then I get down and check underneath. I can't see anyone there or inside. But I make a mental note not to park here again.

On the way out of town I stop off at Martindale's office. Without going into too much detail, I tell him how much help Billy Loo has been. He says he'll see what he can do for him. When I tell him about Cappy's raincoat, he decides to accompany me to Major Crimes.

Talley's willing to meet but decides against Petrillo and Cox sitting in. The television and VCR are still in place in the conference room. From the looks of the pile of videotapes on the floor, I'd say someone's still studying Nick's last night at the Poseidon.

"So what's this all about?" Talley says, once we're seated at the table.

I take the three envelopes out of my jacket and place them in front of him, trying to ignore the look I'm getting. "What the hell's this?" he asks.

"These belonged to Theodore Capetanakis, the man I called Cappy."

"How'd *you* get ahold of them?" Talley asks.

I tell him about Tommy and the raincoat.

"And just *when* was it you came across this raincoat?"

"I didn't know these envelopes existed when I was here yesterday, if that's what you mean. I discovered them afterward. And now I'm turning them over to the proper authorities. Isn't that what a good citizen does?"

"A 'good citizen' calls the cops right away," says Talley, "and doesn't touch a goddamned thing."

"Look, Cappy carried around his most important possessions in that coat. The point is, now *you* have them."

"What do you make of it all, Frank?" Martindale asks, trying to bail me out.

"Two of the envelopes contain personal stuff. As you'll see, he was a bit paranoid. He had a thing about the IRS. The third envelope, the one with the initials "N.D." on it, is the one he was holding for Nick. It has a bunch of old newspaper clippings and a computer print-out from the Poseidon."

"Computer printout?"

"For one of their rated players. Somebody named Jonah Smith."

"Who's he?" Talley interjects.

"It's a phony name, that's all I know."

"We'll have a little talk with this Tommy the Toe ourselves," says Talley.

"Good idea," I say, trying to sound supportive, "he'll probably be more cooperative with the cops."

Talley eyes me intently. "You got something else, Frank?"

"I'd like a small favor."

"A favor? Listen to the guy."

I tell him about the 1975 newspaper clipping in Nick's envelope and the Harry Morrow arson-murder in 1977.

"That's before our time," says Talley, looking at Martindale, "we didn't start here until '85."

"But you have the old case files, right?"

"Upstairs," he says.

"Could I possibly see the Morrow file?"

He thinks a moment, then looks at Martindale. If something passes between them, I'm unable to make it out.

"This is the last time, Frank," says Talley.

After he leaves the room, I grab a cup of coffee and a stale doughnut left over from the morning. In five minutes Talley's back with the file.

"It's cross-referenced with another file," he says. "A 'John Doe.' " He slides the file across the table to me. "Here, take a look. Then I've got to get back to work."

It's a remarkably thin file. No murder case I've ever been involved with, least of all one involving a prominent local citizen, ever produced a mere six pages. There's a case summary, a page itemizing the physical evidence, two pages of witnesses' reports, and a two-page arson investigator's report. No photographs, but there are a few newspaper clippings describing the fire. I glance at the witness reports. The only detailed statement is from the section fire warden, Sandy Maclean. Then I notice something. It's mentioned in the physical evidence inventory as well as the arson investigator's report. I hand those pages to Martindale and proceed to read the case detective's summary. It provides the biggest surprise of all.

Afterward, outside in the parking lot, I ask Martindale for his assessment.

"It's the same MO. The torch, the gasoline, the whole nine yards."

"The same kind of ignition device you found in the lighthouse, too. You notice that?"

He nods his head. "Right. A matchbook with solder wrapped around it. I'm not saying two different people couldn't have used the same device, but it would make for a hell of a coincidence."

"That's what I thought."

"And the Morrow murder was when?"

"1977."

"This guy's got staying power, I'll grant him that."

That's because he's had some help. The case detective's report proves that. It's a study in obfuscation, a mishmash of dates and times, air temperatures and wind directions the day of the fire, useless interviews with nearby Pineys, along with contradictory hypotheses about Harry Morrow's restaurant business and his support of casino gambling in Atlantic City. Even a few rumors are cited to the effect that Christians Against Casinos might be responsible. If there was any doubt about the deceptiveness of the report, I had only to look at the name of the case detective at the bottom of the page. It was signed, "Sgt. Jack Coyle, Atlantic County Major Crimes Squad."

9

I DECIDE ON pasta primavera for dinner. Maybe all the carbohydrates will give me a boost, help me focus on the question of what it was that got Nick killed. Chopping vegetables in the kitchen, my thoughts drift to a New Hope antiques dealer Catherine and I used to know. He died recently, from a stroke, at the age of eighty-eight. We knew him as Mr. Jaffee. He was an old-fashioned gentleman, the kind you'd never think to call by his first name, which I think was Cornelius. Mr. Jaffee had a unique way of assessing an antique. At first he would appear more interested in where it had been over the years than in its authenticity. Had it been hidden in an attic for the past fifty years, buried in a damp basement, or out in plain view in a room frequented by living, breathing human beings? Had it been damaged in any way by sunlight, humidity, chemicals, human abuse? And so on. All this was merely to lay the groundwork for a more de-tailed inquiry into its provenance. "You must go back to the first day," he would say, "every object has a story and every story has a begin-ning." After Catherine died I turned to him for advice on running the shop on Walnut Street. He repeated that refrain to me over and over again: You must go back to the beginning. He knew how diffi-cult it was to reconstruct the entire history of a piece, especially if it had had many owners, but he believed it was essential to try. What he learned about an antique determined how he *felt* about it. And for Mr. Jaffee the subjective reaction was what determined its per-sonal value, its value to *him,* which, after all, was the only value that mattered.

Every story has a beginning. You must go back to the first day.

During dinner I finish off the remainder of the chardonnay from last night. Then I make coffee and rummage through Mr. Cordell's CD collection for some decent jazz. There's a lot of electronic stuff, fusion, which I hate, as well as some early Ellington. I'll opt for the Duke over Chick Corea any day. But just as "Harlem Airshaft" gets started Gwen calls.

She wants to pick my brains, I can tell. So I steer us toward personal chitchat instead. I talk about Bernie for a while. She responds with a sympathetic description of her father. I reciprocate with more about Catherine. Then, as the conversation's flagging she drops a bombshell.

"You know how I said yesterday I was going to do some more checking on my own?" she says.

"Yeah."

"Well, I did."

"And?"

"Have you ever heard of the Ocean View Motel?"

"Yeah, actually I have."

"You have?"

"There was another clipping I came across. It mentioned a rumor that the motel was going to be sold to the Angelina Corporation."

"Well, that sale went through in July of '78. The Ocean View Motel was torn down eight months later to make way for the Poseidon."

"So?"

"Guess who was a silent partner in the Ocean View before his untimely death in the Pine Barrens in 1977?"

"You're kidding."

"That's right. Harry Morrow. It was one of the many businesses he was involved in, besides The Tudor House. His partner was somebody named Henry Bass. After Morrow was murdered, Bass sold the place to old Joe Dante."

At Bass's name a distant image breaks the surface. *Midnight shakes the memory as a madman shakes a dead geranium.* One of the clippings in Nick's envelope mentioned Bass, said he moved to New York after selling out. But there's something else about that name that strikes a chord.

"So, Frank, what do you think?"

"I think this is very interesting."

"*How* interesting?"

"What do you mean?"

I know exactly what she means.

"Oh, come on. How *much* is it worth to you? There's more, you know."

"Tell me what you want to and I'll reciprocate as best I can."

"Promise?"

"Promise."

"Okay, it's a deal. Get this, Frank—the Ocean View was sold for $1.5 million! That's all. One-and-a-half measly million. I mean, hell, at the time the value of property in town was positively *skyrocketing* because of the casino referendum. For comparison's sake, I looked up the sale of the Strand Motel. That's the Boardwalk place Steve Wynn bought in June of '78. You know, the spot where he put up the Golden Nugget? Guess what Wynn paid for his little piece of paradise. Eight-and-a-half million! I figured it out. Old man Dante got his Boardwalk hotel for *eighteen percent* of what Steve Wynn paid for a place of similar size a month earlier."

"Not bad. Not a bad deal at all."

"Okay, I'm waiting."

I have to admit it, I owe her something for this one.

"Okay, look, I'll tell you what I know about the body under the Boardwalk. But there has to be one condition."

"What's that?"

"You've got to keep me out of it. Promise me that."

She's silent a moment. "Okay, agreed. But we're not talking off the record, right? Just not for attribution."

"Right."

"Okay, shoot."

"The victim was Cappy. You remember, the man I mentioned to you, the one who wanted me to get Nick out of town?"

"Yeah, the eccentric who lived at the mission."

"Right. Now pay attention. Here's your scoop. His full name was Theodore Capetanakis."

This time there's a longer silence.

"*The* Theodore Capetanakis?"

"The one and only."

"Jesus, Frank."

"He was doused with alcohol and set afire. Probably by the same killer who got Nick."

I tell her a little about Cappy. And I mention Mr. X with the bushy eyebrows. But I stop short of my encounters with Tony Dante and Jack Coyle, and my foray into the Poseidon's computer files.

"So who do you think's behind this, Frank? I mean, shit, this arsonist sounds like a maniac."

"He's a hired killer. We're not talking Boston Strangler here."

"That's reassuring."

"Don't forget, Gwen, this isn't for attribution."

"Like I promised. But I've *got* to do a story on this, Frank. I can see it now. 'Gwen Olin: the reporter who broke the story on Theodore Capetanakis.' I'll need another source though. I can't just print that some anonymous person gave me a tip on the victim's identity."

I can hear her thinking on the other end of the line.

"That's up to you. Just don't name me."

"Look, I've got to hang up. Got a few calls to make. Oh, and Frank?"

"Yeah."

"You watch out, okay?"

"Okay."

A LITTLE BEFORE eleven Bernie calls. I take it in the kitchen where I'm making a cup of herbal tea before bed.

"I can't sleep, Frank. I'm finally at home in my own bedroom, and I can't get to sleep. Can you believe that?"

"I'm telling you, Bernie, you need a companion. 'Never sleep alone.' Isn't that what Madonna says? Or was it JFK?"

"*Madonna!* How can anyone take a name like that? It's sacrilege. Do you know—"

"It was a joke, Bernie. Don't get upset. It's not good for you."

"Yeah, I suppose you're right. So how's it going?"

I give him an overview of the events of the past three days.

"Frank, you realize something big's going on down there, don't you? I mean big enough to interest more than just the local cops."

"The thought had occurred to me."

"I've done some checking, like you asked. You remember that IRS investigator I introduced you to a year or so ago, the guy with the bow tie we had lunch with at O'Malley's?"

"Yeah, his name was Navaho or something."

"Nardo. Well, Nardo says the whole Capetanakis family's in deep doo-doo with the IRS. Your Cappy, he was different from the rest of the bunch. Seems he didn't believe in taxes. I mean he wasn't just greedy or pissed at having to pay so much. He really *believed* people shouldn't have to pay taxes."

"So he gave his money to the Poseidon instead."

"How'd you know that? Damn, Frank, you're stealing my thunder again."

"What's that noise?"

"What noise? You mean on the phone? I don't hear anything. Anyway, yeah, it was something like that. Nardo couldn't tell me everything but I got the general picture. It's nothing very original, but it takes balls these days, what with all the federal laws and the surveillance. I guess Capetanakis would deposit a large amount with the Poseidon—maybe a million or so—bet a few measly bucks, and walk away."

"Then for a percentage the remainder was transferred to a foreign bank."

"Exactly. Nardo said they're looking at accounts in Switzerland, France, the Caymans, just about everywhere."

I decide to tell him about the Poseidon's computer files on the two Jonahs. It gets his attention.

"Are you saying Dante's behind it all?"

"He's got to be. His casino manager wouldn't be laundering money on his own. On the other hand, Dante's got no business smarts. Matter of fact, the guy's basically stupid."

"And this other Jonah, the guy Nick was following, you still don't know who he is?"

"All I know so far is he's got a big-time gambling addiction."

For a few seconds I can hear Bernie's breathing on the other end of the line.

"Tell me the truth, Frank. You think he's the one who killed Nick?"

"Hard to say. He doesn't look like your typical hit man, at least not on videotape. But arsonists come in all shapes and sizes."

"Don't forget Benny the Match."

How do you forget a serial arsonist who preyed on orphanages? Benny—his full name was Benjamin Harrison White—turned out to be the most unassuming, kindhearted person I've ever met. He ran a newsstand on Market Street and on weekends did volunteer work for youth organizations like the Boy Scouts and Big Brothers. He loved kids. But he hated orphanages. He'd lived in one in Mississippi, we later learned, until he was fourteen. During that time he suffered terribly at the hands of some astoundingly cruel priests and nuns who, thinking he was retarded, decided that his fragile mental state was cause to abuse him. He killed thirteen people in fires at six different orphanages, foster homes, and halfway houses before we finally caught him. When we went to arrest him we found him in the pediatric ward of a north Philadelphia hospital reading stories and handing out balloons to kids with terminal diseases. I felt as if I'd walked onto the set of "Mr. Rogers' Neighborhood" to arrest Fred Rogers himself.

"There's something else, Bernie. It looks like Dante's having me followed."

I tell him what Dante said in his office earlier today about Gwen and me.

"And the girl's being watched, too?" he asks.

"She's not a 'girl,' Bernie. She's at least . . . thirtysomething."

"Right. That's what they all say. Does she do drugs, Frank? All these kids today do drugs. Just watch yourself."

I hear the noise again. This time I recognize it. And it's not coming from the telephone.

"Bernie, I've got to go. Call you in a day or so."

"Just find him, Frank. Find the bastard."

"I will, Bernie."

The sound came from the front porch. It's the same loose floorboard Gwen stepped on, the one near the swing on the beach side. For the first time since leaving Philly I wish I'd ignored the Jersey gun laws and brought my Glock semiautomatic with me. Still, the lights in the rest of the house have been turned off so I may be able to get a glimpse of whoever it is through the porch windows without being seen.

I make my way slowly along the inside wall of the living room, feeling my way like a blind man. I can barely see my hand in front of my face. Trying not to bump into the Shaker end table next to the sofa, I feel around for the brass poker in the rack that holds the fireplace tools. It's solid and reassuring in my hand; holding it helps slow my breathing a little. Edging along the wall, I negotiate around the ship's clock, the America's Cup prints hanging next to the fireplace, and finally the bookshelf filled with Mr. Cordell's collection of ceramic lighthouses. At the end of the wall there's an eighteenth-century tavern table that Catherine and I gave her parents for their thirty-fifth wedding anniversary. It holds a solid brass table lamp from Holland with an anchor light. Fortunately, I know precisely where it is.

When I reach the nearest window, my senses are on edge about something. I ignore the warning, eager to get a look at whoever's there. As I'm about to part the curtains I hear something. It's not a creaky floorboard this time. It's metal on wood, or metal against metal. Something's been set down on the porch. Then I hear footsteps. I can't ignore the smell seeping through the closed windows any longer. It's a harsh, caustic odor. When it dawns on me what it is, I feel as if I've just taken a bullet in the stomach. What I heard was a metal fuel container being placed on the porch. What I smell is gasoline.

At the other end of the porch there's a brilliant flash. Suddenly the living room lights up as if an electrical storm has surrounded the house. For an insane instant I try to recall whether or not there was any forecast of foul weather today. Then the rest of the porch goes up. A yellow-orange wall of flames blankets the entire side of the house.

For a moment I'm paralyzed. Then I move.

The Cordells have an elaborate fire-alarm system that's set off by sensors inside the house. There's a battery-powered backup should the power fail. But what the system won't do is sense heat on the *outside* of the house. The fire department needs to be alerted manually in such a case. So I make my way across the room to the control panel on the wall near the front door, banging my shin on the coffee table in the process. With the flames lapping at the windows I don't have any difficulty making out the numbered buttons. The LED display says AUX, indicating the system has already gone to auxiliary power. The bastard must have cut off the electrical supply. Then, just as I'm preparing to punch in the three-digit alarm code, the screen goes blank. He's managed to take out the entire system. I turn and reach for the telephone on the table next to the sofa. It's dead, too.

By now both outside walls are engulfed. Thick tongues of yellow flames cling to the door and windows like fiery vines.

Do I open the front door and make a run for it? Won't he be waiting for me? Can you go through a wall of fire without getting seriously burned? Do I have a choice? I touch the knob of the front door. It's too hot to hold with my bare hand so I take out my handkerchief and try to turn it. The knob moves but the door won't budge. Something's blocking it. I run into the pantry off the kitchen and try the rear door. It's been barred from the outside, too.

The only thing left is to move to higher ground. I take the stairs two at a time. The flames haven't reached the second-floor windows yet, but the flickering from below is clearly visible. I race down the hall toward the fire escape at the rear of the house. It's either that or I jump from a second- or third-story window.

At the door to the fire escape, some instinct tells me he's been here, too. I'm right. The door won't budge. I peer into the darkness through one of the glass panels. It looks like a two-by-four has been wedged between the door and the outside railing. I run down the hall and take the stairs to the third floor. The door to the fire escape there is wedged shut, too.

There's one possibility left. Outside one of the third-floor towers there's a narrow balcony. It's only about four feet long and two wide, but it's protected by a short railing. A person could get out onto it through one of the tower windows. I might be able to drop from there to the first-floor roof, then jump to the ground.

Across the hall, the door to the tower room is locked. I remember now. This is where Mr. Cordell has stored some of his recent acquisitions. I try hitting the door with my shoulder. It's no good. The oak's too strong. So I smash the knob and lock with the poker.

Inside, the windows have been painted shut. They probably haven't been opened since before the Depression. But they're the large double-hung variety. I could fit through one easily once the glass is broken. I go back and close the door, then cover the crack at the bottom with a small carpet. When I smash the window I don't want to create an updraft like the one that killed Nick. Standing back a bit, I take a shot at the lower pane with the poker. Amazingly, nothing happens. They don't make glass this thick anymore. On the third hit it finally breaks. After several more strokes I manage to knock out most of the big pieces. It takes another minute of hammering and smashing to get rid of the small shards stuck in the frame. Then I find a small throw rug and lay it across the bottom of the window. I crawl through the opening head first, trying to brush aside the pieces of broken glass with my hands. Outside on the balcony I take a deep breath and lean back against the shingled siding.

The fire appears to have made it to the second floor. With the glare from the flames below it's hard to see much, but I think I can make out a man standing in the street. I duck down inside the alcove created by the balcony, trying to hide beneath the edge of the roof. Then I hear someone shout. The man appears to be waving at me.

" . . . fire department . . . don't worry . . . coming . . . save you. . . . "

It's old Mr. Gordon from across the street. The old coot probably saw this entire thing from the moment the flames went up.

Then I hear sirens at the end of the street.

Thank God for nosey neighbors.

THE PINES

BOOK ONE

1

DWF, THIRTY-SIX. Ambitious, strong-minded journalist; smart but cranky; imaginative in bed. Seeks someone who likes antiquing, *real* country music, canoeing in the Pines, and twilight dinners by the Mullica River. Only ex-cops need apply. Age not a problem."

"What *is*?"

"What is what?"

"A problem."

"Oh. Dishonesty, I suppose. And eating Twinkies in bed. I hate that."

It's nearly two in the morning. We're playing Gwen's favorite game, "Let's Get Personal." Each of us has to write down, then read aloud an imaginary advertisement for the personal columns. The idea is to reveal something intimate, something we especially want the other to know. Near exhaustion, I protested at first. But she was relentless, insisting it would help me calm down.

"Soup's even worse. In bed, I mean."

"I know," she says. "There's no chance of sex after you've listened to somebody slurping gazpacho."

Adjusting herself on the sofa, she moves in closer, tucking her legs underneath her. She's wearing a pair of blue cotton sweatpants and an oversized T-shirt that says DO IT IN THE COUNTRY.

"Who's that?" I nod in the direction of her CD player.

"Patsy Cline."

"I've never heard her before."

She nuzzles her cheek against my shoulder. "See, I'm educating you."

"It's okay, the part about age. But you could have left it out."

"I thought you might be concerned about it."

"I'm not."

"Bullshit."

"At least you didn't say anything about height."

"Height's never a factor . . . unless it reflects on other dimensions." She grins lasciviously. "Just kidding. Anyway, you're too conscious of it. Besides, you're only an inch shorter than I am. Maybe not even that. Anything else?"

"The 'imaginative in bed' part, I could have guessed that."

"Oh, really? How?"

"From your hands. You have the fingers of a voluptuary."

"My, aren't we smitten with our vocabulary. A voluptuary? Really?"

"You don't do drugs, do you? Bernie said I should make sure you don't do drugs."

"*Moi?* Well, I smoked pot once but I—"

"Didn't inhale. I know."

She pokes me in the ribs. "Tell Bernie to lighten up. He's going to have another heart attack. Okay, your turn."

I pick up the slip of paper I've been scribbling on and begin reading.

"Recently young WWMG. Short and cocky, one-time academic wannabe, a neoconservative at heart who always votes Democratic. Likes good jazz, baseball, modern poetry, anything Chippendale, and tall women with long straw-colored hair who laugh at the wind. Seeks brilliant up-and-coming journalist who lives alone in the woods. No vegetarians, pseudofeminists, or women who dance with the wolves. Age not a problem."

"I don't get it."

"What?"

"The first part."

"WWMG? That stands for 'widowed white male gumshoe.' "

"I knew that," she says with a straight face. "And 'recently young,' what's that mean?"

"The fire. I defied death. I'm reborn."

She takes her head off my shoulder and looks at me.

"You're serious, aren't you?"

"Very."

"Does that mean you're ready to talk about it?"

"You mean, how did it make me feel? I felt grateful you weren't there."

"But I'd have been saved, too, right? Thanks to old Mr. Gordon."

Mr. Gordon did call the fire department. Thank God for that. It's just too bad he didn't get a better look at whoever started the blaze. "He was driving one of those there whatchamacallit trucks," Gordon said afterward. "A pickup?" I asked him. "Yeah, that's it." But that's all he could remember.

"Yeah, I was lucky. By the time the fire trucks pulled up, the flames had moved past the second floor. They were heading straight for me."

"Where were you?"

"Out on a third-floor balcony. They managed to get me down in a minute or two, but it took a while longer to put the fire out."

By then the flames had burned through several walls. Somehow the frame of the house survived, but the roof over the front porch is gone. The fire chief recommended an off-duty cop to watch the place until things inside can be secured.

"And you don't have any idea who did it?"

"No. But it's a safe bet it was the same guy who killed Nick and Cappy."

"Jesus, Frank. Aren't you even a little worried?"

"Of course I am. That's why I'm here."

"But you sounded so odd on the phone. Anybody else'd be in shock. You sounded . . . I don't know . . . *pleased with yourself.*"

She's right. I *was* pleased with myself.

"It happened once before. Back in the seventies. During a bust my partner—a guy named Russ Naylor—was blown away by a real wacko. I missed taking a bullet by a millimeter, maybe less."

"Oh, Frank, that's horrible. What about your partner, was he a good friend?"

"Yeah, he was. But afterward I felt, I don't know . . . elated. It was weird. I was high for weeks. It was like I'd been given a reprieve from an execution. Death's a funny thing. You know that Woody Allen line? He said dying doesn't frighten him, it's just that he'd rather not be there when it happens. But you've got to be there, that's the point. It's the one appointment you can't miss. And today I nearly got killed again. Two resurrections in one lifetime. You can't ask for more than that."

Gwen's living room is dark, except for a faint glow from the kitchen behind us. Through the screens of her front porch, I can see a light glimmering across the river. She gets up on her knees and bends down to kiss me. I reach around and pull her on top of me. We roll off the sofa onto the carpet. The hollow at the base of her neck looks tantalizingly delicious. I bury my tongue there as my hand explores underneath her T-shirt.

She fumbles around with my belt, then unzips me.

"Frank, I had no idea."

"What can I say? It's in the genes."

"By the way, you got it wrong."

"What?"

"It's 'women who *run* with the wolves.' "

"Whatever."

SOMETHING WET IS wiggling around in my ear. I glance at my watch through a partially lifted eyelid. It's nearly four. Gwen removes her tongue.

"What'd you mean by that 'academic wannabe' stuff?"

I mutter at her to go to sleep, then turn away.

"Frank?"

"Huh."

"Answer me. Did you want to be a teacher once?"

"I *was* one once."

"You were?"

"I taught art history for two years."

"Why'd you quit?"

"I decided to become a cop."

"Oh."

She lies down, curling up behind me, her hand gently stroking the inside of my thigh.

MY EYES OPEN to the sun streaming into Gwen's bedroom. Through the sliding glass doors I can see the river and a small cottage sheltered in the pine trees on the other side. The river is alive with reflections, as if silvery fish are dancing on the surface.

"Morning, sunshine." She's standing in the doorway dressed for work, a beige and yellow sweater-vest, white oxford shirt, and linen slacks. Somehow she manages to look professional and alluring at the same time.

"Hi."

She comes over and sits on the bed. Our kiss is long and lingering.

"Oh, no you don't," she says, pulling away. "I've got to be at the office in half an hour. I'm already late."

She reaches over to the night table and gathers up the torn Trojan wrappers.

"These were my husband's, you know," she says, keeping her back to me. "Did I explain that?"

"I figured as much."

"Just didn't want you to get the wrong idea. There are still a few left. Like a thousand. Toward the end he forgot he was married. We only had sex when he hit it big. Which was never."

"What was he like?"

"I hope you don't gamble. I refuse to sleep with anyone who gambles. Jerry gambled. That's why we divorced."

"I know. You told me." Is it just sleeping together we're talking about here? "So what are your plans for today?"

"I've got to make some more calls about Capetanakis. Still don't have any confirming source besides you. My editor won't run the story unless I get at least one more. And I have to work on a follow-up piece on Sandra Greenberg."

"Busy day. You ever talk to anyone at the mission about this Greenberg kid?"

"Just Tommy the Toe."

"What do you think of him?"

"He seems harmless enough. Why?"

"No reason."

"What about you, what are you going to do today, go back to see what's left of the house?"

"I saw all I needed to last night."

"You never said how bad it was."

"It was bad, but most of the antiques are okay, except for the smoke damage. The house'll require some major structural repairs. I've got to get in touch with the Cordells and see what they want to me to do."

"Frank?"

"Yeah?"

"You sure the person who did it is the one who killed Nick and Cappy?"

"Yeah, I'm sure."

"Does he know you're here?"

"I wasn't followed, if that's what you mean. And I don't think he'd try again. It's too risky. But I think I'd better stay somewhere else tonight, just to keep you out of it."

"No, I don't want you to."

"Why not?"

"I'd feel safer if you were here, really. Please stay, okay?"

She's holding an imitation Shaker bentwood box taken from her dresser. She found it on our antiquing trip to Cape May last Sunday. I tried to talk her out of it, but she wouldn't listen. She refused to dicker over it, offering the dealer the full $85 he was asking.

"Okay," I say, still unsure.

"Good." She leans down, kisses me quickly, then moves away.

"I need to visit a library today. Where's the nearest one?"

"There's a county branch in Hammonton. What're you looking for?"

"I'm not sure yet. I'm going into my scholarly mode."

"Can I help?"

"Isn't Capetanakis enough for right now?"

She studies me a moment.

"I guess it'll have to be."

"I'll cook something for us tonight. What would you like?"

"Pizza and beer."

I frown at her.

"Sorry, Frank. You might as well know the dirty truth about me right now. I'm not the nouveau cuisine type."

"It's *nouvelle* cuisine."

"Whatever."

2

Gwen's Mullica River place is a small vacation bungalow up-graded for year-round living. It's in the southeastern portion of the Wharton State Forest, a 200,000-acre expanse of mostly pine, oak, and cedar that forms the heart of the Pine Barrens and contains, on average, fifteen people per square mile. Except for the ruins here and there of an old iron town or a nineteenth-century paper mill, the remote interior of the forest reveals no signs of industrial man. It remains a nearly pristine wilderness in the middle of the country's most densely populated state. Gwen, who grew up in Newark, talks about her Piney home with the fresh wonder of a recent arrival in paradise. She seems to feel that living here is akin to some sort of religious experience. It's her "back-to-nature" phase, she admits, but it suits her and seems genuine. Of course the Piney, whose defining characteristic is a desire to live free of the pointless distractions of modern life, has the strongest feeling for the timelessness of the woods. People like Virgil Applegate understand the passing of the seasons and know how to accommodate themselves to the cyclical rhythms of death and rebirth. For them there's less a sense of the present or the future than there is of the past repeating itself over and over again. Even for an outsider it's easy in the Pines to imagine you've somehow found your way back to the "first day." My Mr. Jaffee would have appreciated that.

On the way to Hammonton, about fifteen miles from Gwen's on the southwestern border of the forest, I leave the windows down to let the scents of cedar and pitch pine fill the car. But it's another arid

April morning, and the expected springtime aromas are in short supply. Instead, there's a hint of dry decay in the air, as if spring and summer have stepped aside to make way for early autumn. It's windless, too. A young girl on a Sailfish sits motionless in the middle of the river, waiting for a breath of air to catch her sail.

The county library is a flat, rambling contemporary brick structure that could pass for a modern medical clinic or an office complex. Inside, I ask to see the index for the *Atlantic City Star.* The reference librarian directs me to a small reading room in the back.

The rolls of microfilm are labeled and filed in flat, wide drawers in a cabinet in the rear of the room. I take out the ones I want, insert the first roll of film in a reader, and scroll forward to the year 1977. The name "Henry Bass" doesn't appear. It is, as expected, listed for 1978, referencing the sale of the Ocean View Motel. But from 1979 on there are no further listings of his name. Which is not surprising considering the man moved to New York after selling the motel. Just to be safe I check the Atlantic City telephone book at the pay phone out front. No Henry Bass.

At the reference desk I inquire about listings of attorneys by state.

"We have one directory, but I'm afraid it's not current," says Mr. Luro, a tall, emaciated red-headed man of about thirty-five.

"What year is it?"

"Here, follow me."

He leads me to a row of metal shelves containing the library's basic reference collection. I follow him down the fourth aisle.

"Here it is," Luro says, pointing, "it's 1991."

It's something called the *Martindale–Hubbell Law Directory.* Thirteen thick volumes listing all the attorneys practicing in the United States. It's daunting, not to mention depressing, to realize that one country can support this many lawyers.

"Won't hurt to look," I say. "Thanks."

I take down Volume 9, for New York. The "New York, New York" section is by far the largest, Manhattan appearing to have more lawyers per block than any other city in the world. There are seven Basses and Henry R. is right there among them.

The legend at the front of the book explains all the numbers. Bass was born in 1934, first admitted to the bar in 1961, and received his B.S. from Rutgers and his law degree from NYU. At the time of this publication he was a member of the law firm of Turner & Frye.

There's also a professional biographies section, comprising the largest portion of the directory. Henry Bass is listed under the firm of Turner & Frye.

> HENRY R. BASS born Trenton, New Jersey, February 19, 1934; admitted to bar, 1961, New Jersey; 1977, New York.
> *Education:* Rutgers College (B.S., Accounting, 1958), New York University (J.D., 1961). Seminar panelist, New York City Center for Legal Education: "Analysis of a Chapter 11 Case," 1988; "Administering Chapter 13 Cases," 1985; and "Dealing with Powers of Trustees," 1984. Chairman, Governor's Task Force on the Future of Legal Education in New York State, 1990.
> *Member:* Association of the Bar of the City of New York; New Jersey, New York State and American Bar Associations; Bankruptcy Lawyers Bar Association; New York Lawyers Association; National Association of Bankruptcy Trustees; Commercial Law League of America; and American Bankruptcy Institute. *Specializing in Bankruptcy and Commercial Law.*

Henry Bass, Esq., expert in bankruptcy law, is looking more and more interesting. I take the book to the Xerox machine and make a copy of the entry.

Bass must be something of a presence in New York legal circles. Not just anyone gets appointed by the governor to chair a statewide task force. For a prestigious assignment like that he might well have made *The New York Times.*

The *Times Index* is kept on three shelves above a library table in the back of the reading room. I take down the volume for 1990, look under the "B's," and there he is.

> **Bass, Henry. See also**
> Governor, State of New York—Task Force on Future of Legal Education Je 26,22:6

At the citation under "Governor, State of New York" I find a more detailed description.

Governor, State of New York—Task Force on Future of Legal Education
Governor, responding to a recommendation by state law-school deans, appoints fifteen-person task force to study the future of legal education in New York. Task Force will focus on legal needs in the twenty-first century; photo. (M) Je 26,22:6.

Back at the microfilm files I retrieve the *Times* film for June 15–30, 1990. It takes a minute or two to fast-forward to the June 26 issue. When I reach the first page I slow down, inching my way along to page 22. There it is, a two-column headline announcing the appointment of the governor's task force. But it's the accompanying photograph that captures my attention. With the state seal behind him, a smiling governor stands between two men. The man on his right is a prominent law-school dean. It's the image of the third man that jumps off the screen at me. His hairline's a little fuller than when I saw him last, but he has the same pencil-thin mustache, shark's fin nose, and bushy eyebrows he did when he stood across the roulette table from Nick at the Poseidon two weeks ago. It's the elusive "Jonah Smith." The caption under the photograph says he's Henry R. Bass, "senior partner in the law firm of Turner & Frye and legal expert in the field of bankruptcy law." I put a quarter in the microfilm reader and make a copy of the photograph.

"*STAR*, GWEN OLIN speaking."
  "Gwen? It's Frank."
  "Hi there, lover, how are you?"
  "Good. You?"
  "Not bad. Been thinking about you."
  "Nothing naughty, I hope."
  "Nothing but."
  "Slow news day, huh?"

"Don't underestimate yourself."

"It's unseemly for a man my age to be the object of a young woman's fantasies."

"Hey, fella, don't complain."

"Good point. Tell me, do you have time to check something for me with that colleague of yours? You know, Germaine, the one doing the series on the Poseidon's bankruptcy."

"George? Sure. He's just across the room. What is it?"

"Ask him the name of Tony Dante's bankruptcy lawyer? See if it's a certain Henry Bass."

"You mean the guy who was a partner with Morrow in the Ocean View?"

"That's the one."

"Now that would be interesting. Hold on. I'll check."

It takes her a minute. While she's away from the phone I study the material on Bass that I photocopied from the *Law Directory*.

"Frank?"

"Yeah."

"Sorry. No such luck. George says Dante has a whole team of lawyers for the case. Six to be precise. No one named Bass among them."

"Damn."

"Yeah, sounded like you were onto something. Say, what're you doing for lunch?"

"Sorry. I've got a full day ahead of me. I've barely gotten started. See you for pizza and beer tonight, right?"

"Damn straight. And don't be late."

"GOOD MORNING, Turner and Frye, attorneys at law. May I help you?"

"Yes, my name's Frank Sweeney. I'm trying to locate a man named Henry Bass. He was listed with your firm back in 1991. I wonder if he's still there?"

"Mr. Bass, oh no. He's no longer with the firm."

"Could you tell me where I can find him?"

"Let me have you talk to our office manager, Mr. Hobart."

After a short delay, Mr. Hobart comes on.

"May I help you?"

"Yes, my name's Frank Sweeney. I'm trying to find a former member of your law firm, Mr. Henry Bass."

"May I inquire as to what it's about?"

"I need some legal advice. He was highly recommended to me."

"I see. Well, I don't know if he can help, but I'll give you his new number."

It's getting interesting. Bass's telephone number has a south Jersey area code.

A PLEASANT-SOUNDING female answers the phone. She's young, a little unsure of herself.

"Federal Building, may I help you?"

An image surfaces in my memory again. A name buried at the bottom of an article on bankruptcy in the *Wall Street Journal.* Is it possible?

"I'm sorry, but I'm not sure I've dialed the right number. What city is this?"

"Camden, sir."

She sounds irritated.

"Camden?"

"That's right. How may I direct your call?"

"I'd like to speak with a Mr. Henry Bass."

"Just a second, please."

There's a wait, then another voice comes on, this one older, more confident.

"Bankruptcy Court, Mrs. Ogden. May I help you?"

"Is this the office of Henry Bass?"

"This is the office of *Judge* Bass, yes. What may I do for you?"

"*Judge* Bass?"

"That's right, sir," says Mrs. Ogden. "But the judge is out of town. What is it you wanted?"

The last piece has fallen into place.

"Mrs. Ogden, I'm a reporter with the *Linwood Bugle*. I just want to confirm who the judge is in the Poseidon bankruptcy case."

"That would be Judge Bass. He's presiding in the Poseidon case. Is there a problem?"

3

Nick, busted, out of work, and reduced to the bitter equality of mission life, must have thought it too good to be true when he went to table 11 at the Poseidon that night and confirmed what Cappy'd told him. Across the table was a man—someone he might well have recognized from his years of working in Camden—chasing his losses with five-hundred- and thousand-dollar bets much like the mindless steamer Nick himself was. He would have appreciated the judge's dilemma, even sympathized, while envying him the resources he had to throw at his problem. There's a sense of brotherhood among degenerate gamblers, just as there is among the sick on a hospital ward. It can be heartening to witness the way in which others are locked in the jaws of their disease, comforting to find your own misery reflected in their angry eyes. But Nick would hardly have been interested in having the judge share his pain. The judge was going to be his ticket out of the mission and back to the action.

So how'd Nick play it? Did he approach Bass and try to shake him down, threatening to go public with the fact that a federal bankruptcy judge had been discovered gambling at the very casino whose future he would be deciding in the weeks ahead? Or did he take the only other option (it never would have occurred to Nick to play the dutiful citizen and report the incident to the Casino Control Commission or to someone in the federal court system) and come at it from the opposite direction, blackmailing one of the higher-ups at the casino?

No matter which path out of his personal hell Nick chose, I'd bet a handful of Poseidon wheel chips that ultimately it led him to Tony

Dante. Dante, whose employees have been breaking federal law by allowing Henry Bass, aka Jonah Smith, to submit false information on their Currency Transaction Report forms, had to have been in on the scam. No one could have pulled it off without his knowledge and consent. Dante's a bungler, an incompetent, but he's the kind who trusts nobody, who has to know everything his underlings are doing. And his people would have been too terrified of him to try it on their own, having little to gain from it anyway. Besides, the Jonah scam is stupid. It lacks class. It has Tony Dante's name written all over it. The scam must have seemed just right to a mind like Dante's. It was cheap, especially given the level of Bass's losses, and effective, an arrangement that gave Bass what he most needed, anonymous access to a roulette table, in return for a little friendly consideration in bankruptcy court. Add in Cappy's money-laundering scheme, and Dante with his two Jonahs must have figured those trusty instincts of his ought to be bronzed for posterity.

Then Nick met Cappy and everything began to unravel.

But why would Cappy have risked letting Nick in on the scam in the first place? Didn't he realize the threat to his own scheme? Given the fact that he was drunk when he told Nick about Bass, maybe he never gave it a thought. Still, I have to suspect his motives. Was he repaying Nick for saving his life, or was he getting even with someone? Had Bass screwed him somehow, maybe overturned one of his business deals? Or had something gone sour between him and Dante? Whatever it was, Cappy, like Nick, overreached himself. The knife of vengeance cuts both ways.

The biggest question remains: who is this pyrofreak who gets his kicks burning people alive? And how long before he goes after the judge, especially now that he's on the run?

MRS. OGDEN TURNED out to be very helpful, once I assured her of my good intentions. Although the judge was unavailable—"called away for a few days by an emergency"—she sounded a note of loyal concern that half-suggested she needed someone to talk to. The life of a bankruptcy judge must be stressful, I responded, my voice dripping with empathy, what with having to make financial decisions affecting the lives of thousands, maybe millions, of people. Yes, she responded, it's hard on all of us. And his family, I said, they must be feeling it too. Yes, Mrs. Ogden sighed, Mrs. Bass is a saint. Now there's a human interest story, I replied, how might I get in touch with the judge's devoted wife?

AT THE BASS RESIDENCE in Cherry Hill, the maid answers the phone. The judge, she says, is out of town. When I reply that it's urgent, she agrees to call Mrs. Bass to the phone. Waiting, I can hear her shoes click-clacking their way across a marble floor. Then an excited voice in the distance, followed by the hurried sounds of someone rushing to pick up the receiver.

"Dr. Ludlow, is that you?" she says.

Her voice is raised expectantly. I decide to take a chance. I was going to lie anyway. I might as well do it big-time. Taking a deep breath, I summon up my best professional voice: understanding but slightly distant.

"No, Mrs. Bass, this is Dr. Sweeney. Dr. Ludlow's been called away on an emergency. He thought maybe I could help."

I just hope Dr. Ludlow's not her gynecologist. There are limits to my ingenuity.

"Dr. Sweeney? I've never heard of you."

"I'm new to the area. Dr. Ludlow's helping me get my practice started."

"He's not planning to retire, is he?"

"No, nothing like that. Now what can I do? Dr. Ludlow had to rush. He didn't have a chance to fill me in."

There's a long silence on the other end. The sound of her breathing increases, as if she's using the telephone for a respirator.

"Mrs. Bass? What is it?"

"I think I need something. I can't handle it anymore. Can you prescribe some tranquilizers? Maybe Valium or something?"

"Why don't you tell me what the problem is first?"

"I'm worried. My husband's never gone off like this before. I'm afraid he's . . . "

"You're afraid of what, Mrs. Bass?"

"I'm afraid he's going to . . . kill himself."

"What makes you say that, Mrs. Bass?"

Another silence, this time with whimpering.

"He did something. I don't know what it was, but he's in trouble, I can tell. He owes a lot of money. People keep calling. What am I supposed to tell them? He took most of my money. What am I going to do? He's been gone two days now. Suppose he never comes back, then what? How am I supposed to live? Oh, doctor, I need something."

"All right, now, try to calm yourself. Take a deep breath, then we'll talk."

There's no response, but the breathing on the other end seems to slow.

"Mrs. Bass, are you breathing deeply?"

"Yes."

"Good. Now tell me, did you notify the police?"

"Good heavens, no. My husband's an important man, he—"

"I understand. Where do you think he went?"

"I don't know."

"You don't have any idea?"

"No. There were a bunch of phone calls, then he left."

"What kind of car is he driving?"

"He took *my* car. The Jeep Grand Cherokee. He gave it to me for my birthday."

"Did he take anything with him besides money and the Jeep?"

"His shotgun. That's why I'm so worried. He never takes his shotgun with him except during deer season."

"Is he a hunter, Mrs. Bass?"

She laughs. "Henry? No, he just goes to drink and play cards. Far as I know, he's never even used that gun."

"Where is it he goes to drink and play cards?"

"I don't know. Someplace in the woods, I think. Why are you asking all these questions, anyway?"

"It's always helpful to get the full background on a patient, Mrs. Bass."

"Well, Dr. Ludlow, he never— wait, there's another call. It might be Henry. Can you hold?"

"Of course."

I hear a click on the line as she transfers to the incoming caller. When she comes back on, the tone of her voice has changed.

"Dr. Sweeney? I've got Dr. Ludlow on the other line and he says he doesn't know you. Who'd you say you were?"

"Dr. Ludlow? Did you say Dr. *Ludlow*? I'm sorry, I thought you said Dr. *Ludwig*. My mistake."

With that I hang up.

4

It's nearly noon when I get off the phone with Max Hartwick, the Cordells' insurance agent in Philadelphia. We've agreed on a contractor to handle the repairs, as well as a dealer to come and assess the damage to the antiques. Hartwick himself is going to talk to the Ocean County fire inspector. Earlier I called Moira Burnes, a young attorney in the firm of Haskins & Cray. She's my liaison to the Cordells while they're in Europe. Moira was not amused by what I had to tell her, having opposed the idea of me using the house in the first place. She did say the Cordells are somewhere in the Italian Alps and unreachable for now. So any confrontation with them can be put off a while.

Sitting in the car, with my favorite Benny Carter tape playing, I sip a cup of black coffee and consider my options. There are precious few of them. The only certainty is that I have to find Henry Bass before he does himself in. Or someone does it for him. It may be too late. But Bass is all I've got. He's the weak link, the one most likely to turn against the others.

All morning my mind kept returning to last Thursday. There I was, standing across from Lucy the Elephant, waiting for Cappy. How was it I didn't know Lucy had once been moved? Had I failed to make a connection between the dozens of isolated facts I've collected over the years? The fact is, for all my research I didn't go far enough back. *Every story has a beginning. You must go back to the first day.* Perhaps to find Judge Bass I need to go back to the beginning, too. Right now it's all I've got.

IT TAKES FOUR phone calls to learn that Sandy Maclean is now Assistant Division Fire Warden. His office is in Batsto, but today's his day off. An understanding secretary gives me directions to his home in Atsion.

After stopping off for a Big Mac and coffee, I drive north out of Hammonton on Route 206, back into the Wharton State Forest. I'm on a one-lane blacktop that takes me past fields of blueberry bushes, boarded-up farmer's markets, and scrub pine as far as the eye can see. At the Atsion Recreational Area I take the road toward Atco. Here it's all tall pines and oaks. Maclean is supposed to run a tree farm somewhere along this road. Just past the Mill Run Deer Club, a white one-story stucco building, I see the sign. I pull off the road into a gravel driveway, coast past a two-story farm house, and park in the back next to a bunch of rusty farm implements.

In the distance a man is working in a field of scotch pines. He begins walking this way.

"Mr. Maclean?"

"Yeah?"

"I wonder if I could have a few minutes of your time? My name's Frank Sweeney. I'm a private investigator from Philadelphia."

I show him my ID. He takes a long look before returning it to me.

"Okay, I guess. What do you want?"

"I'm looking into a murder that resulted from a forest fire somewhere around here. It was back in 1977. Your name was mentioned at the time as a spokesman for the fire service."

"It was that charcoal pit fire, right? July 1977. Arson. Two men killed. Two hundred-and-fifty acres burned. Took two days to get it under control."

"That's the one. Apparently you remember it."

"You're the second person in two weeks to ask me about it."

"Oh?"

"Yeah, some policeman stopped by a couple of weeks ago. Told him what I knew and showed him the spot where the fire began."

"A policeman?"

"Yeah. He wasn't in a uniform though. He was in plain clothes."

"Was his name D'Angelo?"

"Yeah, that's it. You know him?"

"I used to. I wonder if you could tell me whatever it was you told him?"

"No problem. Actually, I took him to the place where the fire started."

"I'd like that, too. Would you mind?"

"Not at all. I never miss a chance to talk about a forest fire. Give me a minute, I'll go clean up."

He's a tall, overly thin man in his late fifties, wearing a gray, sweat-soaked T-shirt and dirty jeans that he has to hitch up several times on his way into the house. When he comes out he has on a fresh long-sleeve blue shirt and a clean pair of jeans.

"How do you want to do this?" he asks. "I've got to go into town for some tools. You want to follow me? That way when we're finished I can just go my own way."

"Sounds good to me."

I fall in with the Rover behind his green Ford pickup, and we head back in the direction of Route 206.

IT's A SANDY CLEARING, surrounded by a wall of pines, oaks, and cedars. At one point there's a break in the tree wall, revealing a swamp fifty yards in the distance. I'm standing on the edge of a small mound about thirty feet across which, according to Maclean, is the charcoal pit where Harry Morrow met his end back in 1977.

"This is actually the spot where the fire started?"

Maclean looks at me as if I've questioned his manhood.

"Takes more than eighteen years for something like this to disappear in the Pines, Mr. Sweeney. This spot was used regularly for coaling until those murders. After that nobody touched it. You poke around in that sand you'll probably find some of the charred wood from the fire."

"Okay, I believe you."

"Fire index was pretty high that day," he says, kicking at the base of dry pine needles and brush along the edge of the clearing. "Just like now. See, ground here's so dry it won't hardly hold any water. Turns the woods into a tinderbox. We'd been worried that July. You get so you expect a fire sometimes. Of course, nobody expected murder."

"How bad was the fire?"

"Like I said, a few hundred acres. I've seen a lot worse under those conditions. We were lucky, considering. There've been some blazing sons of bitches in these woods, though. Nineteen sixty-three was the worst. Blacktop on the roads was bubbling, the fire was so hot. Damn near jumped the parkway and burned its way to the ocean. I wasn't here then. But people still talk about it."

"How long have you lived here?"

"Moved here in '76. I was born up north near Morristown, but I liked it down here so much I just moved in and looked for work. One day after a forest fire I decided to sign up. I hated what that fire had done. I just love these woods, I guess. I love fire, too. That's the strange thing."

"And you were one of the investigators back in '77 who discovered the arson?"

"I was. I was the one who first spotted the gasoline. The arson people from the city didn't seem much interested. In fact, nobody ever seemed much interested in that case. I don't know that they ever solved those murders."

"They didn't. And what about the ignition device, did you spot that, too?"

"How'd you know about that?"

"I've seen the police report."

"Really? Well, then you must know the right people. Yeah, I spotted it."

"What'd you make of it?"

"Over the years I've seen a few like it. Some used plain old electrical wire wound around a matchbook. That's the only one I've ever seen that used solder."

"So you haven't seen one like it since then?"

"Nope."

"What else can you tell me about the investigation?"

"Not much to tell. County cops came in and took over. After that hardly anything happened."

"Did you have any dealings with the detective in charge? His name was Jack Coyle."

"I remember him. Soon as he came on the scene I was sent packing. Guess he didn't like me. Didn't much like him either."

"Why not?"

"He was careless."

"What do you mean?"

"The *habenaria integra*. He walked all over it."

"I don't understand."

"We've got dozens of different kinds of orchids growing in these woods, Mr. Sweeney. That man Coyle managed to tromp all over one of our rarest. The man never looked where he was going. Real unfortunate trait for a homicide detective to have, if you ask me."

Maclean looks angry. His eyes challenge me to demonstrate that I'm not like Coyle.

"During the investigation were there any theories about why Harry Morrow was murdered?"

"Not that I recall. I never heard of the man until that day. Ain't never heard him mentioned since then either."

"What about the other man who was killed? I understand they never identified him. Even dental records were useless."

"That's right. They said he probably got in the killer's way. I suppose that's possible but it's real sick, if you ask me."

"Do you have any idea who he might have been?"

"I hadn't lived here long enough in '77 to know many people in the woods. But I have a theory."

"What's that?"

"Some people around here are hermits, Mr. Sweeney. They don't see more than two or three people in a year, if that, and ain't none of them dentists, either. A man like that, he wouldn't have no dental records. No, my guess is it was probably someone nobody'd heard from in years. That's why nobody'd know if he was missing."

"Hasn't there ever been any mention of someone missing?"

He shakes his head. "Your native Pineys are real close. They don't like outsiders. Me, I'm *still* a transplant to some of them. I only arrived nineteen years ago." He grins at his own joke. "If they knew somebody was missing they wouldn't have told me about it, not back then. They wouldn't have gone to the police either. Nobody 'round here much trusts the police."

This is getting me nowhere, but I nod and smile anyway. I wish I had the time to stay and talk more. It's tranquil here. I feel relaxed for the first time in days. Perhaps that's why I'm having trouble making the imaginative leap to that day in 1977 when this small clearing saw the beginning of a 250-acre forest fire.

"Okay, Mr. Maclean, I want to thank you for your time."

"Don't you want to see the Sooys?"

"The what?"

"The Sooys. I took that Lieutenant D'Angelo to meet them. You said you wanted me to tell you everything I told him."

"Who are the Sooys?"

"Come on, I'll introduce you."

5

I SHOULD EXPLAIN before you meet them," Maclean says, as we walk in the direction of our cars. "The daughter's name is Ruth. She's been deaf since birth, but she signs and she reads lips. So if you want to talk to her you'll have to speak slowly or go through old Joe. Joe's her father. He's real protective. She's lived here all her life. As far as I know she's never left the house without him."

"Were they questioned after the fire?"

"From what I've picked up over the years, it sounds as if one of

Coyle's men might have stopped by and asked a few questions. But Joe kept Ruth away from it all. I doubt if any of the cops even knew she existed."

"How old would she have been then?"

He thinks a moment.

"Joe told me last month that she'll be thirty-three this June. What's that make her back in '77? Around thirteen or fourteen, I guess. Old Joe's past seventy, I know that. The mother's not around anymore. She ran off after Ruth was born. Couldn't handle the thought of raising a child late in life, not to mention a deaf one. No one's seen her since. Old Joe, he never talks about her."

"And you told all this to D'Angelo when he was here?"

"Pretty much, yeah."

"What'd he say?"

"He was real interested. I took him to meet Joe, but I don't know what came of it. Haven't spoken with Joe since then."

We retrace our steps down the narrow sand road. It leads through the woods away from the charcoal pit and exits out onto the dirt lane where Maclean's pickup and my Range Rover are parked. According to a faded sign a quarter of a mile back, this dirt lane is called Joe's Road. The Sooys' house, a handsome log cabin nestled back in the trees, sits on the other side of the road across from where we're parked. Decorative maroon trim has been added to the cabin's rustic exterior, and the caulking between the logs has been highlighted with white paint. The entire road is surrounded by thick woods on both sides. There's not another house in sight.

We cross the road to the Sooys' gravel yard. I can see someone, a woman, sitting at the front window. When I look at her she darts back behind the curtains. Maclean leads me past a propane gas tank on the side of the house and around to the back.

"Old Joe prefers visitors to use the back," he says. "If you knock at the front he won't answer."

"Why's that?"

"He can get a better look at you from back here," he says, taking the three steps to the door, then knocking. "He's a little fearful, likes to check you out real good before he opens the door."

After a few seconds the curtains part in a window to the right of the door. Old Joe studies us. Finally, the door opens a crack, and a pair of eyes look us over.

"That you, Sandy?"

"It's me, Joe. I've brought someone to meet you. He'd like to talk. You got a minute?"

"You vouch for him?"

"I'll vouch for him, Joe."

The door opens and we step into the kitchen.

"My Lord but that smells good," I say. The aroma of apples and cinnamon mixes with freshly brewed coffee.

"Spent all morning on that strudel," says Joe, grinning proudly. "Maybe you'd like to join me." Stooped over, he looks at Maclean, then me. His ancient face, brown from years of working outside, is a topographical map, full of rivulets and spiky estuaries.

"I'd be delighted," I say, realizing how hungry I am.

Joe turns and shuffles over to a small alcove for some cups and plates.

Maclean smiles at me. "You said the right thing. He loves to bake."

Joe returns and places three plates and mugs on the kitchen table. Then he brings the strudel and coffee over from the top of the stove.

"This here's Frank Sweeney, Joe," says Maclean, taking a seat. "He's a private investigator."

Joe looks in my direction. I take a seat and bide my time. The strudel is magnificent.

"You must make your own dough," I say. "This is too good to come ready-made."

Joe nods, but his eyes give him away. He's pleased at my approval. I sip some coffee and look around. Several oil paintings hang on the wall next to the sink. Two are Pine Barrens scenes done on bread-boards. One's a deer standing in a clearing. The other's a duck caught in midair by birdshot from the gun of a hunter sitting in a sneakbox. Both have been done in a flat, two-dimensional style without any per-spective or foreshortening to provide depth. The details of the deer, the duck, and the hunter's outfit are wonderfully rich and precise. There's also a rendition of DaVinci's *The Last Supper*, which includes one white-haired apostle at the end of the table who looks suspiciously like Old Joe. The painting has been draped with a colorful handmade quilt.

"You do those?" I ask Joe, nodding at the paintings.

"Nope. Ruth's the artist in this family. Ruth's the artist." Then silence. We resume sipping our coffee.

The cabin's small, but feels roomy and comfortable. There's a pantry off to the right and, adjoining the kitchen, a small living room. From here I can see the front window where daughter Ruth observes whatever comings and goings there are on a back road in the middle of the Pines.

"Mr. Sweeney's looking into the murders from the charcoal pit fire," says Maclean.

"Like that last fella was here?" Sooy asks.

"Yes, like him," I say. "Nick D'Angelo was a friend of mine."

"That Lieutenant D'Angelo, he had a way about him. A real smooth talker."

That's never been one of Nick's strong points. I guess when the prize is big enough, even he was capable of rising above his limitations.

"What did Nick ask you about?"

"Oh, he wanted to know about the day of the fire."

"Were you and your daughter here that day?"

"I was here, yes. I was here all right."

"And your daughter?"

I glance into the living room at the chair situated by the front window. He stares into his coffee mug, studying a piece of congealed cream on the surface.

"It's okay, Joe," says Maclean. "It's been twenty years. Time to stop worrying. Time to talk. Mr. Sweeney's not here to harm Ruth."

"I told your friend everything there was," Sooy says to me. "Isn't that enough? Ought to be enough."

"Nick D'Angelo's been murdered. I'm trying to find his killer."

He puts his mug down abruptly and begins to get up from the table. "I always knew that business wasn't over. I knew it. I just knew it."

"Well, you were right. Whoever started that fire in 1977 is still at

223

it. Only now he's doing his killing in Atlantic City."

He sits back down and looks at me. "A little burning would be good for that place. Cleanse it. Purify it. Bible says 'every man's work shall be revealed by fire.'"

"This is murder we're talking about, Mr. Sooy."

His head bobs up and down quickly. "And it's evil ways I'm talking about, Mr. Sweeney, evil ways."

"I'd like your help. Can't you just tell me what you told Nick?"

"Look what it did for him. Got him killed, that's what it did. What about me and Ruth, what'll happen to us?" His voice trembles a little.

"Nothing's going to happen to either of you if we catch this killer. But we need your help for that."

"You saying you work for the police then?"

"No, I'm only a private investigator."

That seems to reassure him. "Don't want nothing more to do with the police, nothing to do with them." He pauses a moment. "You knew this Lieutenant D'Angelo well?"

"His brother is my best friend."

He nods understandingly.

"Friendship's the best bond there is. Next to family, of course."

"Of course."

He studies me a moment, then says, "What do you want to know?"

"For starters, what happened here that day twenty years ago?"

"We was damn lucky that day, damn lucky. Wind was blowing the other way. Otherwise this here cabin woulda gone up with the rest of the woods. That son of a bitch almost killed me and my Ruth."

"Did you see anything?"

"Nothing. I was sick to bed with the sinus. Sick with the sinus. Can't hardly stand up when it gets bad. 'Course, I *had* to get up once we seen how bad the fire was. Then we got on outa here. Got right on outa here. We got outa here then."

"What about your daughter, Mr. Sooy? Did she see anything?"

He ponders this for a long time, then stands up slowly and turns toward the living room. Maclean and I follow him. The room is sparsely furnished with two tattered recliners, a TV, a coffee table showing the nicks and dents of a lifetime's use, and Ruth's straight-backed chair by the window. Along the front wall under the window is a low bookshelf made of unfinished pine boards. I can see a sketchbook there, along with some colored pencils.

The lack of furnishings serves to draw attention to Ruth's paintings. These number several dozen, hanging on the walls and propped up along the floorboards. Most are scenes from the pinewoods—ducks, deer, and snapping turtles in their natural habitats; migrant workers picking blueberries; and flooded cranberry bogs in the rich blood-red hues of the autumn harvest. But several have a fantastic quality to them. In one, the eyes of several animals peer out of the trees at what I take to be an angel tending a smoking charcoal pit. In another, a young woman asleep on a bed of pine needles seems to be dreaming while several strange creatures—one with the body of a deer and the head of a fox, another a songbird with the webbed feet of a duck—watch from the nearby underbrush. Several feature the Sooy cabin, including Old Joe sitting out front in an aluminum lawn chair. In two there are pickup trucks driving by on Joe's Road. A few have religious subjects. One depicts a haloed Jesus hovering above a cedar swamp like an alien who just descended from a UFO. Most of the paintings, like those in the kitchen, have been done on pieces of old scrap wood—cedar planks or pine posts—or on laminated breadboards. Everything is flat, decorative, two-dimensional, and stunningly detailed. All told, it's one of the most remarkable collections of folk painting I've ever seen in one room.

"Is all this your daughter's work?" I ask, moving up close to look at a full frontal depiction of a young girl in baggy overalls holding a Raggedy Ann doll in a smudged hand.

"She's the artist in the family," says Joe, behind me, "she's the artist."

"Has she ever studied art?"

"Nope. Learned it all herself."

When I turn around she's standing in the hallway that leads to the bedrooms. Her appearance makes her look older than thirty-three. She's in a frumpy red-print dress and shabby black sandals. Her long brown hair is tied back with a simple ribbon and in need of brushing. But the vibrant blue eyes and unassuming smile make up for everything else.

Old Joe signs something to her but she ignores him. He stands back, glaring at me. I walk over to her and she accepts my outstretched hand, averting her eyes at the last minute.

"I like your work very much," I say, trying to enunciate each sound carefully. She smiles, then nods.

"I'd like to ask what you know about the fire across the road, the one back in 1977." I turn, pointing toward the woods.

Her eyes go to her father, who looks increasingly helpless. After a long pause, something transpires between them and she begins signing.

"She wants to know if the man who was here is your friend," says Joe.

"I knew him, but not well," I say to her. "His brother is my good friend. That's why I'm here."

Old Joe interprets for me. "She says he was a nice man. He listened to her."

"I understand," I say to her.

Then she turns and disappears into a room at the end of the hall.

"I guess she's going to show you more," says Joe, in a tone that suggests he's washed his hands of the whole business. "I didn't tell her what happened to the other man who was here. That would upset her. She knows you're his friend. That's enough."

I nod my agreement. After a minute or so she returns with a large cardboard box with the top cut off. It holds half-a-dozen paintings sitting upright. She places the box on the coffee table and retreats to her spot in the hallway.

I pull the paintings out of the box and lay them on the floor. Unlike the others, these have been done on canvas. Each one appears to be a depiction of the charcoal pit fire as viewed from the Sooys' cabin. It doesn't take long to arrange them in chronological sequence. The first one shows the woods and the sand road across the way. Above the trees, sparks fly in all directions, as if fireworks had been touched off back in the woods somewhere. On the next canvas, flames depicted as red tongues have appeared above the trees. In the third composition, the woods are ready to explode with the intensity of the growing blaze. The next shows fire trucks and emergency vehicles arriving on Joe's Road. Then men with axes and hoses are shown standing at the entrance to the sand road, the sky black now with soot and flying debris. The last canvas presents the fire's aftermath. It's a view of the clearing and what was left of the smoldering charcoal pit. Four men, two in fire turnout gear, two in plain clothes, stand at the edge of the pit, staring at the embers.

I walk myself through the sequence of paintings one more time, looking for something, anything. Then I feel a tap on the shoulder. It's Ruth, holding one more canvas.

The fire in this one has developed beyond that in painting number one, but hasn't reached the "red tongues" stage depicted in number three. It shows the same view of the sand road and woods, but there's something new in this one. A white panel truck heads away from the fire, down Joe's Road toward the county blacktop, the rear wheels spraying dirt and gravel. On the side of the truck, in large black letters, out of proportion to the size of the vehicle itself, are the words, JERSEY SHORE TRUCKING.

"Did you see the driver of the truck?" I ask her.

She shakes her head, no.

"What about Nick D'Angelo, did he see this painting?"

She glances at her father first, then nods an emphatic yes.

"Anyone besides him?"

"No," says Joe.

"Not even the police?"

He shakes his head. "Especially not them."

"What about the men killed in the fire? Do either of you know who they were?"

"We don't know anything about that," says Joe, quickly, as if he's been expecting the question. He gathers up the paintings and puts them in the cardboard box. Apparently, my time is up.

On the way out the door with Maclean, I offer to put Ruth in touch with a Philadelphia dealer who specializes in folk art.

"He's trustworthy and fair," I say. "You wouldn't have to do anything. He'd want to come down here and look at your work. If he likes it he'd offer to sell it for you. I can assure you it would be a fair price."

Joe will have nothing to do with the idea. But Ruth, I can tell, is less dubious. This results in an extended conversation, filled with a number of intense signs and gestures, particularly on Old Joe's part.

"She says 'no,' " Old Joe reports, after several minutes. "We think they should stay here."

That's too bad. Ruth Sooy may never have the chance to learn just how good she is. And she *is* good. Over the years I bought a number of Pennsylvania Dutch folk-art paintings for Catherine. I know what's good and what isn't. But maybe Ruth and Old Joe don't want outsiders in this silent world of theirs. Maybe they don't even care about the money. I can understand that. I'd even prefer it that way. It fits my sense of the innocence of this place. Still, as I'm following Maclean out the door, I jot down the name and phone number of the dealer and place the slip of paper on their kitchen table. Just in case.

6

I TRY THE COUNTY library again. But Jersey Shore Trucking isn't in any of the south Jersey telephone books. Either the company's no longer in existence or its name has been changed.

"Yeah, we've got some old telephone books downstairs," says Mr. Luro, in answer to my question, "but I'm not sure they go back to 1977."

He picks up the phone and punches a number on the intercom.

"Laura, do we still have those old phone books in the basement archives? Yeah. Really? Okay, thanks."

He hangs up, then comes out from behind his desk.

"Seems we have them for as far back as 1970 but only for Atlantic County. Want me to see if we have one from 1977? It'll take a while. They're all packed away in boxes."

"I'd appreciate it very much."

He disappears into the back of the building, and I head for the vending machines in the lobby. Outside, a cup of black coffee in hand, I find a place on the grass where I can stretch out and think. What I'm wondering is why Nick spent so much time investigating a twenty-year-old murder case when Cappy had already given him more than enough to use against Bass or Dante. He wasn't the crusader type. Nick had more important things to concern himself with, like his own survival. He would have wanted enough money to get back into action, that's all. So what was he doing out here in the Pines playing detective?

Mr. Luro's standing in the doorway waving at me. He's clutching a telephone book as if he just unearthed a rare first edition.

The book turns out to be valuable indeed. It's the 1977 Yellow Pages, and there's a listing for Jersey Shore Trucking. The address is 1710 Commerce Highway, Hammonton.

FOLLOWING MR. LURO'S directions I find Commerce Highway on the south side of town, just past the Hammonton Water Company. The few commercial buildings out this way are well dispersed, separated by acres of farmland and untended fields. I get my bearings at Havens Electronics, whose roadside address identifies its street number as 1550. A quarter of a mile later there's a large sign for Atlantic Coast Trucking, and a smaller one underneath that says PROPANE TANKS FILLED HERE. It's a two-story box-like affair with a flat roof, surrounded by half an acre of blacktop. The first floor features a truck repair bay and an office, while the second appears to include living quarters. Around back there's a small shed and a large fenced-in propane tank. Out front the lot's filled with trailer hitches and a dozen or more vehicles, ranging from one medium-sized van with a refrigeration unit to a small panel truck not unlike the one painted by Ruth Sooy. Most of the vehicles bear the name of Atlantic Coast Trucking. The rest are nameless.

I slow down, trying to read the address, but the numbers on the office door are too small to make out. So I turn around, go back, and pull into the Blue Bell Diner directly across the road. I park the car and get out my binoculars. The number on the dirty glass door is faded but readable. It's 1710.

In the diner no one behind the counter seems to know who owns the business across the way. I find this hard to believe but shrug it off. Maybe I still look like a cop to some people. I buy a large coffee, two doughnuts, and a copy of the *Hammonton News,* then go back outside to watch and wait.

In the next hour I make two more trips into the diner, one for more coffee and another to use the bathroom. Otherwise, not much happens. One of Atlantic Coast's trucks is driven away by two men who are dropped off by a young woman in a blue Buick. Another truck is returned and parked in the back near the propane tank, after which a man in a western hat, walking with a limp, comes out of the office and goes around to check on the returned vehicle. When he comes back he stands outside the office for three-and-a-half minutes talking with the man who returned the truck. Then the he walks around to the side of the building and takes the outside stairs to the living quarters on the top floor. After four minutes he comes back down and goes inside the office. In between this frenzy of activity, I learn from the *Hammonton News* that the superintendent of schools is worried about the use of marijuana among Hammonton teenagers and that the state police captured a car thief from Boston last night after a high-speed chase on the White Horse Pike. Something tells me this is as exciting as it's going to get.

At four o'clock I face facts. This is going nowhere. I don't even know who or what it is I'm watching. So I toss my paper aside and head back into town to do a little more research.

THE TAX ASSESSOR, a Mr. Burline, has his office in the Town of Hammonton Building on Central Avenue. He's a plump, balding, little man whose necktie and collar are so tight the skin on his neck is inflamed.

"Our records go back to 1963," Mr. Burline says curtly, in response to my question. I've caught him in the act of closing up early for the day, and he's not at all pleased.

"What about businesses?"

"Hammonton doesn't require mercantile licenses, but we do require certificates of continued occupancy."

"So you would have those records back to 1963?"

"Yes," he sighs, glancing at a clock on the wall behind him.

"Which means you could tell me who owns a certain business now, as well as who owned it back in 1977?"

"Possibly. If you give me the address."

So I tell him the address.

"You understand, we don't have the full deed here in this office, only the front and back pages. If you want the full deed, you'll have to go to the county clerk's office."

"If the front and back pages are good enough for you, they're good enough for me."

He glares at me a moment, then disappears into a back room. When he returns he has a large, green, canvas-covered data binder in his hands. He lays it on the counter and opens the front cover to the table of contents. Running his finger down a long column of numbers he finds "1710." Then, marking his place, he runs another finger across the page horizontally until he finds what he's looking for.

"Ah ha," he says, unable to hide his satisfaction, "section twelve, parcel nine."

I respect a man who loves his work.

He turns the heavy binder over on its front cover and approaches his prey from the back. Section 12, parcel 9 is about ten pages in from the rear. He flips through several pages of deeds before coming to it.

"Very interesting. The property is commercially zoned. Looks as if it's always been a trucking company. Right now it's listed as Atlantic Coast Trucking, Inc. It's been owned by the same party since 1977, when it last changed hands. The name was changed back then, too."

"Tell me what happened in 1977."

I think I already know.

"Here, see for yourself. It's very interesting." He turns the book around so I can read the deed. "See, in 1977 it was purchased by

Capetan Transport. If that company's the one I think it is, then this is *very* interesting. Look at the signature of the grantee. Do you realize who that is?"

Indeed, I do. There it is, the signature of Theodore Capetanakis.

"I don't recognize the other name though," he says, "the name of the grantor."

"That's okay, I do."

The date of the sale was August 18, 1977, barely one month after the charcoal pit murders. The grantor, or seller, of the property at 1710 Commerce Road, which was then called the Jersey Shore Trucking Co., was Anthony P. Dante. Not the Angelina Corporation, but Tony the Book himself.

"Tell me," I say to Mr. Burline, as I'm heading out the door, "has anyone else been in here to ask about this property?"

"This one? Oh, no."

"You sure?"

"This is the first time I've ever looked at those deeds. I'd remember it if I'd seen that Capetanakis name before. Oh, yes, I'd remember that."

BEFORE I GO BACK to Gwen's, I drive to Beach Haven to check on the house and pick up some clothes. The contractor is there with one of his foremen preparing an estimate. From the way the boss man talks about the high cost of materials and given the fact that he drives a new Cadillac, I suspect the bill for this project is going to set the insurance company back a few thou. He does see to it that the house is safely boarded up before he and the foreman leave, something that I'm sure will be thoroughly covered in the estimate.

I decide to do what I've been dreading all day, which is call Bernie. Like it or not, it's time for him to face the fact that his brother was into blackmail. My guess is he expects the worst, but I'd prefer somebody else be the one to tell him. I'm not up to shielding him from his own guilt anymore. I feel a little like the artist John Singer Sargent must have felt when he said every time he painted a portrait he lost a friend.

7

GWEN AND I have our pizza and beer sitting in lawn chairs out on her dock. It's twilight. The air is still but fragrant. Fiddlehead ferns, slender and motionless, line up along the riverbank like coiled snakes standing on tiptoe. No mosquitoes yet, but every now and then some tiny winged creature flits by, then drops below to begin a miniature dance on the water's surface.

"My article runs tomorrow," she says, sipping her Heineken. She has already consumed three pieces of pizza and is working on a fourth.

"I trust I'm not mentioned."

"Only as an 'anonymous but well-placed' source."

" 'Well-placed.' I like that. Makes me feel significant."

"You are. You said yourself you had a breakthrough today."

"I still don't know who the killer is."

"What *do* you know?"

"I've collected a few details on the 1977 murders. Other than that, not much."

She stares into the blue-gray haze gathering above the river. When she turns back to me, she looks hurt.

"You still don't trust me, do you? No, stop. You don't have to answer that. It was a stupid, unfair question."

I take her at her word but eventually the silence gets to her.

"You're right not to, you know. Not to trust me, I mean."

"Why's that?"

"I don't know exactly. Jerry used to say it was because I hated men."

"Do you?"

"Sometimes. Men have all the power. I hate *that*."

"I don't have any power, not over you anyway."

"How do you know?"

"Isn't there some theory that you have to *allow* others to have power over you?"

"Like that bullshit that you have to turn your power over to someone first?"

"Something like that." I down the last of my beer and decide to change the subject. "Tell me about your article."

"It's good. Very good, actually. And unless someone in Philly or New York already has the same tip you gave me, the *Star* will be the first to break the story. I think I've finally got my editor's attention."

"Did you include much background on Cappy?"

"Everything I could find. There's a short biography, complete with the latest speculation about why he was here."

"Why *was* he here?"

"I talked to a few people in Philly. It was tricky. I didn't want to reveal what I had. But I managed to find out he was on the run from the IRS. My theory—it's only a theory—is he was down here on some tax-evasion thing."

"Really?"

She slides her chair close to mine, then peers into my eyes.

"What am I telling you all this for?" she says, grinning slyly. "You've probably had it figured out for days. Right?"

"Maybe, maybe not."

But I can't help smiling at her.

"I knew it! I'm right, aren't I?"

Even in the twilight I can see the glint in those brown eyes. I reach across my chair and kiss her.

"I must taste like pepperoni," she says.

"Pepperoni's very sexy."

We get to our feet, kissing eagerly. The next thing I know, we're down on the grass in front of the dock and my hand's under her T-shirt.

"You know," she whispers, her hand between my legs, "there's a very prudish, old Christian lady in the cabin next door."

"Nothing she'll see could possibly shock her," I respond, pulling her T-shirt off, the bra along with it.

"Why . . . is . . . that?"

I bury my face between her breasts, eliciting a little squeal.

"If she hasn't seen it before, she won't know what it is."

With Gwen on her back, I get up on my knees and reach down to unfasten her jeans, then slide them off, along with her panties.

"And if she has seen it before," I add, "it won't come as any shock to her."

"That . . . makes . . . sense."

Exploring the inside of her legs, I slowly work my way upward. She moans, her hips undulating to the rhythm of my fingertips.

"Besides," I say, "Christians believe in doing unto others."

Spreading her legs apart, I bend down. Her dark wetness obliterates two years of barren dreams. All the dry springtimes are forgotten.

"Oh God, Frank . . . please don't stop."

"What will your Christian neighbor lady say?" I ask, calling out from that wilderness.

"Praise the Lord," she says, letting out a whimper, then a sob.

As I'm lying on my back gazing up at a rising half moon, a blessed calmness comes over me. It's something I haven't felt since Catherine was diagnosed. Life was choked off at the source then, leaving me gasping for air. I should feel like a traitor now. But all I know is relief. And gratitude.

Gwen, propped up on her elbow, has begun sprinkling little tufts of grass on my chest.

"What are you doing?"

"It's playtime. I always feel like playing after sex."

"Are you serious?"

"Would I be doing this if I weren't?"

"I suppose not."

I reach down and put my hand between her legs.

"What are you doing?"

"Playing too."

"Frank? Is that what this is all about? Us, I mean. Are we just playing with each other?"

"Right now, I believe we're making each other happy. Isn't that enough?"

"I suppose."

She turns thoughtful, so I resume my study of the penumbra of hazy light around the moon's crescent.

"Tell me more about Bernie," she says, returning from whatever distant region she's been visiting.

"Did I tell you I called him earlier this evening? He said to say hello to you."

"What'd you tell him about me?"

"I told him you had a fantastic ass."

She pokes me in the ribs. "You did not. Now what'd you really say?"

"I said I thought you had the makings of a pretty good journalist."

"The *makings*? *Pretty* good? Thanks a lot."

"Know what he said?"

"What?"

"He said, 'Coming from you, Frank, that probably means she's about to win a Pulitzer.' "

"I think I like him."

"I think he'd like you, too."

I also spelled out for him the brutal facts about Nick. He took it very well, considering. But then Bernie has always been bullheaded. Once he has fixed on an objective, he is capable of ignoring anything, even the truth, if it gets in his way.

"Did I tell you," she says, "I have to go to Philly the day after to-morrow?"

"What for?"

"Research. I've got a few friends at the *Inquirer*. I think they can help with a story I'm working on."

"Just be careful. Philadelphia's a dangerous place for good-looking young women."

"Thanks for the warning, old man." She stops and turns her head toward the house. "Did you hear something?"

I turn over, facing the house.

"No. What is it?"

"There it is again."

This time I hear it. All of a sudden I feel pretty foolish lying naked in the moonlight. And except for a couple of empty beer bottles, there's no weapon within reach.

"Just stay put," I tell her, pulling on my chinos.

Crouched down, running barefoot across the grass, I make it to the house and squat next to the wall on the north side. In another ten seconds I'm out front, still clinging to the cabin. I can hear it distinctly now, an automobile engine, but not close by. I peer around the corner but there's nothing except trees on the opposite side of the road. Then I think I see something. It's off the road, facing in the opposite direction. I move out of the shadows and cross into the woods on the other side, staying low to the ground. Immediately I face a problem. I'm no Deerslayer. My soft feet aren't cut out for this kind of primitive stalking. Away from the cushy grass, the twigs and pebbles feel like loose nails under my feet. I peer intently into the darkness, trying to see where there might be a path with a protective coating of pine needles. Unfortunately, the way is not straight, nor is it soft and plush. The only alternative is to inch forward slowly, biting my tongue to keep from screaming out.

About twenty-five yards away, it happens. I step on something sharp and jagged. My expletive can be heard halfway to the Garden State Parkway. The next thing I know, the car's pulling away. Desperate, I limp toward it, hoping to get a glimpse of something. But this guy's too fast for a middle-aged man with tender feet. Still, I get close enough. Close enough to see that it's *not* a car but a pickup truck.

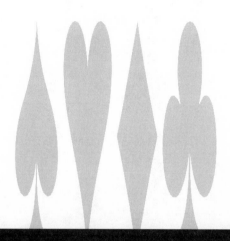

THE PINES
BOOK TWO

1

THURSDAY MORNING I convince Gwen to let me borrow her Toyota for the day. It's my insurance, in case someone noticed the Range Rover yesterday. I transfer my duffel bag, with my technical gear and assorted hats, to her car. After I convince her it would be equally unwise for her to use the Rover, she agrees to get a ride with a coworker. But she can't resist being a tease. Pulling away I can see her in the rearview mirror standing by my car dangling the keys at me.

I get to the Blue Bell Diner by eight and park on the side of the building, leaving an unobstructed view of the activities across the road at Atlantic Coast Trucking. Inside, I buy a large coffee and two newspapers. Today there's a different person behind the counter, an old man with a friendly smile and a willingness to talk. After a minute or two of chitchat about his grandchildren, I learn the name of the man with the limp. It's Angel, Angel Bird. He's the manager, has been for years, according to the old man. Still, nobody knows anything about him, except that he comes over for coffee and doughnuts every morning at ten, "regular as clockwork."

Back in the car, I pull a faded Phillies cap and a pair of sunglasses out of my bag and put them on. Then I scrunch down and settle in for a long day.

Stakeout time is glacial time. It can go by at the rate of cold molasses passing through a sieve. It's a lot like solitary confinement. You can't endure it without the proper attitude toward time. A wise old sergeant I knew when I was a rookie used to say, "There ain't no thing as time, there's only your mind fucking with itself." Someone said there's no future in the past. But there's no future in the future either. When you get right down to it, there's really only now, something the mind tries desperately to escape. One of my favorite Yogi Berra stories has Tom Seaver asking Yogi what time it is. To which Yogi says,

"You mean now?" In his own way, Yogi always gets it right. Goethe claimed the present moment makes a powerful goddess. The trick is to learn how to worship her properly.

The first thing I do is check the *Star* for Gwen's story. It turns out there are actually two stories. The first, as expected, is on the front page. It's a long article on the identity of the Hotel Underwood murder victim, featuring a four-column headline and a photograph of the crime scene. Her confirming source is Cappy's brother. The second, on page two, is a biographical sketch of Theodore Capetanakis, accompanied by the well-traveled 1951 photograph of the mystery man. All told, the Capetanakis items amount to nearly a full page. Gwen's investigative talents are evident everywhere. She must have called Talley with the information I gave her because she quotes his stunned response to her query as an indirect confirmation of Cappy's identity. She was right. It's a good story.

Five minutes before ten, I get out of the car and go into the diner. Timing it carefully, I emerge from the men's room at the moment Angel Bird steps up to the counter. I do a slow walk-by. He's a stick of a man, about five foot ten, 135 pounds tops, with boyish features. I'd guess he's around forty. He's wearing a faded blue denim shirt, black jeans tucked into cowboy boots, and a dirty western straw hat pulled down tightly over greasy brown hair. Balancing himself with his left hand on the edge of the counter, he favors his right leg, which is turned outward slightly. Back in the car I watch him cross the road, clutching his coffee and doughnut as if he thinks someone's going to take them from him.

An hour later, at 11:07 A.M., Angel comes out of his office, locks the door behind him, and walks around to the side of the building where he gets into a red Dodge Ram pickup with oversized rearview mirrors mounted on the doors. He pulls out onto Commerce Road and heads south, away from Hammonton. Tossing the sunglasses aside and putting on a Mets cap, I follow him, trying to keep at least one other car between us. In about a mile and a half we pass under the Atlantic City Expressway. After another mile we're at the Black Horse Pike. Angel heads north on the pike and pulls in at an Italian place, Franco's Ristorante. The pike is narrow here, with no median, so I drive by, make a quick U-turn, and pull in at the Black Horse Tavern across the road from Franco's.

He's still in his truck. From the way he keeps staring into his rearview mirror it's apparent he's waiting for someone. At 11:47 A.M. a black limo with tinted windows pulls off the pike and parks out of sight on the far side of the restaurant. Angel gets out and goes into the restaurant. Then a figure appears from around the corner where the limo's parked. It's a man in a dark suit. Even from across the road I can recognize the perpetually flushed face of Jack Coyle. Coyle stops, waits a few seconds, then follows Angel inside.

I pull my Nikon out of the duffel bag and attach a 135-millimeter telephoto lens. Some stakeouts you wait an eternity and get zilch. Some days you get lucky. I figure I'm due.

The two of them come out together, Angel right behind Coyle. I take four quick shots, one with them saying something to each other. At the bottom of the steps Coyle turns and walks around the corner of the restaurant toward the limo, leaving Angel to return to his truck. For a minute or so nothing happens. Then, as the limo makes its way across the parking lot, Angel gets back out of his truck. He waves to the limo to stop and walks up to the right rear door. The tinted window comes down, and a man's face appears. He's irritated. In fact, he appears to be yelling. I aim the camera and begin shooting. Tony Dante never looked better. I like him when he's angry. He gives off a certain robust animism that you can't fully appreciate in the secluded atmosphere of his office. By the time Angel has retreated to his truck, I have half-a-dozen excellent shots of the two men talking, including one wide enough to take in the limo's license plate and Jack Coyle in the driver's seat.

The day's a success, and it's not even noon yet. Which may be why, as I pull out of the tavern parking lot, I make the mistake of ignoring the little warning light blinking faintly somewhere in the recesses of my mind.

ANGEL'S NEXT STOP is Adult Universe. It's a windowless, gray stucco building, the only one on Harris Avenue, a short cul-de-sac off the White Horse Pike. Its weed-filled parking lot is surrounded by scrub pines and holly bushes. Out front there's a portable plastic sign on wheels, with movable letters proclaiming, RISQUÉ VIDEOS—EUROPEAN MAGS—LIVE ALL-NUDE SHOWS—FETISH—B&D—OPEN 24 HRS. A sign on the glass door, which has been covered with tinted paper, warns unconvincingly, YOU MUST BE 21.

There's nowhere to park without drawing attention to myself. So I have two choices. I can go back to the White Horse Pike and drive back and forth, hoping to be in position when Angel leaves, or I can go inside and pretend to be a customer. Nick would have loved this. It's his kind of stakeout.

Besides Angel's pickup, there are two cars parked in the lot. One's a 1978 Plymouth in need of a paint job. The other's a recently washed and waxed blue Mercedes. It takes all kinds to make an adult universe, I guess. I park Gwen's Toyota next to the Mercedes, as I'm sure she would prefer. Then I put a John Deere cap on and turn my windbreaker inside out so that the reversible red lining is showing. It's a distraction, not a disguise, but every little bit helps.

The inside is a single-room layout with a dirty tile floor, the walls a sickening glaucous green. It's warm, airless, and smells of indecency. On the left a skinny, pimply-faced young man in his early twenties sits behind a small glass counter. He's wearing a T-shirt that says JESUS SAVES and eating Chinese out of a Styrofoam take-out container. I stare at him for a moment, but as far as he's concerned, I'm not here. Under the glass counter is a display of sex toys—rubber dildoes and vibrators, handcuffs, leather whips and assorted straps, and small metal rings and balls whose function I can only imagine.

Along the rear wall there are six small booths, the doors to two of which are closed. They are closetlike compartments, furnished with a folding chair, overhead light, and small TV and VCR. Each room also features a sliding panel about a foot square at eye level in the rear wall. A sign behind the acne-faced kid at the counter explains the terms and conditions for use of these little ecstasy chambers.

Viewing and Reading Booths—$2 for 15 minutes.
Magazine and video rental extra.
Please be considerate of others—
do not tear or soil reading material.

and

The rest of the place is taken up with racks of photos, reading material, and videotapes. Keeping an eye on the two closed doors, I picked up a magazine called Lesbian Lust. It features two naked women on the cover, one handcuffed to a bed, the other wielding a dildo the size of the Washington Monument. I flip through it for a while, and just when I fear I'll never want to have sex again, one of the green doors opens. A good-looking middle-aged man, conservatively dressed, comes out, his suit coat clutched awkwardly in front of him. The blue Mercedes. He hands his videotape to the kid behind the counter and leaves. Then comes Angel, a pained expression on his face, as if he's been looking into the sun. He adjusts his jeans, askew on his bony hips, and walks out. His right leg leaves little dash marks on the dirty floor.

2

AT MELODY'S TAVERN the late lunch crowd is raucous and loud. It's a heavily blue-collar group. Most sit at Formica-topped tables in a large alcove directly off the bar. A few stand around the pool table in the back. Angel, still in his dirty straw hat, is at the bar. When I came in he looked at me, then turned away, giving no indication he's spotted me. He's been on the same bar stool for over half an hour, slack-jawed and stiff-backed, drinking boilermakers and nibbling at an occasional hard-boiled egg that Melody, following some silent signal, takes from a large glass jar behind the bar and hands to him on a paper plate. Four seats away, hatless now, I'm nursing a draft, chatting occasionally with Melody about the Phils' pitching problems this year.

A heavily made-up blond with a smoker's cough is on the other side of Angel. She's been trying to make time with him for fifteen minutes. At first she talked about the weather while he stared at his glass as if he'd dropped his watch in there. When she asked him for a light, he turned away. Then she offered to buy him a drink. He just put his hand over his glass. Now he looks confused, as if he hasn't a clue how to make her go away. When she finally gets up to go to the ladies room, I grab my glass and take the stool next to him.

"Name's Bernie," I say, leaning toward him conspiratorially. "Thought maybe you could use some reinforcements."

A slight grimace wrinkles his babyish features, and his body stiffens. He continues to stare straight ahead.

"Let me have one of those eggs, too—would you?" I say to Melody. I try again.

"Met a woman in a bar once who wouldn't keep her hands off me. Had to spill my beer on her to get her to fuck off. Never saw her again after that."

Melody refills my glass. I tell her to set Angel up with another. He doesn't object so perhaps I'm making progress.

"Hope you don't mind," I say, watching him down the shot of bourbon in one swallow, "but I'm new around here and need some advice."

Lifting his beer, he turns his head toward me slightly. Blank, no-color eyes. Nothing there.

"I don't give advice."

His voice is remote, as if he's coming out of anesthesia. Harsh and uninviting, without emphasis. It reminds me of one of those computer voices you hear over the telephone.

Melody hands me an egg on a paper plate. I break it apart, sprinkle some salt on it.

"Problem is I lost my job. Fucking department fired me. Can you believe that? Nineteen years with the City of Brotherly Love and they fucking fired me. Shit, I put my life on the line for those bastards."

I pause to take a bite of my egg, stealing a look in his direction. His expression hasn't changed.

"I'm a fireman from Philly, see. It's all I know. No one understands what it's like. They said they didn't trust me no more. Big deal, so I had a few problems. Everybody makes a mistake once in a while. They sent me to a shrink. Can you believe that? The fuck do they know?"

The blond has returned to pay her bill. On the way out she leans over to Angel. "Take it easy, handsome."

He ignores her.

"Fucking shrinks," he says, eyes straight ahead, his voice tremulous, "fucking *fire* departments."

Bingo.

"Problem is, I need a job. Now I'm not asking *you* for one, of course. Just trying to get a fix on where it would be best to look."

"What'd he say?"

"What'd *who* say?"

"The shrink."

"Shrink was a woman."

"Fucking bitches. What'd she say?"

"She said I hated my father, or some shit like that."

He considers this, then nods, as if I've confirmed something he suspected all along.

"What'd you do?" he asks.

"What?"

"I said 'what'd you do?' Jesus, can't you hear?"

"Told you. I'm a fireman."

"I mean what'd you do that got you fired, for chrissakes?"

When he turns to look at me, his pupils are dilated.

"Who said I did anything?"

His head jerks around to look directly at me.

"Who the fuck you trying to bullshit? Ain't no fire department in the country gonna send you to a shrink if you ain't done nothin'. Musta done somethin'."

Finally there's some affect in his voice. Maybe the guy's alive after all.

"You ever seen a fire?" I ask him. "I mean a *real* fire. You know, where it's a tall building and the flames are crackling and roaring and sending off sparks for blocks around? Where you can lose yourself in it and forget all your troubles, forget about all the pain? And those flames are shooting up so high you can feel it down here?" His eyes follow me as I reach down and touch my crotch. "It feels *good*, real good. It's better than a shot of the best whiskey you ever had. It's even better than fucking. I tried to explain that to her. But she didn't want to listen. Fucking shrinks."

He's turned all the way around on his stool now, facing me.

"How'd you do it? What'd you use?"

I lower my voice and stare down at my beer.

"Kerosene. Love the smell of that stuff."

"Nobody understands."

"Ain't that the truth."

I sip my beer, giving things a chance to percolate. After a moment or two, he returns to his earlier position on the bar stool. I motion to Melody for another round of drinks.

"You work around here?" I ask.

"Yeah, I'm in trucking. Ain't got no jobs though."

"Not asking for one. I know how it is. Times are tough."

"Bet your ass."

"I can do anything though. I'm flexible."

I give him my best shit-eating grin and he almost smiles.

"Bet you are."

"I'm a real good persuader, know what I mean?"

There's that half-smile again, but he doesn't say anything.

"Once I persuaded this guy to sell me his classic Mustang. Know how?"

He shakes his head.

"He used to keep it in an old garage at the end of a long driveway. You know, one of those detached garages that sits there all by itself? Well, one night I drove by and noticed he'd gone and left the car out. So I paid a little midnight visit to that garage of his. Took my can of kerosene and went and had me a party. Next day I called him up. Said 'Mr. Phillips, it'd be real terrible, now wouldn't it, if that house of yours ever caught fire like your garage.' Know what he said?"

He shakes his head.

"He said 'I ain't selling.' Called me a bunch of names, too. Real bad things."

"Wood can burn," Angel says, his face tightening.

"Exactly. 'Shit happens,' I said to him. He came 'round. I had that Mustang of his the next week. Know what it cost me?"

"Not much."

"Bet your ass 'not much.' Paid him two hundred. Would've paid him three but he kept giving me grief. Had to make my point."

"I used to be a fireman."

"What? You? Jesus, ain't that a coincidence. Where?"

"Right here in the Pines. I was a volunteer."

"No shit. What happened?"

"Ran into some trouble. Nobody ever understands."

"Life's a bitch. What'd you do after that?"

"Got real mad . . . a lot . . . still do, sometimes."

I glance at him. He's rigid with repressed rage.

"Sometimes," I say, "people got to be made to understand."

"Yeah, that's the way I figure it."

The silence builds as we sip our beers. Melody comes by to see how we're doing but walks on after glancing at Angel.

"I know somebody," Angel says, finally.

"What?"

"I know somebody who might be able to help you."

"Who is it?"

"Man in A.C. Sometimes he needs a job done, you know?"

"Know what you mean. I need to know a little about him though. Ain't working for any bastard who can lord it over me again."

He nods. "Don't worry. This guy's all right."

"What's his name?"

"Can't say. Want me to ask him for you?"

"Yeah, you ask and we'll talk again. Where do you work? I could stop by in a few days, see how it went."

I stand up and put a twenty on the bar.

"Atlantic Coast Trucking. Know it?"

"Just outside of town? I think I passed it coming off the expressway. You the owner?"

"I'm in charge."

"What's your name?"

"Angel. Real name's Reginald though. I changed it to Angel when I was a kid. It's not my real name. Don't want you to think I'm fibbing or nothing."

"Okay, Angel. I'll stop by. Nice talking."

He returns to his watchful stance at the bar, leaving me to stare at the back of his denim shirt.

"Martindale?"

"Yeah?"

"It's Sweeney."

"Frank, where've you been? You see this morning's paper? People are looking for you, man."

"I'm not surprised. Look, I need your help."

"No way. This is my day off, Frank. I gotta help the wife with the yard."

"There's a trucking outfit here in Hammonton just crying out for a fire inspection. I can see violations all over the place."

"What're you talking about?"

I tell him a little about Angel Bird. That's all it takes. He agrees to meet me in an hour.

"And bring your evidence kit, too," I say. "You might want to collect a sample of gasoline from this place."

I CALLED MARTINDALE from a drugstore down the block from Melody's. When I come out I remember what it was that bothered me at the Black Horse Tavern earlier. There was a truck there, a black Chevy pickup, parked two rows behind me. This time when I see it it's half a block down the street, pulling out behind Angel's red Dodge Ram. It's too far away for me to read the plates but the driver's profile looks vaguely familiar. Then it's gone.

3

"THIS IS A LITTLE out of my jurisdiction, Frank."

"By the time he figures that out, I'll be out of there. Just don't let him leave that office. Twenty minutes should do it. I need to be sure about this guy."

"I'll do my best."

"And be careful. He's wound real tight."

Once Martindale's ACFD station wagon has pulled out of the Blue Bell's parking lot and crossed the road, I get out of my car and jog over there. In half a minute I'm at the side of the building. Ten seconds later I've climbed the stairs to the landing outside Angel's apartment.

The door has two locks, one a standard key-in-the-knob type, the other a throw bolt. It takes only a few seconds for my picks to work on the doorknob. The door opens easily. He never threw the bolt.

Closing the door carefully behind me, I stop and get my bearings. It's an old storage loft that's been made into an apartment. But somebody forgot to finish the job. The walls are unpainted gypsum boards with the seams and nails still showing. The original wood flooring is visible, too—although it's been partly covered with a threadbare carpet. It's a kitchenette and living area combined, with a single adjoining bedroom. On my left there's an old electric range, a sink, a small refrigerator with rust on the door, some green shelves, and a yellow Formica-topped table covered with a week's worth of dirty dishes and empty beer cans. To the right against the far wall there's a television set and VCR, surrounded by a shabby sofa, an arm chair, and a makeshift coffee table cobbled together out of a single pine board and two plastic milk crates.

Angel's interior decorator must have been Larry Flynt. The walls are covered with some of the raunchiest pictures I've ever seen. Most appear to have been clipped from magazines like those at Adult Universe. A number of them are original photographs, 4 × 4 Polaroid snapshots and 8 × 10 glossy enlargements, most of them blatantly amateurish, all tastelessly obscene. It's a smutty collage of hard women flaunting gargantuan mammillae, shaved pudenda, parted buttocks, and rubicund anuses. If I didn't know better, I'd guess this was the apartment of some crazed first-year medical student preparing for a final exam in gynecology or proctology. Angel prefers his porn undiluted and unadorned, not to mention clinical. For those who like this sort of thing, as Max Beerbohm put it, this is the sort of thing they like.

Nothing labels a person more than his tastes. Or so I used to think. In graduate school I had an art-history professor who was fond of quoting the adage, "Tell me what you like, and I'll tell you what you are." For his part, he collected seventeenth- and eighteenth-century Chinese ceramics, fine, delicate objects, exquisitely decorated. One day he invited me to see his collection. It was stunning, as was his elegant two-hundred-year-old Germantown home. I also met his wife, as fragile a beauty as the ceramics on his glass shelves. Six years later I returned, this time as backup for the homicide team investigating his murder. His wife had beaten him to death with a poker while he slept. It seems he had been sexually abusing his two daughters ever since they were toddlers, and she had finally had enough. I was fascinated by the paradox, that the same man who admired and appreciated *famille verte* could do something as ugly and reprehensible as defile his own children. Had he collected beautiful things to compensate for the moral void inside himself? Perhaps. But maybe there was no connection at all. If there's a moral, it's that beauty can't hide ugliness. Is the reverse true? The question in Angel Bird's case is, where's the beauty part?

I make my way through a trail of dirty clothes toward an improvised bookshelf of boards and bricks next to the TV. Halfway there one of the floorboards gives way, emitting a low groaning sound. Making a mental note to avoid it on the way back, I bend down to take a look at the contents of Angel's shelves. The top one holds pornographic videos, the bottom one a row of how-to books on topics like psychic self-defense, Ninja mind control, and memory development. There's also *The Complete Prophecies of Nostradamus* and the Department of the Army's "Special Forces Handbook."

Stepping around the loose floorboard, I go into the bedroom, where I'm stopped cold. The wall opposite the foot of Angel's bed contains a collage of snapshots and newspaper clippings, most of them yellow and fading. The subject here is local history, of a special sort.

The earliest item is an article from the *Hammonton Journal* dated June 1972. The headline reads, HOUSE FIRE LOOKS SUSPICIOUS TO POLICE. Another, from the *Atlantic City Star* two years later, says, 300-ACRE BLAZE UNDER CONTROL. There's an accompanying photograph of men from the fire service digging a fire line somewhere near Chatsworth. One of the figures in the photo, a thin, lanky man in full fire-fighting equipage, has been circled repeatedly in red ink. Several other clippings cover a number of blazes in the Pine Barrens, including the 1977 charcoal pit fire. There are a few reports, as well, on buildings that went up or automobiles that mysteriously caught fire in the middle of the night. Appended to several of the clippings are stories from professional magazines on the latest fire-fighting techniques. All the material is taped to the wall in circular fashion around an inner core of Polaroid snapshots. Some of the photos were taken up close, implying an intimate relationship between photographer and subject. One shows a fire in the Pines that appears to have originated from a large pyramidal object ablaze in the middle of a clearing.

All that's merely a prelude. My eye makes its way to three recent photos. One is Absecon Lighthouse at dusk. It's a haunting picture, stunningly beautiful, actually. The outline of the red and white beacon looms against a darkening gray-blue sky, while a faint orange glow emanates from the tiny windows. A second photograph, taken in the dark without sufficient flash, is more difficult to identify at first, but in my gut I know what it is. The dark polelike objects off to the right mark the location under the Boardwalk, and the humanoid shape ablaze in the distance tells the rest, its charred hands clawing at the night sky. The third photo, simple and straightforward, shows a beautiful old Victorian home on fire at the end of a street in Beach Haven.

I draw a few deep breaths, then grab the three recent snapshots, as well as the shot of the charcoal pit, and put them all in my pocket.

Time for a quick look around the bedroom. In the bureau drawers I can't find anything but clothes; the closet contains more clothing, a shotgun, a box of shotgun shells, and two cardboard boxes shoved against the back wall. As I'm bending down to slide the boxes out, I hear something. It's the latch turning in the front door. In an instant I'm on my feet, taking up a position on the other side of the bedroom door.

Someone's in the living room. I hear voices, two of them. One is Angel's. The other is Martindale's. He's trying to calm Angel down, but it's not working.

Casually, I make an appearance in the bedroom doorway.

"Angel, I've been waiting for you. Where you been?"

It's not a bad acting job actually, but deep down I know it isn't going to work. Martindale flashes me a look.

"You?" says Angel. "What the fuck are you doing up here?"

"Dropped by to talk. You know, about the job we discussed. I didn't—"

"How the fuck did you get in here?"

"The door was open. Figured you wouldn't mind."

"Like shit it was. Who are you?"

His pupils are dilated, his body flexed. Keeping his eyes on me, he reaches down and pulls out a boot knife. It's all black, the handle and the blade, and from the way he makes the transition into the attack position, I'd say he knows how to use it.

I back up until I'm standing in the bedroom doorway, my right hand on the door behind me. It's obvious what's on my mind. He sees it, and waves me away from the door with his knife hand.

"Move your ass away from that door."

"Can't do that, Angel."

I glance over at Martindale, who's fixated on the knife.

"Who are you?"

"Told you, Angel. Name's Bernie."

"Bernie who?"

"Just Bernie."

"You were up here looking around. What for?"

"I'm just looking for a job, Angel."

"Bullshit."

Angel's about to lunge, but Martindale's one step ahead of him. He's produced a Smith & Wesson Model 60 Chief's Special from a shoulder holster.

"Hold it. Everybody freeze."

Angel turns around.

"What the——"

"I said freeze! Now put down the knife, Mr. Bird. Just put it down."

Angel complies, tossing the boot knife onto his ratty sofa.

"Good," says Martindale. "Now, let's talk. You know this man, Mr. Bird?"

Angel shakes his head. "Never saw him before. Bastard broke into my apartment."

"He's lying," I protest.

Martindale ignores me. "Did he take anything?"

Angel glances around the apartment, then says, "Don't know."

Martindale comes up behind me and performs a body search.

"Doesn't seem to have anything on him. You want to press charges? I can arrest him for you right here. I have the authority."

This catches Angel off guard. Martindale grabs my right arm and holds it behind me in a hammerlock, keeping the revolver in my ribs.

"Okay, then, here's what I'm going to do. I'm going to take Bernie here down to my car and run a check on him. See if he has a record. Maybe we can get him on something else. Otherwise I ain't got nothing, you see? The two of you got stories that don't agree. He says he knows you. You say he doesn't. He says he's been waiting for you. You say he broke in. See? Ain't got nothing but your two stories."

Angry and frustrated, Angel turns his head away.

Martindale, one arm gripping mine behind my back, gives me a shove. Keeping an eye on Angel's boot knife, I stumble toward the door. When we're in the doorway, Martindale turns back to Angel.

"You did just fine on the inspection, Mr. Bird. No problems there at all. Have a nice day."

"You sounded like a fucking elephant up there, Frank. That floor must've creaked three, four times."

Martindale draws on the straw in his chocolate milk shake. He's already finished off a Big Mac. I'm on my second cup of black coffee. After my adrenalin gets flowing, my appetite usually disappears for a while. Later I'll be ravenous.

"Damn near had to tie him down," he goes on. "It didn't work."

"I noticed. Thanks again. You always carry a piece, by the way?"

"Arson investigators are sworn in as full-time police officers. We're encouraged to carry a weapon."

"The burger and shake are on me. I may even buy you a beer later."

"You sure he didn't make out who you are?"

"He would have said something if he had. This guy's not capable of that kind of dissembling."

"He may figure it out now."

"Only if he talks to Dante. But he's never going to let Tony D. know what happened. That'd mean the end of his usefulness. He wouldn't risk that. He needs the work. It's what he lives for."

"Still think I should have gone back and arrested the fucker. Now we'll never be able to get a warrant."

"Doesn't matter. Stuff's gone by now. Besides, what would those clippings and photos prove? Any half-decent lawyer's going to argue that Angel's just a fire buff. He goes to fires and takes pictures, that's all. There wasn't anything that actually proved he was the one to *start* those fires."

"Shit." He puts his milk shake down and stares at the floor.

"By the way, did you notice a black pickup drive by as we came out?"

He looks up. "A black pickup? No, why?"

"Just curious."

"You've got to tell Talley, you know. This time it's not optional."

"Tell him what?"

"Everything you've told me."

"Can't you tell him?"

"I could. Is that the way you want it?"

"Fact is, Ray, I'm busy. There's somebody I've got to find."

"You read the paper this morning?"

"Yeah, I read it."

He studies me a long time. I return the gaze. Eventually, he just shrugs.

"Okay, okay. Maybe it wasn't you that did it. Did you know the FBI and the IRS were interested in Capetanakis?"

"I'm not surprised."

"Petrillo's in hog heaven. He sees himself and Cox doing the talk shows, telling everybody how they solved the Capetanakis murder case."

"Have they? Solved it, I mean?"

"Shit, no. But they're going to be real interested in Angel Bird. You'll have to talk to them soon, Frank. They'll come looking for you otherwise."

"I know. I'm just asking for a little more time."

"I've got to tell them what I know, Frank."

"I wouldn't have it any other way."

"Anything else? Anything you maybe haven't told me?"

"If I think of anything, I'll let you know."

"You want to nail this creep yourself, don't you?"

I just look at him.

"That's not smart, Frank."

"He burned two of my friends alive, Ray. Jesus."

"Leave him to us, Frank. We'll get him."

"How?"

"For starters, there's the gasoline samples. The lab'll do dye comparisons. If Bird's gasoline matches up with the residues from the lighthouse fire, we've got a start."

"How long will the tests take?"

"One or two days."

"It wouldn't be enough, though, would it? Even if you had an iron-clad match, you couldn't prove Bird was the one who actually *used* the gasoline. It could have been anyone with access to those gas pumps."

The fact is, just about everybody's untouchable right now. Angel, if he's got half a brain, will have destroyed or removed the evidence on his bedroom wall. And Dante will have seen to it that his computer records on the two Jonahs have been erased, or at least sufficiently altered. The IRS might get Dante for breaking the currency transaction law, but that's about it. That leaves Judge Bass. And he may have blown his brains out by now. Even if he hasn't, I still don't know where he is. But I'll bet Jack Coyle could find out for me.

"So what you're saying, Frank, is that you're going to play Lone Ranger on us? Shit. Captain Talley's been real good to you, real good. Lot of PIs wouldn't have had half the attention you got from him. Hell, your average PI, he wouldn't have had *no* attention. I know he owes you and your captain but—"

"Cut the bull, Ray. Look, you can tell Petrillo and Cox this. Tell them to check out Harry Morrow some more. They'll find he owned a motel, the Ocean View, back in 1977. It's the one that used to be where the Poseidon is now. And tell them Morrow had a silent partner by the name of Henry Bass. The Angelina Corporation bought the Ocean View from Bass right after Morrow was killed."

"You shitting me?"

"Why would I do that?"

"Bass? Why does that name sound familiar?"

"Henry Bass. Just give them that name. Trust me. They could look it up."

I get up and toss our trash in the plastic bin.

"Where you going?"

"I've got to get some film developed."

4

AFTER MY FILM'S developed, I find a meat market and pick up some lamb for dinner. When I get back to Gwen's, she's in the bedroom working at her desk. She's been on the phone with George Germaine at the *Star*. It seems Tony Dante, who refused in January to approve a scheduled pay raise for his employees, has arranged a $200,000 bonus for himself. Germaine's article will run tomorrow, blowing Dante's cover.

"What do you think will happen?" I ask her.

"There may be a strike. I've heard rumors. Dante's got it coming."

He has balls, I'll grant him that. But just about anyone's capable of screwing his employees. To get away with it you have to be better endowed in the cranial compartment than he is. The bonus thing could bring him down. At the very least it's a large nail in his coffin. Either way it makes my job easier.

"Anything new on the Greenberg kid?"

She shakes her head. "No, still missing. The bastard's ruined that kid's life. Dammit all." She slams her hand down on the desk. The anger seems genuine but somehow misdirected.

"Is that what you're working on?" I ask, noticing a file folder stuffed with notes.

"What? Oh, yeah. I've got to do a follow-up piece on her."

She pushes the folder aside.

"You work, I'll go cook us some dinner."

We kiss but she's distracted. Savoring her indignation, I suppose. I leave her to it and head for the kitchen.

"You don't like it."

"It's not bad," she says, studying her plate. She takes a large swallow from her glass of Chardonnay.

I've made roast lamb with a peppercorn crust. My first attempt. The recipe calls for raspberry vinegar and soy sauce, neither of which Gwen has in the house. So I improvised, something beginners shouldn't do.

"How's your story going?"

"Which one?" she asks, not looking at me.

"The Sandra Greenberg thing."

"Oh, I'm working on something else." She reaches for some bread, her fourth piece. She's barely touched the lamb. "How was your day?"

"I made some headway."

"Good."

259

"So what'd you do this morning?"

"Talked with Brother Stephen."

"Why?"

"My editor still thinks there's a story there. Human interest and all that. I keep telling him the real story is down the Boardwalk at the Poseidon."

"How so?"

Finally she looks at me.

"What do you mean 'how so?' You've met Dante, for God's sake. You know what's going on."

"What *is* going on?"

"They're scum, Frank, the whole rotten bunch of them. They *use* people." Suddenly she glances toward the living room. "Did you hear something?"

I get up and go check. There's no one that I can see. When I come back she's at the sink rinsing her plate.

"What the hell's the matter?" I ask, coming up behind her.

"Too much fucking garlic."

"That's not what I meant."

"I know."

She turns and goes back into the bedroom, closing the door behind her.

LATER IN BED she's frantic: grabbing, biting, moaning. Normally, I'd trade a couple of days of my life for sex like this, but it's as if I'm not here. When she's finished I feel like a distant onlooker. Afterward, she buries her face in the pillow. The bed shakes with her sobbing.

5

IN THE MORNING, after Gwen has left for Philly, I call the Poseidon security office. Coyle isn't in yet. The receptionist, after a little coaxing, gives me his home phone number.

"Jack? This is Frank Sweeney. Remember me?"

"Shit. How the fuck did you get my number?"

"It's my job. Look, how'd you like to have lunch today? It's on me."

"I've got other plans."

"Really? Well, that's too bad. I thought maybe we could talk about restaurants."

"Restaurants?"

"You know, *Italian* restaurants? Like the one I saw you and Tony Dante at yesterday?"

Silence.

"Jack? You there, Jack?"

"Whaddya want, Sweeney?"

"I just want to talk, Jack."

"You talked to Dante about this?"

"Not yet."

"Well, don't. It wouldn't be smart."

"So, you want to have lunch or not, Jack?"

"Where'd you have in mind?"

WE MEET AT A Chinese place called Chong's House on the White Horse Pike. It's near Egg Harbor, more or less halfway between Hammonton and A.C., with the shorter portion of the trip in my favor. I'm not about to accommodate Coyle and drive all the way into the city.

He arrives in a glistening white Caddie. I wouldn't have expected anything less from someone of Jack Coyle's taste and discernment. After all, this is a man who's wearing a chocolate-colored suit that's a size too big in the shoulders. No matter how hard the guy tries, he's always going to look like an ex-flatfoot.

Coyle doesn't see me waiting in my car and walks straight into the restaurant. By the time I get inside he's found a booth in the smoking section, lighted his first cigarette, and ordered himself a double Chivas on the rocks.

"Jesus, Sweeney, why'd you pick a Chink place?"

"It's good food. And it's Chinese, not Chink."

"Don't give me that PC shit. I'm already in a bad mood."

The waiter arrives with Coyle's scotch, so we order. Coyle picks the Mongolian barbecue and I order the mandarin pancakes. To appear accommodating I ask for a bottle of Bud, too. Coyle, his face flushed, downs half his scotch and sits back in the booth, breathing heavily through his mouth.

"You look tired, Jack. You ought to take a vacation. Maybe go to Vegas, check out the casinos there."

"That's fucking funny, Sweeney. Ain't no way I'm going nowhere right now." He lights up another Marlboro.

"Why's that?"

"You see the paper this morning? See that shit about Tony giving himself a raise?"

"I heard about it."

"Well, the union's shitting bricks." He looks at his watch. "As of half an hour ago they are officially on strike. Fucking pickets were already out front when I left."

"He's not going to survive this one, Jack. You know that, don't you?"

"Tony'll land on his feet," he says, halfheartedly. "He always does."

"Right. Business is down fifty percent. You've got a negative cash flow. The employees are walking out on you. And there's the little problem of a casino license. I've done some checking around, Jack. The CCC has had it with Tony Dante. But even if they do renew his license, he can't make it in bankruptcy court. Not anymore."

He looks up from his drink. "What's that supposed to mean?"

"You know perfectly well what it means. Judge Bass is lost to you. And the next judge isn't going to be in Dante's pocket. It's not wired anymore, Jack."

"I don't know what the fuck you're talking about." He picks up his drink, finishes it off, and waves to the waiter for another.

"Let me spell it out then. I'll tell you a story."

"This gonna take long?" he says, glancing at his watch.

"Relax, Jack. Pretty soon you'll have all the time in the world. Now, I've done my homework so most of this I know for a fact. But you'll forgive me if I fill in here and there with a little imaginative reconstruction. The story begins late in 1976. The gambling referendum in New Jersey has just passed and certain people in Philly, New York, and south Jersey have begun to salivate like Pavlov's dog after the dinner bell's gone off. The gravy train is on the way, and it's headed for the Atlantic City station. About this time there's a certain family down in Florida. Let's call them the Dante family, just for discussion purposes. They're in the cosmetics business. Angelina Cosmetics they call it. The head of this family is a crafty old salesman named Joseph Dante. Well, Joe, he smells a real good thing coming along up here in Jersey. His son Anthony does, too. But Anthony, forward-looking entrepreneur that he is, comes up here on his own and goes into the trucking business, figuring to get rich, I guess, delivering toilet paper to the big hotels. I'm afraid Anthony never was real strong in the brains department. Daddy already knows that, however, and decides that the Dante family is *not* going to provide any services to the casinos. They are going to *be* served. So he tells son Tony to scout out a place on the Boardwalk where they can put up a casino of their own. This is where Tony really lets loose. He decides there ain't no way the Dante family's going to pay full price for a hotel or motel in such an inflated market. I mean, hell, Jack, here are these dumb schmucks in a dying city, these so-called businessmen, who'd nearly gone bankrupt in the sixties and early seventies. And suddenly they're asking millions for fleabag hotels and greasy-spoon restaurants just because they're on the Boardwalk. Who the hell do they think they are, right?"

The waiter arrives with our meals. I stop and take a sip of my beer. Coyle empties his drink, orders another, then lights up again.

"So, Jack, am I getting it right so far?"

He ignores me and tackles his barbecue. I've got to give him credit. He isn't letting anything affect his appetite.

"Anyway, our Tony checks out what's available and discovers this place called the Ocean View Motel, a piece of prime Boardwalk real estate. It's owned by somebody named Harry Morrow, an A.C. businessman, and a silent partner named Henry Bass, a local nobody lawyer. But there's a problem. The principal owner is thinking of going into the casino business himself. He doesn't want to sell, at least not for what Tony's willing to pay. But Tony's undaunted. He does a little research and checks out the silent partner. Maybe he talks to some friends in Philly. Maybe he checks out things in Vegas. Anyway, somehow he finds out that Bass has a gambling problem. Bass makes a lot of trips to Nevada, and he's heavily in debt to some bad people in Philly who like to hurt you when you don't pay up. It turns out Bass would be happy to sell his share of the motel at just about any price. As long as it's enough to get his ass out of the ringer it's in with these dudes in Philly. If there's a little left over after the sale, well, that wouldn't be too bad either. He could use that to get back into action at the roulette tables. So Tony makes Bass an offer. He'll take care of Harry Morrow if Bass will let the motel go for a reasonable price once it's his to sell. Now I ask you, what gambler could turn down an offer like that? Certainly not Henry Bass, who must have been convinced his luck had finally changed."

Coyle's paying attention now. He has stopped eating and is concentrating on the ice cubes in his tumbler of scotch. The mere fact that he hasn't gotten up and walked out tells me something.

"Now the story takes an ugly turn. I'll skip over the grisly details. The gist of it is that Tony gets one of his drivers—a certain psycho with the unlikely name of Angel, a demon with a penchant for matches and gasoline—to carry out the hit on Harry Morrow. Angel, who's about as bright as Tony, takes one of his boss's Jersey Shore trucks, kidnaps Morrow, and takes him into the Pines, where he burns him alive in a charcoal pit."

I stop and take a look at Coyle.

"Doesn't this part make you queasy, Jack? Not even a little bit? Well, it gets worse. Eventually even you may find this story a little nauseating."

I take a sip from my water glass and continue.

"When Tony returns from wherever it was he was hiding out while Angel did the dirty work, he discovers that his boy was driving a company vehicle at the time of the killing. So what does our Tony do? Why what any other nimble-witted retard with an eighty IQ would do. He *sells* his trucking company and gets the new owner to change the name! Is that brilliant or what? Jersey Shore Trucking no longer exists. It's now Atlantic Coast Trucking. That'll show those asshole cops. Of course, the cops never do catch on to him. Why? Well, the one clever thing Tony *did* do was buy off the case detective. You can't really make a trucking company disappear, but you can derail a murder investigation if you own the lead investigator. Since the cops never come calling on our Tony, it doesn't much matter that his truck might have been noticed near the crime scene. And this cop that Tony buys off—let's just call him Jack, for discussion purposes—how does Tony repay him? Well, get this. Jack is promised the job of head of security at the new casino that will go up right on the spot where the Ocean View Motel stands, a motel that will soon be sold by its new owner, Henry Bass, for a *very* reasonable price. Meanwhile—"

"This is all bullshit, Sweeney. Who the fuck do you think you're kidding? You can't prove any of this."

He shoves his plate aside and sits back, lighting up another cigarette.

"Be patient, Jack. It gets real interesting now. You see, Tony sells Jersey Coast Trucking to Capetan Transport. In fact, the deed shows the signature of Theodore Capetanakis. I see I've got your attention. Yeah, I've actually seen the deed. And it seems that in the process Dante and Capetanakis get to know each other. They find that—how shall I put it?—their separate and unique personal quirks and professional endeavors can be mutually beneficial. Over the years a business relationship evolves. I doubt if it ever becomes a friendship. Cappy's too discriminating, and too distrustful, to enjoy the company of someone like Tony Dante. But Dante serves a purpose. Cappy likes to gamble now and then, but more important, he likes to avoid people. He's basically a hermit. He moves around a lot, traveling incognito more and more as he gets older. He needs places to escape to, places where he can get lost in the crowd or where someone's willing to shield his identity. A casino-hotel can sometimes provide that, though he often hides out on the street, too. In return Cappy provides a few business favors. Maybe he sees to it that Capetan Transport sends certain 'discounted' shipments Tony's way, items that fell off the back of somebody else's truck, stuff like that. As time passes— we're in the nineties now—Capetanakis becomes more eccentric, more paranoid. He's terrified of the IRS. He begins to look not only for ways to avoid paying taxes, but for ways to hide his money *before* it can be taxed. Am I on the right track, Jack?"

"Fuck off, Sweeney. Like I said, you can't prove anything."

"Have some tea, Jack. Remember, it's on me."

I signal to the waiter who brings us two teas.

"You want some dessert, too, Jack? No? Okay, now, where was I? Oh, yeah, money-laundering."

"The fuck you get all this—

"That's right, Jack, money-laundering. Hard to believe, isn't it? I keep telling myself Dante has balls. This proves it. It's just brains he lacks. Anyway, back to my story. I have to digress a little now. All the time that Dante and Capetanakis have been chummy with each other, something else's been going on. Henry Bass has been kept on a string. Now, this is where I have to speculate a little, since I've yet to meet the good judge myself. Maybe Dante used Bass's professional services over the years, maybe not. I really don't know. I do know that Bass kept gambling, no doubt doing some of it at the Poseidon. But despite a heavy addiction, he managed to move up in his profession. Most men with a problem like his would've ended up in jail. Not Bass. He did himself proud in New York, getting appointed by the governor to a task force and all. In 1991 he was even with a reasonably prestigious law firm, Turner & Frye. Then guess what? Suddenly he's *Judge* Henry Bass. And not just any judge, but a *bankruptcy* judge. And not just any bankruptcy judge, but the *Poseidon's* bankruptcy judge. Now I ask you, is that coincidental, or what? How could it have happened? First off, you have to be appointed to those judgeships, and someone pretty influential has to recommend you. What do you think, Jack, did Capetanakis see to it that Bass got that judgeship? I'll have to ask the judge himself when I see him. I do know this was one hell of a happy confluence of events for Tony Dante. If the man weren't so bloody stupid, I'd be tempted to think he planned the whole thing back in 1977."

"Tony's not stupid. He's just . . ."

"Just what, Jack? Lucky, maybe? I don't think so. Not any more at least. So tell me, who came up with the idea for the Jonah scam?"

Jack still isn't talking, but some of the defiance has gone out of him.

"Okay, Jack, I'll give you my theory. It's only a theory, mind you. I think the Jonah scam was Cappy's idea. *He* was capable of thinking ahead. He knew that in the years to come he'd have to find ways to keep his money out of the hands of the IRS. The Poseidon provided a perfect means to that. He couldn't use any of the other casinos. None of them knew who he was, and they wouldn't be dumb enough to buy into the money-laundering idea anyway. But there were problems. First of all, even Dante knew it was risky. So Cappy had to make it worth his while. I'm assuming Dante got to keep a good percentage of the money that was laundered. He's smart enough to have figured *that* out. But Cappy gave him another inducement, one that was in Cappy's interests as well: Cappy would see to it that Henry Bass got appointed to bankruptcy court in Camden, the jurisdiction that would hear the Poseidon's case. The only condition Cappy stipulated with Dante was that Bass had to be allowed to gamble *anonymously* at the Poseidon, because by this time the man's gambling was out of control. Most of the other casinos wouldn't have him, and besides, as a bankruptcy judge, he shouldn't have been seen gambling at all, least of all in one of the places whose future he might have been deciding. It would have meant the end of his career. So Cappy and Bass took on phony identities: Jonah Jones and Jonah Smith, respectively. This lasted for a few months, then something went wrong. My guess is Dante crossed Cappy, crossed him big time. And for that simple reason Cappy wanted revenge, otherwise why would he put Nick onto the judge? Am I right, Jack?"

"I said I got no idea what the fuck you're talking about."

"Start with the fact that Cappy liked Nick. They'd been hanging out together in the mission, going to ball games, getting drunk together. They found they had a lot in common. To top it all off, Nick—like Cappy—had been screwed by Tony Dante. It all crystallized for Cappy when Nick saved his life. That was just too much for him. One night when he was drunk he felt he had the chance to pay Nick back. So he told him about the judge and how he shows up at the Poseidon every Tuesday night. He didn't tell him anything else, certainly nothing about the money-laundering scam. He figured this was enough for Nick to get some big bucks out of you guys and break free of the mission. But when Cappy sobered up he realized he hadn't done Nick any favors at all. Quite the contrary. That's when he called me."

"Jesus, Sweeney, you ought to go on a fucking talk show or something. You tell a hell of a fairy tale." But his voice has lost its edge. He's subdued now, considering his options.

"Nick really got into it, didn't he? He went over to the Poseidon, checked to see that it really was Judge Bass there on Tuesday nights, and then did some serious investigating of his own. Then he came to you. He came to you and scared the shit out of you and Dante."

"Look, Sweeney—"

I take the photos from my shirt pocket and spread them out on the table. Coyle, Dante, and Angel frozen for eternity in front of Franco's Ristorante.

"Jesus."

He quickly scoops them up, crumpling them in his hand.

"It's okay, Jack. You can keep them. I have the negatives, and plenty of copies."

"Doesn't prove shit. A picture of Tony and me with some third party doesn't mean dick."

"It does when the third party is the bastard who killed Nick and Cappy."

"And how you gonna prove that?"

I take another picture out of my pocket, holding it out of his reach.

"Here, how's this? Uh, uh, Jack, hands off. What do you think? Think it would make a good postcard? It's not your usual shot of the lighthouse, is it? You'll never guess where it came from. It's from the wall in Angel's bedroom. I've got others, too. There's one of Cappy in flames. And one of my house on fire. Oh, and there's one of the charcoal pit fire back in 1977 where Harry Morrow and some innocent bystander were murdered. You know all about that, Jack, don't you?"

"Shit."

"And believe it or not, I also know where there's a picture of Angel's truck coming out of the Pines just after he started the charcoal pit fire."

"What the—"

"Trust me, Jack. The picture exists. Someone else was there. Nick figured that out, too."

While Coyle's mulling this over, I sip my tea, pushing his cup toward him.

"Drink up, Jack. Best to have a clear head when you consider these things. By the way, was it your idea to burn down my house?"

Coyle shakes his head. "Fuck no, that was Tony's. I don't go in for that kind of shit. All I wanted to do was rough you up a little, give you a few bruises. I never figured you for this kind of stunt."

"What about Harry Morrow? Were you in on that ahead of time?"

"I swear, Sweeney, I had nothing to do with that. Not until—"

"Not until Dante bought you off?"

He shrugs. "I got this visit in the middle of the night. It was Angel with ten grand. Do you know how I was living back then, Sweeney? A fucking efficiency apartment, cockroaches and all. My ex-wife had all the money. Alimony, the works. So along comes Tony with all this dough, tax free. Shit, what could I say?"

"You could have said 'no,' Jack."

"Kiss my ass, Sweeney."

"And what about Nick? And Cappy? Were you in on those hits?"

"That was all Tony's idea. He don't consult with me on shit like that."

"But you knew?"

"Yeah, he told me after. What was I supposed to do, call the cops?"

"Might not have been a bad idea, Jack."

"What the fuck do you want from me, Sweeney?"

So I play my last card. I pull Gwen's miniature tape recorder out of my shirt pocket and show it to him, the spindles still turning. All this time he's been speaking into the button-microphone on the cuff of my shirt sleeve.

"You fucking bastard. You son of a fucking bitch."

"Keep it down, Jack. People are staring."

He makes a move for the recorder. I pull it back quickly.

"Careful, Jack. There are lots of people around. You don't want to make a scene here, do you?"

"You can't use that, Sweeney. That tape would never be admissible in court, and you know it."

"Maybe, maybe not. But I'm not a cop. I'm a private citizen. The cops can legally use any evidence I turn over to them, no matter how it's acquired. At the very least, this tape's certain to get your license revoked. You'll never work in a casino down here again, Coyle."

"You fucking bastard."

I switch the recorder off, pop the tape cassette out, and put it in my coat pocket.

"You working for the cops? Is that what the fuck you're up to?"

"It's personal. I'm in this for a friend."

"You're hotdogging it, aren't you? A real fucking freelancer."

"Who'd you rather deal with, me or the cops?"

"I don't fuckin' believe this. So what is it you want?"

"I want Henry Bass, if he's still alive. He's going to help me nail Dante and Angel."

"And what about me?"

"You I'm willing to trade for a couple of bigger fish."

"Meaning?"

"Meaning, you cooperate and I'll give you a head start, let you make a run for it. The way I figure it, Jack, in another day or two you're gonna be looking for work anyway. Dante isn't going to be in business much longer. You cooperate with me and maybe there'll be a tomorrow for you in some other town. Maybe you can make a fresh start in Vegas. I'm not asking you to turn in your boss. Just lead me to Bass, that's all I'm asking. What's it going to be, Jack?"

I give him a moment to stare into the watery remains of his scotch glass.

"I don't know where Bass is."

"But you can find out, right?"

"Maybe."

"I'll give you till tonight."

"Jesus, Sweeney, that's not enough time."

"I don't hear from you by tonight, I go to Talley with the pictures and the tape. In the meantime, they'll be someplace safe. So don't bother coming after me. Here's where I can be reached."

I write Gwen's phone number on a napkin and give it to him. For the first time since we sat down he looks unsure of himself.

"Cheer up, Jack. It's almost over. You know, your mistake was one I would have made, too. You underestimated Nick. You never imagined he'd dig deep enough to figure it all out, did you?"

"Shit, he didn't get half of it right."

"He did dig up the story on the Harry Morrow killing."

"Nick? He was nothing but a fucking degenerate gambler, chasing the big score."

"You saying he didn't try to blackmail you guys for the Morrow murder?"

"If he did, Tony and I musta missed it. All we ever heard about was the judge. Nick just wanted his old job back, that's all. That and some credit at the tables. The guy had no imagination."

I study him. If he's lying I can't find any sign of it.

"Tell me something else. Who was the second victim in the charcoal pit fire?"

"Some dumb Piney, I suppose."

"You never tried to ID the body?"

"Why should I? I had my orders."

"And your ten grand."

"Fuck you, Sweeney."

"Get back to work, Coyle. I'm going to sit here a while. It's safer."

He considers his options, then gets up.

"Too bad you left the force, Sweeney. You'd have made a hell of a shakedown artist."

"With patsies like you, Jack, anybody could do it."

I watch from the window as he gets into his Caddie. In a few seconds he pulls out onto the White Horse Pike, heading back to Atlantic City. I stay in the booth for a while, sipping my tea, wondering why he didn't put up more of a fight.

BACK AT GWEN'S I sit by the phone all afternoon, trying to read, occasionally dozing off and falling into crazy half-dreams about burning roulette wheels and blazing panel trucks with JERSEY SHORE TRUCKING printed on the side. During one languid stretch I see Catherine standing in a clearing in the Pines somewhere, dressed in a fiery red robe, speaking words I can't understand. I sit up with a start, perspiring. It's been days since I've thought about her.

By seven Gwen still hasn't returned. I cut up some cheese and fruit and nibble at it, sipping a small glass of the Chardonay left from last night. At eight I turn the TV on. The Pirates are visiting the Vet. The season's barely three weeks old and already the Phils are in last place. So I doze some more. When the phone rings, jolting me awake, it's the middle of the seventh inning. A man, a friend of Gwen's, is on the line. He sounds surprised. Welcome to the club. When I don't explain myself, he says to tell her Bill called and hangs up.

At midnight, praying for oblivion, I fall onto the bed without bothering to take my clothes off.

WHEN THE PHONE RINGS again, it sounds miles away. I sit up, unsure of where I am. The clock radio on the night table says 3:34 a.m.

"Sweeney? That you?"

"Coyle? Jesus, it's almost four in the morning." There's some odd background noise on the other end. "Where the hell are you?"

"I'm at a pay phone out on the Boardwalk. Whaddya think, I'd call from my own fucking office?"

I can distinguish the sound of gulls and waves in the distance.

"That's using your head, Jack. What do you have for me?"

"We still got a deal?"

"Just like I said, Jack."

Silence for several seconds.

"Okay. He's at the Serenity Gun Club."

"Where's that?"

"It's in the Pines. I think it's a hunting club he uses during deer season."

"Who knows he's there?"

"Just Tony, now you. Tony's letting him use the place as a hideout. The judge let things get a little out of hand. He owes more sharks than even Tony can help him with. If you want him alive you'd better get your ass in gear. Sounds like he's trying to find the balls to blow his fucking brains out. Tony figures it'll be no big loss. It'll save him the trouble."

"Is he alone?"

"No, Einstein, he brought his whole fucking family along."

"Okay, Jack, I'll check it out."

"Look, Sweeney, you got to cover for me. You got to buy me some time."

"I told you I would. Now how do I find this Serenity Gun Club?"

"You can't find it alone, not unless you're a fucking Piney. You're gonna have to get help."

"What are you trying to pull—"

"It's the best I could do, Sweeney. All I can tell you is it's in the woods somewhere near a place called Hidden Swamp. Look, I've done my part, now you gotta do yours."

"I'm doing it, Coyle. It's hide-and-seek time and I'm starting to count."

After I hang up and look around the bedroom, it hits me that Gwen still hasn't returned.

6

I FEEL AS IF I've just been kicked in the groin. The face of Henry Bass stares up at me from the front page of the morning *Star*. It's the old photo from the *Times*, with the governor and the law-school dean. The headline reads,

FEDERAL BANKRUPTCY JUDGE
HAS TIES TO ANGELINA CORP.

It's Gwen's story and she has named names. Besides Judge Bass, there's one "Frank Sweeney, former Philadelphia homicide detective turned private investigator." I'm credited with having unearthed the connection between the judge and Dante's casino enterprise. So much for my status as an "anonymous but well-placed source." Then I remember the copies I made of the Bass material at the library. I stashed them in the glove compartment of the Range Rover. And Gwen had access to my car on Thursday while I was using her Toyota. Bernie warned me.

She's done some research of her own, too. The story includes additional details on the sale of the Ocean View Motel, as well as the confirmation by a "highly placed source" at the court of appeals, third circuit, that Bass's appointment to bankruptcy court was accomplished at the behest of Theodore Capetanakis. There's a "no comment" from Talley. Dante, too, refused to talk, showing some intelligence for once. Gwen counters that with some innuendoes from a new source, Charlie Bishop, who apparently has been fired. She ends by revealing that Judge Bass has not been seen or heard from since last Monday. All in all, it's a hell of a story, a real coup for Gwen, female Judas that she is. No wonder she hasn't come home yet. She probably fears for her life.

I decide on a diversionary strike against Talley and his boys. Actually, it's self-defense. Once Talley sees the story I'll be on his "Most Wanted" list. I find a large Manila envelope in Gwen's desk and address it to him at Major Crimes. Into the envelope I put the photographs I took of Dante, Coyle, and Angel at the restaurant, as well as the snapshots taken from Angel's bedroom. I also include the tape recording of Coyle at lunch yesterday. Jack's had enough of a head start by now. I never said how long I'd give him anyway. Then I scribble out a short cover note (no apologies, just the facts), seal the envelope, and look in the Yellow Pages for a delivery service.

MACLEAN'S WIFE, half-asleep, picks up the phone. After some mumbling and rustling around, Sandy comes on.

"Sandy? It's Frank Sweeney. Sorry to bother you so early but it's urgent."

"Huh? What's urgent?"

"Have you ever heard of the Serenity Gun Club?"

"Huh?"

"The Serenity Gun Club."

"Ah, yeah, I've heard of it."

"Can you tell me how to find it?"

"What's this all about?"

"I need to find this gun club, that's all."

"You ever traveled in the Pines alone?"

"No."

"Then forget it."

"Could you take me? I'll pay you."

"Yeah, I could do it. When do you want to go?"

"In about half an hour."

He groans, then covers the phone. There's more mumbling. I can hear the level of his wife's voice rising in the background.

"Sorry. Saturday's my day with the kid."

"I said I'll pay you."

"Doesn't matter. Tomorrow would be okay though."

"That might be too late."

For a few seconds I review my options, all two of them. I can either risk it on my own or I can wait until tomorrow. I don't like either choice. Then I think of a third.

"Sandy, you know a guy named Virgil Applegate?"

"Virgil? Everybody around here knows Virgil. He's a good old woodjin. He could get you there."

"Woodjin?"

He laughs.

"That's Piney talk. A woodjin's just a local who works as a guide."

"Do you have his telephone number?"

More laughter, this time louder.

"Virgil doesn't even have electricity. No indoor plumbing either. Virgil's a character."

"So how do I get ahold of him?"

"His place isn't as hard to find as the gun club. I'll give you directions."

After I put the phone down, Martindale calls. He's worried.

"Talley wants to see you. It took a lot of bullshitting to keep this phone number from him, Frank."

"I'll call him when I can."

"He's not real patient right now, Frank."

"What's up?"

"What's up? You see the morning paper yet? You're featured on the front page, for chrissakes."

"Yeah, I saw it. Didn't you tell him about Judge Bass?"

"I never had time."

"Well, tell him I'm sending him something better than the judge. It's on its way by messenger. I'll fill him in myself tomorrow. Today I'm on the road."

"Frank, look—"

"It's the best I can do, Ray. What else do you have, anything?"

"We've got a match on the gasoline from Atlantic Coast Trucking. It's the same as the residues we took from the lighthouse."

"Good. Look, I'm sorry if you're caught in the middle of this, Ray."

"I ain't in the middle no more, Frank. I'm getting out of the line of fire. Effective immediately."

EVERY ONCE IN A while back in Philly you hear about some brainless city slicker who had one too many and ventured into the interior of the Pine Barrens on his own, never to be heard from again until some Piney stumbled over the body. Apparently, the lure of the forest is so strong for some self-styled urban woodsmen that, without thinking, they will leave the relative safety of a sand road in order to head deeper into the woods. What they don't know is that sand roads sit below the level of the brush that runs alongside, so it's possible to walk twenty or thirty yards into the Pines, then turn around to learn that the road you were just on has disappeared from view. What's worse, having penetrated the forest, the outsider soon discovers there's a dangerous sameness to it all. The things a Piney counts on to guide him go unnoticed by someone untrained in the use of anything but

276

maps and road signs. All of which is why I pay close attention to Sandy Maclean's directions to Fox Chase Ridge.

I make it to Jenkins, which seems to be comprised of no more than a tiny roadside chapel and a gun club. About a mile past the chapel I turn left. Then it's half a mile over disintegrating macadam to Deer Run Road. Along the way I see a few cabins set far back into the woods but nothing else. On Deer Run Road I drive until I come to the third unmarked gravel road on the left. After about a hundred yards I reach the fingerboard, an intersection of three gravel roads. On a small pitch pine there are three weather-beaten signs. One says FOX CHASE RIDGE in faded white lettering. I head that way, down a narrow lane with the underbrush closing in on both sides. After two hundred feet there's another hand-painted sign, this one on a cedar shingle. It says HEAVENLY ACRES. The arrow points to an old tar-paper shack about a hundred feet down a sandy trail.

Along the trail are more signs, made of pieces of old scrap wood nailed to trees, with warnings like NO TRESPASSING AFTER DARK and ABSOLUTELY NO FOX HUNTING. Just before the shack there's a large window shutter nailed to a cedar. It has several lines of Biblical verse printed on it in faded black letters. I stop the car to read it: HE IS THE ROCK, HIS WORK IS PERFECT—FOR ALL HIS WAYS ARE JUDGMENT—A GOD OF TRUTH—DEUT. At the end of the trail, one last sign fixed to a fence post reads, V. APPLEGATE—U.S. CITIZEN.

The gravelly, weed-filled yard is blanketed with junk. There are two rusty automobiles, one a 1958 Ford sedan without the top. The second car has been stuffed with used two-pound coffee cans and cardboard boxes, all filled to capacity with tools and assorted nuts and bolts. Scattered about are a number of old appliances—including an ancient ringer-type washing machine and the remains of a Philco TV set, circa 1950—as well as tires and crates of various sizes, more tools and garden implements, the bottom half of a wooden swivel chair, two metal washtubs, and dozens of other items whose function I can't figure out. Up close, the house is more substantial than it looked from the road. It's a small but sturdy saltbox, about thirty feet on each side, neatly covered in tar paper.

Applegate is on the other side of the house, near his pickup, using a wooden rake to turn over some sort of grass or moss that's been spread out on the ground. He's wearing the same clothes I saw him in the night we met: black leather cap, red flannel shirt, dirty black work pants, and gum shoes. In the daylight I can see a touch of gray in his hair, and his face looks wizened.

"Got to turn this stuff over once or twice a day, you know. 'Specially with this good sun. Ain't no good if it don't dry."

He acts as if I'm an old friend who's been standing here all morning. A black-and-tan hound paces back and forth behind him while he works.

"What is it?"

"Sphagnum. Here, squeeze it."

I take a piece and squeeze, watching the brownish-red water run through my hands. The hound comes over and licks at the wet spot by my feet.

"Go ahead," he says, "squeeze it dry."

No matter how hard I try there still seems to be some water left.

"Can't do it," he says.

"What do you do with it?"

"Sell it down to the nurseries. They wrap plants and seedlings in it. Used to be big business 'round here once. No more. Don't find hardly nobody gathering moss anymore. Not anymore. It's a shame. You know, walking on this stuff it's just like carpeting. Ain't no rug prettier than sphagnum."

"I don't know if you remember me, Mr. Applegate—"

"Name's Virgil. 'Course I remember you. You're that fella was with Miz Olin at The Homestead. How she be?"

"Fine, Virgil. Look, I came by to ask a favor."

"You need something out there?" He points to the yard. "Help yourself."

"No, it's not that. I'm trying to get to some place in the Pines. The Serenity Gun Club. You know it?"

"Serenity Gun Club? 'Course I know it. Don't we know it, Pete? It's right near Hidden Swamp. That's a real nice hard-bottom swamp, just off Ford's Crossway. I used to help old Ford take cedars out of those woods before that gun club was even built. I've run one or two deer drives there myself over the years, too. I seen the biggest tree frog of my life there once. It was the biggest of my life. Yessir, the biggest. There's a big deadfall right nearby. Rattler's Deadfall. That's one way of finding it."

"Well, I'd like you to take me there, if you're available."

He looks around at the moss spread out at his feet.

"Pete and I got a lot more work to do before I can go traipsin' all the way out there."

The hound comes up and sits proudly next to Virgil, demonstrating his solidarity with his master.

"I'm prepared to pay you for your time."

He takes one more look at the ground, then says, "Let's go inside."

I follow him through a low, narrow doorway into a small vestibule cluttered with tools and tin cans containing balls of string, nails, assorted fasteners. Beyond this entranceway lies the kitchen and beyond that the rest of the house, which is a single open room. The kitchen has a stove that runs on bottled gas and an unconnected sink with no faucets that sits up on a wooden bench. Water has to be brought in from a well outside. The combined living and sleeping area adjoining the kitchen is furnished with a wooden table and three chairs placed next to an old-fashioned potbellied woodstove in one corner of the room. Against the opposite wall are two tattered easy chairs. The wood flooring is covered with several small, braided throw rugs that appear relatively new. Virgil's "bedroom" is a small daybed placed under one of the front windows.

He pours some water from a jug into a small saucepan and places it on the gas stove to boil.

"You like tea or coffee?" he asks. "I got both."

"Coffee's fine."

When the water comes to a boil, he pours it into two stained mugs and brings them over to the table where there's some instant Folgers, a jar of sugar, and a bottle of powdered nondairy creamer sitting next to a kerosene lamp. As we each make our own coffee, my eyes wander around the room. The walls, which appear to have been papered with the pages from a Sears and Roebuck catalogue, are filled with nearly as much junk as the yard outside.

"You a collector, Virgil?"

"Oh, yeah, I can't throw nothin' away. That's the way I think, see."

"I know what you mean."

There's a religious motto taped to the wall. Above it a dime-store version of the ubiquitous *Last Supper* hangs framed in black plastic and mounted behind a set of deer antlers, giving it the effect of being framed twice. I liked Ruth Sooy's quirky rendering better.

"I figure it's half a day to Hidden Swamp and back," Virgil says. "By the time I get back here it'll be too late to go to gathering moss. No sir, it'd be too late by then. Too late by then. That's a full day of gathering sphagnum. I'd have to charge you for the full day of work I lost. This'll cost you money."

"How much money are we talking about, Virgil?"

He stirs his coffee and thinks about it for a long time. When he responds he looks up and stares me straight in the eye.

"I figure about twelve dollars. That's cash money."

"Make it fifty and you got a deal."

"Oh, no, I don't want no big-city charity. I said twelve. Take it or leave it."

"Okay, Virgil, I'll take it."

7

Hoping to see what the Range Rover can do, I suggest to Virgil that we go in my car. Any four-wheel drive capable of adjusting to five different ride heights ought to be the vehicle of choice for a trek into the woods. He thinks about it a long time, glancing back and forth between my car and his rusty pickup.

"Okay, I suppose. But even that there luxury jeep a yours won't do no good in sugar sand. She'll go all the way down to the axle in that stuff. All the way down. And there's a lot of it near Hidden Swamp. Gets close to the gun club, we'll have to go on foot."

I agree, and Virgil, paper lunch bag in hand, follows me to the car.

He edges slowly into the passenger's seat while Pete jumps eagerly past him into the back.

"Got to tell ya something, though," he says, looking over the wood and leather interior.

"What's that?"

"Wouldn't want you to leave this thing behind."

"Why not?" I expect some horror story about the fate of cars left unattended in the Pines.

"Wouldn't want people thinking I'm getting uppity."

"I understand, Virgil."

There's a steady breeze out of the south. The sun has begun to burn through the morning overcast, creating jagged arrows of light among the trees and along the side of the road. As I head back in the direction of the fingerboard, Pete puts two paws up on the back of the seat and stares straight ahead, panting into my ear.

"My gracious, ol' Pete, he loves to travel," says Virgil. "I tell you where I got him from?"

I shake my head. "No, you didn't, Virgil."

"I got him from the old man Cramer over to Bulltown. He raises these Maryland foxhounds, see. I got me Pete in trade for some work I done for the old man Cramer. I hate fox hunting. But I love ol' Pete. Feel bad for him, though, not having his rightful work. Man and dog oughta have their rightful work. Feel bad about that. Feel bad about the old man Cramer, too. His woman passed away a year ago. Ain't never been the same since. No sir, ain't never been the same. He's got his dogs, though. He's got his dogs."

When I reach the county road, Virgil says to drive south for a while. "We'll go past Hog Wallow about a couple of miles," he says, "then there's a shortcut oughta save us some time."

"So tell me, Virgil, what's the significance of that one sign back at your place, the one that says V. APPLEGATE—U.S. CITIZEN?"

"Ain't no significance. That's what I am, is all."

We drive over a small creek that Virgil identifies as Little Hauken Run, then turn right onto Pine Swamp Road. In a quarter of a mile, he says to go right again, onto a dirt road. In a minute or two we're passing a cranberry bog, a number of separate bogs actually, a vast network of reservoirs, raised roads, and flood gates built on sandy soil that was once a cedar swamp. Now it's all walled in by dikes that also serve as roadways between bogs. At the sight of it all Pete begins to bark.

"I done some work here a few years back. Pete, he remembers. My daddy used to work this bog, too—back when they still did scoopin'. That was before they developed the water method."

"I thought you said your father was a bayman."

"He was. But come the fall we needed the ready money, just like everybody else."

"Have you lived in the Pines all your life, Virgil?"

"All my life. Ain't hard to make your living here. No one bothers you. If you don't want to, you don't have to work. There's wealthy men here. Yessir, there's wealthy men here. There's poor, too. But nobody starves. Can't starve in the Pines so long as you know the woods. You want some food you just take up your gun. In season, of course. Me, I don't do no outlawing. I got a neighbor does. He and his brothers go out shooting deer from their jeep. They just stand up and shoot. I seent them once." Pretending to have a gun in his hands, he takes aim out the window and fires. "Just like that. Just like that. Except they stand up. Theirs is one of those without the top."

"I expect you must know just about everybody in the woods, Virgil."

"I know a lot of them, tell you that."

"You ever come across a man by the name of Angel? Angel Bird?"

"Man with a limp?"

"That's him."

"I know of him."

I look over at him but he's staring out the window, avoiding my gaze.

"What do you know about him?"

"I know some people don't belong here. That's all I'm gonna say."

"What about the men who hunt at the Serenity Gun Club, you know any of them?"

"I worked for them once or twice in deer season."

"You recall their names?"

"Didn't have names."

"What?"

"They called themselves Smith and Jones, stuff like that. Didn't want me to know who they was. That's my guess. It's okay by me. They paid good. Who's it you're looking for?"

"The one named Smith. Real name is Bass, Henry Bass. Ever heard of him?"

"Nope. What makes you think he's going to be there?"

"Friend of his told me he's there. Just hope he was telling the truth."

It's a misnomer to call Jack Coyle a "friend" of Henry Bass's. A man like Coyle doesn't have friends, a telling point in his character and the reason why it's risky to be here on his word alone. Still, it's all I've got right now.

Beyond the cranberry bogs we come upon some woods that have been burned recently. Many of the trees are gone, and the ground cover is sparse. There are blackened snags everywhere.

"Had a fire here last year. Same time a the year as this. Worst fire we ever had in the Pines was in April, too. Back in 1963. The fire here was okay, though. It's mostly junk wood. Gum and maple. Some fires are good. Helps the cedar push out the junk wood."

"How'd it start?"

"What?"

"How'd this fire here get started?"

"Don't know."

He turns away again and stares out the window.

"Fire's a sensitive subject with you, isn't it Virgil?"

"Anybody starts a fire deserves hangin'. That's my feelin' on it. Fire's a part of life here, but nature don't need no help from no crazies. I fought my share of forest fires. I know."

I keep quiet, letting him go wherever he wants with the topic.

"Still, you get your best berries after a fire's been through the woods," he says, finally. "There's some good in everything, I suppose."

Having put the subject to rest, he pulls an apple out of his paper bag. Pete jumps up on the back of the seat and whines at him. Virgil makes a little clicking noise, and the hound retreats to the backseat where he sits up and begs. A string of red licorice materializes out of the paper bag. Virgil rips off a piece and gives it to Pete, who sits back and chews it methodically.

"You want some fruit?" Virgil asks, beginning to cut his apple with a pocket knife. "Got bananas and apples."

"Thanks, I'll take a banana. That's a fine-looking knife you've got there, Virgil."

He holds it up proudly. Its handle has been finished in scrimshaw. On each side the ivory has been intricately incised with a similar hunting scene: ducks flying over a waiting hunter who's poised with his shotgun inside a sneakbox concealed in tall swamp grass.

"My daddy carved this for me. Gave it to me on my tenth birthday. It's been places and seen things, this knife has. I could tell you some stories about this here knife. I could tell you some stories."

All of a sudden we're on a short downgrade. Then the hardtop disappears and we're on a combination of gravel and sand. Just as suddenly the road rises and the hardtop reappears.

"Road back there ought to be oiled," says Virgil. "Used to do that. Worked for the state highway. Good money."

He points out a wooden sign at the entrance to a sand road. It says MERION GUNNING CLUB.

"Used to track deer for those folks during hunting season."

"You a good tracker, Virgil?"

"That's an art in itself."

"How do you do it?"

"You look for the best acorn patches. You find droppings. You find buck rubs. Stuff like that."

"Buck rubs?"

"Yeah, the deer get the fuzz off their antlers by rubbing it against these saplings. These young trees are about this thick." He holds his thumb and forefinger about two inches apart. "Their bark gets all rubbed off and polished. The buck, he gets that fuzz off before he fights for a mate."

The road has veered off to the right. We're in a swampy area now, passing a small lake surrounded by cedars, then a wide low-lying area that seems to be a system of marshes and small ponds.

"See that, that there's a dry-bottom swamp," says Virgil, "not like Hidden Swamp. Hidden Swamp's a hard-bottom."

He turns around to give Pete another piece of licorice.

"What's the difference?"

"No hassocks here. There's cedar hassocks in Hidden Swamp. About this wide." He holds his hands a foot apart.

"What are they?"

"Roots from the cedars. They get all tangled up. They're like stumps. Good for hangin' moss out to dry."

I smile, marveling at all the esoteric information. It's like being in a foreign country, made worse by the fact that I've lost my sense of direction. I thought we were heading southwest, but with the sky overcast again and the sun gone from view, I wouldn't want to bet on what direction we're traveling in.

"Gonna take a shortcut up ahead," says Virgil. "There's a sand road with a couple of old Jersey bull pines standing guard, like a gate."

I turn in where he says to, and suddenly visibility is down to fifty feet, less when there's a curve in the road. It's extremely narrow, with the trees and undergrowth encroaching from both sides. Occasionally a branch brushes against the car. When that happens Virgil glances over at me with a twinkle in his eyes.

"We ain't even reached sugar sand yet," he says. "This is solid stuff, packed down over dirt and grass."

"That's reassuring."

"This is one of my favorite spots."

I glance around. We're surrounded by a dense growth of trees.

"You want to experience something in the woods," says Virgil, "all you got to do is stop and be still." He stares out of his open window. "And wait. Be still and wait, that's what my daddy always told me. Somethin' will always come along to surprise you."

The only surprise I want is for this sand road to end immediately and place me at the front door of the Serenity Gun Club.

"Wind's changed," he says, looking at the trees. "Comin' out of the west now. Picking up, too."

As the trees rustle in the mounting breeze, the sweet mix of pine and cedar wafts through the car. There's a harsh beauty to these woods. I can sense a promise of tranquility lurking out there in the stark landscape somewhere. Still, I can't imagine actually living here. I'm not ready for the kind of freedom Virgil takes for granted.

"Gotta be patient," says Virgil, noticing me glance at my watch. "We're gonna get there when we get there. Got a turn comin' up in a hundred yards."

Soon we're on another sand road, this one perpendicular to the last. In a hundred feet we come to another, which crosses at a slight angle.

"This is a plowed lane. Fire service makes them. They help break up fires. Real good for fox and deer hunters, too."

I get onto the plowed lane, which is no wider than the sand road was, and turn right, heading southwest, according to Virgil.

"See some real good-sized rattlers out this way," he says, no doubt to cheer me up. "Gray fox and pheasant, too."

"So where the hell are we, Virgil?"

"Comin' up on Rattler's Deadfall. That's when we'll know we're close."

The holes are getting deeper, the bumps higher, so I hope he's right. My back's beginning to ache. Up ahead the trees appear to thin out, and I can see what looks like a stream or small river off to the right.

Virgil looks out the window. "That little river there feeds into Hidden Swamp." Then he points. "There it is, right in the middle of all that drowned land."

I can see it now. The steady sameness of the tree-lined path is broken abruptly by a low-lying marshy tract of fallen trees and entangled bushes about ten yards from the river. Rattler's Deadfall sits back from the plowed lane about twenty or thirty yards. Before I can ask the obvious question, Virgil explains.

"Was a young man name of Jarner in there. Back in '68. He was harvestin' some of that dead timber. Rattler bit him. Don't usually see them in such wet spots but they can swim, I know that. I seent one in the water once. Went right through his boots. He'd a lived if he'd known how to suck out the venom. I know who found him. It was days after. Jarner's body was all stiff and gray. That rattler'd done his job."

Instinctively, I accelerate, but the jarring from the road only aggravates my back. Past the deadfall the plowed lane returns to its tunnellike constriction, closing back in on us. A little voice in the back of my head begins screaming for space, for a way out.

"How much longer?"

"This is it," says Virgil.

I don't see anything but the enveloping trees and underbrush. Then, without any warning, the Rover barrels over a small rise and descends to an intersecting gravel road on the other side. It's not exactly center field at the Vet, but at least the sense of total enclosure is gone. I can see the sky without having to crane my neck and look straight up through the windshield.

Virgil points left. So I steer the car into two ruts in the middle of the road. About fifty yards down on the right there's an opening in the trees, yet another road into the woods. But this one's made of pine poles laid crosswise on a path about twenty feet wide.

"Fred Ford knew cedar farmin'. He died a few years back. This is his corduroy road. Goes straight to the Hidden Swamp. People around here still call it Ford's Crossway. My father used to come here to get cedar for his garveys. Cedar's the best wood there is for boats."

"You mean this doesn't take us to the gun club?"

He looks down the road, motioning me on. "That way."

My heart sinks. But in a quarter of a mile we come to the last sand road. This time there's a sign: DO NOT ENTER—DEAD END. Finally, we've gone as far as we can go.

As I pull off the road I feel the difference immediately. The car slows a little, sinks, then the wheels begin to spin. I can hear the automatic traction system go into effect.

"Keep going," says Virgil, "it ain't real bad yet."

After fifty feet the dirt road's no longer visible in the rearview mirror. In a hundred feet we come upon a black Jeep Grand Cherokee parked in a little cutout area.

"We'd best stop here," says Virgil. "Time to get out and walk."

I pull the Rover into the cutout just ahead of the Jeep.

"How far is it?"

"A hundred yards, maybe less."

Pete jumps out first and heads for the nearest tree. I get out and walk into the woods, too, following Pete's example. When I return he's running back and forth around Virgil, waiting for a signal to get started. Virgil raises his hand. Pete stops in his tracks and hunkers down. Then Virgil crouches on the sandy ground next to the hound and doesn't move, keeping his balance with one hand on the sandy surface. After a minute or two he stands up.

"You hear that?" he asks me.

"What?"

"Don't know for sure. Might've been a deer. It stopped, though. But we're downwind, so it couldn't have picked up our scent."

Motionless, we stand there for another minute listening. I don't hear anything but the wind, which is stronger now.

"Guess we'd better get goin'," Virgil says, "can't keep your Mr. Bass waiting."

After one last look over his shoulder, he takes up the lead, heading down the sand road. Pete and I take up the rear.

8

THE ROAD CURVES, goes straight, then curves again. Still no gun club in sight. How long can it take to walk a hundred yards? With dense woods all around, it's like making your way through an endless topiary maze. The sand seems to get finer and softer the farther we go, too. Virgil was right. There's no question about being able to drive through this stuff. I can hardly walk on it.

Finally, we emerge into a sandy clearing surrounded on all sides by dense woods. The club sits in the middle, a well-turned-out modern log cabin, the kind advertised on TV for soft city folks who want a place where they can pretend to rough it. It's a simple setup. There's a large propane tank next to the cabin for heating and cooking and a gasoline-powered generator around back. The tank and generator would have to have been rolled in from the road on logs, no small feat. I can't see an outhouse anywhere, which means somebody's dug a well and a septic tank, and installed indoor plumbing. All the modern conveniences. The cabin itself has only one story but runs to about one hundred feet on all sides, large enough to house six or eight men comfortably.

While I'm trying to decide how to approach the place, Pete takes off on a run for the front door, barking all the way.

"Pete, get back here. Bad dog."

Pete, bored by all the time spent in the car, would rather check out this new object on the landscape than wait for Virgil.

Motioning Virgil to stay behind me, I make my way around to the rear of the cabin. The back door's locked. I can't see anything through the rear windows except a room full of bunk beds and bare mattresses. Around front Pete's pacing back and forth at the door, alternately whining, sniffing, and barking. Virgil pulls him aside while I knock. After half-a-dozen tries I test the handle. It's unlocked.

Inside, it smells like a fraternity house the morning after an all-night stag party. The stench of urine and liquor permeates the room. It isn't hard to figure out why. Off in a corner on a stained mattress lies the unconscious body of Judge Henry Bass, dressed in white boxer shorts and black socks. On the floor next to him, two empty Jim Beam bottles lie on their sides. His hair is greasy and disheveled, his eyes lusterless and unfocused. His mustache and bushy eyebrows, which weeks earlier lent an air of class to the man, now look merely outlandish.

He's breathing laboriously, but he *is* breathing. Pete immediately goes over and gives him a thorough sniffing. Unapproving, he returns to stand next to Virgil.

"He a friend of yours?" asks Virgil.

"Never met the man."

"Be grateful for that."

I call out his name. There's no response, so I try shaking him. After several good pokes in the ribs his eyes open.

"Judge? Judge Bass?"

"Huh? What the—"

The judge tries to sit up. His stomach balks at the effort. He puts his hand to his mouth but it's too late. Last night's bourbon ends up on the floor next to the mattress.

"Waste of good sippin' whiskey, you ask me," says Virgil.

"Who the hell're you?" says Bass, wiping his mouth on his forearm, gasping for air.

"Name's Frank Sweeney. This is Virgil Applegate. I'm here to help you, Judge."

His expression remains blank, uncomprehending.

"Virgil, how'd you like to check in the kitchen and see if there's any coffee. I think the judge could use some."

"Wouldn't mind some myself," Virgil says.

He disappears down a narrow hallway and reappears at a server's window cut out of the connecting wall between the kitchen and living room. I stand up and take a quick look around. The living room is really a rec room. There's some rustic pine and oak furniture along the walls, but the majority of floor space has been given over to three felt-topped poker tables in the middle of the room. The exposed log walls are bare except for some empty gun holders, several multi-pronged buck racks, and a few tattered and faded centerfolds from *Playboy* and *Penthouse.* Across the room is the door to the sleeping quarters. Down the hallway past the kitchen are a bathroom, a storage area, and the rear exit.

"Need a drink, for chrissakes," says Bass, on his back again.

"That'll have to wait till you and I have a talk."

"Who the hell're you, anyway?"

"I'm a private investigator, a friend of Nick D'Angelo's. I knew Theodore Capetanakis, too."

"Who?" Even those milky bloodshot eyes can't conceal his startled reaction. "Shit."

He turns his head away and stares at the log wall. I pull up a chair from one of the poker tables.

"I know about the Jonah scam. So do the police."

"How'd you find me?"

"Jack Coyle told me. He had to. I have some compromising state-ments he made to me on tape."

"*Coyle* told you I was here?" He manages to sit up without vomit-ing. His expression is a mix of fear and incredulity.

"That's right."

"That's impossible. Nobody knows I'm here."

"What?"

"I didn't tell *anybody*."

"Not even Tony Dante?"

He shakes his head, then begins to laugh.

"What's so funny?" I ask.

"You know *why* I came here?"

"To kill yourself."

He laughs again, louder this time.

"That's right. Now Dante'll take care of it *for* me. That's okay. What the fuck do I care who does it? Trouble is—" he grins, his eyes sud-denly alive, "now you and your Piney friend there are going to die with me."

"Nobody's gonna get killed, not if we get a move on."

"You don't know Tony. We've been set up, Mr. Sweeney. That psy-chopathic cretin, Angel, must have been tailing me the whole time. And now he's got you here, too."

"Listen to me—"

He stands up.

"Save the bullshit." He stumbles, then makes his way toward the sleeping quarters. "Don't worry. I'm just going to put some clothes on. Can't go to my last reward dressed like this."

I follow him into the room and watch while he pulls on some pants and a shirt, then steps into a pair of bedroom slippers. Out in the liv-ing room, Virgil is waiting with three mugs of coffee and a box of cookies.

"All I could find," he says, putting everything down on one of the poker tables.

Pete scratches at the front door, so Virgil goes over and lets him out. "You want me to leave, too?" he asks me.

"Stay if you want."

"I'll just sit over there and rest a bit, if you don't mind."

He takes his coffee and cookies and sits in the corner of the room under a five-point buck rack. Something flashes through my mind from this morning: *The Last Supper,* framed in deer antlers on the wall of Virgil's cabin.

"Virgil, that picture of *The Last Supper* you had on your wall?"

"Yeah?"

"Is it some kind of Piney tradition to drape it with something?"

"Lots 'round here do it, I guess."

That's three versions of DaVinci's *The Last Supper* I've seen since I've been down here. And each was draped with something different.

"Jesus," says Bass, "what the fuck—"

I force him to sit back down.

"Okay, Judge, let's talk."

"Isn't anything to talk about. It's all over."

"I need to know some things."

"Why bother?"

"Suppose I suggested a way for you to cut your losses?"

"How?"

"I may be able to cut a deal for you, if you agree to testify against Dante and Bird."

He begins laughing again, then stops.

"I didn't kill anyone, you know."

"I didn't say you did."

"I never imagined Tony would have Nick and Cappy killed like that. Angel's scum. He'd put a match to his own mother."

"Answer a few questions for me. Who's idea was the Jonah scam?"

His eyes roam around the cabin, and for a moment he looks almost wistful. Virgil's asleep in his chair.

"You know, we had some good times here back in the old days. Every deer season. All of us hanging out."

"Who's 'us'?"

"Tony, Jack, Cappy, me. Sometimes Tony would bring Angel along, but we always gave him hell about that. Hardly anybody ever did any hunting. Mostly we just drank and played cards. We were like a club, you know, like when you're kids and you have a hideout?"

"This was *after* Dante had opened the Poseidon?"

"Yeah. Anyway, it was Cappy who had the idea for the scam. He was paranoid, poor bastard, really paranoid. Always thought somebody was cheating him at poker, that kind of thing. So he gave Tony this idea, and Tony went for it. Cappy told Tony it was like an insurance policy. I'd become a judge, Cappy said. He knew somebody at the court of appeals. Then Tony would have someone to look after his interests when the Poseidon's case came up. He set the whole thing up for Tony. All Tony had to do was keep Cappy's money out of the hands of the IRS. He even came up with the idea for the 'Jonah' name. We were supposed to be 'whales.' You know, high rollers? Cappy thought it'd be funny if a couple of whales were named Jonah."

"And you, you got to gamble at the Poseidon all you wanted."

"Hell, I'd been blacklisted in Vegas. I owed everybody. Wasn't anywhere else to go. Cappy saved me."

"*Saved* you?"

"When I walked into that casino, everybody knew me. Course, I wasn't Judge Bass. I was 'Mr. S' to them, but they *knew* me. It was always 'Hi there, Mr. S,' 'Howya doing today, Mr. S.' In a few seconds a waitress would be there with my Cutty and water. All the waitresses knew me. And I made it worth their while, too, I'll tell you. 'Make room for Mr. S,' they'd say at the table. 'You want a sandwich, Mr. S?' I never wanted to leave. Then it all fell apart. . . ."

I almost feel sorry for the poor bastard.

"What happened?"

"Tony ruined it all. He tried to stiff Cappy. It was a stupid thing to do. I'd still be playing at the Poseidon Tuesday nights if that asshole hadn't panicked. He thought he could solve his cash-flow problem by stealing from a man like Cappy. I think he actually believed he could get away with it. But you don't do that kind of thing to a man like Cappy. That was a mistake, big mistake."

"How'd Dante do it?"

"He just *took* Cappy's money. Half a million at first, then another million. He put it in his own account. The money never made it to the Swiss bank. Big mistake." He laughs.

"Why'd Cappy use Nick to get back at Dante?"

"What was he going to do, report Tony to the police? Hell, he was in just as deep. Besides, Cappy was strange. I think he was more interested in humiliating Tony than getting his money back. He was funny that way. When he drank he did weird things, even weirder than when he was sober. So one night he and Nick got pie-eyed and Cappy spilled the beans."

"Did Cappy know about the murder of Harry Morrow?"

"I think he suspected."

"Did he tell Nick?"

"Who knows."

"Were you involved in the Morrow murder?"

"Tony and I were both in Vegas at the time."

"Very convenient. Can you prove that Tony gave the order to Angel to kill Harry Morrow?"

"I was in the room when he made the phone call."

"Good. That's all the cops'll need."

"Tony went ballistic when he heard what Angel had done, how he'd driven the company truck into the woods and all. Tony damn near put out a contract on *him*. Instead, he decided to sell the company to Capetan Transport."

"Enter Cappy."

"Right. I learned all this later. Too late to warn the dumb guinea that it wasn't exactly the smartest thing in the world to do. I just kept out of it."

"Until now. Now you're gonna save your ass, right? Okay, look—"

There's a noise outside. It's Pete whimpering, then barking. Suddenly Virgil's awake and on his feet.

"That's Pete," he says. "What's wrong?"

"I don't know."

He goes to the front door and opens it.

"Sweet Jesus."

9

Moving to the open door, I look southward toward the sand road. The sky is filled with rising plumes of white smoke moving this way. A visceral fear sinks its pincers into my gut. Glancing instinctively at the line of dense trees on the edge of the clearing, I confirm what I already know: there's no way out except to go deeper into the enveloping maw of the forest.

Bass pushes past me and out the door. At the top of the steps he stops and stares to the south. "We've been set up," he says, turning toward me, his eyes wild with excitement. He dashes down the steps. Virgil tries to stop him, but Bass shoves him aside and takes off on the run.

"He'll never get out," says Virgil. "He's headed right into it."

"How far away do you think it is?"

He looks up at the spires of smoke. It's dark gray now. In the distance it's turning black.

"Wind's picked up. Be here in fifteen minutes, maybe less."

I look at my watch. It's 1:35 P.M.

I look down the road to where Bass has disappeared from sight. "I've got to stop him. Without him I've got nothing."

Blind to my own unreason, I take off at full speed. Virgil's protests recede into the distance as my mind shifts gears.

The woods are filled with the frantic sounds of terrorized animals on the run. About fifty feet down the road, I'm forced aside into the underbrush as three crazed deer race by. The air gets thicker and my eyes begin to sting. In the distance there are two loud popping noises, one right after the other. Then a third. Exploding automobile tires. Forcing them from my mind, I shout to the judge, screaming at him to turn around and come back.

At a bend in the road I stop and shield my face in the crook of my arm, trying to see ahead. Dense blackness looms like an approaching thunderhead. The smoke is multicolored, dark gray nearest the top, a sickly yellow at ground level. For the first time I can hear the fire. This is as far as I go.

Then I see him. He's about fifty feet away, on the ground by the side of the road. I yell and he turns, but from the look on his face I can tell he's in shock. When I reach him he stands up limply and stares into my eyes, trying to figure out who I am.

"Come on, Judge, we've got to go back."

Somehow he manages to run alongside me. With the wind at our backs, it's easier going, but we've wasted precious time. When we emerge into the clearing Virgil and Pete are where I left them. Bass breaks free and stumbles into the cabin.

"Can we head into the woods and make a run for it?" I yell.

Virgil shakes his head grimly, looking fatalistic. "Can't outrun the beast."

The air's heavy with smoke and falling ash. Along the edge of the clearing, a few spot fires have started. Blowing embers have landed on the roof of the cabin. I look around desperately for some sort of fireproof shelter. Nothing. The clearing alone, although free of consumable fuel, is too small to protect us. And even if the flames don't get us here, the smoke will.

"What the hell do we do?" I ask him.

"Get to the swamp," he says.

He's calm. His eyes are intense but focused. When he turns toward the cabin I follow him. At the front steps he stops and says, "Got to get us something wet, some towels or something."

Then there's an explosion somewhere in the rear of the cabin. My first thought is the gas generator. Virgil sets me right.

"Shotgun," he says.

With Pete right behind him, Virgil reaches the sleeping quarters first. At the doorway he glances in, then moves on, his priorities clear. It takes me a little longer to absorb what's happened. Inside the room, the judge lies spread-eagled on the bottom bunk of one of the beds. There's a Remington 12-gauge next to him on the bare mattress. Hungry for one last spin of the wheel, he swallowed the barrel of his own gun. The rear half of his head has been splattered across the wall behind the bed. I guess he never intended to go back. My own gamble hasn't paid off either. Death always draws the high cards.

In the kitchen Virgil's at the sink, wetting two large towels. He hands me one and keeps the other for himself. Then we leave by the back door.

Outside, the wind and heat have increased. We have to raise our voices to be heard. And the air's so thick with smoke it's difficult to see more than ten yards ahead. How can we possibly find our way through the woods in these conditions? Pete seems worried, too. He's crouched at Virgil's feet, whimpering.

I take off my windbreaker and shirt and toss both aside. Virgil does the same, dropping his red flannel shirt on the ground. He walks ahead in a sleeveless V-necked undershirt, still wearing his black leather cap.

"When it gets real bad," he says, shouting into my ear, "get down on all fours—there's always a little oxygen down close to the ground."

When it gets real bad? What the hell does he think *this* is?

Somewhere behind us there's a loud popping, then a frightening roar, followed by a whooshing noise. It sounds like a gigantic blowtorch.

"The dickens," says Virgil, looking worried.

"What was it?"

"The propane. Valve's blown. That tank explodes anywhere near us and we're goners. Come on."

With the wet towel draped over my head, I stay close behind Virgil and Pete. We make it to the edge of the woods where small spot fires have broken out, threatening to burgeon into full-fledged ground fires at any moment. The wind is strong and searing on our backs, pushing us forward, keeping us off-balance. Overhead, treetops burst into flame as flying embers land in the crowns of the tallest cedars and oaks. An endless roar fills the air. It's like walking through a flaming wind tunnel. Glancing over my shoulders through the trees, I can see the roof of the cabin in flames. I hope the judge's funeral plans included cremation.

The world has been reduced to elemental noise and heat. It's the earth's last hour. Air and smoke glow orange and red like the inside

297

of a blast furnace. The roar is deafening. Trees and branches pop and crackle out on the flanks of the fire. Debris and ash dance furiously in the heavy air, landing on clothing, striking us in the face whenever we look out from behind our towels. Resin-choked pines explode behind us, a not so distant warning that the worst has yet to reach us. Then a series of rapid explosions erupts from the vicinity of the cabin—the gas stove or maybe the club's ammo stash.

If I believed in Hell, I'd have to say this is it. But I don't. Right now, I believe in Virgil Applegate. Virgil seems undaunted, as if he's been preparing for this all his life.

Desperate, I look for a break in the wall of smoke, something to run through and make it back to safe ground. When an opening does appear, the roaring is weaker there, as if the powerful locomotive coming up behind us has slowed or entered a tunnel. Virgil seems to read my mind.

"Straight ahead," he shouts. "We got to go straight to the swamp. Don't make no turns. That's Hades back there."

"How the hell do you know which way to go?" I yell back.

"Been here before. I can feel my way."

I trudge on, head down, eyes half-closed, my lungs burning. The towel's no longer wet but at least it provides some protection for my face. Progress is impossibly slow and awkward. Trees and snags appear without warning, tearing into my clothes, knocking me aside. My feet become entangled in vines and small bushes. Still, nothing seems to hinder Virgil. He plods on steadily, slowed only by my clumsiness.

After a few more yards, he grabs my hand and places it on the trunk of a tree. I can't see anything but it feels like the heads of several large metal spikes.

"Feel those?" he yells. "They're for a tree stand. Put them in during deer season back in '79 when I was guidin' here. We're on the right track."

God bless this man.

"How far?"

"It's comin' up. You'll know it when you're walking on sphagnum. It's better than store-boughten carpet."

Suddenly, we're propelled forward through the dense air as if we've stepped on a land mine. I end up next to a thick pine tree, on top of Virgil. Pete barks madly at us, then licks our faces. I look down to see blood on my bruised hands. My watch, shattered, has stopped at 1:51 P.M. Our fifteen minutes are up.

"Propane blew," says Virgil, struggling to get up. He glances back for an instant, then moves on.

I stand up too, trying to appear unfazed, but a strange feeling has come over me. It isn't fair. I shouldn't have to die like this. I should be allowed to pass peacefully away in my sleep as an old man. Tears well up. I'm exhausted. I can't walk another foot. I won't. Insanely, some lines of Beckett's pop into my head. *I can't go on like this,* says Estragon. *That's what you think,* responds Vladimir. "I'll go on," says Sweeney.

Then suddenly I feel it. Under my feet. The ground has become soft and springy, as if we're walking on damp sponges.

"Got to get to the deep water," Virgil shouts.

The air's dense with thick black smoke now. I yell to him to stay close. I can barely see his silhouette two yards in front of me. Bent over, cringing from the heat, I'm desperate for the better air near the ground.

We make our way through thick strands of swamp grass over a canopy of oozing moss. It feels like a deep shag carpet under foot. After a while I can feel the wetness cooling my feet. It's wonderful. I reach down and grab a large hunk of the stuff and squeeze it over my face and towel. Thank God for sphagnum.

"Gonna get tricky up ahead," yells Virgil. "It's like quicksand."

He picks up Pete, who's been having a tough time making it on his own across the soggy terrain. I move closer and put my hand on Virgil's shoulder to make sure we don't get separated. We're moving very slowly now, the mucky surface pulling us down deeper and deeper with each step. When it seems we can't go any farther without getting permanently stuck, Virgil stops and turns, his face illuminated by the approaching firestorm. For the first time I sense something like fear or doubt.

"Can't stop now, Virgil."

"What's gonna become of Pete? I can't hold the hound and make it into the swamp, too."

"Give him to me." I take the dog, who clings to me like a terrified newborn. "Let's go."

"Head for them hassocks out there."

I can't see anything except smoke, but it never occurs to me to doubt him.

"How far away are they?"

"Not far. 'Bout fifty feet. Water's only ankle-deep there, though. We want to be farther out. Footing's bad, so we gotta jump across them stumps. When we reach the deeper part, get yourself way down in the water."

I can barely hear him. But I think I get the gist of the plan. I give him an encouraging pat on the back and push him forward.

With the water up around my feet, I'm curiously euphoric. A raging firestorm is seconds away, and I can't discern fear, thirst, or even the need to stop and rest. Perhaps this is sheer exhaustion. Or maybe it's the relief of knowing the end is near.

My eyes sting so badly I can barely open them. With Pete under my left arm, I'm forced to feel my way with my right, causing me to trip over the first hassock. It's a gnarled tangle of slimy roots and grass. I climb up carefully, holding tightly onto Pete, who seems to understand that his job is to stay limp. With one hand on the trunk of a nearby cedar, I make my way to the next hassock. Then the next. And the next. Sensing that I'm nearly out of time, I jump to one last stump. By now I have no idea where Virgil is so I say a little prayer for all of us, hug Pete to my chest, and plunge into the swamp, hoping I haven't circled unknowingly back to shallow water.

In an instant I'm waist-deep in the cooling balm of Hidden Swamp. There's no getting a foothold on the slippery bottom, so I grab the nearest hassock with my free hand, clutching the trembling Pete with the other, and wrap my legs around the submerged stump. Pete and I sink up to our chins, blanketing ourselves in a watery cocoon. All that remains is to avert our eyes from the approaching apocalypse.

When the firestorm passes over, some demonic force tries to lift me out of the water, pulling and tearing at my legs. But the suction of the swamp is like an anchor holding me in place. The roaring rises in my ears. My face is seared with gusts of molten air.

Time slows, stops. Then nothing. No flames, no scorching wind. Only darkness, black as the end of the world. And silence, blessed silence.

10

I HAVE NO IDEA how long we were in the swamp. It seemed like hours, though I know it wasn't. Virgil and Pete are okay, but Virgil's still throwing up cedar water. He ended up clinging to a hassock about twenty feet away from me. Before the smoke cleared I could hear him thrashing about, gagging on swamp grass. It turns out he hates the water. Pete was a real trooper. He stayed put until he heard Virgil. Then he began a furious doggy paddle toward his master. After Virgil and I finally made it to the crossway and collapsed, Pete ran back and forth between us, licking our faces gratefully.

The crossway—Fred Ford's corduroy road into Hidden Swamp— survived with only a few sections scorched. Its brown bark surface is the brightest thing in view. Everything else on the landscape exists in shades of black and gray. As far as the eye can see, there's nothing but smoldering snags and charred poles that were once fully decked-out trees. Only the swamp's salvific waters are untouched. A living oasis embraced by the dead land.

With my eyes stinging badly, it's difficult to see things in any detail. I am able to distinguish the outline of what remains of the cabin. It's been reduced to a few smoking timbers and a stone chimney. The fire itself is a smokey trail in the distance, burning its way in a southeasterly direction into the Pines. Except for the ringing in my ears, everything is deathly quiet, punctuated now and then by the loud crack and pop of a tree exploding.

I'm afraid if we don't make an effort to move soon, we may never get up. So, red-eyed, ashen-faced, and wet to the bone, Virgil and I stand and begin the long walk back, craving nothing more than clean air and fresh drinking water. All along the crossway the mystery of the woods' interior is cruelly revealed. There's the charred black body of a deer, its bloated carcass split open at the midsection. And black pine snags and smoldering cedars everywhere. It was a fire sermon we endured, the birth of Hell. Now is the afterlife.

Then through the haze, voices. And somewhere dimly on the other side, lights.

". . . trucks on the way . . ."

"How long . . ."

". . . second chopper . . ."

". . . Atsion tower . . ."

I cry out like a child waking from a nightmare.

"Maclean, is that you? Sandy?"

"Jesus Christ. Someone's there. Who is it? Who's there?"

Virgil, Pete, and I emerge through the haze on Ford's Crossway. Three Orpheuses ascending from our Piney Hades.

"My God! Jesus, it's Virgil Applegate. And, you— Hal, run and get Bill. Tell him to bring the oxygen and some blankets."

"And some water," I yell.

"My God, were you actually here when the fire passed through?" Maclean asks.

"Made it to the swamp, thanks to him." I point to Virgil, who's sitting down again, near tears.

"I don't believe it."

"Believe it. And he charged me twelve dollars for the trip."

"He's in shock," Maclean says, checking on Virgil. Then he stands up and studies me.

"I'm okay. Take care of him."

I wrap myself in a blanket and breath deeply from the oxygen mask offered by Hal. It's the first decent air I've had in my lungs for hours.

"This thing was arson," I tell Maclean. "There's a body, too, back in what's left of that cabin. It was suicide."

"We already spotted the gasoline cans back by the road."

"I can give you the bastard who did it. He drives a red Dodge Ram truck."

Maclean looks at me.

"A Dodge Ram?"

"That's what I said."

"You well enough to walk?"

"Yeah. I just want some water."

"Follow me."

I take a quick look at Virgil, who's being treated for shock by one of Maclean's men. Pete's by his side. They'll be okay. I follow Maclean to one of the emergency vehicles where someone hands me a bottle of water.

"Feel better?" Maclean asks, after I've emptied half the bottle.

"Much."

"Good. I want to show you something."

At the end of the crossway we get into his pickup and take the rutted gravel road in the direction of where Virgil and I parked. It's eerie, on one side of the road there are plenty of healthy woodlands, on the other nothing but smoldering devastation.

The two four-by-fours are right where Virgil and I left them on the sand road. The tires on Mrs. Bass's Jeep Grand Cherokee have exploded, leaving the car on its axles. The Range Rover is there, too. What was once eggshell white is now scorched earth black. The windows are shattered and both rear tires are gone, disintegrated in the heat. It's a total loss. And with twenty more payments due on it.

At first I don't notice the other charred vehicle. It's shielded by an ambulance and a fire-service wagon. Even when I finally see it, the truth doesn't sink in immediately. Maclean gets out, and I follow him over there. We walk around and stop on the other side. It's a truck, a Dodge Ram. Whether or not it was once red is impossible to say.

On the driver's side door someone has been handcuffed to one of the braces holding the oversized rearview mirror. Whoever it once was—it appears to have been a man—is nothing but a slab of barbecued meat now. His knees are drawn up in the pugilistic pose. The free arm is curled up toward his face, the fingers turned inward, clawlike. Raw flesh and gums are drawn back at the mouth, exposing the teeth and charred tongue in a gruesome death grin. Only the feet give away his identity. Despite the fusing of clothing with charred flesh, it's still possible to see that he wore western boots. The rhinestones have lost their luster and melted into the leather stitching, but the basic outline of the boots is still distinguishable. This Angel has ridden his last chariot of fire.

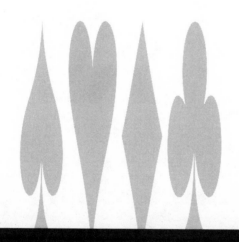

THE BOARDWALK

1

THERE'S AN ANCIENT Taoist principle I've always found reassuring: it doesn't matter how slowly you go, so long as you don't stop. Right now, I'm clinging to that for all I'm worth, because by the time Sandy Maclean gets me back to Gwen's I'm losing power like a steam engine with a leaky boiler.

Gwen's car isn't in sight when we pull up. I invite Sandy in but he prefers to wait in the pickup with Pete. He has offered to take care of the hound until Virgil's released from the hospital. Virgil was still in shock when we left him, and the emergency crew felt he should be watched for the next twenty-four hours.

Inside, on the kitchen table I find the remains of lunch for one— tomato soup, some crackers, a half-eaten ham sandwich, and part of an apple. I gather up the leftovers and put them on a plate. There's a stale doughnut on the counter too, and a nice fillet in the fridge. I put it all together and take it out to Pete. He nearly knocks me over getting to it.

Back in the cabin I notice Gwen's briefcase and unopened overnight bag on the bed. Her work clothes have been tossed on the floor. Her jeans and sneakers are missing.

A little lightheaded, I get out of my clothes and into the shower. As the warm water laves my burning eyes, I begin laughing. Then suddenly I'm shaking uncontrollably, trembling like Pete during his immersion in Hidden Swamp. Crouched in the corner of the shower stall, I rock back and forth on the balls of my feet. "It's okay," I say over and over again. "It's okay. You're going to be all right. Now it's his turn."

AFTER PUTTING ON a clean pair of chinos and a rumpled blue polo shirt, I make a ham sandwich and drink three glasses of water. I feel as if I may be thirsty for the rest of my life. I grab the sandwich along with the rest of my things, and on the way out the door leave the key Gwen gave me on the kitchen table.

"Thanks for waiting. I really appreciate this, Sandy."

"You sure you don't want to borrow my truck? I can use my wife's car for a while."

"No, I'd feel better in a rental."

"I still can't believe what you told me. You sure?"

"I'll be certain after I talk to the Sooys again. Now, tell me more about that cop who came to see you, the one who claimed he was Nick D'Angelo."

MACLEAN DROPS ME OFF at one of those rent-a-junker places. I drive away in a snappy little yellow number, a 1980 Ford Escort. It's not a Range Rover, but the radio works and it handles beautifully. Maybe there's a moral in this.

The first bookstore I try is Darien's, half a mile down from the car rental. It turns out they carry nothing but New Age stuff. No art books. A middle-aged flower child at the counter refers me to a store in McKee City two miles away on the Black Horse Pike.

The McKee City store features an entire wall of art books, including half-a-dozen on American folk art. I decide on *American Folk Paintings*. I like its landscapes.

WHEN I STEP OUT of the car in front of the Sooys' cabin, the air is leaden, thick with the smell of burned timber, as if the fire had passed right through here. Joe is outside wetting down the roof with a garden hose. It isn't necessary, but after what I've just been through, I'd do the same thing. Out of the corner of my eye I can see Ruth peering at me from behind the curtains of the front window.

"I have to talk to you and your daughter, Mr. Sooy."

He won't look at me.

"What for?"

"I'm trying to catch the man who started the fire today. I think you and your daughter can help."

He laughs. "We ain't got nothing to do with no fire."

"No, but I think the two of you met the man who started it. Wait—" I raise my hand. "What I'm trying to say is that he might have come here under false pretenses."

"Ain't nobody been here under any pretenses."

I ask him to describe Nick D'Angelo, the 'smooth talker,' the man with 'a way' about him. He gives me the same description Sandy Maclean did. Then I hand him Nick's photograph.

"Here, I'd like you to look at this."

He takes the photograph, examines it, then hands it back.

"Never saw this man before in my life."

"This was Lieutenant Nick D'Angelo."

Now he's confused.

"*This* is Lieutenant D'Angelo?"

"That's right."

"But . . ."

"Could we go inside and talk? I brought something for Ruth."

Ruth's ready for us. She's wearing a bright green dress and the same black sandals as before. Her hair, no longer tied back, has been brushed out and reaches down to her shoulders. She seems pleased about something. I have the uncomfortable feeling she's been waiting for me. Joe signs something to her, and her expression changes. She looks confused now.

"I ain't done any baking today," says Joe, "but I got coffee."

"I'd love some."

Joe goes into the kitchen, and I walk over to where Ruth is standing.

"I brought you something."

When I show her the book her eyes brighten. She takes it over to the couch and sits down. By the time Joe returns from the kitchen with coffee, Ruth no longer knows we're here. For her it's the shock of recognition: Edward Hicks, Grandma Moses, all those primitive landscapes, the realistically delineated plants, the eyes of fantastic animals peering out of the woods.

"It's called *The Peaceable Kingdom*," I say, after noticing her eyes on one page in particular. She watches my lips closely. "The artist was Edward Hicks. He was a sign painter. He was self-taught. Like you."

She seems confused.

"How's it feel," I ask, "to know there are others who paint the way you do?"

After letting that sink in, I say, "I want you to have this. It's a gift."

She smiles at me, then turns and speaks haltingly. It comes out in a deep nasal tone, but it would be impossible to misunderstand it.

"Thank . . . you."

"Will you do me a favor in return?"

She nods her head. I look over at Joe, but he's resigned to it.

"Do you remember when I was here last time, you showed me the painting of the truck leaving the scene of the forest fire across the road?"

She nods again.

"I'd like you to tell me the name of the second man who died in that fire. You know, the man who built the charcoal pit?"

Without looking at her father, she gets up, goes into the kitchen, and returns with a small notepad and pencil. She writes something down, tears the top sheet off, and gives it to me. I barely have to glance at it. I can make out the large, bold hand from where I'm sitting.

"Thank you, Ruth. You did the right thing."

"The man who was here," Joe says to me, "the one who said he was Lieutenant D'Angelo? He asked about the collier, too."

"Did Ruth know him?" I ask, pointing to the name on the piece of paper before putting it in my pocket.

"They were friends. He was a hermit. So's Ruth. She was about the only person he ever talked to. She was just fourteen at the time. Sometimes she'd go over and help him watch the charcoal pit."

Thankfully for her, she wasn't there the day Angel showed up with Harry Morrow.

"But he had a family, didn't he?"

"There was a son. His woman ran off with the child. Just like my Anna." There are tears in his eyes now.

Ruth watches us, then turns, walks to the far wall of the living room, and takes down one of the paintings, the one showing a young woman asleep on a bed of pine needles. The woman appears to be dreaming as several fantastic creatures look on from the bushes.

"She wants you to have it," says Joe.

"No, Ruth, I don't think you should give this away."

Her eyes plead with me to accept it.

"Okay, but only on one condition. You have to let me show it to a dealer in Philadelphia. Okay?"

She thinks a moment, then nods at me with a smile.

2

IT'S NEARLY 9 P.M. before I leave the hospital. When I come out the air feels different. It smells like rain. Virgil's doing fine, but he lost the pocketknife with the scrimshaw handle that his father gave him. It's somewhere on the bottom of Hidden Swamp. He's being philosophical about it, considering he could have lost much more. But I can tell it bothers him.

I'm exhausted, desperate for sleep. Still, there's one more stop to make.

This time she's home. Her Toyota's out front. I can hear music coming from somewhere inside. It takes a lot of pounding on the door to get her attention.

"Hi," she says, her voice noncommittal. "I never thought I'd see you again."

I guess I expected something more. Even a little false remorse would do. Billie Holiday's singing "Gloomy Sunday" somewhere inside. Right song, wrong day.

"I saw it on the news," she says, backing away from the door, drawing me inside. "You okay?"

"Tired."

"How's Virgil?"

"I just saw him. He'll be out tomorrow. What'd they say about the fire?"

"It's under control. About three hundred acres gone. Guess somebody doesn't like you."

"Looks that way."

"Couldn't have been your buddy, Tony Dante. I was interviewing him at the time of the fire, it turns out."

"No, it wasn't him."

"You've been getting phone calls all afternoon. Martindale, Talley, somebody named Petrillo."

"I'll call Talley later."

"Want a drink? Glass of wine or something? Coffee?"

She sits down on the couch. I take the easy chair across from her.

"No, I had something at the hospital cafeteria."

"So—"

"So you—"

"Sorry."

"Go ahead."

"No, you go."

"So you got an interview with Dante."

"Yeah, he even let me have a photographer along. The man's crazy. Thinks a little good publicity now can save his ass. Not that he's going to get any. Good publicity, I mean. It's a little late for that. Rumor is he's going to close down in the morning."

"Tony Dante's history, no matter what he does."

"You sure about that?"

"I'm sure."

She waits, hoping I'll volunteer more.

"You hear about Sandra Greenberg?" she asks, after the silence gets unbearable.

"No."

"It was just on the news. She's dead."

"What?"

"They found her in one of the high-roller suites at the Poseidon."

"What was it?"

"Champagne and cocaine."

"Jesus."

"Fucking Dante, he probably knew it the whole time he was talking to me. The mission's planning a prayer vigil on the Boardwalk in

312

the morning. A going-away present for the little prick. He deserves far worse."

"You saying he killed the kid?"

"I'm saying he let her gamble. The booze and coke were gratis."

"Too bad you can't prove that. It'd save the cops some trouble."

"You really don't care about *her,* do you? All you can think about is getting Dante."

"I have to parcel out my compassion. You should do the same."

"You think she was a lost cause from the start, don't you?"

"Aren't you still a little close to this story? What happened to the reporter's vaunted objectivity?"

"Bullshit. I'm talking about *you.* You can't feel anything."

"What? Unless I missed something, I'm the one here with the legitimate bitch. I mean you *are* the one who betrayed me."

She winces. Maybe she never thought I'd see it in those terms. I'm beginning to wonder just how far apart we really were.

"It's my job, Frank. What did you expect? You left the damn photocopies in your car."

"That doesn't give you the right to break into my glove compartment and take them."

"It's my job to find things."

"Oh, give me a break."

"What about us?" she says, her voice still sharp and accusing.

"What *about* us?"

"You know what I did while I was in Philly, Frank? After I finished at the *Inquirer,* I went to see Bernie."

"What? You saw Bernie?"

"That's right. Do you know what he said when he saw me? He said I look just like her, Frank. Just like your dead wife! Jesus, I look just like a dead person, the dead person you're still in love with. All along there was someone else in bed with us, Frank. Isn't that a kick in the teeth!"

"You broke our agreement. You used me."

I study her face in the shadows. There is something of Catherine in the way the hair falls over the forehead. She has her eyes, too. But that's all. Catherine's nose was smaller, her mouth less full. And as for temperament, there's no comparison.

"It appears we've *both* been using each other," she says.

Silence.

"It's all of a piece, Frank, your dead wife and your obsession with the past. I understand it now. This thing you have about old Atlantic City, Lucy the stupid fucking Elephant, and all that. It's like the thing with your wife's suicide. And Nick's death. And Cappy's. You're obsessed with the dead, Frank."

"You don't know what you're saying."

"And all that bullshit about Zen and the art of cooking, all that stuff about meditating while you're chopping carrots. I never believed a word of it. Besides, you're a terrible cook. Where are you going?"

"To find a motel. I'm exhausted."

"Please stay." Her voice is suddenly soft and inviting.

As the door closes behind me I can hear her saying, "I'm sorry, I'm sorry."

3

You look like shit, Frank."

"Thanks a lot, Captain."

"Understand you had a rough day yesterday," says Cox, grinning, a piece of jelly doughnut showing between his teeth.

Cox is in good spirits. Me, I don't function well at seven in the morning after a day spent running from a raging inferno. I'm still having trouble with my eyes. And I have a headache that extends out to the tips of each gray hair.

"I apologize for meeting at this ungodly hour," Talley says, looking around the table, ignoring me, "but under the circumstances there wasn't any choice."

I get a few glares from Petrillo, as well as the newcomers, two nightshift detectives named Hal Sutton and Mavis Fredericks. Even Martindale looks a little pissed. He and his wife were planning to spend the day in Philly with some relatives. Except for Petrillo, who's wearing a new tie, everyone's dressed casually in jeans or khakis and sporting 9-millimeter Sig Sauer automatics in shoulder holsters.

Talley's arms encircle a pile of papers on the table. Ever since he walked in he's been shuffling through them, sorting and reordering. When he resumes there's a hint of a smile on his face. "Let's dispense with a few related items before getting to the biggie. I do have some good news. Last night Sutton and Fredericks arrested Jack Coyle. The DA's had us on the case around the clock. It's paid off."

Smiles and nods of approval all around. Sutton, a short man with a pointy, balding head, and Fredericks, a sallow-complexioned woman with cringing eyes, turn and look at each other, giving the thumbs up sign.

"Caught the son of a bitch on the expressway. On his way to fucking Philadelphia." Sutton, whom I've never met until this morning, glares down the table at me. "Should have heard that bastard in the car on the way back, yelling something about a deal he cut. Guess he thought he could get better treatment from the cops in the City of Brotherly Love."

Never apologize, especially in situations like this. It's a losing proposition. I gave them the tape and the pictures. What more do they want?

"A few other details," says Talley, glancing at a piece of paper, then placing it at the bottom of his pile and looking straight at me. "Strictly off the record. This makes it into the papers or onto the tube and I'll personally break somebody's legs. FBI and IRS are preparing a case on Dante. Money-laundering, tax evasion, for starters. They're working on more. They had Bass and Capetanakis in their sights, too, until somebody went and killed them."

"Bass killed himself," I interject, but nobody seems to notice.

"So who the hell whacked all these assholes anyway? We make a case on anybody?" asks Mavis Fredericks. Talley waves her off for the moment and proceeds with his notes.

"Talked to the ME a few minutes ago. No IDs on the two bodies burned to a crisp in the Pines yesterday. Sweeney's is the only testimony we've got on this. It's going to take some dental records to prove it."

"So who the fuck were they?" Sutton asks, looking at me.

"Judge Bass for one," I reply. "He shot himself inside the gun club before the fire reached him. The other victim was a psycho named Angel Bird. He was Dante's hit man. He killed Harry Morrow back in 1977 and, more recently, Nick D'Angelo and Capetanakis."

Fredericks looks my way, this time with a little more respect. "And who the hell did him?"

"That's why we're here," says Talley. "I know I'm stretching procedure by asking Frank to join us, but the fact is he can help. The DA agrees. Frank?"

I look at Martindale.

"Ray, you remember that black pickup I thought was following me after we left Angel's apartment?"

"Yeah."

"I was wrong. It wasn't following me. It was following Angel."

I tell them about the mystery man who visited Sandy Maclean and the Sooys, claiming to be Nick, and how Coyle said Nick really didn't have all the facts when he blackmailed Tony Dante. All of this should have triggered a warning bell. The Nick I knew was lazy, prone to cut corners, just like Coyle said. He'd never have gone to all the trouble of investigating a pair of killings that dated back to 1977. He had more than enough to blackmail Dante with, anyway. The man using Nick's name, the man who *was* investigating those murders, wasn't interested in blackmail. He wanted revenge.

I tell them what Ruth Sooy saw watching from her front window back in 1977. Then I put the slip of paper on the table.

"She knew the second victim, the collier who was burned alive with Harry Morrow. She wrote the name down for me."

I pass the piece of paper down to Talley who reads it aloud. "Jeb Leeds."

Petrillo looks down at me.

"As in 'Brother Stephen Leeds'?" he asks.

"Jeb Leeds was Brother Stephen's father."

4

I APPRECIATE THIS, Captain."

Talley, in the driver's seat, turns and nods.

Amazingly, droplets have begun to appear on the windshield. Finally. *Stirring dull roots with spring rain.* Or lulling us into accepting the lesser gift.

"This is absolutely it, understand?" he says. "After this, we're fucking even."

"Understood."

"Guess you deserve to be there at the bust. After what that bastard put you through yesterday."

He has no idea.

Last night at the hospital Virgil and I waded through fifteen minutes of meaningless chitchat before one of us finally mentioned what had happened. Virgil was the first to speak.

"That was a dickens of a fire," he said. Tears rolled down his weathered face like rain cascading over a rocky ledge.

"It was, Virgil, it certainly was."

For an instant, the room began to shift under my feet. We were in the woods again, that infernal red-orange smoke all around us, the roar of the approaching firestorm at our backs. Virgil, unwavering, in his black leather cap and V-necked undershirt, was outlined in the smoke like some preternatural shape from another world come to guide me out of Hell.

I looked down at the man on the bed. He was staring out the window, contending with his own memories. Neither of us could find any more words. I bent over, hugged him, and left quietly.

"You gotta keep away from Brother Stephen," says Talley. "You stay by me, okay? I got your word on that?"

"Okay," I lie. My loathing for Angel has been redirected to Brother Stephen, putative shepherd of lost souls and reckless avenger.

"I've got enough problems now with the DA, thanks to that damned reporter," Talley says.

"I understand." And I do, I really do.

We're doing eighty on the expressway, heading east toward the city. Petrillo and Cox are several car lengths ahead of us. It's their bust. They deserve it after missing out on Angel, says Talley. He's along for the glory, hoping the press will cover this one to the hilt. Then it's on to the Poseidon to nail Tony Dante for the murder of Harry Morrow and Jeb Leeds. Talley thinks my testimony, along with the photos, the taped conversation with Coyle, and what Bass told me, is enough to convict Dante, if the FBI doesn't lay first claim. I'm not so sure, but this isn't my case, as people keep telling me.

"I understand you know this reporter broad?"

"We're no longer friends."

"A wise decision on your part."

First she fucked me, then she screwed me. What was to decide?

He's silent for half a mile. We pass low-lying wetlands—Absecon Bay, Lakes Bay, Shelter Island Bay—guarding the entrance to the one-time Queen of Resorts. Sodom and Gomorrah in neon now.

"You know something about Pineys, Captain? They're fond of religious icons."

"Icons?"

"Yeah, like cheap reproductions of Leonardo DaVinci's *The Last Supper.*"

"Really? I thought a Piney's idea of art was a picture of Pee Wee Herman on the outhouse door."

"You ever actually met a Piney, Captain?"

"A few. They're strange."

"It was a Piney who saved my life yesterday."

"So I understand. What's your point, I mean about the religious icons?"

"My point is there's a copy of DaVinci's *The Last Supper* in the mission, right outside Brother Stephen's office."

"So that's how you figured him for a Piney?"

"It helped. There's also the more obvious fact that he actually told me where he grew up. I didn't pay any attention to it at the time,

318

though. It was near a town called Nesco. That's in the Pines. Close by the Sooys, actually. Near where Jeb Leeds was killed. It took a while before I remembered that. Then there're the hunting photos in his office. Leeds and his hunting buddies with their shotguns. In one he's actually in front of a building. It was his gun club in the Pines."

"You ever looked in the phone book? There are lots of Leedses in and around the Pines. Lots of Sooys, too. How'd you know this particular Jeb Leeds was Brother Stephen's father?"

"A man fitting Brother Stephen's description had pretended to be a cop investigating a twenty-year-old murder. It was the only possibility left."

Somehow, Brother Stephen found out what Cappy told Nick. He probably learned about Nick's visit to the Poseidon to scope out the judge, too. But, as I said, he wasn't interested in blackmail. After twenty years he finally had a lead on what had happened to his father, and he wasn't about to surrender his rage in return for something as trivial as money. Not that Dante ever would have complied. Brother Stephen would have known that, too. He's smarter than Nick ever was. Vengeance is a higher passion than greed.

"He's not here," says an incredulous female voice. "Don't you know? There's going to be a prayer service on the Boardwalk this morning. Out in front of the Poseidon. Everybody's there."

"Everybody" means the entire mission, residents and staff, trucked down the Boardwalk in a sixties-style protest caravan, filling vans and borrowed cars, whatever could be scraped together. Led by an enraged Brother Stephen in his black pickup, the taste of vengeance still fresh in his mouth from yesterday.

Petrillo and Cox stick their noses into Brother Stephen's office to see for themselves, then resume grilling the helpless receptionist. Talley listens from the doorway.

Light streams into the hallway from the office next to Brother Stephen's. Sister Felice's desk and bookshelves have been stripped bare. Cardboard boxes are all over the floor. She's in jeans and a navy blue Notre Dame sweatshirt. Crow's feet are visible on her ashen face.

"Sister, you're leaving?"

319

"That's right." She clutches a Bible, then decides to put it in one of the cardboard boxes.

"May I ask why?"

She stops what she's doing.

"Things have changed."

"With Brother Stephen?"

"Yes. With him. I . . . I guess I never really knew him. God, that sounds so trite."

"When did you find out?"

She puts down a handful of file folders and takes a seat behind her desk.

"That's a pretty open-ended question, Mr. Sweeney."

"Answer it anyway, would you?"

"Okay. It might help to tell it to someone. I've known Stephen since the late '70s. Until a month or so ago, he was merely an unhappy man. Bitterly unhappy. Then Cappy came along. And after him, Nick. Nick confided in me. Said he had this hunch. 'Just a hunch,' he said. I told it to Stephen. I shouldn't have but. . . . Well, we were . . . we shared things. I thought. . . ."

"You thought he could help you keep Nick from doing something foolish."

She smiles gratefully.

"That's right."

"Instead, Stephen became obsessed, began investigating Cappy's claims on his own."

Brother Stephen with his own demon memory to exorcise.

"I had no idea that what Cappy told Nick was somehow connected to the disappearance of Stephen's father. I mean, it's true he's always talking about it. But he could never be sure how or when the old man died. Not until all this happened. He wasn't even around when his father disappeared. He was in Africa. His mother was a missionary. She took him away from the father when he was a boy and went to Nigeria. She sounds like a fanatic to me. Stephen never forgot his father. They wrote to each other. Jeb—that was his name— he sent pictures. Stephen still has them. Old Jeb in front of his charcoal pit."

320

I'll bet I know who took those pictures, too. Ruth Sooy, one of the few people the old hermit ever spoke to, except on the fateful day he encountered Angel Bird.

"Odd thing is," says Sister, "Stephen had given up hope of finding the answer to Jeb's disappearance until Nick came along."

"Didn't he ever suspect Dante?"

"When he came back from Africa he learned about the fire and the Morrow murder. He figured it was connected to the casinos somehow. He suspected the second dead man was his father but he had no way of knowing. There weren't any dental records. The old man never saw a dentist. And Stephen could never find out anything more. At the time, Tony Dante was an unknown. It was the father, Joseph, who started the Poseidon. Nobody ever heard of Tony until after the father died. Stephen *had* heard of Henry Bass, though. When I told him Nick had mentioned that name, he changed. That was when it all started. I can see that now, though I didn't at the time. Stephen never said anything about his father. He just went off and began doing research, checking the newspapers, court proceedings, everything. He wouldn't tell me what he found. But now I see what it was. He'd finally confirmed that his father was the one killed in that fire. I still don't know who told him."

"The old man had one friend, a young girl named Ruth Sooy. Stephen finally tracked her down. She confirmed it for him."

She shakes her head, as if it's all a great mystery, then resumes packing.

"What do you know about yesterday, about the fire?" I ask.

She stands up, suddenly pale.

"He told me last night. I made him. He swears he didn't know you and that other man were there. He only wanted that Angel person. And the judge. I screamed at him. I nearly clawed his eyes out. He was playing God. Or the Devil. I don't know which."

"And he isn't finished."

"What?"

"There's still one left."

"You mean . . . oh, my God."

Outside in the hallway, I fall in next to Talley who's on the way to his car with Cox and Petrillo.

"Did you hear all that?" I ask.

"Every word."

5

I T'S DRIZZLING STEADILY now, darkening the ribboned surface of the Boardwalk. The warm rain acts as a balm to my parched skin and stinging eyes.

Out in front of the Poseidon, protesting mission residents have joined arms with striking casino employees, forming a circular human chain. I estimate 200 people, counting bystanders. Inside the circle, dozens more mill about, placards and signs rifling the air. REMEMBER SANDRA GREENBERG! THE POSEIDON IS DANTE'S INFERNO. CLOSE *ALL* THE CASINOS! The people in the crowd display a noisy bravado, like cheerleaders at a rainy spring pep rally.

What the mission's receptionist said is true: everybody *is* here. Lady René, her ampleness planted precariously on a folding chair, sits inside the circle next to Brother Stephen's pickup. She's carrying on an animated conversation with Busty Barkley and Harry LaRue. Behind them, white-haired Harriet rests passively in her wheelchair, coin cup in her lap, a plastic rain hat on her head. Tommy the Toe stands next to her, with Julius from the kitchen and Sol the card counter nearby. Even Billy Loo and Leonard Pitkin have shown up, arms around each other's waist. Dozens of Poseidon workers roam aimlessly about. On the periphery, two uniformed cops, outnumbered and ignored, warily observe the action.

Over by the casino entrance Charlie Bishop looks on, no doubt unsure whether it's his funeral or his liberation he's attending. Gwen stands next to him. Meryl Sarbanes, shielded from the rain by the canopy, sits at her electric keyboard, connected by an extension cord to a power source somewhere inside the casino. She's poised to play.

A local TV station is setting up its equipment next to her. Gwen looks my way, then turns back to Bishop.

Inside the circle, Brother Stephen's crew-cut head rises above the crowd. He's standing on the back of his pickup, sporting a khaki hunter's vest and holding a bullhorn in his hands. He looks the crowd over, then gets down.

Talley whispers something to Petrillo and Cox. The two detectives separate, Cox going over to stand under the canopy, Petrillo moving to the opposite side of the crowd, near the beach.

"We've got to wait him out," Talley says. "It'd be worth your life to try to break through that line of people. And I don't think they'd take kindly to seeing their leader carted away by the cops right now." He pauses a moment. "I think I'll call for backup."

"Good idea."

When he returns from his car, he wonders out loud what Brother Stephen is planning to do.

"Maybe he doesn't have a plan," I respond. Wishful thinking on my part.

Music begins issuing forth like a challenge from the speakers under the canopy. It's the initial premonitory lyrics of "Let's Face the Music and Dance," warning of trouble ahead. Dante's on the offensive, with Ol' Blue Eyes leading the charge.

People in the crowd begin looking up, sighting along the Poseidon's angled façade of opaque glass. A few point to the fourth floor, shouting and jeering, waving fists. A young man wearing jeans and a mission T-shirt arrives carrying a stepladder. As a small group gathers around him, he positions the ladder under the edge of the canopy. Suddenly, Tommy the Toe appears from inside the human chain, ready to climb the ladder. In an instant, he's up onto the top of the canopy, holding onto the base of Dante's plastic god. From somewhere a coil of rope materializes. It sails through the air toward the outstretched hand of the elderly Baby Titus, Child of the High Wire. The counterattack by Sinatra continues in the background.

Brother Stephen is on his feet again, surveying his flock. He looks in the direction of Meryl Sarbanes and gives a signal. She bends over, tongue extended, and begins to play, diving for notes like a demon bobbing for apples. The crowd quiets, and monotones of "Amazing Grace" rise from under the canopy.

Dante ups the volume, a megadecibel assault. Brother Stephen, furious, glares skyward just as Tommy, his arm through the coiled rope, begins to shinny up Poseidon's trident. Tommy pushes off from the plastic toga, and grabs the outstretched arm holding the ace and king of spades. He loops a noose over the three-pronged spear, lassoing a giant sea god.

Down on the Boardwalk the musical slugfest continues. Sinatra versus Sarbanes. People try to sing along with Meryl. But Frank croons on, taunting the crowd with the mellow tones of "Why Try to Change Me Now."

Finally, Brother Stephen puts an end to the competition with his bullhorn. "Quiet, everyone, quiet please! Quiet!"

Meryl's tongue takes a rest, leaving only the sounds of Sinatra and the surf breaking in the distance.

"I'd like to open with a prayer," says Brother Stephen. "Please bow your heads. Heavenly father . . . remember your servant, Sandra Greenberg . . . and grant her today the peace and glory of your Son, Jesus Christ."

Inside the circle, Tommy begins playing out the rope, moving away from the building. He hands the end to Harriet, who grips it tightly while he pushes her in the direction of the beach, making the line taut. She looks like an elderly Lilliputian in a wheelchair trying to bring down Gulliver.

Despite the fact that the rain has gotten heavier, the number of on-lookers has increased, many clutching opened umbrellas. Bleary-eyed players from neighboring casinos have been stumbling into the Sunday morning rain, delighted to find they haven't missed the Boardwalk's best floor show. Somewhere chanting begins, drowning out Brother Stephen, Sister Meryl, *and* Brother Frank.

"We want Toe-neee. We want Don-tay."

Sinatra counters with "Try a Little Tenderness."

Half-a-dozen people are clustered around Harriet now, pulling and jerking at the god's tether. But Poseidon stands firm.

Looking desperate, Brother Stephen holds up a photo of Sandra Greenberg, pleading for attention. Proud Poseidon begins to sway, but the assault lacks leverage. Tommy directs his platoon to move farther away from the building.

"We want Toe-neee. We want Don-tay."

Suddenly, Brother Stephen is gone. I glance around. Cox is near the casino entrance, talking to a cop in uniform. A TV cameraman roams the crowd, getting close-ups. But no sign of Brother Stephen. I wave Petrillo toward the entrance to the casino.

Then there's a scuffle on the perimeter of the circle. People begin backing away.

"Look out!"

"He's got a gun!"

Head down, Brother Stephen comes out of the crowd, striding stiffly toward the row of glass doors under the canopy. His 12-guage Ithaca pump gun is at his side, pointed downward along the length of his leg.

I make a dash for the casino entrance. Behind me, Talley's protests are drowned in the rain. I'm about fifty feet away when Brother Stephen reaches the door. The last thing I see before he disappears inside are the bulging flaps over the shell loops on his hunter's vest.

At the glass doors Cox and Petrillo rush past me, guns drawn. Inside, nearly all the slot machines are silent. A few lonely bells ring eerily in the distance.

"The escalators," I shout to Cox and Petrillo, "he's probably headed there. Watch out, he's carrying enough ammo to take out the entire Boardwalk."

Cox weaves in and out among the rows of slots. Petrillo's right behind him, shouting at two elderly women to get out of the way. Weaponless, I'm a distant third. Zigging and zagging past straight slots, progressive slots, MegaPoker slots, Denizens of the Sea, and Quartermania. Then across the elevated walkway and through a wide archway into a vast room with Players' Edge Draw Poker, Pokermania, All-American Poker, and Louisiana Jacks or Better.

Sinatra is still in the air. Now the song is "It Had to Be You."

My eye is on the escalators up ahead, where a giant sign features

Tony Dante's grinning face and the message, AT THE POSEIDON YOU WIN EVEN WHEN YOU LOSE. Something moves, a glimpse of steel. There's a flash from the open well above the escalators.

"Down! Get down!"

The blast is deafening, as loud as yesterday's firestorm, but briefer, more merciful. Shattered red-white-and-blue cowgirls fall from their golden stallions on the video poker machines behind me. A jackpot every forty-five seconds. The remaining players in the casino head for the exits. Cox and Petrillo hold their fire.

Then Brother Stephen shows his back. He's making a run for the high ground, probably figuring he can't stop us down here. Or else, like the late Judge Bass, nothing matters to him anymore. Nothing except checking out on his own terms, making one last wager before he goes.

The escalator passes the second floor. When we reach level three, the Neptune Casino, Brother Stephen isn't in sight. I stay crouched down behind Cox and Petrillo. Cox, down on his hands and knees, makes his way toward the blackjack table nearest the tropical fish tanks. As Petrillo prepares to follow, Brother Stephen pops up from behind a craps table and fires. Tank water and shattered glass fill the air. The floor around Cox turns into a tropical lake bed, zebra fish, swordtails, mollies, and angelfish flopping about on the soggy carpet. Brother Stephen makes a dash past the poker tables and disappears through the private door.

That's two shots. I figure he started with four or five rounds in the gun if it was fully loaded. But it doesn't matter, I tell myself, because he's carrying extra shells.

"That's an office wing he went into," I yell, running between the tables. "It's one floor up to Dante's office. Take the stairs."

Petrillo turns, prepared to stop me, but I give him a look. He thinks better of it and heads for the door to the office wing.

In the hallway outside the personnel offices it's blessedly silent. No Sinatra, no employees. Everybody's on indefinite leave. There's only our own heavy breathing to mar the quiet.

At the end of the hall we take the stairs next to the elevator two at a time. On the fourth-floor landing, Cox and Petrillo finally wave me back.

"This is as far as you go," whispers Cox. "You gotta stay the hell out of the way from here on."

He stands to one side of the fire door, both hands extended, gripping his Sig Sauer. Petrillo, automatic in his raised right hand, reaches for the knob. Once the door's open far enough, Cox takes a position in the doorway and quickly sights up and down the hall. He nods to Petrillo, who follows him into the hall, letting the door close behind him.

Wait a few seconds, I tell myself. Stop and listen, then proceed.

With the door barely open, I look up and down the hall. Brothel red carpeting and faux Louis XIV furniture. This is the place.

Down the hall Petrillo disappears through the door to Dante's outer office. I head that way, staying close to the wall. Standing to one side, I push one of the double walnut doors open slightly, revealing part of the gilt-edge side table with the simulated French antique telephone. No one's in sight. With the door all the way open, I can see down the narrow hallway, past the ante rooms to where Petrillo and Cox are positioned. They're hugging the wall outside the closed door to Dante's office.

As I take up a position in the outer reception room, Cox waves me off, but I ignore him.

"Stephen Leeds, this is the police!" Cox shouts. "We know you're in there. Come out now and nobody'll get hurt."

Inside Dante's office there's another blast from the 12-gauge, followed by the sound of exploding glass.

Cox stands aside while Petrillo kicks at the door. As it flies open, Cox tumbles into the office, staying low. There's another shot. Petrillo screams and reaches down, clutching a bloody knee, then falls backward toward me.

Keeping out of Brother Stephen's line of fire, I inch my way along the wall to Petrillo. Undoing his necktie, I wrap it tightly around his leg just above the knee. Ashen-faced but conscious, he grimaces, eyes fixed rigidly on the ceiling. He doesn't see me pick up his Sig Sauer.

I put it behind me in the waistband of my chinos, letting the wind-breaker cover it.

"Jesus, gimme some fucking help in here. Somebody take this son-of-a-bitch down, for chrissakes!" It's Tony the Book. He's a taxpaying citizen now and wants his rightful protection under the law.

Just inside the doorway, Cox is crouched down, out of Brother Stephen's view. Rain mixed with salt air blows through the room. I can see Brother Stephen's khaki hunting jacket and the back of his head. He turns around, waving the shotgun, so I pull back.

"Stephen, it's Frank Sweeney. I'm not armed." I give him a glimpse of raised arms, then pull back. "We just want to talk to you. Give us a minute, okay?"

"I've got nothing to say. Get out. I have no quarrel with the po-lice."

"You will if you kill Dante," I respond.

"Doesn't matter now. I've already killed. Got to pay for one. Might as well pay for two."

Curse God and die, again. It seems to be his motto.

I can see Dante now. He's on his knees. Behind him, with the plate-glass window gone, gray-black rain falls on his cringing back.

"What the fuck do you want, Leeds?" Dante shouts from the floor. "Tell me and it's yours."

"You killed my father."

"The fuck I did! I didn't kill nobody's father. You got a gripe, give it to me, we'll talk. Maybe I ain't been so charitable. Maybe I shoulda helped the mission more. What can I say? I been busy. It's not a good time for me. Case you can't see, I'm about to go outa fucking busi-ness."

Brother Stephen lowers the gun and points it at Dante's head.

"Jesus, no!"

"Don't shoot," Cox yells.

Brother Stephen turns his head toward Cox, the gun still aimed at Dante. "Get out! All of you get out, do you hear?"

Dante tries again. "Look, Leeds, let's talk, huh? You and me, we can have a sit-down. Maybe I can help. You know, speak out, use my influence. I've been too quiet all these years. I shoulda complained more about what's happening 'round here, you know. I never made a beef to the city. I can talk to them now. Am I right or am I wrong?"

"You killed my father."

"I swear to God!"

Cox begins crawling toward a bookshelf against the wall where he'll have a better line of sight. But he's not stealthy enough. Just as he raises his gun, Brother Stephen turns and fires. Cox's rain slicker flies back, blood splattering the bookshelf. The left side of his chest turns a pulpy crimson. He's unconscious when he hits the floor.

I yell from the hallway. "Stephen, I'm coming in. I'm not armed. I just want to talk." I lower my hands. "See," I say, slowly pulling my windbreaker aside, revealing a sweaty imprint under each armpit.

"You shouldn't be here. This has nothing to do with you."

"You're wrong. Tonyboy there had my best friend's brother killed. I'd like to see him pay for that."

"I'm about to take care of it for you," says Brother Stephen.

I read conviction and determination in that gaunt face. He means what he says, which leaves me in a difficult situation. To my way of thinking, each of these bastards needs to pay, but I want to be the one to collect. Brother Stephen had *his* day of vengeance yesterday. Today it's my turn.

"What I had in mind was him rotting in prison for the rest of his life. It's a hell of a lot worse than a quick death at your hands. You kill him and *you're* the one who rots."

"Gonna rot anyway. I have to pay for what I did."

He turns back toward Dante. I estimate he's thirty feet away, maybe more, too far for me to rush him. Gradually, I let my arms drop to my sides, the right hand pushing my windbreaker aside.

"Stand up," he yells at Dante, waving the barrel of the gun at him.

Dante, eyes pleading, looks back and forth between Brother Stephen and me. He stands up slowly, clutching his gut as if he's about to puke. My hand's behind my back now. Feeling for Petrillo's automatic, I stay focused on the 12-gauge. Then, with a firm grip on Petrillo's Sig Sauer, I extend the gun and yell, "Hold it, Leeds! I've got a—"

I see his finger move. So I fire. But there's a millisecond's lag between the blast of the Ithaca 12-gauge and the shot from the Sig Sauer. It's true what they say, timing's everything.

Dante flies backward as if someone has jerked a rope tied to his waist. The shotgun blast flings him through the opening in the shattered window, into the briny rain, and down to the waiting crowd.

Brother Stephen falls forward, a red circle spreading outward on the back of his head. When I reach him he's lying facedown on the damp carpet. I kick the shotgun aside, then turn him over. He's dead.

Petrillo has managed to drag himself over to Cox. He looks up from the body and shakes his head. That's when I hand him his gun.

"*You* fired at Brother Stephen," I tell him.

He looks at me.

"It's your gun, son. I saw you do it. You managed to drag yourself over here, pull yourself to your feet, and get off one shot. You were a moment too late, but you got him. Hell of a shot."

"But—"

"Trust me. It's easier this way." I look down at Brother Stephen bleeding on the floor. "Besides, it really doesn't matter."

With the salt air and rain in my face, I walk over to the window and take a look out of the gaping hole in Dante's glass wall. One last surprise remains. Dante never made it to the Boardwalk below. A few feet beneath the window, Tony the Book hangs skewered like a shish kebab by the god of his own creation, the tips of the rusty trident protruding through his chest.

Below on the Boardwalk, the crowd resumes its roped assault on Dante's plastic icon.

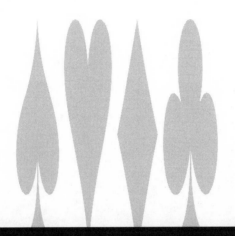

EPILOGUE

APRIL 30, 1996

BEACH HAVEN, NEW JERSEY

APRIL 30, 1996

D IE IN YOUR THOUGHTS every day and you'll no longer fear death. So goes an old Zen maxim. I've been mulling that one over for two days, in between debriefings at Northfield, phone calls to Bernie, and talks with the bank and insurance people about the Cordells' house. Talley says I was "damned lucky" not to get my brains splattered all over Tony Dante's office. He's reluctant to attribute my survival to the keen aim and wise-beyond-his-years judgment of young Detective Petrillo. He knows better than that. But he's keeping his doubts to himself. For his part, Bernie says my whole experience down here reminds him of the monks who used to sleep in their coffins in order to keep their minds focused on Last Things. I told him in two weeks' time I've experienced enough Last Things to do me an eternity. That was when I remembered the anniversary of Catherine's death. Last week was two years. I'll stop off at the cemetery on the way back. No matter how fast you're running, when you turn around death's always there right beside you.

A few good things came of it all. Martindale, who knows one of the managers at the Emperor's Inn, a restaurant at the Showboat, found Billy Loo a job there. Billy's now serving Chinese dishes to overweight tourists from Philly and the Big Apple. He loves it, says he wouldn't go back to dealing even if Tony Dante walked into his apartment and held a gun to his head, which, I assured him, won't ever happen. Speaking of Tony the Book, the image of him impaled in midair on a rusty pitchfork somehow managed to make it onto the air at CNN. But it was shown only once because someone from the

Atlantic City tourist board called Ted Turner immediately and complained. Then there's Sister Felice. She's getting herself to a nunnery, the old-fashioned kind where people pray and think about the meaning of life and death. It's where she belongs. She's a contemplative, and her kind have no place mucking about in the real world's cesspools with the rest of us sewer rats.

As for me, I'm planning to attend an estate auction in Bucks County next week. I've been away from the antiques business too long. It's time to earn some money. Besides, collecting is what I love best. Cooking hasn't panned out as a diversion for me. Maybe it was Rami and all that Zen stuff. I'm thinking of trying yoga instead. I bought a couple of books yesterday. Kundalini sounds intriguing—the yoga of the inner fire.

Bernie insists I bill him for my expenses. I guess I will, considering what it cost me. Just make it fair, he says. Don't pad it and don't omit anything. I've begun a list: automobile rental, gasoline, motel, meals, long-distance phone calls, Virgil's services as a guide, one folk-art book for Ruth Sooy, and my per diem. The only question is how to list the car.

Loss due to fire—one 1995 Range Rover County LWB . . . $40,800 (estimated book value).

See what he says about that.

It's late Tuesday afternoon before I'm ready to leave. The beach house is looking better every day. You'd hardly know there's been a fire. Except for the smell, of course. That'll be around for a while. The antiques appraiser who looked everything over says the damage is minimal. When I relayed that assessment to the Cordells in Sicily, they didn't sound convinced. They're cutting their trip short to come back next week and see for themselves. It doesn't look as if I'll be invited back.

As I begin putting my things in the rental car, the green Toyota appears at the end of the block. I watch it make its way up the street. After Gwen gets out, I walk over and give her a kiss on the cheek. She seems relieved.

She looks as foxy as the day I first saw her: cream slacks, blue silk blouse, and hair tucked up under a straw hat.

"Read your story. It was good, really good."

"Think so? Thanks. Detective Petrillo gives a good interview."

"He's got potential."

She studies me.

"What he told me, was it the truth?"

"Why do you ask that?"

"Somehow I can't see him as the *Die Hard* type. You know, the movie?"

"Gwen, if you're going to become a great newspaperwoman, you've got to stop trusting your instincts so much."

"Well, sometimes your instincts . . . oh, damn you."

Finally she smiles.

"That's better."

She paces back and forth for a few moments, kicking at the gravel in front of my car.

"I thought maybe we could play 'Let's Get Personal' one last time," she says.

"If you want."

"Really? Good. Okay, here goes. 'VADWF. (That's 'very apologetic divorced white female.') Still likes antiquing, real country music, and romantic dinners for two. Has space in river cabin for occasional out-of-town guest. Only ex-Philadelphia cops need apply.' "

"I like it."

"I'm glad. And you?"

"Okay. Try this. 'Suddenly much older WWG. (That's 'widowed white gumshoe.') Looking for a place to visit on trips to the Jersey shore. Only future Pulitzers will be considered."

"Thanks, Frank." She gives me a quick hug.

I watch as she gets back in her car.

"Give my love to Bernie," she says from the driver's seat.

"I will."

"Watch out for yourself, Frank. There are a lot of unscrupulous women out there just looking for a man like you."

"I wish."

I HAVE ONE STOP to make before heading home. Virgil isn't expecting me so I hope he's not off gathering moss or picking pinecones. I have something for him, and for Pete. Pete gets a bag of red licorice. For Virgil I have twelve dollars, payment for services rendered. I have something else to give him, too. It's a pocketknife with a scrimshaw handle. I visited five different stores before I found it. In the end they had what I wanted at an antiques shop in Cape May. The design depicts a hunter and his dog walking through a field. The woods in the background look a lot like Rattler's Deadfall. I had the blade engraved. It says V. APPLEGATE—U.S. CITIZEN. A story went with the knife Virgil's father gave him. Now one will evolve around this one, too. I plan to come back and hear Virgil tell it.

After Fox Chase Ridge, it's on to the A.C. Expressway. Heading west, leaving the neon dream kingdom. Past the casino billboards. Past The Donald waving goodbye. Past a smiling Merv saying, "You've been a great audience. Hurry back!"

Philadelphia, fifty-five miles.